Praise for Susan Carroll

♥

"Ms. Carroll is a more than welcome addition to the ranks of favorite Regency authors."
—*Rave Reviews*

"Award-winning author Susan Carroll makes our heart sing."
—*Romantic Times*

"Susan Carroll is a masterful storyteller!"
—*The Literary Times*

By Susan Carroll
Published by The Ballantine Publishing Group:

CHRISTMAS BELLES
MISS PRENTISS AND THE YANKEE
THE VALENTINE'S DAY BALL
BRIGHTON ROAD/THE SUGAR ROSE
THE PAINTED VEIL
MISTRESS MISCHIEF/THE LADY WHO HATED
    SHAKESPEARE
THE WOOING OF MISS MASTERS/THE BISHOP'S
    DAUGHTER

THE WOOING OF MISS MASTERS

♥

THE BISHOP'S DAUGHTER

Susan Carroll

FAWCETT CREST • NEW YORK

A Fawcett Crest Book
Published by The Ballantine Publishing Group
The Wooing of Miss Masters copyright © 1991 by Susan Coppula
The Bishop's Daughter copyright © 1990 by Susan Coppula

http://www.randomhouse.com

Library of Congress Catalog Card Number: 97-90888

ISBN 0-449-00155-0

Manufactured in the United States of America

First Edition: January 1998

10 9 8 7 6 5 4 3 2 1

Contents

THE WOOING OF MISS MASTERS

♥

THE BISHOP'S DAUGHTER

THE WOOING OF
MISS MASTERS

To my uncle Sam and to Mark Petersen,
the gentleman who helps me take care of him.

Chapter 1

The Duke of Raeburn was in a black humor.

The signs had been noted by His Grace's household through-out the castle that morning, as carefully as sailors reading the sky, then battening down the hatches for the approaching storm. Most of the staff strove to stay out of the duke's way, from the laundry maid to the stately butler, all of them walking about on tiptoe.

The only one who remained unaffected was John Farley, the head groom. But then he had been employed at Castle Raeburn some fifty years. He had known the present duke since the days when he had been but Lord Simon. Consequently, while the rest of the servants skittered about doing their tasks, Farley lingered near the suit of armor mounted in the front hall while he chewed meditatively on a wisp of straw.

His cap doffed, there was no disrespect in his mien but no fear either as he watched the duke come stalking through the archway at the far end of the vast chamber.

Early morning light filtered through narrow windows, which were sealed with heavy leaded glass. The gloom-ridden hall was the only surviving part of the medieval section of the castle with its barrel-vaulted roof and stark stone walls displaying a formidable array of swords, halberds, and battle-axes. Farley thought most modern gentlemen in their yellow breeches and frilled cravats looked rather foolish in such a setting.

But not so His Grace.

The duke was a large man with massive shoulders, built like a block of granite. As he strode into the hall, one half expected to see a squire come rushing forward to tug gauntlets upon those powerful hands, to toss a coat of chain mail over that broad chest.

Despite the fashionable cut of his dark blue riding coat, His Grace conveyed the impression of one who had stepped from another century when men were bred of iron. His hair swept back from his brow and shagged against his starched collar, the unrelenting blackness of those thick locks broken only by flecks of silver at his temples. He had inherited the Raeburn hawklike nose and square jaw, but the heavy forbidding brows and the eyes of blue-tempered steel were all His Grace's own.

His face had tanned so deep as to almost give him a foreign appearance like some Barbary Coast sea captain, deep crags set at either side of his mouth. Most said those weather-beaten lines were the result of His Grace having traveled so much in heathen climates, but Farley allowed as it was because the duke rarely ever smiled.

The groom had heard tell once how some fancy gentlemen in London had proposed a wager as to when if ever His Grace might be likely to grin. But nothing had come of it as no one had dared write Raeburn's name in the betting books, the duke's temper being as legendary as his famous frown.

Farley noted that that ominous scowl was more pronounced than ever as His Grace's top boots rang out upon the hall's rough stone floor. He tapped a riding crop against the leg of his buckskin breeches, the look of barely restrained anger upon his face enough to put most men into a quake. Therefore it was not surprising that the pretty young lady who trailed in the duke's wake appeared highly discomfited.

Looping the train of her riding habit over her arm, she fairly ran to catch up with His Grace while essaying a laugh, which Farley supposed was meant to be a flirtatious giggle, but came out more as a nervous titter.

"I never meant to be such a trouble to Your Grace. Goodness me! I simply don't know how I came to be lost upon your estate or have my horse pull a shoe."

"Nor I, either, madam," came the cold reply. "But I shall have my carriage brought round to see you home."

6

"Oh, n-no, pray, you must not go to such bother. I do not mind in the least waiting until my horse has been reshod." She gave the duke a look that would have melted a heart of stone, but Farley reckoned that the young lady had never come up against a man entirely made of granite before.

"Believe me, it is no bother at all to send you upon your way, Miss Long." The duke seemed to produce the housekeeper out of thin air with a gesture of the riding crop, but in truth, Mrs. Bede had been hovering anxiously in the background the entire time.

"Your Grace?" The housekeeper ducked into a hasty curtsy.

"See to Miss Long's comfort until the carriage is brought round."

Miss Long started to emit a faint cry of protest but His Grace favored her with one of his daggerlike stares while running the length of the crop suggestively between his fingers.

The lady stared at the crop, swallowed, and said no more.

"Your servant, madam." The duke made a stiff bow as the housekeeper led the girl away. It was difficult to tell whether the expression upon Miss Long's lovely face reflected more of disappointment or relief.

As the two women vanished beneath the arch, the duke's gaze turned toward Farley. When His Grace beckoned, Farley snapped to attention.

"What progress have the stables made with that young woman's horse?"

"The mare will be reshod in no time, Your Grace." Farley scratched one of his few remaining tufts of hair. "It's a curious thing, Your Grace, but that horse appears to have been outfitted recently with a new set of shoes. How one could have worked loose so soon—"

"I am sure you know as well as I how that horse came to be missing a shoe, John. What I want to know is whether the mare is fit to be led back to Miss Long's home?"

"Yes, Your Grace."

"Then dispatch one of the stable boys to do so at once and have Parker hurry along with that carriage."

"Yes, Your Grace."

Farley whipped about smartly to execute these orders. But he had not taken two steps when he was halted by the sound of the duke's voice.

"And John . . ."

Farley glanced back.

"If any more young ladies lose their way in my woods—"

"Yes, Your Grace?"

"Throw them into the moat."

"Very good, Your Grace." Farley gave a respectful touch to the side of his cap. Not until he was well outside the castle walls did he permit himself to break into a broad grin.

"I don't see anything amusing about the entire incident." Simon Arthur Lakeland, the sixth Duke of Raeburn, was still growling long after the intrusive Miss Long had been transported from his castle. Ensconced behind the glossy surface of a mahogany writing desk in his library, he glared at his companion who made no effort to disguise her mirth.

The library afforded an excellent selection of comfortable divans and settees, but Lady Augusta Penrose had drawn up a quaint maid of honor chair, well suited to her petite frame. A dark-haired woman, her elegant clothes spoke of town bronze, her twinkling eyes of unfailing good humor.

Lady Augusta was one of the few who dared to laugh at Raeburn. But then Augusta never could be brought to show a proper respect for her older brother, even if she was just a bit of a thing, scarce coming up to his shoulder. She had the Raeburn nose, but not the family height.

When the duke had complained to his sister about his unexpected visitor, Lady Augusta had immediately gone off into whoops from which she had yet to recover.

"Oh the p-poor girl," she managed to gasp out. "Imagine all the t-trouble she went to, discovering your habit of riding out early, removing her horse's shoe, setting up the scene for a romantic rescue, awaiting her fair knight. And instead she gets you, l-looking like the very devil, I daresay."

"It was a vulgar ploy merely to make my acquaintance— even worse than that chit in the inn yard yesterday."

"Oh? You didn't tell me about her."

"Some yellow-haired wench I'd never set eyes on before. She feigned a swoon in front of me."

"What!" Lady Augusta's eyes danced. "Right into your arms?"

"Not in my arms," Raeburn said with grim satisfaction. "I let her plop onto her bottom into the mud. *That* I assure you, roused her fast enough."

This sent Augusta off into fresh peals of laughter until tears stood in her eyes. "Oh, Simon, you are so dreadfully unchivalrous."

"I can be chivalrous enough to a *lady*, but these baggages! What is amiss with these modern hurly-burly females? Don't any of them possess delicacy of mind or regard for proper conduct?"

Lady Augusta dabbed her handkerchief at her moist eyes. "Oh, dear. You are beginning to sound more like Papa every day."

Since their late, esteemed parent had been both high in the instep and full of starch, Simon did not take this to be a compliment.

"Besides," Augusta added. "All these vexing incidents with the ladies throwing themselves at your head are entirely your own fault."

"My fault?" Simon said, thunderstruck. He straightened so abruptly, the leather of his chair creaked in protest.

"Yes, my dear." Smiling, she quoted, " 'It is a truth universally acknowledged, that a single man in possession of a good fortune must be in want of a wife.' "

Simon winced. He had enjoyed the wry humor to be found in *Pride and Prejudice* as much as his sister, but the gentle gibe contained in the novel's opening sentence did not seem near so amusing when applied to himself.

"Blast it all," he said. "Looking for a wife is exactly what I've been doing, this past month and more." He was fully conscious of the fact he would turn thirty-seven before the year was out, and the nursery upstairs yet remained empty.

Although Simon did not always do his duty with the best of grace, at least, by God, he did it.

"It's only that I never expected to be regarded as some sort of a prize," he continued to complain. "Sometimes I think we might just as well set up a greased pole competition, only award me instead of the pig."

Augusta threw up one hand imploringly. "Please, Simon. You have made my sides ache enough already."

"It is all very well for you to laugh. I think you are more to blame for the antics of these blasted women than anyone. That confounded notion of yours that I should give a ball! You've got 'em all stirred up."

"Why, you ungrateful wretch!" Augusta exclaimed. "And after I have been wearing myself nigh to the bone planning the affair for you. Remember it was you who commanded me to find some way of introducing you to all the eligible ladies in the county. What better way than inviting them all to a ball at Castle Raeburn? It seemed such a romantic notion, rather like that prince in the faery story."

"Rather like you are bent on making a damned cake of me," Simon groused.

Lady Augusta sniffed. "Well, if you feel that way about it, I am sure I don't know why I should go to such bother. Stanton was loath to let me come to you for so long anyway. I am sure he will be quite glad to have me home again." She arose, briskly shaking out her skirts. "You may just hie yourself to London next Season with all the other bachelors and visit the Marriage Mart."

"Almack's? Good God! You know I look ridiculous in knee breeches. Besides, I cannot abide London."

Augusta merely lifted her shoulders in an expressive shrug. When she really did appear on the verge of leaving, Simon bolted out of his chair, positioning himself in front of the door. He had never been any good at coaxing, but he gave her the half grimace that passed for his smile and said, "Don't fly up into the boughs, Gus. You know how I get when something happens to disrupt my early morning ride."

"Surly as a distempered bear," she agreed affably.

"That ride is my one solitary pleasure before I am set upon by bailiffs, land agents, and complaining tenants. I didn't appreciate being plagued before breakfast by some scheming female, but I don't mean to snap at you. You must know how grateful I am for everything you've been trying to do for me. It's just this whole business of being in the market for a bride." He expelled his breath in a heavy sigh. "Well, it's not exactly like going to the horse auction and picking out a good hunter, is it?"

As much as she struggled to repress it, Augusta's dimpled smile peeked out again. "Poor Simon," she mocked, but her eyes warmed with sympathy.

"Why can't you just pick out some chit for me?" he appealed to her, only half jesting. "Some sensible young woman who would know how to conduct herself, one who wouldn't chatter too much. She wouldn't even have to be a beauty as long as she doesn't have a face like a monkey. God knows I don't have many requirements."

"No, you don't," she agreed sadly.

"Would you like me to have more?"

"I would like you to fall in love."

Simon pinched her chin. "Stanton's been reading you too much of that romantic poetry again."

But this time Augusta didn't smile. She said rather thickly, "I had always hoped, Simon, that you would find the happiness in marriage that I have found."

"Ah, but yours is a match made in heaven, my dear. Extremely rare. I never looked for such a thing, I promise you. I never expected to have to marry at all." His mood darkened again. "Any more than I ever expected to awake one morning and find myself the Duke of Raeburn."

Abruptly he turned away from her and strode to the window to stare out. Set between the bookcases, the tall, mullioned panels of glass overlooked the vista at the rear of the house. Castle Raeburn was one of the few manors in Sussex, perhaps all of England, to be still surrounded by a moat. Just below Simon, swans sailed by in regal splendor, barely seeming to raise a ripple in the cloudy waters. In the distance loomed the

11

shadowy outline of the deer park and woodland—oaks, larches, and elms stretching as far as the eye could see.

The lord of all he surveyed, Simon thought with a bitter sneer. Except that he had never felt himself to be anything other than a usurper, filling a pair of shoes cut to someone else's size.

Lost in this gloomy contemplation, he wasn't aware of Augusta slipping up beside him until she spoke softly, "Even after all this time, it's never gotten any easier for you, has it, Simon?"

His only reply was a curt shake of his head. But then Augusta knew better than anyone how little he had ever coveted the title, or these lands, how much he loathed his inheritance, especially the way it had come to him.

Almost as one, the two of them turned involuntarily to stare at the portrait mounted over the fireplace. Encased within an ornate gilt frame was the painting of a man with dark curls, the infamous Raeburn nose set between laughing blue eyes. He sat perched upon a wooden stile, a hunting dog at his feet, a riding crop held carelessly in his grasp. The artist had captured all of Robert Lakeland's impatience with posing so well, Simon frequently expected his brother to leap out of the frame and go tearing off in search of more exciting pursuits.

Except, of course, that the late Duke of Raeburn would never do so again.

Simon averted his gaze, feeling the familiar ache of loss, little dulled by seven years' passage of time. He felt Augusta slip her arm comfortingly through his.

"I was still in the schoolroom when Robert died," she mused. "He was so much older than me I never felt as if I got to know him very well. What was he like?"

"Oh, top of the trees," Simon said gruffly, unable even for Augusta to find the words to convey what Robert had meant to him. He still carried with him much of the younger brother's awe for the older sibling who had taught him to ride, to shoot, to drive to an inch. When Simon had received his first black eye at Eton, it had been Robert who had descended upon the

12

school in a blaze of magnificence to teach Simon to be so handy with his fives, he had never been milled down again.

It had been Robert who had come to sit up with him all night when their father and mother had died of a fever within days of each other. The two brothers had shared a bottle of port even as they had shared their grief in a silence that needed no words. And it had been Robert who had proudly buckled the sword to his little brother's side when Simon had received his first commission as a cavalry officer.

But these memories of Robert faded as they always did in the face of that final grim one. Simon supposed he ought to be grateful at least that he had been home on leave from the army that cold winter's day, or else he would never have been there at the castle, never been able to bid his brother . . . farewell.

Simon had always told Robert he would be brought home on a hurdle someday, all because of that neck-or-nothing way in which he rode. It had been a jest between the two of them, nothing more, the younger brother presuming to chafe his elder.

But all laughter seemed to have stilled forever that morning when Robert was borne back from the hunting field upon a litter. His neck had not been broken; that perhaps would have been a mercy compared to the agonizing hours that followed.

His ribs crushed, bleeding inwardly, Robert had descended painfully into the arms of death, and there had been naught Simon could do for him but remain at his side, bringing what comfort he could. Simon had never been given to displays of emotion, but he had allowed the tears to course down his cheeks, unashamed, making no effort to check them.

Despite his agony, Robert had possessed enough strength to touch Simon's hand while summoning up that familiar lopsided smile.

"It'll be all right, Simon. Truly it will," he had whispered. "You'll make a far better duke than me. . . ."

But then, hadn't that been just like Robert? *He* had been the one who lay dying, and yet he had struggled to reassure Simon. The memory of those final moments with his brother still had the power to bring a burning ache into Simon's throat.

13

He coughed to clear it. Realizing that Augusta regarded him with anxious eyes, he sought to change the subject. He tried to make his voice light. "Yes, Robert was a splendid fellow, though it was damned inconsiderate of him not to have left a son behind to save my neck from the matrimonial noose."

"But he left two charming daughters," Augusta reminded him.

"True. How do Maria and the girls get on in their new home?"

"Quite wonderfully. Maria enjoys being nearer to town."

Simon was glad to hear that. After his brother's death, he had entreated his sister-in-law and nieces to consider the castle still their home, but Maria had gently refused. Simon knew she had been wise to do so. It had been painful for her seeing another take her husband's place, as painful as it had been for Simon to assume that role. After living for some years in the Dower House, Maria had recently moved to Kensington.

"Both the girls have grown so," Augusta enthused. "Do you realize that Elizabeth will be ready to make her come-out next Season? I wish Maria would let me present her. It will be ages before my own Emily is old enough for her first Season."

"It confounds me how you could be looking forward to such a thing, Gus. You positively enjoy making the rounds of all those infernal balls, hostessing crushing parties, helping insipid young misses and gawky youths find partners. I believe you were born to be one of those dreadful matchmaking mamas."

"I suppose I was," Lady Augusta said cheerfully, in no way troubled by the charge. "That is why I leaped at your invitation when you wrote to ask my help." But her face clouded over as she added, "However I shan't enjoy it in the least if I think the prospect of finding a bride makes you so utterly miserable. If you are not feeling quite ready, the ball could still be canceled, Simon."

Her words presented to him an awful temptation. Indeed he did wish the ball could be set aside, that he could simply close up the castle again and resume his travels on the Continent. But he had been running away for too many years.

14

"What! And disappoint all those ladies who seem to regard me as the catch of the Season?" Raeburn raised his brows, his voice laced with self-mockery. "After all, I am the sixth Duke of Raeburn. And we all know, a duke must have his duchess."

He stretched his arms, flexing his back muscles. "But enough talk of balls and weddings for one morning. Why don't you fling on your shawl and take a walk with me out to the paddock? I acquired a new bull at the market yesterday. A most capital fellow. He promises to do much for raising the stock of my cattle. If the heifers prove only half so eager as the young ladies hereabouts—"

But Augusta clapped her hands over her ears, greatly scandalized. She refused his invitation, saying that far too many details for the ball yet required her attention. "So you may cease your lewd comments and go view your horrid bull by yourself."

Simon nearly smiled. For all her acquired sophistication, Gus was still an adorable little prude. He was halfway out the study door when he turned and belatedly asked if there was anything he could do to help with the preparations.

She must have detected the reluctance with which he made the offer, for she grinned. "No, nothing, except to stay out of the way. Though you might practice being a little more gracious with the ladies. Your manners have gotten a trifle rusty."

"I never had any. It was always Robert who possessed the most address with your fair sex. I fear that I frighten most of the poor dears to death."

"And take great pleasure in doing so," Augusta said severely. "You can be perfectly charming when you wish. You might begin by being more gallant to the next lady who loses her way in your woods."

"Not on your life! I can tolerate being hunted, but I'll be damned if I'll be pursued when I've gone to earth on my own coverts." As he strode through the door, he added darkly, "God help the wench who ambushes me on my own lands again."

15

Chapter 2

The ball to be given at Castle Raeburn had formed the chief topic of drawing room conversation for the past sennight. It was inevitable that the subject would be discussed at Meadow Lane Lodge even though the lodge's current tenant, Miss Audra Leigh Masters, had no interest in dukes, eligible or otherwise.

That particular afternoon Audra felt as if her front parlor was stuffed full of chattering females. Her younger half sister Cecily sat upon the settee before the hearth, discussing the merits of lace and ruching with her dear friend Phoebe Coleby.

Phoebe's mama had stationed herself near the tea caddy on the parlor table, Lady Sophia Coleby's heavy perfume at war with the young ladies' rosewater, tickling Audra's nose, making her want to sneeze. She inched open the long window leading out into the frost-blighted garden and took a bracing gulp of the cold fresh air before returning to her task of pouring out the tea.

Sophia Coleby talked on while reaching for the plate of tea cakes. Her plump, beringed fingers closed about her third, as she scarce missed a stroke in her endless flow of words. "And when the Vicar told me that the Duke of Raeburn had returned, bringing with him his sister and twenty trunks, I was never more astonished in my life. You could have knocked me down with a feather."

"Indeed," Audra murmured, smiling faintly. Feathers be hanged. Nothing less than a battering ram would serve to dislodge Lady Coleby, especially when she was ensconced in someone's parlor for what she termed a "long, comfortable prose."

Audra had long since lost the thread of Lady Coleby's somewhat erratic conversation. Usually she could summon more toleration for her visitor's volubility, but her ladyship would choose today of all days to pay a call. Audra had recently acquired the latest work by the author of the Waverly novels. Even now the second volume of *Ivanhoe* lay nearby upon the caned surface of a Hepplewhite chair, obscured from view by a soft cushion.

She had been lost for hours in a far different world of banished knights, tournaments, and besieged castles. It was very difficult to drag herself back to the clatter of tea cups and Lady Coleby.

When the rap had come at her front door, Audra would have simply denied she was at home, but her seventeen-year-old sister Cecily had fairly leaped to admit Lady Coleby and her eldest daughter. Now Cecily (the little traitoress) had dragged Phoebe off to look at dress patterns, leaving Audra entirely to the mercy of Lady Coleby's loquaciousness. Tucking away a stray tendril of her chestnut-colored hair, Audra resisted the temptation to pull her spinster's cap further down over her ears. Lady Coleby talked on. She never seemed to need to pause for breath, only an occasional sip of tea.

Wistfully, Audra's gaze traveled to where her book lay concealed. She could not resist shifting it onto her lap and opening it to where she had marked her page. Surely it could do no harm to read just a few more paragraphs. All she need do was continue to smile and nod. It would never occur to her ladyship that Audra was not hanging upon her every word.

Audra had discovered that it was possible with many of her callers to read and appear the perfect hostess at the same time. She supposed she ought to be ashamed of herself and was likely to be embarrassed if she was ever caught out. But at the age of eight and twenty, she had come to regard with a cynical eye some of the views of the world.

In others such behavior as hiding books in the folds of her skirts beneath the table might be considered intolerably rude.

In a wealthy spinster such as herself, it would merely be termed charmingly eccentric.

Lady Coleby droned on, her voice as soothingly monotonous as the crisp breeze rustling the chintz curtains. Turning another page, Audra eagerly pursued the perils of the beautiful Jewess Rebecca as she tried to repulse the advances of the lustful Bois-Guilbert.

That, reflected Audra, was one problem she had never had. As tall as many gentlemen of her acquaintance, Audra had a trick of looking them straight in the eye in such a manner as to quell even the boldest heart. Nor did she possess such a degree of beauty as to make a man so far forget himself. Her nose was a little too straight, her face a little too angular. With her prominent cheekbones and heart-shaped chin, she possessed none of that dimpled plumpness the gentlemen seemed to find attractive.

She had been told frequently that her best feature was her eyes, with their thick-fringed lashes and deep gray coloring. During her one Season in London, a young admirer had actually gone so far as to write an ode to her eyes, comparing them to the mists of London. When Audra had tartly asked whether he referred to the fog or the coal smoke, that had mercifully nipped all further poetical offerings in the bud.

With so limited experience in inspiring unbridled passion, Audra refrained from passing judgment on the way Rebecca dealt with the ardent villain. Threatening to leap from the castle walls seemed a little extreme, but Audra could not help admiring Rebecca's calm determination and courage.

It was incredible that the hero, Ivanhoe, should prefer that blond ninnyhammer Lady Rowena to Rebecca's fire and intelligence. The lovely dark-haired Jewess seemed so much more suited to the bold knight.

"One hardly dares to hope for such a thing, but it would make an excellent match, don't you think so, Miss Masters?"

Engrossed in the book, it scarce surprised Audra when Lady Coleby's voice penetrated her haze, the woman in apparent agreement with her.

"Yes, it would," Audra murmured. "Though I suppose there could be some objection on the score of religion."

Lady Coleby gave a startled gasp, setting her teacup down with a loud clatter. "My dear Miss Masters, I know the Duke of Raeburn has traveled forever in heathen lands, but I daresay he is as devout a member of the Church of England as the next man."

Audra, wrenching her eye from the book, slowly raised her head like someone surfacing through a sea of confusion, aware of one thing only, that she had just made some remarkable blunder.

Lady Coleby leaned forward conspiratorially, the plumes on her poke bonnet fluttering. "Unless, my dear, you have heard something to the contrary about His Grace? You may tell me. I wouldn't repeat it to a soul."

"Wh-why no," Audra stammered. "I haven't heard—that is, I don't even know the man."

"Of course, you do," Lady Coleby said reproachfully. "He is your landlord."

"I *know* that. I meant that I had never met him." When Audra had taken the lease upon Meadow Lane Lodge two years earlier, all the details had been handled by the duke's estate agent; His Grace himself was traveling abroad. The only interest the duke had ever aroused in her was a pang of envy of anyone who had the freedom to travel so extensively and reportedly to such exciting places, Greece, Rome, Egypt. . . . There was much to be said for having been born a man, Audra often thought.

Since she had no idea how she came to be discussing the duke with Lady Coleby, Audra decided that she had best pay a little more heed to her ladyship's conversation. Suppressing a sigh, she nudged her book closed and reached dutifully across the table to refill her guest's cup.

"You must be thinking me the most foolish old woman," Lady Coleby gushed, "to be running on about the duke in this fashion."

"Not at all, ma'am," Audra said politely.

" 'Tis simply the most exciting news I've had in an age. Everyone in the entire countryside is agog."

Everyone but herself, Audra thought. But that was not unusual. Forever buried among her books, she could name to the day what had occurred in Tudor England, but she never seemed to know what had happened in the neighboring village of Haworth Green just last week.

It was on the tip of her tongue to ask Lady Coleby just what was so exciting when it occurred to Audra that very likely that was what her ladyship had been relating for the past quarter hour. Despite a niggling of curiosity, Audra swallowed the awkward question.

It scarce mattered in any case, for in her usual quicksilver fashion, her ladyship's attention had already shifted direction. Nodding toward the opposite end of the room where Cecily and Phoebe were giggling over some new frock design, Lady Coleby trilled, "Don't our girls present a charming picture?"

Audra swiveled around to observe the two young women settled upon the sofa, Phoebe's dark curls an excellent foil for Cecily's honey-blond tresses. With their heads bent together over the pattern book, and Cecily's foolish little pug curled up between them, twitching its corkscrew tail, they did indeed make a pretty picture.

"How becoming that frock is to your sister," Lady Coleby said. "Quite in the latest mode."

"Very fashionable," Audra agreed, but she caught herself frowning. The sprigged muslin, a confection of lace, and the embroidered trim were wholly unsuited for the chilling breath of November as much so as the dainty green kid slippers Cecily had slipped upon her feet. Staring at her sister, Audra was hard put to recognize the madcap little hoyden their mother had bundled off to boarding school two years ago. Although Audra had never taken much stock in her own appearance, she could have been fiercely proud of Cecily's beauty if her sister had not acquired a parcel of missish airs to go along with it. As it was, Audra found herself missing the little scapegrace with smudged frocks and flyaway curls that Audra had looked after in her mother's frequent absence.

When Cecily glanced up from the patterns long enough to feed her pug part of a biscuit, Lady Coleby said frankly, "I would give half my income for Phoebe to have your sister's complexion and those golden curls. Cecily is so lovely. She looks nothing like you."

"I suppose she doesn't."

"Oh . . . oh dear. That is, I didn't mean—"

"It is quite all right, ma'am," Audra said, laughing a little at Lady Coleby's flustered expression. "I understand exactly what you meant. I take more after Mama while Cecily favors her papa, my late stepfather, Mr. Stephen Holt of Dover."

"Indeed? That would have been your dear mother's second husband?"

"Her third," Audra correctly flatly.

"Oh, that's right. I keep forgetting about Lady Arabella's second marriage to that squire from Worcester. But the poor man only lasted two months so I daresay he shouldn't even count."

Audra refrained from informing Lady Coleby rather tartly that it certainly had counted, at least as far as Audra was concerned. It had meant another upheaval in her childhood, another new house, another stranger to call papa. Sometimes she felt as if she had lived under more roofs than an itinerant peddler, and none of them had ever felt like her home.

Coming from any woman other than Lady Coleby, Audra would have presumed such remarks about her mother's marital escapades to be prompted by a sly malice. But she knew her ladyship was merely curious, and who could blame her for that? There were not many like Lady Arabella who had managed to outlive four husbands and then embark upon a fifth marriage, all before the age of fifty. Audra sometimes feared that if Mama lived to a ripe old age, she might manage to outdo even that notorious king, Henry the Eighth, with his six wives.

She did not enjoy discussing her mother and was relieved when Lady Coleby changed the subject. Her ladyship continued to coo over the two young women. "Such prettily behaved girls, your sister and my Phoebe. Your mama did well to send Cecily to that academy. Girls learn so much at a good school."

"Do they?" Cecily had been with Audra a month now at

21

Meadow Lane Lodge, and Audra had yet to see any sign that her sister's mind was stuffed with a vast store of knowledge.

"Oh, certainly," Lady Coleby said. "Phoebe became so clever upon the harp—to say nothing of her prowess with a brush. Only fancy. She learned japanning. There is scarce a stick of furniture in our house that is not adorned with one of her creations, a posy or some woodland creature. Though I must admit her papa was a trifle vexed over the little bears she put on his escritoire."

"I suppose he might be," Audra said with a glimmer of amusement. Sir John Coleby, being the local magistrate, was a gruff no-nonsense sort of fellow. She could well imagine how he must have bellowed to discover his daughter's artwork upon his favorite desk.

But as for herself, Audra thought she might have borne it better if Cecily had gone about wielding a brush, ruining all the furniture. Even that would have been a far more sensible accomplishment than learning to blush, simper, and flutter one's fan.

Despite these stern thoughts, Audra could feel her expression soften as Cecily danced gracefully up from the sofa. She did not even scold when Cecily closed the French doors. Cecily was forever shutting the house up tight lest her pug escape. In vain did Audra point out to her that that was where a dog belonged, out of doors. Cecily was convinced some dreadful fate would befall her pet.

After one final tug to make sure the door was secure, Cecily tripped over to Audra, Phoebe trailing in her wake, the color in both girls' cheeks heightened by excitement. For once Cecily abandoned all affectation, her blue eyes sparkling with child-like enthusiasm.

"Oh, Audra," she said thrusting the pattern book forward. "Do look at this gown. Wouldn't it be just perfect for Phoebe?"

Audra took a peek at the sketch and crinkled her nose. "Too much lace and surely a little too fine for the local assembly."

"I wasn't thinking of it for the assembly, Miss Masters," Phoebe chimed in. "But for the ball."

"Oh? What ball is that?" To Audra, it seemed the most inno-

22

cent of questions. But she became uncomfortably aware that all three of the other women were staring at her.

"Why, you know. *The* ball," Phoebe said. "The one to be given at Castle Raeburn. Mama and I received our invitation just this morning."

"Just as I have been telling you, my dear," Lady Coleby added.

Cecily, who had caught sight of the book tucked upon Audra's lap, shot her a look of blistering reproach. "You must pardon Audra, your ladyship. She—she is sometimes a little hard of hearing."

"My advancing years, you know," Audra said dryly.

The good-natured Lady Coleby did not appear in the least put out to have to repeat all that she had said and at a slightly louder volume. "And we were so thrilled to receive our invitation. It was an honor we scarce expected."

"My congratulations, ma'am," Audra said, striving to show all the enthusiasm and wonder that appeared to be expected. "So the Scowling Duke is to give a ball. Only fancy that."

"Audra!" Cecily gasped, looking mortified. "You should not call His Grace that."

"Why not? Everyone else does. He scarcely seems like the sort to host any entertainment. And what a shabby affair it is sure to be, a parcel of dancing and no supper until past midnight."

"That's what balls are, Audra," Cecily said in suffocating accents.

"Well, if that is His Grace's notion of amusement, I am sure he is welcome to it."

"Ah, but there is more to this particular ball than mere amusement." Lady Coleby raised both of her finely plucked brows, looking arch. "Mrs. Wright believes the duke is finally hanging out for a wife."

"Mrs. Wright has six unmarried daughters. She thinks every single male under the age of ninety is seeking a bride. And what on earth does a ball have to do with that?"

Lady Coleby exchanged a look with Cecily and Phoebe, all three of them seeming to despair at Audra's obtuseness. Her ladyship kindly set herself to explain, "Why you see, my dear, it appears the duke doesn't care to go to London looking for a wife. Hopefully, by giving this ball, he will find a lady that will suit."

"Isn't it romantic, Audra?" Cecily chimed in.

"It sounds like a perfectly cork-brained notion to me," Audra said. "His Grace must have maggots in his head if he expects to become that well acquainted with anyone in a crowded ballroom."

This forthright speech made Cecily look ready to sink, but Phoebe giggled and Lady Coleby smiled, shaking her finger at Audra, terming her a naughty creature.

"But always so droll." Gathering the ends of her shawl, her ladyship heaved herself to her feet. "I fear we must be going, Phoebe. Your papa will wonder what has become of us."

Audra's heart gave a grateful leap, the pages of her book seeming to call out to her, but she tried to disguise her eagerness. "Must you be going and so soon?" Not allowing her ladyship a chance to reply, she leaped to her feet. "We won't keep you then. I shall ring to have your carriage brought round at once."

No matter how short a stay her callers paid, Audra always insisted their coachman employ the hospitality of her stables. She couldn't abide the notion of horses being kept standing about, waiting upon dilatory human beings.

But in this instance, Audra had allowed herself to forget what a task it could be, sending Lady Coleby upon her way. Even after she was bundled into her shawl, her ladyship remembered at least half a dozen more important things she needed to tell Audra. Then a search had to be commenced to find Lady Coleby's missing reticule. It had become lodged beneath the settee cushion. After that, her ladyship insisted that she must write down instructions for Audra's housekeeper on an infallible new method for getting berry juice out of muslin.

By the time Audra managed to sweep Lady Coleby and Phoebe through her front door, her ladyship's fine bays had been kept pawing in the traces for a full quarter of an hour.

Concealing her fret of impatience, Audra stepped out onto

the lane and waved cheerfully as the two ladies were handed into the carriage. "I hope you and Phoebe enjoy yourselves splendidly at the ball," she called. "You must drop round for tea again very soon."

With Cecily by her side, the two of them continued to wave until the carriage lumbered into motion. As soon as the coach vanished down the lane, Cecily's smile faded and she turned upon Audra a look of pure exasperation.

"Oh, Audra! How could you!"

"How could I what? Invite her ladyship back? It seemed the civil thing to do, and I might as well. She'll come anyway."

"You know that is not what I meant."

As Audra headed back into the house, Cecily trailed after her, still scolding. "I am talking about all those outrageous things you said about the duke, all those horrid jests, and to Lady Coleby, of all people. You know what a notorious gossip she is. Your remarks will be all over the neighborhood before tomorrow morning."

"Nonsense. Why would she bother talking about me?" Audra chuckled. "I assure you I am nothing compared to a duke who travels with twenty trunks."

She was already dismissing Lady Coleby from her mind, her thoughts on one thing only. Hastening to the parlor, she found the room odiously stuffy and managed to inch the long windows open a crack before Cecily joined her there. With Cecily following her like a small dark cloud, Audra retrieved her book and mounted a search for her wire-rimmed spectacles.

"And that is another thing, Audra," Cecily continued to scold. "You have been *reading* again!"

Why did her sister always make that sound as though Audra had been doing something disreputable, like tying her garter in public? Locating her glasses, Audra perched them on the bridge of her nose and peered at Cecily over the rims. "It wouldn't hurt you to occasionally look between the covers of a book yourself, miss."

"No, thank you. One bluestocking in the family is quite enough. You are ruining your eyes. I quite detest those spectacles you have taken to wearing and . . . and, oh, Audra, don't

25

you understand? You will get the most dreadful reputation for oddity."

Audra forbore to remind her sister that she had had that reputation for years and that Cecily had never minded it before, at least not until she had returned from Bath, a graduate of Miss Hudson's Academy for Fashionable Young Ladies.

But she didn't want to quarrel with Cecily again. They seemed to squabble too often of late. Instead Audra chose to ignore her sister's comments, seeking out the sanctuary of her favorite wing-back chair drawn close to the hearth.

She was on the verge of plunking onto it when she was startled by a reproachful yip. Glancing down, she discovered Cecily's pug curled up on the velvet cushion.

"Down!" Audra snapped in a tone of command that would have reduced any of her own hunting dogs to a state of prompt obedience. The pug merely yawned. When she reached out to haul the dog off, the beast emitted a low, menacing growl.

"Audra! You're scaring her," Cecily cried.

"Then have the goodness to remove the little bitch from my chair."

Cecily let out a horrified shriek, but swooped to rescue her pet. Cuddling the dog in her arms, she murmured endearments. "The poor little thing. She's quivering. I've asked you not to shout at her, Audra, or call her anything so horrid."

"But that is what a female dog is called."

"I don't care. It sounds vulgar. Besides, she has a name."

"So she does," Audra grumbled as she settled in her chair. "But I could never bring myself to call anything *Frou-frou*."

With an injured sniff, Cecily whisked her dog away as if she feared Audra meant to do the animal some harm, which was ridiculous. Audra was notoriously tenderhearted toward all four-legged creatures, a trait she found slightly embarrassing to admit. She was likely the only person in England who kept a pack of hunting dogs and never hunted. She could not even endure the thought of destroying the vixen who made repeated raids upon her henhouse. Although she could not say that she was fond of Cecily's dog, she would never have wrung its neck, no matter how often she threatened to do so.

26

After being much petted by Cecily and adjured not to mind "crosspatch Audra," Frou-frou settled into the corner of the settee to resume her nap. Audra, flicking through the pages to where she had left the imperiled Ivanhoe, wished her sister would alight somewhere.

But Cecily hovered over her, hands on hips. "I cannot believe you are going to bury yourself in that book again, especially after we have had such thrilling tidings."

Never glancing up from her volume, Audra searched her memory, but she could recall nothing more thrilling than a complaint from her housekeeper. "I would call it vexing rather than exciting. That is the second time the cow has got into the garden this week. It is all the fault of Sir Ralph Entwhistle and his blasted hunt. If he does not remember to close the gate next time he crosses—"

"Audra! How can you be so provoking! You know I am not talking about any cow or— Do put that book away and pay attention. You never talk to me. I am nigh ready to perish of loneliness."

Audra would have thought that the recent onslaught of Lady Coleby would have been enough to cure anyone of loneliness for a twelvemonth, but she was not proof against the dejected pout of Cecily's lips nor the tiny catch in her voice.

"I am sorry if I have been neglecting you, Muffin," she said, then immediately had to apologize again for letting slip the now-hated childhood nickname.

"For you know I am far too old to be called that anymore, Audra," Cecily said indignantly.

"So you are," Audra said, suppressing a smile and a twinge of wistfulness at the same time. Although she didn't close up the book, she removed her spectacles and reluctantly tried to accord Cecily her full attention.

"What is it you wish to talk about?" she asked, hoping it was nothing to do with the cut of sleeves or the length of hemlines this year. Audra couldn't abide discussing furbelows.

Cecily brightened immediately, sinking gracefully onto the settee opposite. "Why, the ball. The ball to be held at Raeburn Castle. Was there ever anything so delightful?" She did not give Audra a chance to reply but immediately began to enthuse over the pleasures of waltzing in the great hall, sipping champagne, and eating lobster patties. But when she reached the point of wondering at what silk warehouse they should order the material for their gowns, Audra felt obliged to interrupt.

"But Muff—I mean, Cecily, you should not get that excited. There is not the least likelihood we shall be invited."

"Why ever not? After all, your papa was a viscount, and mine was second cousin to an earl. It is not as if we are beneath the duke's touch. I am sure we are every bit as good as the Colebys."

"I never said we were not. What I do say is that His Grace is completely unaware of our existence."

Audra didn't add that if this duke meant to involve them in a foolish round of balls and dinner parties, she was content to remain unknown.

Cecily, however, looked quite crestfallen. "There must be some way of obtaining an introduction," she urged.

"I suppose I could call at the castle and leave my card."

"Oh, no, Audra. You couldn't. A single lady calling upon a gentleman. It simply isn't done."

"Of course, it isn't. Do credit me with some notions of propriety, you goose. I was only funning you."

Cecily glared at her, and Audra sighed. With all the grown-up airs she had acquired, Cecily seemed to have entirely lost her sense of humor. Audra tried to recall if at seventeen *she* had taken everything so deathly serious.

Her brow puckered in thought, after a moment, Cecily asked, "Why can't Uncle Matthew wait upon the duke? I believe he would if you asked him to, Audra."

"Oh, Cecily," Audra said reprovingly, and the girl had the grace to blush. The Reverend Matthew Arthur Masters, who was actually Audra's great-uncle, was pushing ninety and rarely ever went into company these days.

"Then I do wish Mama would come home now," Cecily fretted.

Audra tensed as she always did at any mention of their mother. Arabella, the Contessa di Montifiora, was currently traveling through Naples with her fifth husband, on an extended bridal tour. So extended, in fact, that Mama had not been home in over two years. And even if she had, Audra thought somewhat cynically, Lady Arabella would not have been the least use to either one of her daughters. She was too caught up with her own amours. But as Cecily had yet to suffer the same disillusionment with their erratic parent, Audra held her tongue.

Instead, she said, "Missing one ball is not the end of the world, especially this one. I have told you His Grace is likely a most disagreeable man." Audra spoke with a marked authority, although she had only once ever set eyes upon His Grace and that had been a mere glimpse obtained six years ago when she had been fortunate enough to attend the York Races. But she yet retained an impression of a tall, dark-complexioned man with massive shoulders, his thick black brows drawn together in a perpetual scowl.

But Cecily could not be brought to believe that an eligible duke could be other than handsome and charming, the ball to be held at the castle other than a glittering event. The girl's shoulders drooped, and with some trepidation, Audra recognized all the signs of Cecily descending into a state of being absolutely crushed. From there it was only a step away to utterly devastated.

"Never mind, Cecily," she tried to comfort, settling back with her book. "We have other things to look forward to. The strolling players will be returning to Haworth next month, and there is going to be a horse auction at the fair."

To Audra's astonishment, her sister burst into tears. "Oh, Audra, you never understand anything! This place is so h-horridly dull. That ball was the only thing that . . . oh, if I wasn't going to London for my come-out next spring, I-I should simply want to d-die." Upon a final great sob, she stood up and rushed toward the door.

"Cecily! For heaven's sake—" Audra began in exasperation, but her sister had already fled from the room. Audra half started to go after her, but she knew it would do no good. She was a poor hand at consoling Cecily these days. Telling her such bracing things as not to be a widgeon and threatening to dash cold water over her head never seemed to serve the purpose.

"Oh, hang it all. She'll get over it," Audra muttered, flouncing back against the cushions. Cecily's maid would cosset her with cool cloths to the brow and cups of tea, then that would be the end of the matter.

Thus assuring herself, Audra tried to resume her place in the book. But even in the depths of the dungeon at Torquilstone Castle, Ivanhoe in his most dire peril yet, Cecily's unhappy face swam between Audra and the pages. When the bold knight should have been shouting defiance at his enemies, instead he seemed to be mewing, "I simply want to die."

After spending ten minutes trying to read the same paragraph, Audra slammed the book shut in disgust. Rubbing her fingers against her eyes, she wished that the Duke of Raeburn had sunk into the sea before returning home to so cut up their peace at Meadow Lane Lodge.

But she was too honest to entirely blame the present difficulty with Cecily upon the duke. Cecily had been discontent with life at Meadow Lane before Raeburn's return, perhaps even from the moment she had joined Audra there three months ago.

It is so h-horridly dull here. Audra realized Cecily had spoken those words out in pique, and she should ignore them. But the remark stung all the same. Audra had worked very hard to establish a snug, agreeable home for Cecily when the girl should have finished her schooling.

It had never occurred to her that Cecily would dislike Meadow Lane. From the time Audra had first taken the lease, she had found the property perfect, near enough to her Uncle Matthew of whom she was fond, far enough away from other interfering relatives who found it shocking that a spinster should live alone.

Of course, the black-and-white timber lodge was small, having been no more than a hunting retreat. Yet Audra liked the deep masculine tone of the paneled walls. She had scattered about ruby red rugs and hung bright chintz curtains, bringing warmth and light, rendering the house cozy. Here she had enough room for her horses, her dogs, her library. What more could one want?

A companion to share it with, someone whose interests matched her own. The thought came unbidden, but as ever Audra was quick to reject it. She had long ago given up conjuring masculine images in the dark of her room, faces with sympathetic eyes and understanding smiles. And if occasionally she was beset by a peculiar feeling of melancholy or emptiness, she had only to pluck a book from her shelves and bury herself within the pages.

She had been foolish to hope that Cecily would likewise be content with such a reclusive existence. Audra tried to understand, knowing that she was the oddity. Most young women naturally craved the same things Cecily did: society, waltzing balls, handsome suitors.

Perhaps what rendered Audra so frequently irritable and impatient was the realization that she could not give Cecily all those things. Muffin was counting so much upon a London Season. Audra had not as yet found the courage to tell her that she was doomed to disappointment. There would be no coming out for Cecily next Season or perhaps any other. It was not a question of funds, Cecily had inherited a respectable portion and Audra was a considerable heiress in her own right. Audra had to allow her mother that much. Lady Arabella never had thrown her cap over the windmill for a poor man.

The difficulty with Cecily's coming out lay in finding a respectable matron to present her. Audra placed no dependence upon Mama returning to assume the responsibility. The only other likely candidate was Mama's sister. But Aunt Saunders had quite washed her hands of her nieces after the debacle of Audra's own presentation. Audra knew she had been a most reluctant debutante and very difficult, as gawky as a wild colt with her tongue as unbridled as her gait.

When asked her opinion of Almack's, she had replied that she found it very like Tattersall's, only that she thought the horses derived a great deal more amusement at being auctioned off to the highest bidder. Unfortunately, the remark had been overheard by Lady Sefton, one of the all-powerful patronesses of Almack's, resulting in Audra's being denied admittance to those hallowed walls.

Aunt Saunders had been furious. Never had any protégée of hers been refused vouchers. After stigmatizing Audra as a "devil's daughter" in the most icily well-bred accents, she had sent her packing and had never spoken to her again, a circumstance Audra had never regretted until now.

That had been over seven years ago, and her aunt still seemed to be holding a grudge. Shortly after Cecily's return from school, Audra had swallowed her own pride and had written a letter upon Cecily's behalf, pleading with her aunt to present Cecily the following spring. Aunt Saunders had not even deigned to reply.

Audra did not know what more she could do. She had never found the charge of her sister a burden before, but she had to admit it had been much easier looking after Cecily when all her hurts could be healed with sticking plaster, all her desires satisfied by an extra cake at teatime.

"You grew up entirely too fast, Muffin," Audra said with a melancholy sigh. But there was no use dwelling on that or she would end by becoming as blue-deviled as Cecily.

Reopening her book, she made one more effort to seek solace as she always did and put the recent frustrating scene with Cecily out of her mind. But she met with no more success than before, being interrupted this time by her housekeeper.

The dour Mrs. McGuiness thrust her head inside the parlor to announce that one of Miss Cecily's suitors, "that there Mr. Gilmore," had stopped by with some posies for her.

Audra grimaced. Until Cecily's arrival, she had never realized so many callow youths inhabited the county.

"Tell him Miss Cecily is indisposed," Audra replied.

"Very good, Miss Audra." Before ducking out again, the housekeeper added, "You might also want to know Jack Coachman said he saw Miss Cecily's dog running off, a-heading for Raeburn's Wood."

"Jack Coachman needs spectacles. Miss Cecily's dog is right over—" Audra began to point toward the settee, but froze in midgesture. The settee was empty.

Mrs. McGuiness clicked her tongue with the usual relish she seemed to take in any impending disaster. "Miss Cecily will be that upset," she predicted with dark satisfaction before bustling off to dispose of the suitor.

Ignoring the woman's grim comment, Audra leaped up, convinced that she would find the little beast still lurking somewhere beneath the furniture, ready to growl at her again.

But she looked under all the chairs without finding any sign of the pug. It was then that her gaze fell upon the window that she had cracked open earlier. With a sinking heart, she saw that it had been shoved much wider than she had left it.

"Oh, blast and perdition!" Stomping through the long window into the garden herself, she placed her fingers to her lips and emitted a series of unladylike but expert whistles.

Of course, there was no response. Audra prepared to retreat to the house, shrugging her shoulders. Surely the little bitch could not be so stupid as to be unable to find her way back home.

Yet uneasily she recalled the report of Jack Coachman. The pug had been seen heading for Raeburn's Wood. It might easily become confused or worse. It might encounter a *real* dog who would make a meal of it.

Audra muttered imprecations under her breath, but she saw no other remedy. She was going to have to go look for the foolish beast. Cecily was distressed enough already. Audra could hardly face her over the supper table and inform her that her beloved Frou-frou had gone missing.

Pausing only long enough to snatch up her old crimson shawl and a leash, Audra bolted through her front door and down the steps. In her haste, she nearly collided with the young gentleman who lingered in the lane.

Mr. Gilmore had yet to take his leave. His cherubic face wistful above his strangling neckcloth, he stood gazing up toward Cecily's window.

Although startled by Audra's sudden appearance, he recovered, sweeping his curly brimmed beaver from his pomaded locks. "Oh, Miss Masters! Good afternoon. I was so distressed to hear that Miss Cecily—"

"Your pardon, sir." Audra thrust him unceremoniously aside, having neither the time nor patience for lovelorn youths at the moment. "I cannot stop now. The little bitch has escaped. I have to haul her back by the scruff of her neck."

Audra rushed on, oblivious to Mr. Gilmore's open-mouthed expression. He followed her progress down the lane, slowly returning his hat to his head. He had heard stories about the eccentric Miss Masters, how stern she could be, even cruel to her younger sister, but he hadn't credited a word of it. Now he could see plainly those tales were all too true.

Chapter 3

Several hours later, Audra tramped along the lane skirting Raeburn's Wood, dried leaves crunching beneath her feet. She had lost both her lace cap and her temper, but was no nearer to recovering Cecily's wretched dog.

Clenching the leash tight in her fist, she muttered, "When I get my hands upon that little bitch, I'll wrap this about her throat." But beneath this fierce threat was a growing sense of unease. The pug had never strayed this far afield before.

When her continued whistles and calls met with no response, she was almost on the verge of doubling back when she heard an answering bark. But such a deep baying could hardly come from Cecily's dog.

While she hesitated, listening, any doubts she may have had were put to rest. Rounding the turn in the lane came two sleek hounds with plumed tails waving. The beasts were hard followed by a rider, a short stocky man mounted upon a gray hunter.

Audra stiffened, having no difficulty in recognizing the local master of the hunt. Sir Ralph Entwhistle was as notorious for his poor seat as for his unruly pack of dogs. Audra had an urge to dive for cover, but it was already too late.

Sir Ralph had spotted her; and man, horse, and dogs bore down upon her at full cry.

"Miss Masters! Huick halloa!"

Audra could never decide what annoyed her most, the way he always greeted her as if she were a vixen on the run or his loud, braying laugh.

She skirted back as he reined his sweating mount close beside her, his dogs barking and leaping at her frock with their muddied paws.

"Here, now. Ratterer! Bellman! Down." When the dogs failed to obey his command, he slashed out with his whip. Audra emitted a horrified protest, but the hounds were already slinking away.

Beaming, Sir Ralph tipped his tall hunter's hat, revealing carroty waves of hair, his bluff features nearly the same shade of red.

"G'day Miss Masters. What're you doin' afoot? Lose your horse?" The baronet guffawed at his own wit.

"No! But I fear you are about to lose yours." She reached up to stroke the nose of Entwhistle's hunter, the beast lathered with sweat, obviously badly winded. She exclaimed indignantly, "Fie upon you, sir. You have nearly ridden this poor creature into the ground."

"Not this lazy brute. I but showed him a good run. Oh, but we had excellent sport today, Miss Masters. Cub hunting. You should have seen it."

"What I did see was my cow, wandering loose. You left my gate open again when you crossed my land."

"Pish!" Sir Ralph dismissed her complaint with a wave of his hand. "Forget about the cursed cow. I keep telling you, you ought to ride out with the hunt one morning. Exhilarating! Nothing like it. Many wenches do so nowadays."

"Wenches, certainly, but not ladies."

35

"Bah! I thought you'd a bit more of a dash than to be bothered by any stuffy notions of propriety. B'gawd, madam. I've seen you ride. Good seat, light hands."

"Unfortunately, I cannot return the compliment." Upon further inspection of Sir Ralph's horse, she was nigh sickened to see how the creature's mouth had been ruined by the way he jabbed at the reins.

"Even a performing monkey could be trained to ride better than you," she said. She was a little appalled by her own bluntness, but Sir Ralph only roared with laughter.

"Ha, Miss Masters! What a complete hand you are. Always jesting."

Audra stepped back, pursing her lips. She might have known that it was impossible to insult anyone with a head thicker than last Sunday's pudding. Feeling that she had already allowed him to distract her long enough, she said, "If you will excuse me, sir. I am on rather an important errand."

"I know. I noticed the leash. Searching for Miss Cecily's dog, aren't you?"

Something in Sir Ralph's grin rendered her uneasy. "Why, yes. You haven't by any chance seen it?"

"Dashed well believe I did. Mistook it for a rabbit and set my hounds after it."

Audra felt herself go pale. "You what!"

Sir Ralph shook with chuckles. "Never thought one of those little lap dogs could move so fast. Streaked off into that thicket yonder like a bolt of lightning."

Biting back a curse, Audra whirled in the direction he pointed. "Best make haste, ma'am. That little cur is likely halfway to London by now."

"Why didn't you tell me so at once, you . . . you . . ." But before Audra could think of an epithet strong enough, Sir Ralph emitted another of his donkeylike brays, slashed at his horse, and galloped off, his hounds tearing after him.

Seething with frustrated rage, Audra could only glower at his retreating form. She was angered enough to wish the earth would be rent asunder and send that heedless dolt to the devil—that is, as long as the dogs and horse could make it to safety.

But she had little time to waste cursing Sir Ralph. Hiking up her skirts, she raced toward the spot where the baronet claimed to have last seen Cecily's dog. Audra plunged deep into the thicket herself. Sharp twigs scratched her hands and one low-lying branch tangled in her hair.

Pausing long enough to free the stray tendril, she consigned Sir Ralph to perdition. He and his galumphing hounds had made her task thrice as difficult. Cecily's poor pug could be cowering anywhere, by now too terrified to even respond to Audra's calls.

Yet she kept pausing to whistle, kept struggling forward. She figured she must have come better than five miles all told. An indefatigable walker, the distance itself did not bother her, but she viewed with dread the sun sinking lower behind the trees. Raeburn's Wood was not exactly an untamed forest, but it was no place to wander after dark either.

Yet the alternative was unthinkable. How could she return to Cecily without the dog? Perhaps, though, she should at least work her way back to the lane. While she was pondering this course of action, a sound carried to Audra's ear above the evening song of the lark.

She tensed, listening. It was the bark of a dog and not the full-blooded cry of anyone's hunting hound this time. No, such a disagreeable yipping could only come from Cecily's pug. Audra hesitated only long enough to determine the exact direction of the sound, then charged after it.

Shoving branches aside, Audra made her way forward. Her head bent down, she was in nowise prepared to suddenly break free into a clearing. Stumbling a little, she gazed upward and caught her breath.

The Castle Raeburn itself loomed before her, those turrets of white stone bathed in the last golden light of the dying sun. Never having been so close to the castle before, Audra could only stare. It was like something out of Ivanhoe or a faery story. The crenellated battlements, the arched, leaded-glass

37

windows, the whimsical cone-capped towers all shimmered in the murky waters of the moat.

Tendrils of ivy crept up the walls, giving the impression of a place abandoned to the mists of time. Almost unnaturally silent at the twilight hour, the castle conveyed an aura of enchantment, whispers of a most delicious danger to any foolish enough to invade its mystical circle. Although generally not given to romantic fancies, even Audra hesitated to take a step nearer.

But the spell was broken by the sight of Cecily's pug scampering alongside the moat, growling. Far from appearing overcome by her recent encounter with Sir Ralph's hounds, the idiotic dog was harrying one of the majestic swans swimming past the bank. The creature arched its long white neck, beat its wings, and hissed.

Relief to find the pug unharmed mingled with a sharp sense of irritation. Her reluctance to trespass forgotten, Audra rushed forward, covering the dozen yards or so between herself and the dog. Too late did it occur to Audra that she should have approached with more caution.

Spying her, the leash in her hand, the pug made a break for it, taking refuge beneath a clump of thick bushes along the moat's edge.

Audra swore and began snapping off twigs as she fought to part the branches. "Come out of there, you little—"

Barely she managed to curb her temper, realizing that her angry tone of voice was only making the situation worse. The pug crouched deeper beneath the bush, growling at her. Audra hunkered down. Although the thought made her nigh ill, she knew she would never be able to coax the dog out unless she employed Cecily's manner and made her voice sticky sweet with endearments.

Gritting her teeth, Audra managed to coo, "Come here, darling. That's right. Come on out to me, sweetheart."

"I appear to already be out, madam."

Audra started, momentarily disconcerted by the deep male voice that seemed to issue from the dog. Then she heard a footstep from behind, a large shadow falling over her. Audra rocked back on her heels, nigh losing her balance. She put her hand down on a sturdy boot, the rolled-down tops bespattered with mud. Yanking her fingers back as if she had just touched a snake, her gaze locked on a pair of well-honed thighs encased in tight buckskin breeches.

Her dismay only deepened as she looked upward and found herself kneeling as if in homage to a tall, powerfully built man, his silver-flecked temples emphasizing the night blackness of his hair, his dark eyes boring into her.

For a moment she couldn't move, could scarce breathe. She could not have felt more discomposed than if she had conjured up some black-hearted wizard, the genie who guarded the castle, and he looked about to reduce her to cinders with one flick of his mighty hand.

Those harsh, leathery features, that hawklike profile she had glimpsed only once before, many years ago. But it astonished her how well she recalled his face. The Scowling Duke. Only his frown was much more formidable than she remembered. Even after hearing Lady Coleby's lengthy account of His Grace's return from abroad, it was still unnerving to have him spring up so suddenly before her.

When Audra found her tongue, she blurted out, "Where the deuce did you come from?"

"I was about to ask you the same thing." Placing one gloved hand beneath her elbow, he hauled her none too gently to her feet.

Vague thoughts chased through Audra's brain of the proper way to greet a duke and she knew full well that had not been it.

"Your Grace, I beg your pardon," she faltered, hoping that despite the fearsome expression, he might prove gallant enough to help her through what was a most awkward moment.

He wasn't.

"Your Grace?" he mocked. "I thought I was your darling."

If there was anything Audra hated, it was to blush, but there was no willing down the hot tide of color that surged into her cheeks.

"Of course you must know I was not addressing you. I

was—" She nearly choked to admit it. "I was talking to the dog."

"Dog?" His heavy black brows arched upward, his voice patent with disbelief.

"Yes, a small brown pug. She ran off. She's hiding right over there in those bushes."

Far from appearing convinced, the duke continued to regard her as if she had come to pinch his silverplate. Self-consciously, Audra smoothed back her hair, supposing that in her current disheveled state, she must look far from respectable. Anxious to prove her tale, she bent down and began parting the branches.

"See? The dog's right down . . ." Her voice trailed off as for the second time that day Cecily's despicable dog was not where she should have been. Nothing lurked beneath the bushes but a scattering of fallen leaves.

"She *was* there only a moment ago," Audra said desperately, unable to meet Raeburn's skeptical gaze. She began to stalk up and down whistling, beating the bushes, even going so far as to peer into the moat. All the while she was miserably conscious of Raeburn watching her every move, his arms folded across his chest in a posture of strained patience. As if he had indeed been a sorcerer conjuring his own sudden appearance, he seemed to have caused the dog to vanish as well.

"Damnation!" Audra exclaimed, frustrated beyond endurance. "Now I shall have to begin searching for her all over again. If you hadn't distracted me—" She bit her tongue, trying to recall whom it was she addressed. But Raeburn did not appear offended so much as disgusted.

"A creditable performance, madam," he snapped, "but I don't intend to spend the rest of my evening watching you hunt for a dog that has no existence outside of your imagination. Now what the devil are you really doing here?"

"I *told* you, " Audra said crossly, still scanning the line of the woods for some sign of the pug. "And if you don't mind, Your Grace, I am not accustomed to being sworn at."

"No? You swore at me first," he reminded her. He stepped in front of her, the implacable wall of his shoulders blocking her

40

line of vision. Until that moment, Audra had not fully appreciated how tall or how intimidating a figure His Grace could be.

She hated the way her pulse fluttered, her cowardly urge to retreat. She had never been a pudding-heart before and wasn't about to begin now. Refusing to yield an inch, she gazed defiantly up at him, although the front of her bodice nigh grazed against his waistcoat.

"Whatever your excuse for being here," he said, "I fear you are too late. All the invitations have gone out."

"Invitations?" Audra frowned. Talking to this man was worse than trying to follow one of Lady Coleby's conversations. "Invitations to what?"

"Doing it rather too brown, my dear. I am talking about the ball, as you well know."

"Oh, *that*. Yes, I had heard something about it."

"I'll wager you have. Well, I congratulate you, Miss . . ."

"Miss Audra Leigh Masters of Meadow—" Audra began, then stopped, thinking it perhaps less than wise to inform His Grace she was his tenant. In his present ill humor, he might be likely to evict her.

"Miss Masters, your approach is a little more original than the others. At least I have not had to endure your swooning or pulling your horse up lame."

"I never faint. I take excellent care of my horses and . . . and I haven't the vaguest notion what you are talking about."

"Take care, madam," he growled. "You have already tried my patience to its limits. I assure you I have been beset all week by *ladies* such as yourself. Apparently the word has gone out there is a vacancy here for the post of duchess. Since you have gone to such effort, I suppose I should give you due consideration."

Before Audra could react, he seized her by the chin and forced her head up. Studying her through narrowed eyes, he murmured, "Hair, tolerable, although it could use a thorough brushing. Teeth appear to be good, eyes an unremarkable gray." His gaze dipped in a quick appraisal of her figure. "Rather a Long Meg, but I like that. I get tired of stooping down to talk to people."

41

Momentarily dumbfounded, Audra could only stare at him. She had heard tell the duke was a disagreeable man, but it had never been bruited about that he was quite mad. As the full import of his accusations finally sank in, she gave vent to an outraged gasp, striking his hand away.

"You think that . . . that I only pretended to . . . that I came here a-purpose to seek you out so . . . Why, you . . . you are the most despicable coxcomb I ever met, or else a raving lunatic. Let me tell you, sir, if I was in the market for a duke, I would scarce be searching for one beneath the shrubberies, while carrying a leash."

Although he continued to regard her with that infuriatingly sardonic expression, a shadow of uncertainty flickered in his eyes.

Trembling, Audra could scarce find words adequate to express her indignation. "I-I am a spinster, Your Grace, and fiercely proud of it. I have a fortune of ten thousand pounds a year, a stable with several fine horses, and a kennel full of dogs. I do not need a husband."

"I beg your pardon," he drawled.

"So you should. And furthermore, even if you had sent me an invitation, I would not come. Neither I nor my sister have any interest in attending your odious ball." Audra considered what Cecily's reaction would be if she were privileged to hear Audra saying such a thing, but in her present anger, Audra gave it no more than a fleeting thought. She finished up by loftily informing the duke, "I wouldn't come to that ball even if you got down on one knee and begged."

The stern set of his mouth twitched with something akin to amusement. "Since there is little likelihood of my doing that, I fear I will be deprived of the pleasure of your fair company."

Audra glared at him. "You have to be the most conceited person I have ever met. But there! What more can be expected of a man who travels with twenty trunks full of clothes?"

He looked a little confounded at that, and feeling as if she had at least gotten a little of her own back, Audra started to flounce away from him when she caught sight of a movement by the edge of the woods. Cecily's pug darted into sight, this time in fierce pursuit of a frog. Feeling vindicated, Audra could not refrain from flashing the duke a look of triumph.

"If Your Grace will excuse me, I must see about recovering my imaginary dog."

But she had not taken two steps nearer to the little beast when, as usual, the pug began to growl and back away as if it had never set eyes upon Audra before. A peculiar choked sound came from the duke's direction. If it had been anybody else but Raeburn, Audra would have sworn the man smothered a laugh.

"Come here, Frou-frou," she called through clenched teeth.

"Frou-frou?" the duke echoed. His Grace might not know how to smile, but he certainly could smirk.

"I assure you I never named her that," Audra began hotly, then broke off. What was the use? It was a complete waste of time trying to explain anything to that man. Besides, with a jaunty flick of its tail, the pug was racing back into the woods again. Audra charged after it, not even troubling to bid the duke farewell.

Raeburn watched as both the pug and the woman vanished into the twilight, leaving the glade behind his castle seeming strangely deserted. A rueful half smile escaped him. He scarce knew whether to laugh or curse, his amusement tempered by an uncomfortable feeling that he had just made a thorough ass of himself.

"How was I to know there really was a dog?" he muttered. It was all the fault of Miss Long and her scheming kind, their foolish stratagems rendering him suspicious of any woman he chanced upon. He had never before been wont to think that every stray female was eager to cast herself into his arms.

Even if he had, Miss Masters had certainly set him straight on that score. Simon did laugh then, as he recalled the lady's indignation when she had informed him she had no use for a husband. She had looked rather magnificent, that wild mane of chestnut hair tumbling about her shoulders, her eyes flashing scorn. Not a beauty by any means, but he had lied when he had said her eyes were unremarkable. Far from it, he thought they were the most honest gray he had ever seen.

He supposed he ought to set off after Miss Masters and tender her some explanation of his boorish conduct, even extend an apology. But he had too great a regard for his own nose. In her present humor, the lady was likely to draw his cork. Besides he doubted he would catch up to her, and he had no notion where she lived.

Simon shrugged, telling himself it was of no great consequence. He hardly need worry about currying the good opinion of a woman he'd scarce met and one, moreover, he was unlikely ever to see again. Dismissing the incident from his mind, he followed the line of the moat, heading for the wooden bridge that crossed to the inner court of the castle.

He returned to his bedchamber to change for dinner, as they kept country hours at the Castle Raeburn. While he struggled into a fresh white shirt, he was surprised to find himself still thinking about Miss Masters, recalling some of the things she had said to him. What was it she had called him? The most conceited person she had ever met, but then what more could be expected of a man who traveled with twenty trunks?

Simon frowned, wishing he had informed her that nineteen of those twenty trunks she had spoken of belonged to his sister. But then, what business was that of Miss Masters's? Still it irked him all the same, he who prided himself on his good sense and the plain manner of his attire, being accused of being a popinjay.

He could not help brooding about it as he descended belowstairs to lead Lady Augusta into the dining room. Was Miss Masters partly correct? Not about the trunks, of course, but about his conceit. Had he become a little too puffed up of late, too full of his own consequence as the duke?

Annoyed with himself for giving any weight at all to what Audra Masters had said, Simon attempted to shake off his air of abstraction. Linking his arm through Augusta's, he led her into the small dining chamber. Simon much preferred its simple paneled walls to the more ostentatious formal one with its gilt and trim and overwhelming chandeliers.

Waving aside the footman, he held the chair for Augusta

himself and then settled at the opposite end of the gleaming satinwood table.

During the course of turtle soup, Augusta made cheery inquiry as to how his walk had gone. "You were absent so long. I am sure you could not have spent all that time just looking at a bull. What did you do with yourself all afternoon?"

"Nothing of import, merely made a fool of myself."

"Oh." Augusta took a spoonful of creamy broth. "I thought you might have done something different for a change."

He accorded this sally no response. He considered regaling Augusta with his encounter with Miss Masters but thought better of it. Gus had already enjoyed enough mirth at his expense for one day.

Instead he could not refrain from asking abruptly, "Gus, do you find me conceited?"

"No, dear. Only impossibly arrogant."

Simon grimaced. Trust a sister to provide all the reassurance one needed.

Augusta looked up from her soup dish, regarding him with a puzzled look. "Whatever makes you ask such a thing?"

"No particular reason." Simon was quick to change the subject, asking how the preparations for the ball were going.

It served the trick of diverting Augusta's thoughts, but he was almost sorry. She launched into a lengthy account of her concerns about acquiring enough lobster.

"And I still cannot make up my mind how to decorate the ballroom," she lamented. "Would simple floral arrangements be enough, or should I try for something more exotic?"

"Hanging the room with black crepe seems appropriate." His suggestion met with no more than a disgusted look from his sister.

Even though he had inquired, Gus ought to realize all these details about the ball did not interest him in the least. Not a single aspect of it except perhaps . . .

To his own astonishment, Simon caught himself asking, "Have you sent out all the invitation cards?"

"Of course. But if you have recollected someone else you wish to invite, I suppose—"

"Oh, no. No!" Simon made haste to disclaim. A vision of Audra Leigh Masters danced through his mind, only to be quickly dismissed. "Why the blazes should I want any more infernal females invited?"

"Well, I did think we might have asked the Marquess of Greenwold. He has two charming daughters, though they do live a little far off."

"Then no matter how charming, let them stay there. I don't want to be plagued with any overnight guests." Clearly bored with the subject, Simon summoned a footman to refill his wineglass.

"You might show a little more concern, Simon," Augusta complained. "At least in what ladies will be in attendance."

"Why? I fear that the only female that has roused even a passing interest in me has already said she'll be damned if she's coming."

"What!" Startled, Augusta dropped her fork, clattering it against her dish. "Simon! Who is she?"

But Simon already looked as if he regretted having said so much. He attacked a joint of lamb instead, maintaining a most maddening silence. Augusta knew that stubborn look too well to badger him with any more questions. Consumed with curiosity, her own dinner went untasted, and she glowered at him. If she did not murder her brother before this visit was over, it would not be because he hadn't done his utmost to goad her to it.

Chapter 4

For several days after her encounter with the Duke of Raeburn, Audra's thoughts still turned on all the crushing retorts she should have uttered. The arrogance of that man! That he should have supposed for one minute that she had come creeping about his estate, merely to throw herself at his head, assuming that she was like all these other foolish chits hereabouts, panting to make his acquaintance.

Audra's cheeks burned anew whenever she recalled the duke's insolent manner, subjecting her to his inspection. Had she been a vain woman, she would have been quite devastated by some of his remarks about her person. A Long Meg with unremarkable eyes indeed! She was fully aware of her own defects and did not need them pointed out.

Although she had given him a blistering scold, she had not said near enough. This frustrating feeling was coupled with a dread that she had said perhaps too much. Apparently he had not realized she was his tenant, but there was no saying that he wouldn't by now since she had so stupidly furnished him with her name. She did not know if His Grace was a vindictive man, but he obviously had a formidable temper. She lived with the hourly expectation of a notice arriving, demanding her immediate eviction from Meadow Lane.

Yet she doubted she need fear any such grim messenger today. Rain was coming down so hard, one would have to be a madman to venture forth. Water cascaded down the long windows in the parlor like a waterfall. Audra regretted the fact she had invited her great-uncle Matthew to travel from his home in the village to spend the day with her and Cecily. She hoped that elderly gentleman would have the good sense to send his excuses.

But her relative seemed short of that commodity, for shortly after noon Mrs. McGuiness popped her head into the parlor to announce that the Reverend Masters's carriage was fair floating down the lane. Biting back a dismayed exclamation, Audra joined the housekeeper at the front door to hustle her uncle inside, helping the plump elderly gentleman to remove his drenched cape and rain-slicked beaver hat.

His flowing waves of white hair were pulled back into a slightly bedraggled queue. Beneath brows as thick as a drift of snow, his pale blue eyes twinkled up at Audra.

"Stap me, m'dear, but I believe I should have brought my oars."

"Uncle, you are fair drowned," Audra said. "Come by the fire at once."

"Don't fuss, girl." Reverend Masters paused to chuckle and pat the round belly straining beneath his waistcoat. "A man of my girth is hardly like to be washed away."

Nonetheless he permitted himself to be led to the chair before the parlor hearth. His cherub's face glowed from the heat of the crackling blaze, his complexion remarkably smooth for a man of ninety-odd years. It was hard for Audra to remember sometimes that he had been her father's uncle, not her own. Reverend Masters attributed his longevity to the fact he had never listened "to a demned thing" the fool doctors told him, always stuffing himself with as much pastry and Madeira as he desired.

"Ah, that's better." He sighed as he held his hands over the blazing fire. His nose turned a bright red as it always did when he was too warm or had drunk too much port.

Although he protested, Audra insisted he remove his boots. As she knelt down before him and tugged them off, she continued to scold. "It isn't that I am not glad to see you, Uncle, but you should never have come out on such a day."

"I had to, m'dear. Another day closeted at the parsonage, and I would be fit for naught but Bedlam. Would you believe it, I was so desperate to fill my hours, I nearly thought of writing a sermon."

Audra laughed, too accustomed to such outrageous comments from her uncle to be shocked. There had never been anyone less suited for holy orders than Matthew. But as he had explained to Audra once, "What the devil else is there for a younger son besides the army? I could tolerate being shot at by some irate husband, but by a total stranger I had done nothing in the least to offend? No, no, m'dear. That is asking entirely too much."

He was something of a reprobate, her uncle Matt, and greatly scandalized the rest of her father's family. Those same fusty relatives did not approve of Audra either, which perhaps was why she and Uncle Matthew got on so famously. Whatever the reason, Audra was immensely fond of the old gentleman. His proximity had proved one of the chief inducements to her signing the lease on the lodge.

Without making her solicitude so obvious as to vex the old man, Audra removed his boots and took great pains to make sure he hadn't taken a chill.

She had just settled upon the settee opposite him when Cecily tripped into the parlor, Frou-frou ambling at her heels.

"Was that Uncle Matt's carriage I heard arriving?"

" 'Deed it was, miss." Uncle Matthew's broad face fairly beamed. "Bless me, the child grows lovelier every day. Come here, my pretty niece, and give your uncle a kiss."

Cecily dutifully complied, bestowing a soft peck on his cheek. Audra watched with tolerant amusement. Although he was not in truth Cecily's uncle, Reverend Masters had "adopted" her, ever having a soft spot in his heart for a lovely girl. Never averse to receiving compliments, Cecily gave him a dazzling smile.

But Audra was forced to admit that Cecily had been nothing but charming these past few days. She had never mentioned a word about their quarrel, her disappointment over having to miss the upcoming ball, or any of her dissatisfaction with life at Meadow Lane. Her disposition had been of such a sweetness, so cheerful, so obliging, it was enough to make one wonder if the girl was up to some mischief.

Yet Audra was immediately ashamed of herself for harboring such a suspicion. She was becoming as evil-minded as his horridness, the Duke of Raeburn.

Cecily seated herself upon a footstool, near the arm of Reverend Masters's chair, playfully calling upon Frou-frou to "make her curtsy to Great-uncle Matt." The dog actually deigned to wag her tail for him. It was apparently only Audra at whom the little beast chose to growl.

That did not disturb Audra, who still felt like doing some growling herself, every time she recollected how Frou-frou's escapade had led to her disastrous meeting with Raeburn.

It didn't help to hear Cecily merrily regaling Uncle Matt

with the story, at least as much of it as she knew. Giggling, she said, "And naughty Frou-frou led my sister on quite a chase through Raeburn's Wood. Poor Audra was out looking for her until well after dark."

"Oh, brave woman!" Uncle Matt's gaze shifted toward Audra, clearly taking a wicked relish in her discomfiture. "What? Were you not afraid of the Scowling Duke leaping out to demand a forfeit for your trespass?"

To her dismay, Audra felt a hint of red creep into her cheeks. Was it possible that Uncle Matthew had actually heard something of her meeting with Raeburn? It had never occurred to her that the duke might be so ungentlemanly as to spread the tale of their infamous encounter.

Audra squirmed in her seat. "Wh-what makes you ask me such a thing, Uncle Matt?"

"Nothing, m'dear. 'Twas only a jest, certainly naught to make you look as if you had just swallowed a fly."

"You will have to excuse me," she said stiffly. "I found the whole affair less than amusing."

"Why, Audra, it's quite unlike you to take snuff over such a trivial thing. What's happened to your sense of humor, child?" Her uncle shot her a puzzled but penetrating look that rendered Audra extremely uncomfortable. She felt relieved when Cecily inadvertently came to her aid by explaining, "I fear Audra has reason to still be cross. While she wore herself to the bone tramping the woods, my wicked little Frou-frou doubled back." Cecily dotingly rubbed her pet's neck. "Audra returned in despair, only to discover Frou-frou curled up in her favorite chair."

Uncle Matt and Cecily both chuckled at that, laughter in which Audra was quite unable to join. She glared at Frou-frou, muttering, "That dog is lucky to still be alive."

"I daresay." Uncle Matt chortled. "Especially knowing you m'dear, I don't doubt but what the search interrupted your reading." The rector reached down to pat an open book that was, as always, left littering the small chairside table. Uncle Matthew squinted at the spine. "Why, by my faith, is this still *Ivanhoe*? I thought you received this book days ago. With your habit of devouring books, you ought to be done and ready to lend it to me."

"I have been a little distracted of late," Audra said. She was not about to admit the distraction was of a most disturbing and curious kind. Poor Ivanhoe was indeed a sorely vexed man with his sweetheart and father held prisoner at Torquilstone. But that was no reason that every time she pictured the knight's scowling face, the image should turn into Raeburn's dark frown. Nor why at the turn of every page, her traitorous mind should keep conjuring up a hero with black, silver-flecked hair and fierce bushy brows. It was not only annoying but foolish to keep imagining Ivanhoe in Raeburn's massive proportions, that deep chest, those broad shoulders, and those brawny forearms. Audra had seen samples of armor before. If Ivanhoe had been such a strapping figure of a man, the metal plating would never have fit him.

Since she quite detested His Grace, she didn't know why Raeburn should assume the role of Ivanhoe in her mind. If he must invade her head, she should imagine him as the black-hearted villain Front-de-Boeuf. Better still she should not think of Raeburn at all.

It disconcerted her to realize that her inability to concentrate had not gone unnoticed, even by Cecily. She informed Uncle Matthew in grave tones, "Audra has been so restless of late. But I suppose that is the sort of crotchets that older, er, I mean that more mature ladies have from time to time."

"No, it's only the damp," Audra retorted. "My rheumatism, you know."

Uncle Matt choked at that, and Audra took the opportunity to change the subject by challenging him to a game of chess. He was a skilled player, and Audra had enjoyed many lively skirmishes with him in the past, neither giving much quarter.

Lining up the ivory pieces upon the board, she and the old gentleman were soon engrossed in the game. The afternoon passed pleasantly enough despite the rain that beat against the glass. The parlor was silent but for an occasional snort from Frou-frou, the crackle of the logs on the fire, the tick of the clock on the mantel.

Even Cecily sat quietly engaged with her stitching. If she was bored, she concealed her occasional yawns behind her hand. Audra lost all track of time, breathlessly watching her uncle's hand hover over his bishop, waiting for him to fall into her trap.

She did not notice when the rain stopped until her sister pointed it out to her. Springing up from her seat, Cecily skipped over to the windows.

"The sun is trying to come out. Perhaps there will be a rainbow." Cecily flattened her nose against the glass. "Oh, Audra, do come and see."

Since Uncle Matt had somehow managed to turn the tables upon her and Audra discovered her queen in peril, she was too preoccupied to stir. In any case, Cecily's raptures seemed a little excessive for a bit of colored sky.

"Pray, don't bother me now, Muffin," Audra murmured. "I am sure the rainbow will still be there later."

"It isn't a rainbow. It's a coach and four coming down the drive."

Audra's and the rector's heads jerked up simultaneously. Her own groan was echoed by Uncle Matt.

"If it's that Coleby woman, I warn you, Audra, I'll hide myself in the wine cellar until she's gone."

"Shame on you, Uncle," Cecily said. "You are as bad as Audra. It isn't Lady Coleby's carriage at all. It is—" She broke off with a gasp. Retreating a step from the window, she stood pale, transfixed.

"Cecily?"

When Audra received no response to her sharp inquiry, she became concerned enough to abandon the chessboard and join her sister at the window. "Whatever is the matter, Muffin?"

Too overcome to speak, her eyes round as saucers, Cecily could only pluck at Audra's sleeve and point out the window. Audra looked out and froze, feeling as if she had just turned to stone herself.

Pulling to the front of the cottage was a shiny black coach with a team of gaily caparisoned white horses in the traces. An outrider led the way, blowing upon his trumpet. Emblazoned upon the carriage door was a coat of arms, but the insignia was no more impressive than the coachman and the two footmen who rode behind all garbed in sapphire blue livery.

"Audra," Cecily quavered. "Do you think it is the— the—"

"The devil!" Audra cried. She could not imagine that it was the King of England come to call. Only one person hereabouts was likely to have such a rig-out as that.

"Raeburn!" she said.

Cecily gave a shivery sigh and looked likely to swoon. Audra wanted to shake her sister for being such a goose, but she could scarce do so. Not when her own heart was racing in such idiotic fashion.

Uncle Matthew had obviously not heard her pronouncement for he called out testily, "Are you two girls just going to stand there like stocks or are you going to tell me? Whose coach is it?"

Before Audra could say a word, Cecily trilled out, "It's the duke's carriage, uncle. Isn't it wonderful? Oh, Audra!" Cecily's blond curls bounced with her excitement. "Why do you think His Grace is coming here?"

Audra could imagine several reasons, none of them good. "I don't know," she said glumly. "But perhaps we had best go upstairs and start packing."

"What?!"

Audra ignored her sister's startled exclamation. Not wanting to be spied ogling, she inched further behind the drapes. Holding her breath, she watched one of the footmen spring forward to open the coach door, bracing herself for the sight of that familiar arrogant profile.

But the man who alighted was a stranger to her. Although of distinguished bearing, his garb was simple, marking him as no more than a servant himself. Yet with a great parade of self-consequence, he marched toward the lodge's front door.

"Oh!" Cecily's shoulders slumped with chagrin.

Audra felt she could have echoed that sentiment, but whether from relief or a similar sense of disappointment she refused to consider.

Impatiently, Uncle Matthew stumped over to join them. "What the deuce is t'ward?"

Audra shrugged, being as ignorant as he. But it seemed none of them were to be kept in suspense for long. Whatever errand the duke had sent this man upon, it was discharged promptly. After disappearing from view for a moment during which Audra heard muffled sounds of her front door being answered by Mrs. McGuiness, the duke's man popped into sight again.

Clambering back into the carriage, the coachman whipped up his team, and the impressive entourage departed as suddenly as it had come. Audra caught a last view of the vehicle vanishing down the lane by the time Mrs. McGuiness entered the parlor.

The dour housekeeper appeared a little awed herself as she approached Audra. She bore a missive of some sort upon a silver tray much to Audra's wry amusement. Apparently Mrs. McGuiness had not thought it good enough to hand over a letter from the duke as she always did the regular mail. So she had employed the silver serving tray normally used for holding the tea service.

The housekeeper thrust the tray at Audra, too overcome to say more than, "For you, Miss Masters."

"Thank you." Audra took up the letter gingerly as though it were likely to explode. If it were an eviction notice, never had one been sent so elegantly as this square of creamy vellum with the duke's heavy seal imprinted upon the wax closure. Was it just possible . . . ? No, it seemed utterly incredible to even imagine that the overbearing duke might have penned her an apology.

Whatever the contents of the missive, one thing was certain. She would never find out by simply turning it over and over in her hands. Audra started to break the seal, when she became aware of three heads crowded close to hers. Mrs. McGuiness was the worst, nearly toppling into Audra in her efforts to see.

"Shouldn't you be starting the tea?" Audra asked repressively.

Mrs. McGuiness pursed her lips, but she took the hint, beating a disappointed retreat. Now if only she could be rid of Cecily and her uncle as easily.

At a look from Audra, Uncle Matthew did appear a trifle

sheepish and stepped back a pace, but nothing could discourage Cecily from hanging on Audra's sleeve.

"Oh, Audra, do you wish to kill me with this suspense? Do not wait any longer. Open it. Open it!"

Although fearful of what the note contained, Audra broke the seal and unfolded the vellum. She strove so hard to focus on the elegantly inked lines, it took some moments for the sense of the words to sink in.

"*His Grace, the Duke of Raeburn, and Lady Augusta Penrose,*" Audra mused aloud, "*request the honor of your presence at—*"

She got no further, for Cecily fairly shrieked in her ear, "At the ball! Audra! It's an invitation to the ball."

Audra stared. When she realized for herself what it was she held in her hands, she dropped the vellum as if her fingers had been scorched. While she stood stunned, Cecily snatched up the invitation.

Waving it wildly over her head, Cecily danced about the room, breathless with joyous laughter. "The ball! Oh, Uncle Matthew, we're going to the ball."

Cecily flung her arms about the rector, causing the old man to laugh with delight himself. He patted her shoulder indulgently, saying, "Are you indeed, my pet?"

Audra had scarce time to brace herself before Cecily rushed wildly at her as well, enveloping her in a crushing hug.

"Oh, Audra, I knew you would find some way to arrange the invitation when I so wished for it. You are the best, kindest, dearest sister in the whole world."

Audra's mind whirled as she struggled to make sense of all of this. Gasping, she eased herself out of Cecily's strangling embrace. "Cecily, do control yourself. This has to be some kind of mistake."

"How could it be?" Cecily waved the invitation before Audra's eyes. "Both of our names are clearly marked." Audra tried to see, but Cecily would not stay still long enough for her to get a good look at the blasted thing again.

Audra frowned, knowing full well she had done nothing to

55

secure that invitation. Far from it! If Cecily had any idea of half the things Audra had said to His Grace . . .

So how had their names come to be added to the guest list? Had someone else put in a word on their behalf? Audra glanced toward her uncle with sudden suspicion.

But Uncle Matthew shrugged. "Do not look at me thus, Audra. I had naught to do with it. You know my infernal gout keeps me from getting out as much as I would like. Though long acquainted with the Lakeland family, I have not even seen His Grace since his return."

Nigh delirious with happiness, Cecily continued to frolic about the parlor, her activity causing Frou-frou to yip while Audra wracked her brains for some explanation.

The only one possible was that after meeting her, the duke himself had somehow traced where she lived and discovered the name of her sister. But why, after Audra had insulted him, should he take such pains, sending the invitation when she had sworn to turn it down?

"Plague take the man," she muttered. "He must have sent it just to vex me." Whipping round, she snapped, "Cecily, do cease this unseemly display at once."

Cecily subsided enough for Audra finally to grab the invitation away from her. She crushed it in her hand. "There is no chance whatsoever of our accepting this thing."

Cecily's bright smile faded. Young Juliet could not have looked more stricken when discovering her Romeo was dead.

"Audra! Wh-what are you saying?"

"I'm saying we are not going. It would be . . . wholly improper."

"Improper! I see nothing in the least objectionable in attending. Do you, Uncle Matthew?"

But the Reverend Matthew Masters, sensing a storm about to brew, wisely retreated back to his chessmen, determined not to be caught in the middle.

"It's improper because . . ." Audra groped for some plausible excuse. "Because you are not even out yet."

Cecily's face flushed with indignation. "As if you ever cared for such fustian notions. Besides this is a private ball, not at all like you were taking me to an assembly."

"It is of no avail arguing with me, Cecily. My mind is made up. We are not going because I do not wish to—"

"You never wish to go anywhere," Cecily cried with a stomp of her foot. "You keep both of us cooped up in this dreadful house. It's . . . it's horrid and . . . and wicked of you. My entire life is passing me by."

"What utter nonsense. You are only seventeen."

"I'll be eighteen soon, and before I know where I am at, I'll end up an old maid just like you."

After which passionate speech, Cecily spun on her heel, bolting for the door.

Uncle Matthew sprang to his feet. "Here now, Cecily. What a dreadful thing to say. You come back and apologize—"

The door had already slammed closed behind her.

"Let her go, Uncle," Audra said dully. "She's right. I am an old maid, and I don't mind it in the least."

Her voice did not carry its usual conviction though, and she gave vent to a weary sigh. "I suppose Cecily will spend the rest of the afternoon weeping again."

"I fear 'tis all part of being seventeen, m'dear."

"Is it? I don't recall. Sometimes I don't think I ever was that age."

"No, you were never given the chance to be. I always said your mama saddled you with too much responsibility too young. Why doesn't Lady Arabella return to take charge of Cecily?"

Audra shuddered. "Please, don't wish such a thing upon me. More likely I would end up taking care of Mama as well."

She meant it as a jest, but memories crowded forward all the same, assuring her that her words were not far from the truth. Lady Arabella had ever been a flighty creature, given to acquiring herself the most doting, elderly husbands. It had always fallen to Audra's lot to prevent her mother from overspending or creating a scandal with her latest handsome lover.

It might be most unfilial to admit, but she was quite content

57

to have Mama continue her latest bride trip indefinitely. Rousing herself from these disagreeable reflections, Audra moved to chuck the invitation into the fire. She was astonished when Uncle Matthew's hand shot out to prevent it.

Those pale blue eyes, usually so merry, were clouded with trouble. "Don't be so hasty, m'girl. You might want to reconsider attending that ball."

"Uncle!"

Ignoring her exclamation, he continued, "Though I cannot approve of Cecily's manner, behaving like a spoiled child, some of what she said is true. 'Tis not good the way you live here, so much alone. You are a young woman still, Audra."

"Not that young. You have only to ask Cecily. I believe she thinks I am a contemporary of Methusaleh." Audra's wry smile coaxed no like response from him.

"You are not going to commence scolding me, too, are you Uncle Matt?" she asked. "I have heard enough regarding my shocking manner of life from Lord Sunderly."

Indeed, the cousin who had inherited her father's title had thought it the most outrageous thing since the Gunpowder plot, that Audra should set up her own establishment with only a housekeeper for a companion. But since neither Lord Sunderly nor any of Papa's other relatives had ever troubled themselves about Audra's welfare before, she did not feel obliged to regard their disapproval.

But her uncle Matthew had rarely ever lectured her. Consequently Audra found his words not so easy to dismiss. "You know well enough that I never preach propriety, Audra. But a companion would enable you to get out more, receive more people. Heavens, child, you see no one but myself and that Coleby woman. And that is only because no one can keep that dratted chattering female out."

Audra drew herself up proudly. "You mistake, sir, if you think me unhappy. I am quite content with my quiet way of life. My only concern is about Cecily. I know that she should have more gaiety, a Season in London, perhaps."

She lowered her eyes, coming down from her high ropes a bit. "I even wrote my aunt Saunders about it, but unfortunately

58

she has not replied. I suppose she still remembers the debacle I made of my own Season."

"That was scarcely your fault. Your mama never did anything to prepare you. Letting you closet yourself in the schoolroom and without a proper governess to even teach you the way to get on."

Audra rarely felt the urge to defend her mother, but in all fairness, she could not let her own social failure be laid at Arabella's door. "I learned everything I ever wanted to out of my books," she said. "And you can hardly blame Mama for my clumsiness. Even the best of tutors cannot turn a goose into a swan."

Uncle Matt looked as if he wanted to argue that point, but instead he said, "Well, I suppose that's all water under the bridge. It is the future I am worried about. How are you and your sister ever to meet any eligible gentlemen shut away here at Meadow Lane?"

Audra smiled. "We have gentleman callers all the time. Young Sir Worthington, Mr. Gilmore, Mr. Blake. And I play chaperon to Cecily as a proper old-maid sister should."

"And which of those youths do you want Cecily to marry? That silly ass Gilmore or that boy with the spots?"

The question startled Audra. "Why, none of them. They are all but callow boys, scarce out of the nursery."

"Well, you had best brace yourself, m'dear. I fear Cecily is not as strong-minded as you. If she is given no other choice, you are likely to end up with one of those boys for a brother-in-law."

Audra started to hotly refute his prediction, but she found she couldn't. It wasn't as if she didn't want Cecily to have better opportunities.

"I tried to get Muffin a London Season," Audra said. "What more can I do?"

"You could make the most of this." Her uncle tapped the vellum she yet held crushed in her hand. "Give me one good reason, miss, why you and your sister should not attend that ball."

"There are several—" Audra began, but incurably honest,

she recognized the chief one, her stiff-necked pride. How could she turn up so humbly on Raeburn's doorstep, after all her expressions of scorn, informing him she would not come if he begged her? The duke would be bound to think her no better than all these other fluttery chits after all. But she could not admit these qualms, not even to Uncle Matt.

She finished lamely, "It would be most uncomfortable, taking Cecily alone, with—with no male escort or older relative to—"

Her uncle puffed out his chest. "What do you take me for—the pantrymaid? It so happens, miss, that as a courtesy, I am always invited to functions at the castle. I had no intention of attending this ball myself, but now I can see where it would be a very good thing."

"Oh, Uncle Matt, Cecily and I couldn't possibly drag you off to such a fatiguing affair."

"Fatiguing, be demned. I would quite enjoy it. I am scarce in my dotage yet, miss." His eyes turned suddenly misty with memories. "Faith, it has been a long time since I have stood up with a lady. Did you know that his majesty, that is, the late king, poor mad George, once told me I was the most skilled dancer to ever grace St. James?"

"I am sure you were, Uncle." Audra reluctantly smoothed the vellum out again.

His Grace, the Duke of Raeburn requests the honor . . .

Was it possible that the words meant just that? That perhaps instead of being another gibe, this invitation was a peace offering, Raeburn's awkward manner of making amends for his insulting behavior?

As Audra's doubts made her hesitate, Uncle Matthew poured forth the full force of his persuasion, stressing how much social good it would do Cecily, to say nothing of how happy Audra would make him. Audra sighed. The Reverend Matthew Masters did not possess the ability to thunder from the pulpit, but Audra was convinced her uncle could have wheedled Satan himself into forsaking his fire and brimstone.

She flung up one hand at last in surrender. "All right. All right, Uncle. I can hardly withstand both you and Cecily. I suppose I should go tell her at once that I have changed my mind. I only hope she doesn't choke me in her ecstasies."

The old rector nodded in approval, not permitting a sage smile to crease his lips until his niece had gone. He had definitely taken the right tack to persuade Audra, emphasizing Cecily's needs. It wouldn't have done at all for him to admit it was Audra that he was really worried about. He had been observing her solitary habits for some time. The girl was becoming as sequestered as a nun. But if he dared hint that attending that ball would do her more good than Cecily, why, Audra would take his head clean off.

Chapter 5

By the evening of the ball, if Lady Augusta Penrose had been a female of lesser fortitude, she would have indulged in a fit of the vapors. A blight in the hothouse had ruined many of the flowers she had counted upon for decoration, the extra champagne ordered had failed to arrive, and the French chef she had imported was engaged in such a dreadful row with the duke's own cook, it was unlikely that any supper at all would be served that night. But then, she supposed it was all to be expected when one was giving a ball in the middle of the wilderness instead of more civilized London.

These disasters were capped off when she discovered the duke's valet, Bartleby, had given in his notice . . . again. On the way to make one last harried inspection of the ballroom, Augusta met the lordly looking manservant stalking down the hall, his portmanteau in hand.

"Not again, Bartleby," Augusta groaned. "You have not been quarreling with His Grace tonight of all nights."

A rather spare individual with the face of a suffering artist, Bartleby drew himself stiffly upright. "Far be it from me to cause you any distress, m'lady. I am a patient man. I am accustomed to being sworn at, to say nothing of having a boot shied at me from time to time. But when the master that I have served faithfully all these years, the same one as I have always endeavored to turn out as becomes a gentleman of modest habits, when he accuses me of rigging him out like a *fop* . . . Nay, 'tis too much even for a saint to endure."

"Oh, Bartleby," Augusta cried, but when he made her a smart bow, stalking on his way, she made no effort to stop him. The valet would never get any further than the kitchens where he would permit the housekeeper to offer him tea and a sympathetic ear. And heaven knows, Simon was not the sort of man unable to function without the services of his valet. Still, it was another vexation.

The folds of her silver gauze ball gown rustling, Augusta made her way to the duke's bedchamber door and knocked. Upon her identifying herself, her brother bellowed, "Come in."

Augusta grimaced. She knew Simon would not be enthusiastic about the ball, but if he was going to be in one of his difficult moods, they might as well bar the doors to the castle and be done with it.

She entered to find Simon in his dressing room. He was in his stockinged feet, attired in nothing but a white shirt and black breeches. His expression waxed thunderous as he snapped the starched ends of a stock, preparing to tie his cravat.

"Simon," she demanded, without preamble. "What have you done to poor Bartleby now?"

"That silly ass. I threatened to boil him in his own starch. The dolt kept insisting that in the honor of the occasion, I should allow him to do something special with my cravat arrangement tonight, some damn fool thing he called 'a waterfall.' If I wanted a waterfall about my neck, I'd dump a bucket of water over my head and be done with it."

"Simon!" But Lady Augusta bit back her vexed exclamation, knowing it would not do a particle of good to scold. Besides, she had to admit that Simon's taste regarding his attire was impeccable. Having studied the portraits of her ancestors, she might deplore the passage of an age when men garbed themselves in more brilliant colors, rich brocades, cuffs dripping with lace. She often thought that Beau Brummell had done the gentlemen of England no service, persuading them to adopt evening attire that was infinitely more boring. But in Simon's case, the more severe style—the unrelenting black—somehow suited his rugged, dark masculinity.

While Lady Augusta admired her brother's appearance, she saw that he was far from returning the approval. He paused in his exertions with his cravat to scowl at her own gown, his gaze fixed on the plunging neckline.

"Shouldn't you drape yourself with some sort of shawl," he growled. "Or—or stuff a bit of lace there?"

"No. Let me remind you, Simon, I am a married lady, not some chit fresh out of the nursery. Do not attempt to be playing big brother to me tonight. I assure you I am frazzled enough what with everything going wrong."

He turned back to the mirror with a shrug. "All will come right in the end. I have never attended any function of yours that came off less than elegant, Gus. You are ever the perfect hostess."

Although somewhat mollified by the compliment, she said, "I fear the success of this particular function depends more upon its host."

Simon bent closer to the glass, adding another fold to his cravat. "Oh, I'll be so charming, the ladies will be nigh ready to bust their stays with delight." Since this pledge was accompanied by a frown dark enough to shatter the mirror, Augusta did not feel much reassured.

She fidgeted with the things on his dressing table, the silver-handled Sheffield razor, the jars of snuff, the small knife he used for paring his nails, his comb.

Simon felt a twinge of conscience. His placid sister appeared unusually ruffled. Perhaps he could forgo the pleasure of tormenting her, at least for one night.

"I promise you, Gus," he said, "although I may not exactly

be the perfect host, I shall endeavor to uphold the honor of the dukes of Raeburn."

"If it is not asking too much, I should also like to see you enjoy yourself a little."

"Ah, that is entirely another matter," Simon said, removing the razor from her grasp before she managed to cut herself. He attempted a taut smile, but could already feel the tension stiffening his neck muscles. Usually he never put himself into such a bother for a mere ball, finding such entertainments a boring nuisance. But this one had somehow attained an importance all out of proportion to the event. He was too much aware that every eye would be trained upon him this eve, all those fond matchmaking mamas, all those coy young maidens tremulous with hope. Simon had been catching enough disturbing bits of gossip during the last fortnight. There was an absurd notion firmly fixed in nearly everyone's mind, that he would award the palm to some eager female this very night.

Simon had never flinched when facing the entire French line, but all this rampant speculation was enough to make him want to bolt.

Seeing Gus so fretful only added to his feeling of being damnably on edge. He barked out an order for her to be still, at least until he had finished dressing. Although she subsided into a striped-silk chair, she kept stealing uneasy glances at him. Uneasy? Nay, more like sheepish.

When he stepped back for one final look, subjecting the severe style of the cravat to his approval, Gus cleared her throat.

"Simon . . . do you recollect that young woman you told me about, the one you found so fascinating?"

"Who the blazes was that?"

"Miss Audra Leigh Masters."

"I wouldn't exactly say that I told you anything about her, Gus. More accurately, you bedeviled the life out of me until I mentioning having met the young woman out—er—walking her dog. But I believe I said no more than that. Certainly nothing about fascination."

"It was rather what you didn't say," Augusta replied. "You didn't call her a hare-brained fool or a die-away ninny. After hearing your opinions of the other ladies hereabouts, I found such reticence positively heartening."

"And so? What about Miss Masters?"

"Nothing," Augusta said airily. "I only thought you might be interested to hear that I found out where she lives."

"I hadn't given it much consideration," he said, reaching for his white satin waistcoat and proceeding to struggle into it. That wasn't precisely a lie. He hadn't thought much about Miss Masters, only caught himself looking for her and the dog, every time he passed by that part of the moat.

Although he was curious, he refused to question his sister as to what she had discovered. He didn't have to. Augusta was determined to tell him.

"Miss Masters happens to be your tenant. She lives at Meadow Lane Lodge."

Meadow Lane. Simon's fingers stilled in the act of buttoning his waistcoat, the mention of that place threatening to bring forth a dangerous flood of memories. The old hunting lodge had been bought up by his father "to prevent rackety young men from coming down from London and scaring our birds." The cottage had been Robert's private retreat, away from the castle. Many times he had entertained Simon there, the pair of them playing truant from the old duke's stern gaze.

"I didn't know the place had been rented," Simon said.

"Did you not instruct Mr. Wylie to do so?"

"I suppose I did." Simon straightened, giving himself a mental shake. He assured himself it would have been sentimental folly to do otherwise, but when he thought of Robert's special place inhabited by a stranger. . . . Sometimes being practical did not come easy.

"So Miss Masters lives there now?" he mused. Practically on his own doorstep. She must keep rather close to the place or surely he would have seen her in the village or come upon her in the lane. But it was not as if he had been deliberately looking for her.

"She lives at Meadow Lane with her younger sister, but no older companion. Rather odd," Augusta said. "But they say she is a considerable heiress."

"Ten thousand pounds a year," Simon mumbled under his breath. His lips twitched as he remembered Audra's indignant speech.

"Her father was the Viscount Sunderly," his sister continued to enlighten him. "Her mother came from good family as well. She was one of the Exeters. Do you recall, Simon? The woman everyone used to call Lady Arabella because she went through husbands at such a rate, no one could ever recall her married name."

"*Her?* The one that now calls herself Countess Monta something?"

"I fear so."

Simon pulled a face. "I met her once when I was traveling through Italy. Good God, the woman is as vulgar and lascivious as Princess Caroline."

"The poor princess. I sometimes think her highness is judged too harshly. They are saying the king will never permit her to be crowned with him."

But the ton gossip held no interest for Simon. He was still digesting the startling information that the absurd, painted female he had met abroad was Miss Masters's mama.

He surprised himself by saying fiercely to his sister, "It makes no odds. Miss Masters is not in the least like Lady Arabella."

"I am pleased to hear it. I shall look forward to making Miss Masters's acquaintance to—" Augusta clapped her hand over her mouth.

When Simon subjected her to a hard, suspicious stare, a guilty flush stole into her cheeks. She rose hastily. "I had best put a few finishing touches onto my own toilette."

"Not so fast, my dear sister." Simon seized her by the elbow. "What d'you mean by that, Gus? Just when do you expect to meet Audra Masters?"

Her smile was a little uncertain, but her eyes danced with mischief. "Why, tonight, of course. I invited her to the ball."

"You what!"

"Don't roar like that, Simon. You hurt my ears."

"Augusta!" His tone became almost as pleading as fierce. "Tell me you didn't. You never sent—"

"I am afraid I did," she said cheerfully. "In quite the grand style, too, I might add. I sent your own secretary Mr. Lawrence to deliver the invitation in your best coach, with footmen in attendance."

Simon emitted a low groan. "So what did she do? Meet poor Lawrence with a loaded blunderbuss?"

"Certainly not, you silly man." Augusta gave a tinkling laugh. "She accepted with the greatest of civility."

Simon was so thunderstruck, he relaxed his grip on Augusta's elbow, permitting her to pull away. With a well-satisfied smile, she made good her escape before Simon could recover his wits enough to bluster, "Blast you, Gus, and your infernal meddling—"

But the door had already closed behind Lady Augusta. In truth, Simon thought grimly, there was little more he could say. He supposed he had furnished Gus with a meddler's license by asking her to arrange this ball in the first place.

But what imp had induced her to invite Audra Masters, and perhaps even more to the point, what had made Miss Masters accept?

"So she wasn't going to come, eh? Not even if I got down on one knee and begged."

As he faced the mirror, a slow, wicked smile spread over his features, but it was nothing compared to the devil's glint in his eyes. This ball that had promised to be such a tedious affair had suddenly taken on an entirely new aspect.

Whistling softly, he finished dressing, taking more pains with his appearance than he ever had in his life.

The Masters's carriage rumbled past the castle gate, moonlight rendering the road a ribbon of silver spiraling toward the great stone keep beyond. The cone-capped towers rose above the line of autumn shorn trees, the stone battlements held spellbound by clouds whispering across the inky sky. It was a night formed for enchantment, adventure, romance. . . .

And Audra wished herself a thousand miles away. As the

67

coach rattled over the ancient drawbridge, she blotted out the chatter of Uncle Matthew and Cecily, her hands clenching tight the nosegay her courtly uncle had presented to her. Why had she allowed Uncle Matt to persuade her into coming? She had wondered that more than once during the past days of preparation, being dragged through silk warehouses, endless fittings with the dressmaker.

And all for what? She detested balls. She was dreadfully awkward at dancing, even more so at the art of making social conversation with strangers. And to add to her discomfort at attending this particular function, *he* would be there.

Raeburn. His Grace of the dark, sardonic eye. The notion of meeting him again made the bodice of her russet-colored gown seemed laced too tight, not allowing enough room for the host of butterflies that had taken up residence beneath her rib cage.

Despising her nervousness, Audra sought to quell it. She'd be hanged if she would permit herself to be intimidated by the mere thought of the man. After all, she had cornered the dragon once in his lair, felt the scorch of his fiery breath. She would daresay that she could survive a second encounter.

Besides, she kept reminding herself, she was only enduring this misery because of Cecily. And it already seemed worth it to see Muffin looking so deliriously happy. Cecily appeared a veritable princess tonight, all garbed in filmy white from her gown to her satin cloak. A spangled ribbon caught up golden curls framing a face so shining with innocent dreams that most strangely it brought a lump to Audra's throat.

She knew too well that dreams were seldom what they seemed, but she hoped that for just one night, it might prove different for Cecily.

When the coach at last lurched to a halt in the castle courtyard, bewigged grooms sprang forward to open the door. But it was Uncle Matthew who alighted first to offer up his hand to Audra and Cecily. The old man had a most youthful spring to his step tonight. From some ancient trunk, he had unearthed satin knee breeches, a shirt frothy with lace, a brocaded frock coat. But the old-fashioned attire suited him far better than if he had attempted to ape the fashions of the younger men. His excitement at attending the ball seemed not one whit less than Cecily's.

"My ladies," he said, sweeping off his tricorne with a courtly bow that caused his stays to creak.

Cecily giggled as her uncle handed her down. She paused midway upon the coach steps to gape up at the castle. The high arched windows seemed almost iridescent with the glow of myriad lights.

"Oh, Audra," Cecily breathed. "It's all so wonderful. Just as I imagined. There's magic, a certain something in the air tonight—"

"It's called frost," Audra started to mutter, then bit her tongue. No, she had resolved she would say or do nothing to spoil this night for Cecily or her uncle.

"Indeed, it is all most charming," she agreed, giving her starry-eyed sister a gentle prod to get her moving down the steps.

Within the castle hall, liveried footmen hastened forward to take cloaks and hats. This was the newer part of the castle, and although the architecture without had been cleverly designed with the old, Audra noted that the interior could have been part of any Georgian mansion.

When she handed over her own mantle, she felt a tug on the train of her gown. Turning to politely request the gentleman next to her to move his foot, she drew up short, staring into the grinning countenance of Sir Ralph Entwhistle. It had never occurred to Audra that the baronet would be present. She had never known him to do other than tear about the countryside, making some poor horse's life a misery. It was astonishing to see him out of his top boots and buckskins, his stocky frame garbed in tight yellow pantaloons with matching coat. With his wild red hair brushed back, he resembled nothing so much as a squat yellow candle.

"You!" Audra could not helping exclaiming in accents of dismay. "What are you doing here?"

Not in the least taken aback by her bluntness, Sir Ralph chuckled. "I was invited o' course. Thought my sisters may as well have a touch at the duke, too. It'd be a fine thing to have

Sophy or Georgy settled here at Raeburn. Good hunting land. Worth the nuisance of attending a ball."

"Indeed?" Audra leveled him a frosty stare. She meant to sweep past him, but the dolt was still standing on the hem of her gown.

"Aw, here now, Miss Masters," he coaxed. "B'gawd, woman, you can't still be vexed with me over that little jest I played with Miss Cecily's dog. Why don't you promise me the first dance and we can be friends again?"

"That would be rather difficult since I don't recall our being friends in the first place. Now kindly get off my train."

For a second, she feared Sir Ralph might be too boorish to comply, but he stepped aside at last. However, as she stalked away from him, he emitted one of his hee-haw laughs and called after her, "The first dance, Miss Masters!"

Audra longed to tell him if he attempted to stand up with her, his first dance was going to be his last. With difficulty, she checked her temper, recalling her resolve not to cause Cecily any embarrassment this evening.

By the time she joined her sister and the Reverend Mr. Masters, taking their place in the receiving line, Audra managed to regain a semblance of calm.

Lit by a massive chandelier, a sweeping marble stair curved upward to the ballroom above. The steps already seemed thronged with silk skirts and fluttering fans waiting to be presented to His Grace.

Audra reflected it was a pity that Raeburn's drawbridge these days was only for ornament, no longer capable of being raised. Of course it had been many centuries since the castle had been attacked, but it was definitely under siege tonight . . . by an army of women.

None of them might be so vulgar as Sir Ralph, admitting that they were also here to have a "touch at the duke." But soft smiles did little to disguise predatory gleams and Raeburn's name was on everyone's lips.

The game was afoot, but the prize tonight was no mere stag or dog fox, but a duke, replete with accompanying lands and titles. Faith, if Raeburn had not shown himself to be so impossibly arrogant, Audra could have felt sorry for the man. But since he had courted this sort of pursuit by giving this silly ball, she did not waste a moment of her sympathy.

As she waited in the reception line, she tried to ignore the fact that her dancing slippers had already begun to pinch her feet. Her heavy chestnut locks done up in a crown of braids seemed to have a dozen hairpins impaled in her scalp. To take her mind from these discomforts, she amused herself by trying to guess which of these women Raeburn might be likely to choose for his duchess. The buxom girl with the shocking décolletage? The icy blonde who was looking down her nose at the rest of the assemblage? Or perhaps that lively little brunette with the voice as shrill as a starling.

As the line inched forward, Audra soon caught a glimpse of Raeburn himself at the head of the stairs. He towered above most of his guests, even the gentlemen, the powerful frame of his square shoulders encased in a black evening coat. The glow of candlelight picking out the flecks of silver in his glossy dark hair did but little to soften the harsh cast of his countenance. Audra sensed he was trying to appear affable as he greeted so many chattering females, but it was difficult. His scowl seemed to come so much more naturally, but perhaps that was all a trick of those heavy black brows.

Still, he looked magnificent, as blazingly fierce as any conqueror of old, very much the duke, the lord of his castle. It suddenly occurred to Audra that she had felt much more on an equal footing when she had just blundered into him out by the moat. He seemed much more formidable looming at the top of the stairs, and her heart gave a flutter of trepidation.

She could have slapped herself for it. After all, she wasn't an intruder this time. She was here by his invitation. That reminder did not seem to help, and she started unreasonably when Cecily plucked at her sleeve.

"Audra," Cecily whispered. "Is that the duke?" She indicated an excessively handsome young sprig near the top of the receiving line, his curls as golden as Cecily's own.

"No!" Audra was appalled that her sister could mistake such

71

a stripling for the Duke of Raeburn. "He's right over there, by that petite lady that I suppose must be his sister."

Cecily followed Audra's pointing finger. "Oh," she said, her voice considerably subdued.

Audra was not surprised that her sister should be awed. Though not classically handsome, Raeburn possessed one of those striking countenances no woman could forget. Audra felt obliged to drop a word of warning in Cecily's ear.

"Now, I know you have been weaving a great deal of romantic fantasies in your head, Muffin. But I pray you, don't go losing your heart to the man."

Cecily gave her a very odd look. "N-no, of course not, Audra."

Audra did not have time to say more for at that moment she became aware that a footman was intoning the names of her own party.

"The Reverend Mr. Masters, Miss Audra Masters, and Miss Cecily Holt."

Uncle Matthew made his leg, but he did not waste much time upon the duke, the old rogue moving straightaway to bend over the pretty Lady Augusta's hand. Cecily seemed to have frozen with terror, but at a gentle nudge from Audra, she sank into her curtsy.

Faced with Raeburn's scowl, she only managed to blush and stammer, "Th-thank you for inviting me. You have a very nice castle. I-I have always liked antiquities."

"You are very welcome, young lady," Raeburn said, "but I am not quite that old."

His gruff jest completely discomposed Cecily, and she all but stumbled in her haste to get away from him. Raeburn rolled his eyes heavenward, and Audra bristled. What more did he expect from the poor child when he had looked as if he were about to have her for breakfast?

Her own nervousness dispelled by anger, Audra determined he would not find her so easily intimidated. When his attention shifted in her direction, she dropped a stiff curtsy.

His eyes skated over her, then started as though in sudden recognition. He then subjected her to a more thorough and,

72

Audra thought, more critical inspection. His gaze locked with hers at last, and her chin came up. She felt like a duelist about to raise her pistol, but she managed to snap out, "Good evening, Your Grace."

"Miss Masters. I almost did not know you. What have you done to your hair? I liked it better down."

"I did not fix it with any thought of pleasing you."

"Indeed?"

She hadn't offered him her hand, but he took it anyway, engulfing it in the calloused strength of his own. His mouth actually twitched in the semblance of a smile.

He asked, "So have you come here tonight for my head or merely to dance?"

"Neither," she said. "I came to chaperon my sister."

"Sister?" Raeburn's gaze shifted to where Cecily now stood talking to Lady Augusta. Under the older woman's kindness, the girl had recovered and appeared once more aglow with excitement.

"Ah, yes," Raeburn said. "Would that be the same sister who also didn't want to attend the ball?"

Audra refused to rise to this baiting, merely wrenching her hand away. Raeburn bent, making an elaborate show of examining the knees of his breeches. Audra was certain she would be sorry for asking, but she couldn't seem to help herself.

"What, pray, are you doing?"

"Checking for smudge marks." His eyes danced wickedly. "I don't recall getting down on my knees, but I suppose I must have done so. After all, you did say something about being reluctant—"

"I said I would not come if you begged, and I'm beginning to wonder why I did." Audra glared at him. "Did you only invite me here to continue our quarrel?"

"I fear I didn't invite you at all. It was my sister's notion."

Audra felt her face wash red with humiliation. Forgetting all her noble resolves about spoiling her sister's evening, she turned, preparing to gather up Cecily and Uncle Matthew to leave at once.

But Raeburn seized her by the wrist, preventing her. With a

73

soft laugh, he said, "All the same, Miss Masters. I am deuced glad you came."

The look in his eyes was steady, unexpectedly sincere. Audra found it more unnerving than when he mocked her. She said, "I only accepted the invitation, Your Grace, because I believed you would behave like a gentleman."

"No! What did I ever do to give you such a foolish idea as that?"

The thunderstruck expression he feigned coaxed a reluctant smile from her.

"That's better," he approved. "Put up your sword, madam, and I shall do the same. What do you say? Shall we call a truce?"

Audra merely arched both brows. For the second time that evening, she regained possession of her hand from him. Since the next cluster of ladies pressed closer, eager to be presented, he was obliged to let her go.

Simon watched Audra gather up her sister and vanish into the crowded ballroom. It was harder than ever to return to his task of greeting these other insipid females, but he managed. Seeing Miss Masters had given his spirits an odd lift, rendering him almost gracious.

He had nearly given up on her arrival, thinking she must have changed her mind. Since he scarce heeded the names flung at him, he had not been aware of her presence until he had glanced around to find her standing before him.

Even then he hadn't recognized her at first. She looked so different in that rather drab brown gown, her hair done up so primly in those braids. He had been disappointed, wondering if memory had failed him, if he had been incorrect in fancying her something out of the common way.

But one look into those forthright eyes had reassured him. He should be ashamed of himself for how he had teased her, deliberately provoking her. But her eyes turned the most delightful storm gray when she was angry, like a warrior queen dispensing her thunderbolts.

Simon never thought he would look forward to such a thing

as the first dance, but he became impatient for the orchestra to strike up the music.

He was drawn to the last few guests straggling in when his sister stole a chance to whisper to him. Lady Augusta's smooth brow was marred by a frown.

"I must say, Simon. Your Miss Masters was certainly a pretty little thing with engaging manners, but I scarce expected such an infant to capture your attention."

"You got the sisters mixed up, m'dear," Simon murmured back. "Miss Masters was the other one."

"The tall one with the flashing eyes who looked like she wanted to poleax you." Augusta brightened at once. "But, Simon, how delightful."

Simon gave his sister a wry glance. "Just don't be handing her any weapons."

He made a smart bow to the last late arrival, then excused himself. As he stalked eagerly across the ballroom, the crowd parted and fell back for him.

A hush seemed to fall all over the room and, at any other time, Simon would have found the air of breathless expectation embarrassing. Every lady present craned her neck, waiting to see whom he would favor with the first dance.

But they were as doomed to disappointment as himself. The strains of the first cotillion struck up, but in a room full of eager females, Simon could not locate the one lady he sought.

Miss Masters appeared to have vanished.

Chapter 6

Audra never had any intention of trying to hide when she first entered the ballroom. Having survived the ordeal of seeing

Raeburn again, she had merely meant to blend in with the elegant frieze adorning the walls.

She felt that she could in good conscience do so, having done her duty by Cecily, seeing the girl suitably partnered. Unlike many of the other more coy maidens waiting to see whom the duke would choose, Cecily had been glad to award the first dance to the poetic Mr. Gilmore.

"Though I know he can be a bit silly," she had confessed to Audra. "I would far rather stand up with him even if the duke should ask me. I fear I would find dancing with His Grace most terrifying."

Audra could scarce blame her sister after the way Raeburn had overwhelmed Cecily with his fierce scowl when she had made him her curtsy. Yet Audra had to admit the man could be unexpectedly charming after his own gruff fashion. She could not help recalling that brief moment he had looked straight into her eyes, remarking that he was "deuced glad she'd come."

The memory had a strange effect on her, bringing a rush of warmth to her cheeks that she fought to quell. She still concurred with Cecily's view that it would be remarkably uncomfortable to have to dance with Raeburn. Any lady foolish enough to do so tonight would be a marked woman, the focus of much critical staring and speculation. Cecily had been quite wise to prefer the more bland, but less notorious attentions of a Mr. Gilmore.

As for Audra, she had no intention of dancing with anyone, despite how her Uncle Matthew scolded. When Cecily moved off to take her position in the first quadrille, Audra took up hers beneath the shadow of one of the room's towering pillars.

Uncle Matthew followed, frowning. " 'Tis not necessary for you to linger there, m'dear. Those pillars have been holding up the roof for a long time without any assistance from you."

"You are quite right, Uncle. As soon as the dancing begins, I mean to find a chair."

"What! Be seated among the quizzes and dowagers. I won't hear of it, Audra—"

"Now, Uncle, I warned you before we came that I meant to do no dancing, not even with you. So I suggest you seek out some other lady to bedevil. There will be many needing your gallant consolation once the duke makes his selection."

Although the old rector pursed his lips with disappointment, he did as she asked. She could hear him grumbling as he moved away and kept a wary eye upon him. She was still not certain the old man would not return with some sprig in tow, attempting to partner her off. But as she watched her uncle's retreat, Audra realized she stood in far more immediate danger.

Pressing past a plump, turbaned dowager, Audra saw Sir Ralph Entwhistle heading in her direction, his bright red hair a beacon even in the crowded ballroom. The vacuous smile on his face and the determined set to his chin left Audra in no doubt of his intentions.

The fool thought he was coming to claim his dance. Audra tensed. Was there any way of discouraging a man so completely dense? Audra could think of but one. Unfortunately, drawing Sir Ralph's cork would just attract the sort of attention she most deplored.

Only one other alternative remained to her, and that was flight. Frantically she glanced around for a suitable retreat. Spotting what she thought was a curtained alcove, Audra headed for it.

Behind her, she heard Sir Ralph's baffled cry, "Miss Masters." As persistent as one of his own hounds, he kept coming. Audra quickened her steps. Darting beneath the curtain, she discovered that the arch led not to an alcove but a long corridor.

She'd never make it to the other end before Sir Ralph spotted her. Instead she raced to the first door she saw, opened it, and hurled herself inside. Leaning up against the oak portal, she attempted to still her breath, putting her ear against the wood to listen.

Presently she heard the tread of heavy footsteps and Sir Ralph calling, "Halloa! Miss Masters?" He sounded so very like a mournful dog, baying because he had lost the scent, that Audra had to stifle a gasp of laughter.

She waited, scarce daring to breathe until she heard his footsteps recede. Flooded with relief, she still did not stir, determined not to make her way back to the ballroom until she was certain Sir Ralph would have had enough time to inflict himself upon some other unfortunate female.

Shifting slightly, she glanced about her, for the first time taking stock of the place in which she had sought refuge. Light from the fire left blazing upon the hearth cast flickering shadows up the walls, walls lined from the floor to ceiling with shelves of books.

Audra stood transfixed, pressing her hands to her heart. She had heard tales of the magnificent library to be found at Castle Raeburn, but never in her wildest imaginings had she ever fancied a treasure trove such as this.

Shivering with delight, she stepped away from the door. Locating a branch of candles, she lit the wicks, then like a pilgrim approaching a shrine, she paced reverently along the stacks, breathing in the heady scent of leather, caressing the embossed lettering on the spines.

Any number of intriguing titles leaped out at her, causing her head to spin. Chaucer and Milton nestled side by side with Fielding and Shakespeare. Among some of the newer-looking books she found Byron.

With a tiny sigh, she pulled a volume of *Ivanhoe* from the shelf. What with all the hubbub over this blasted ball, she still had been unable to finish the book. Wistfully, she thumbed to the page where she had been obliged to leave off on far too many occasions. As she fingered the book, she became aware that an armchair stood just at her elbow, its overstuffed cushions looking far too inviting.

She half started to sink into it and stopped, horrified at herself. No, truly, she couldn't. Even now she could hear distant strains of music coming from the ballroom, reminding her where she ought to be.

But by now Cecily must be moving through the steps of the quadrille with Mr. Gilmore. Likely Uncle Matthew was also agreeably engaged. Who would miss Audra if she were to take a few minutes, just long enough to finish the end of one chapter?

Perching gingerly on the edge of the chair, Audra was tempted to ease off her shoes for a moment. The slippers had begun to pinch abominably, but she feared that once removed, she might never get the wretched things back on. As she perused a few lines of the book, she soon forgot her aching feet. Becoming ever more absorbed, she settled deeper against the cushions. After a time the muted sounds of music and laughter coming from the ballroom faded. She scarce heard the mantel clock chiming out the passing of the hour.

Torquilstone Castle was in flames. The villain, Bois-Guilbert, managed to seize Rebecca as he made his escape and Audra rode with them, flinching at every arrow that whizzed past her.

Caught up in the tale, Audra did not notice the library door swinging open until it was too late. It slammed to, alarming her so that she nigh jumped from her chair.

For one dreadful moment, she feared it might be Sir Ralph come looking for her or, at the least, some lofty butler who would demand to know what she was doing in here. As she peered round from her chair, she wished she could shrink to the size of inkprint and vanish into the book.

Worse than any supercilious servant, it was Raeburn.

Oblivious to her presence, he strode in, looking like a harried fox gone to ground. With grim purpose, he moved to a cabinet against the opposite wall and drew forth a brandy decanter. As he sloshed some of the liquid into a glass, Audra froze, unable to move a muscle, which was quite absurd. As soon as Raeburn whipped about, he was bound to see her, no matter how still she sat.

She was correct for as he shifted, preparing to toss down the brandy, he paused with the glass halfway to his lips, staring at her. His brows rose in astonishment.

"Miss Masters," he said. He set the glass down with a sharp click. "I wondered where the deuce you were hiding."

"I-I wasn't hiding." Audra flushed, annoyed with herself for stammering and even more so for the guilty impulse to whip the book behind her like a naughty child caught pilfering sweetmeats.

But as Raeburn's gaze tracked from her discomfited face to the book she clutched, he looked more amused than vexed.

"You do seem to have a habit of making yourself quite at home upon my estate, madam."

Audra shot to her feet. "I beg your pardon. If I had any notion *you* would come in here—"

"I know. You would have fled to the Antipodes. Oh, do sit down, Miss Masters. We called a truce, remember?"

When she didn't comply, he barked, "Sit down."

Though disgusted by her own meekness, Audra obeyed him. Not that she minded being bellowed at, but Raeburn seemed exactly the sort of man to back up his commands with force if necessary. Besides, she was not about to let His Grace think she could be so easily frightened away. She settled back in the chair, resting the book on her lap with forced casualness.

"I didn't mean to intrude," she said. " 'Tis only I have never seen anything like your library. And the fire had been left burning in here. It was all so inviting."

"The fire is always left kindled for me. I spend a great deal of my time here, though I always doubted the place would hold much interest for my guests, especially the ladies."

"Perhaps it wouldn't for most. I always seem to be different."

"So you are, very different." Raeburn was not the only person to tell her so, but he was the first person to sound so approving. She felt more strangely flustered than if he had paid her a lavish compliment.

When he stalked toward her, her heart gave a disconcerting thud, although all he did was pluck the book from her hands, glance at the title, then return it to her.

"*Ivanhoe.* I've had no opportunity to examine that one myself. Is there any merit to it?"

"I can scarce say. I have been interrupted too many times. But it was wrong of me to be reading when I should be in the ballroom."

"Why? I am sure you are feeling no more eager to return to that tedious affair than I am."

"Tedious? But if you feel that way . . ." She trailed off, knowing it was none of her concern, but she couldn't refrain

80

from asking, "Why the deuce did you ever have the blasted thing?"

"Be hanged if I know." He grimaced. "It seemed like a good idea at the time. I fear that as a duke, I am not blessed with your freedom and independence. I have certain obligations, even though I, too, am a bachelor and fiercely proud of it."

"Yes, I had forgotten. Your legendary search for a bride." Audra could not prevent a smile escaping.

"Do you find it that amusing? I admit I have a face and temper like the devil, but I can surely find some wench who will have me."

"Likely too many of them. I only smiled because it all seems so silly—Er, that is, I mean . . ." Audra floundered, trying to recover from her want of tact, but Raeburn would have none of it.

"Come, Miss Masters. You have never hesitated to insult me before. Why turn shy now?"

Very well. He had asked for it. She crossed her arms, her voice laced with scorn. "Did you really believe you were going to find a wife tonight in that ballroom? That all it would take was one look, one glance, and you would immediately know which lady to choose? Forgive me, but you scarce seem the sort to be prone to such romantic nonsense."

"I am not, any more than you are. The idea that one would come across one special person that one would find so intriguing . . . Well, of course, it is absurd. And yet . . ." His eyes locked with hers. "And yet," he added softly. "One must begin somewhere."

"I suppose one must," Audra replied, surprised to hear her own voice sound so breathless. She had never realized it before, but it could be rather dangerous to stare too long into any man's eyes, especially eyes possessed of such fierce, dark passion as Raeburn's. She felt oddly lightheaded and was quick to lower her gaze.

"It will scarce aid Your Grace in your search to linger here. You should get back to the ballroom. After all, you are the host."

81

"Justly rebuked, Miss Masters." He held out his hand to her. "Very well. Come on then."

Audra only stared in dismay at those long, tanned fingers, their latent strength quite evident. "Oh, n-no. I had rather hoped you might permit me to remain—"

"The devil I will. I fear I am not that generous, madam." He took the book from her and dropped it on the side table. Seizing her by the hand, he tugged her to her feet. "If I must suffer through this cursed ball, so must you."

Audra opened her lips to protest, but what could she say? After all, it was his castle. She permitted him to lead her from the library with great reluctance. But as they started down the hallway, she did complain.

"There is no need to keep such a grip upon my arm, sir. It is not as if I were planning to run away."

"Truly? It seems to me you have a very bad habit of doing so, Miss Masters. I wouldn't want to lose you again. I believe we will be just in time to take our places in the next set forming."

"You may do so, but I am not engaged to stand up with anyone."

"I didn't think you were or you could hardly be going to dance with me."

"What!" Audra came to an abrupt halt beneath the arch that led back into the ballroom, her dismay only second to her astonishment. Dance with *her*? Was His Grace often given to these mad starts?

"You cannot mean, that . . . that is I am honored, but I don't dance, Your Grace."

"Neither do I," the duke said pleasantly. "So this should prove a most interesting exercise."

Maintaining a firm grip upon her arm, he propelled her inexorably forward. Audra could already sense the eyes fixing in her direction, heads nodding together, the whispers behind fans. She sought to quell a hot blush.

"Your Grace, I fear I have not made myself clear. I don't want to dance."

But with his customary high-handedness, he led her to the

head of the set. Too proud to plead with him, to confess her own clumsiness or even how sore her feet already were, Audra held her head up high. When he finally released her arm, she could do naught but remain. To flee from his side would only cause the whispers to increase.

As the music began, Raeburn swept her a bow full of mocking challenge. Audra sank into a furious curtsy, hissing between her teeth. "You are going to be very sorry for this, Your Grace."

His lips twitched in infuriating fashion. He was still smiling when they came together in the movement of the dance. Audra smiled sweetly back at him, then stomped on his foot. His smirk vanished in an astonished gasp. "You vixen! You did that a-purpose."

As they separated, Audra skirted round him, managing to deliver a swift kick to his shin.

Raeburn choked back an oath, his brows crashing together. "I'm warning you, madam . . ." But the rest of his threat was lost as the steps of the dance took them apart.

When they next came back together, she caught him square on the ankle.

"Damnation!" Raeburn growled. His black scowl would have daunted anyone else, but Audra was far too caught up in her own anger. In fact, she could never recall taking such a militant pleasure in any dance. She paraded down the line, planning her next assault.

Approaching Raeburn again, she prepared to aim for his instep. But, his eyes narrowed, Raeburn struck first, treading upon her toes. Audra stifled a yelp. Simmering with indignation, she readied for the next skirmish, a sharp kick that caused him to falter.

His thunderous expression boded ill for her, and Audra almost knew a craven impulse to retreat. But there was no help for it. The perfidious patterns of the dance brought her back to his side where he tromped upon her other foot.

Audra bit her lip to keep from swearing. Her poor toes, already pinched tight by the slippers, were in no condition to tolerate more of Raeburn's abuse. Much as she hated being the first to cry enough, she became uncomfortably aware of the shocked stares of the other dancers in their set.

When next she came face-to-face with Raeburn, she curbed her temper, settling for a glower rather than a blow.

"You, sir, are no gentleman," she snapped.

"And you, madam, are assuredly no lady."

After which exchange of insults, they finished out the dance in grim silence, more after the manner of a pair of duelists, circling each other with wary respect.

As soon as the last notes of the dance sounded, Audra made the briefest of curtsies, preparing to stalk away as fast as her throbbing feet would let her. But Raeburn linked his arm roughly through hers.

"It is my habit, madam, to escort my partner from the floor, no matter how ill-used I have been."

Audra longed to shake him off, but she supposed she had already created enough of a scene for one evening. Clenching her teeth, she permitted Raeburn to lead her to the side of the ballroom.

"If you feel ill-used, it was entirely your own doing," she said. "I told you I didn't want to stand up with you. I can make enough of a spectacle of myself without your assistance."

"I don't doubt it, especially if you treat an offer to dance as if a man had offered you an insult."

"Offer! More like demand. And it was an insult. You only did it to torment me."

"Can you imagine no other reason?"

"No!"

Having guided her to the side of the ballroom, he subjected her to a hard stare. "It might have occurred to you that ... Never mind." His jaw tightened. "Your servant, madam."

Sweeping her a curt bow, he stalked away. Still seething, Audra watched him go, but her anger was tempered by the uncomfortable feeling that she had somehow wronged him. Even if he had forced her to dance, she had behaved in an abominably unladylike fashion, even for the eccentric Miss Audra Leigh Masters. Perhaps she even owed the duke an apology.

But at least, he would have the good sense never to demand that she dance with him again.

That thought, however, did not offer her the satisfaction that it should have. Rather, it only seemed to add to her misery, especially when the strains of a waltz filled the room and she observed Raeburn leading another lady onto the floor.

She was a dark-haired beauty, willowy, graceful, a diamond of the first water. But the way the creature simpered, looking up at Raeburn with such toad-eating deference, was enough to turn Audra's stomach. Unable to endure watching anymore, Audra limped off to find an obscure corner of the room.

Locating a small gilt settee half-hidden by a spray of flowers, Audra sank down upon the cushion. She never carried anything so frippery as a fan, but for once she wished she had one of the blasted things. The room seemed unbearably warm, but whether from her recent exercise or her bout of temper, Audra could not have said.

Bending over to massage the toe of her slipper, realizing she had the devil of a blister forming, Audra would have been content to pass the rest of the evening in quiet obscurity. But she had completely forgotten her initial reason for escaping to the library—that is until Sir Ralph suddenly loomed above her to remind her.

The baronet looked for all the world like a sulky red-haired troll. "B'gawd, Miss Masters," he accused. "You forgot our dance."

Audra thought if she heard the word "dance" upon a man's lips one more time tonight, she would have a fit of apoplexy. Stretching out one slipper, wriggling her sore foot, she said, "You must hold me excused, sir. I fear I will be doing no more dancing tonight."

"I shouldn't wonder. I watched you dancing with Raeburn." Sir Ralph brayed a laugh. "The squire and I got up a wager which of you would be the first to lame the other."

"Wonderful," Audra muttered. "I am pleased to have provided you with such diversion, sir."

She winced when Sir Ralph plunked himself beside her with

such force the entire settee seemed to tremble. "Well, it doesn't matter a ha'penny about the dance. I'd far rather sit and talk."

Audra nearly groaned aloud, wishing she had claimed sore ears instead of feet. At any other time, she could have dealt with Sir Ralph, but she was feeling far too wearied from her quarrel with Raeburn. Naturally, the baronet's conversation settled upon one thing: his fox hunting.

Audra thought of telling him once and for all that she found his notion of sport cruel and disgusting, but she knew it would be a waste of breath. The fool would never comprehend her feelings. So she listened in dour silence while Entwhistle lamented the dearth of foxes.

"Not many new cubs. It's going to be a bad year," Sir Ralph said. "Which is why you must no longer ever speak to Mr. Cecil. He's a vulpicide."

"A *vulpicide*?"

"He shot a vixen raiding his henhouse."

"But you kill foxes all the time," Audra protested indignantly.

"That's different. I do it proper, hunting them with hounds. Cornered a feisty cub just the other morning, but some of my young dogs aren't so well trained. B'gawd, Ratterer and Bellman tore that fox to shreds before I could even claim the pads and mask."

When Entwhistle went on to describe the scene in more vivid detail, Audra felt herself go pale. By the time he reached the part about what remained of the cub's blood-soaked brush, Audra truly thought she was going to be ill.

Rescue came from an unexpected quarter, an acid voice interrupting Sir Ralph's boisterous flow of words.

"I don't believe Miss Masters cares for your hunt stories, Entwhistle."

Both Audra and the baronet glanced round to discover the Duke of Raeburn leaning up against the back of the settee. How long he had stood there listening, Audra had no idea. She despised herself for the way her heart leaped, how foolishly glad she felt to see him.

As for Sir Ralph, although he rose respectfully to his feet, he

thrust out his lower lip. "Pish, Miss Masters takes a keen interest in the sport, which is more than can be said for some, Your
Grace. What's this foul rumor I've been hearing tonight that
you may start forbidding my hunt to cross your land?"

" 'Tis no rumor, but a fact, sir," Raeburn said levelly. "Besides the fact you ruin my tenant's crops, I heard young Worthington near snapped his neck jumping one of my hedges the
other day. If anyone is carted off on a hurdle, it's not going to
be on my estate."

"Damme!" Sir Ralph roared. "B'gawd, I've never heard
such an attitude. 'Tis positively un-English." When Raeburn
stiffened, the baronet managed to lower his voice, assuming
a more placating tone. "Not that I don't understand. Your
brother's unfortunate accident and all. But a man can cut his
stick a hundred other ways than hunting, and it happened so
many years ago."

Audra thought she detected a flash of pain in Raeburn's
eyes, quickly shuttered away. But all he said was, "I believe
you are keeping my sister waiting, Entwhistle. She is expecting
to dance with you."

Though clearly prepared to argue the hunt question all night,
Raeburn's words took Sir Ralph aback.

"The Lady Augusta?" The baronet's eyes rounded. "Is she,
then? B'gawd, I wouldn't want to offend my hostess." And
looking immensely flattered, Sir Ralph bustled off.

Audra angled a reproachful glance at the duke. "What an un-
handsome thing to have done to your sister."

"Wasn't it, though?" Raeburn's grim expression relaxed into
the barest hint of a smile. "It scarce signifies, for if I know Gus,
she has already promised every dance by now."

The mischief in those dark eyes almost invited her to smile
back at him. Just barely Audra recollected that she and Raeburn were supposed to be at odds with each other.

He folded his arms, staring down at her. "Well, aren't you
even going to thank me?"

"For what?"

"Rescuing you from the company of that redheaded oaf."

"I am quite capable of dealing with Sir Ralph myself."

Audra started to stand, preparing to stalk away. But her foot twisted just enough to rub the slipper against her blister. She sank back down, sucking in her breath between her teeth.

"What the deuce is amiss?" Raeburn asked. "Are you hurt?"

"No, 'tis nothing. Only my blasted foot."

He settled beside her on the settee, his brow furrowing with concern. "I'm sorry. It is all my fault for being so cursed rough. Do you have a sprain or only a bruise?"

Audra shrank away, whisking her slippers further beneath the hem of her gown. "There is no need for you to be so concerned. My injury is none of your doing. It is only these dratted shoes. They have been paining me all evening. They are about two sizes too small."

"Of all the confounded folly. Why the blazes didn't you have them made to fit?"

"Because." Audra's cheeks stung with mortified pride. She blurted out, "Because it is bad enough being so tall, without having my feet seem so large as well."

There! Now that she had made confession of this one small but foolish vanity, perhaps he would leave her in peace. Though he looked a little astonished, he said gruffly, "There's no disgrace in being tall, and I prefer women to have large feet rather than mince about."

"You are utterly ridiculous, sir." But a laugh escaped Audra in spite of herself.

Raeburn nodded with approval. "I wondered if I would ever be able to persuade you to smile at me again."

Audra tried to resume her pokerlike expression, but it was hopeless, especially when Raeburn continued, "Whether your afflicted foot is my fault or not, I suppose I do owe you an apology for what I did earlier, forcing you to dance. My sister, Gus, will tell you I do have a tendency to be a bit of a bully."

"Pray don't apologize, at least not for tramping my toes. I fear I asked for that. As my sister would tell you, I have an infernally bad temper."

"You were right to be angry. I was being selfish, consulting only my own feelings and not yours. Contrary to what you might believe, Miss Masters, I didn't ask you to dance with me just to enrage you. I did so because I wanted to stand up with you more than any other lady present."

"Oh," was all Audra could think of to say. Her reply seemed foolishly inadequate even to her. "I can't imagine why Your Grace would—I am sure there are many more charming women present."

"Aye, I have near been charmed to death tonight. I've never been so flattered, so fawned over. 'Yes, Your Grace. No, Your Grace. The sun is blue if you say so, Your Grace.' I swear the lot of these females would court the devil himself, if the title of duchess came with it."

"Poor man! I could kick you again if it would make you feel better." But although she sought to mask a sudden bout of shyness beneath her flippant tone, Audra did not want him to think her wholly unsympathetic. "I do understand," she said. "I was pestered nigh to madness with unwanted suitors my first Season. All because of my fortune, you know."

"Ten thousand pounds a year," Raeburn agreed with a quizzing smile.

Although she blushed to be reminded of her vulgar boast, Audra continued, "But since there was no reason I had to be married, I eventually managed to drive everyone away."

"Rather like the princess in that old story, living in her castle behind her wall of thorns."

"Yes, if you like. Only I would never be caught napping. If there were any prince fool enough to scale my wall, I would greet him with an unsheathed sword."

"Would you? I give you fair warning, Miss Masters. I am a fair hand with a blade."

Audra started, scarce knowing how to interpret such a remark. If it had been anybody else but Raeburn, she almost might have supposed him to be flirting with her. A little daunted, she suddenly realized how close he sat. Of course, the settee was rather small.

Sitting rigidly upright, she gave a nervous cough to clear her throat. "This is getting to be a very silly conversation. Perhaps we had best talk of something else. Why don't you tell me about your travels abroad?" she suggested desperately.

"My dear Miss Masters, you are a glutton for punishment. Hasn't this ball provided you with boredom enough?"

"No, truly, I would not find it boring at all. That is one of the drawbacks to being a spinster," she said wistfully. "One can never go anywhere, unless one drags along some dreadful companion. Certainly not anywhere exciting like Greece . . . or Rome."

"But surely you could visit Italy anytime you chose. Doesn't your mother live—" Raeburn broke off, looking mighty uncomfortable, as Audra found gentlemen often did when mentioning Lady Arabella.

"Y-you know my mother?" she faltered.

"Well, er . . . yes, I did meet her just once during the course of my travels." It was an innocuous enough statement, but it was what His Grace was not saying that seemed to speak volumes.

Audra knew she should just let it rest there, but she couldn't seem to do so. She attempted a smile that was more a pain-filled grimace. "Such a small world, isn't it? My mother is so high-spirited. I-I suppose she flirted with you most shockingly."

"Of course not," Raeburn said almost too quickly. "Only look at my face, Miss Masters. Do I appear the sort of man a woman would want to flirt with?"

Audra did scan his features most intently, from that hawk-like nose to the harsh lines carved by his mouth, to the lowering dark brows that could not quite disguise the kindness in his eyes as he lied to spare her feelings. Yes, Audra was disconcerted to discover, he was exactly the sort of man she would wish to flirt with if she were at all adept at the art.

That realization was almost as embarrassing as her suspicion that likely her own mother had cast out lures to the duke. When he tried to lighten her mood by launching into an anecdote of how he had once nigh fallen into the canal in Venice, she stopped him.

"I am afraid I have kept Your Grace here talking long enough. You should be paying more heed to your other guests. Dancing or some such."

Raeburn's dark look showed exactly what he thought of her suggestion, so she hastened to add, "All these determined ladies might wax dangerous if deprived of your company for too long. I daresay your absence has already been remarked."

Raeburn did glance about him as if half expecting to find some predatory female ready to spring at him from the floral arrangement. Though he scowled, he rose to his feet, the gesture rife with resignation.

"Very well. I shall go do my cursed duty, but only under one condition."

Audra regarded him warily. "Which is?"

"You will let me take you into supper later."

Caught somewhere between delight and dismay, Audra stammered. "Oh, n-no, I couldn't."

"Why not? All right, so you don't dance. But even you, my redoubtable Miss Masters, must eat."

"Of course, I do," she said with a reluctant laugh. "But—"

Her protest was silenced when he captured one of her hands. "As my one true friend, Miss Masters, after flinging me to these ravening hordes of women, you should at least promise me some respite."

His words might be light, teasing, but his gaze was intent. Audra sighed. Was there ever any other man who knew how to use his eyes to such advantage?

"All right. I shall sit with you at supper."

He smiled, carrying her hand to his lips. Then, as if he feared she might yet change her mind, he bowed and was gone.

Audra sat perfectly still for long seconds after the duke vanished, staring at her hand as if she had never seen it before. Raeburn's kiss had not been in the least romantic, but rather brusque. Yet her skin still tingled from the rough brush of his lips. She drew in a tremulous breath, feeling more strange than she ever had in her life, as if she wanted to laugh and cry all at the same time. She, who had never been given to any excess of emotion.

She told herself she should have remained firm, refused Raeburn's demand to take her into supper. But he had called her his "one true friend." Was there any higher compliment a man could pay to a woman? Audra liked the sound of it as a thought suddenly occurred to her. Given her reclusive lifestyle, she had never had many friends.

Glancing up toward the window panes, blackened by night, the ball suddenly seemed more interminable than ever, but for a different reason. With an almost feverish impatience, she tried to calculate how much time remained until midnight, the hour supper would be served.

It would seem longer if she just sat here, ticking off the minutes. She supposed she ought to go look out for Cecily, especially considering she had not seen her sister for some time. A very poor chaperon she was turning out to be. Standing up, she emerged from her hiding place, preparing to skirt across the center of a ballroom where another lively waltz was taking place.

Odd that she had never noticed, but there was something rather delightful about a ball, the whirl of colors, the graceful way the dancers dipped and swirled. Her feet were feeling a little better, and she was almost sorry she had sent Raeburn in quest of another partner.

As she made her way past the column of pillars, she caught herself humming with the music. She saw Raeburn in the midst of the dancers and had to choke back a laugh. He had a rare and charming smile upon his face as he waltzed with a sweet-faced elderly dame who looked old enough to be his grandmama. Audra could only begin to imagine what must be the indignation of all the young ladies present. What a teasing devil he was.

But Audra's amusement was tempered by the fact that nowhere amid all the circling couples did she spy Cecily. Granted the ladies outnumbered the men tonight, but Audra had never expected that her lovely sister would have to sit out a dance.

Imagining what Cecily's chagrin must be, Audra hastened to find her. Most of the partnerless ladies were clustered in disconsolate groups to one side of the ballroom. As Audra made her way toward them, she squeezed behind several gilt-trimmed chairs where some of the women had taken refuge.

She overheard the dark-haired beauty whom Raeburn had

danced with earlier complaining in peevish accents to a formidable dowager in a purple turban.

"We may as well go home, Mama. Since the duke has stopped dancing with any of the eligible ladies, it is obvious he has settled upon his choice."

"What utter nonsense, Charlene. Whom do you think he has chosen?"

"That tall, plain creature, the one who stepped all over him during the cotillion. His Grace was over there in that corner, talking to her forever. Alicia Wright even saw him kiss her hand."

"That Masters woman? The eccentric spinster who lives like a hermit. Ridiculous! Good Lord, I have heard that she is even *bookish*."

Audra knew she should not listen to any more of this, but she suddenly felt rooted to the spot with dismay, unable to move.

Another older woman whom Audra vaguely recognized as Mrs. Wright, the mother of six unwed daughters, leaned forward to join in the conversation. "Eccentric Miss Masters may be, but also possessed of a large fortune, according to Lady Coleby."

The turbaned one sniffed. "Sophia Coleby is a wicked gossip, but she does usually know everything. But surely the duke need not take fortune into account in his choice of a bride."

"My dear," Mrs. Wright sneered. "The gentlemen always take that into account."

No! It was all Audra could do not to break in upon the women and protest. Raeburn wasn't counting upon any such thing, because he had not chosen Audra for anything other than a friend. It was horrid of these old tabbies to be implying otherwise.

But worse was to follow. Mrs. Wright lowered her voice, but remained disastrously audible. "Of course you know whose daughter Miss Masters is. That vulgar creature known in London circles simply as Lady Arabella. Widowed four times and married again, to say nothing of . . ."

93

Behind the cover of her fan, Mrs. Wright whispered something to the turbaned dowager which caused that lady to stiffen with shock.

"Well," she huffed. "That explains why Miss Masters is so shameless in setting her cap at the duke. Like mother, like daughter, I always say."

Mrs. Wright gave a sour laugh. "I fear Miss Masters will never be able to rival Lady Arabella in the number of marriages. The poor dear is getting such a late start, and the duke is a remarkably healthy specimen." Mrs. Wright stood up, shaking out her skirts. "I grow stiff from just sitting here. Shall we take a turn about the room?"

"We might as well." The purple turban also rose. "Come along, Charlene. Perhaps if you keep moving, your want of a partner will not be as noticeable."

The two dowagers rustled off, the pouting dark beauty trailing in their wake. Audra stepped slowly forward, then leaned on the back of one of the vacated chairs for support. She touched a hand to her cheek, astonished to find it was possible to blanch and still burn at the same time.

If things had been arranged more fairly, it would be possible for her to stalk after those creatures, slap Mrs. Wright with her glove for bandying Audra's name about, challenge her to a duel. But the world only favored gentlemen with such an outlet. A lady was ever obliged to smile, confining her barbs to her tongue, and the heavens help those possessing no claws to defend themselves.

Audra knew she shouldn't pay any heed to malicious gossip. She flattered herself that she was usually tougher than that. But Mrs. Wright's remarks were not all easily dismissed. To have herself compared to Lady Arabella, to be said to be like her mama! God save her, that was one raking of claws that had drawn blood.

And yet she had to absolve even those two harpies. No, the fault was her own, entirely hers. She had known any woman Raeburn bestowed attention upon tonight would attract undue attention, jealous criticism. At what point had she allowed herself to forget that—when he had smiled too deep into her eyes, when he had teased her into forgetting her shame about Mama's behavior, when he had kissed her hand?

It scarce mattered when she had become a fool, only that she had. Most heartily did she now regret her promise to Raeburn that he could take her to supper. She might possess neither beauty nor charm, but one thing she did have was pride.

Supping with the duke would really set tongues to wagging. But far worse than any gossip were the doubts that had been sown in Audra's mind.

Was she so sure herself that Raeburn's only design in courting her was friendship? The kiss to her hand, forcing her to dance, repeatedly seeking her out, could those have any other significance? She couldn't bring herself to think of Raeburn as a fortune hunter, or even that he would consider marrying her for any reason.

It was all so absurd, so confusing. Only one thing was certain. The prospect of facing him again filled her with a sensation of panic. If there was only some way she could vanish before midnight, be far away from here. Yet Cecily would never forgive Audra for tearing her away from the ball that early.

She was still pondering what to say to the girl, when she finally located her sister. Or rather Cecily found her first, fairly hurling herself into Audra's arms. Before Audra could speak a word, she was dumbfounded to hear Cecily's declaration.

"Oh, Audra, I want to go home."

Audra blinked, attempting to recover from her astonishment. But instead of relief that her own escape should be made so easy, Audra felt alarmed. Cecily was quite pale, with a glazed look in her eyes.

"Muffin, what's wrong? Have you not been having a good time either?"

"I have been having a wonderful time." A large tear escaped to trickle off the end of Cecily's pert nose. "B-but now I feel like I am going to be s-sick."

She clutched a hand to her stomach, her face going from white to hintings of green.

Audra slipped her arm about Cecily's waist. "Don't cry, love. I will take you home at once. Where is Uncle Matt?"

"In the card room, I th-think."

"Well, there is no need to disturb him. We can send the coach back to fetch him later. Come on."

Bracing Cecily, she led the girl toward the main door of the ballroom. Although her concern for Cecily was quite real, Audra experienced a sense of shame as well. Her solicitude was perhaps a shade too eager, as if she exploited Cecily's illness to cover her own cowardly desire to flee.

Guiding Cecily down the long, curving stair back to the lower hall, Audra despatched a footman to send for her coach and fetch their cloaks.

Cecily sagged against Audra, a picture of misery. "Shouldn't we take our leave of Lady Augusta and the duke?" she asked.

"No!" Audra lowered her voice, managing to add in a calmer tone, "We will send round our excuses later. You don't want to be sick here all over His Grace's marble tiles, do you?"

"Oh, n-no, Audra." She stood, listlessly docile while Audra swept her cloak about her shoulders. Audra pulled up the hood, hiding drooping blond curls, a face most woebegone. Audra tried to be gentle, hoping her own nervousness was not apparent. Her chief dread was that Raeburn would somehow detect her flight and swoop down for explanations.

Not that she did not have an adequate excuse. Anyone could see how ill Cecily was. But she feared that His Grace might have an uncanny knack of seeing other things as well, the desperation that surely must lurk in Audra's own eyes.

Bundling up in her own mantle, Audra hustled Cecily toward the door. Just as she felt herself nigh safe, her worst fear was realized. Raeburn appeared on the landing above her, casting a long shadow down the curve of the stairs.

Audra didn't look back, didn't hesitate, but shoved her sister out into the night. Over Cecily's muffled protest, Audra fairly dragged the girl across the flagstone courtyard to where the coach awaited them.

"Audra," Cecily moaned, but Audra scarce heard her over the wild thudding of her own heart. She was moving so swiftly that she stumbled, painfully wrenching one slipper half off her feet.

Cursing, Audra had to pull up. Hopping on one foot, she reached down to right it, but at that moment she thought she heard Raeburn calling her name. Calling? Nay, bellowing.

Swearing, she yanked one slipper off, then the other one, hurling both the cursed things in the direction of the moat.

Able to move more quickly in her stockinged feet, she got Cecily to the coach door.

"But Audra," Cecily said. "I think the duke is—"

Audra gave her sister no chance to finish, part pushing, part hurling the girl into the carriage. Shouting up to the coachman not to spare the horses, Miss Cecily was deathly ill, Audra vaulted into the carriage herself unassisted. As a footman slammed the door, she glimpsed Raeburn emerging into the circle of lantern light.

With an oath, the duke rushed forward, but his shouts were lost in the rattle of carriage wheels. Miss Masters's coachman whipped up his team, tearing out of the courtyard as if a thousand demons were in pursuit.

No, not a thousand, only one, Simon thought grimly as he pulled up short to catch his breath. He raked his hand back through his wind-tossed hair in frustration. Hands on hips, he watched the coach vanish into the night.

Now what the deuce had gotten into that woman? Bolting off without a word after having pledged to dine with him. Forever running away. If it had been any other female avoiding him, he would not have been surprised. But Miss Masters was not frightened of him. Far from it. Though not given to vanity, he had begun to flatter himself that she even liked him a little.

Well, the devil with her, he muttered, spinning on his heel. He could not stand out here all night staring after her like some lovelorn sot. There was a nip in the air, and some of his footmen were gaping at him as if he had run mad, which perhaps he had.

But it was harder than ever to steel himself to return to that ball. The evening that had begun to hold such promise seemed again unendurably flat. And all because she had gone. Raeburn was man enough to admit that. Miss Masters's company held great attraction for him, although at times he felt ready to throttle her. Yet they had been getting on rather well at the last. So why had she fled?

Perhaps it had something to do with that one moment when she had mentioned her former suitors. Her chin raised in defiance, Raeburn wondered if she had any idea how vulnerable she had looked when she declared, "I drove them all away."

Just like the princess hiding behind the wall of thorns. Raeburn had been teasing when he had said that to her, but now he realized that it was not that far off from the truth.

"Except, Miss Masters, I am no prince," Raeburn murmured frowning. "I am more of a dragon, and there is no blasted way you are going to keep me out." His jaw set with grim purpose, Simon was striding back to the castle when he was approached by a timid stable boy,

"Beg pardon, Yer Grace. But that last lady as what left here in such a hurry. Why, she forgot these."

The boy's eyes were round as saucers as he extended something toward Simon. When he saw what the objects were, Simon emitted a soft bark of laughter.

At that instant, Lady Augusta emerged from the house, slightly breathless. "Simon, I saw you go running down the stairs. Is something wrong?"

"No, nothing, Gus. Nothing at all." He astounded Augusta by planting a smacking buss on her cheek. With a puzzled frown, she watched as he strode past her whistling a tuneless song.

She was further confounded to note he had a pair of lady's dancing slippers tucked under his arm and he was smiling, smiling in a way that he had not for ages . . . not since Robert had died.

Chapter 7

The morning was well advanced, and Audra could not seem to rouse herself from the lassitude that had overtaken her. She had no inclination to venture down to the stables and go for a ride or even to walk into the village to see what might be newly arrived at the local lending library.

She might at least have delved into her book. The house was quiet enough with Cecily still abed. But *Ivanhoe* lay unopened upon the small parlor table, Audra not even possessing the energy to lift the cover.

Muffin had passed a bad night after leaving the ball, being sick several times, once in the coach going home and once in her room. Heavy-eyed herself from ministering to Cecily's needs, Audra had been left too exhausted to even think until now.

Slouched in the armchair before the parlor fire, she sat listlessly regarding what remained of the nosegay Uncle Matt had given her. The flowers were already wilting, a sad reminder of last evening's festivities. Audra had heard of some sentimental maidens pressing flowers into books to remind them of a particular night. But Audra thought she would as soon forget the event where she had made such a roaring fool of herself.

When some of the drooping petals came off in her hand, Audra chucked the whole bouquet into the fire, watching as it was consumed with a sharp crackle and an angry hiss. She supposed by this time the entire county would be clacking over her hasty departure from the duke's ball, wondering, speculating. Likely they would all conclude it was just another example of her odd behavior. What more could be expected of a woman who preferred books to men?

Far better that they think that than continue to link her name with Raeburn's. Hopefully, after a time, some fresh piece of gossip would divert their minds, and the mad spinster of Meadows Lane would be entirely forgotten again.

And Raeburn? Would he forget? Likely he was quite vexed with her for running off with no explanation. At this thought, Audra nearly laughed aloud despite her melancholy humor. In view of Raeburn's temper, which rivaled her own, saying that the man would be vexed was rather like calling the conflagration that burned down the house a trifle warm.

But no matter how furious he was, he would get over it. No man could tolerate as many snubs as she had dealt him. He would curse her, but then he would direct his attention elsewhere, back to his task of finding a bride, filling the castle nursery with heirs.

As for herself, she needed only to put the events of last night from her mind. The infamous ball was finally over. She could go back to her own quiet existence.

But that was the very deuce of it. She was not sure that she could, whether she was destined to be haunted forever by the feeling she might have lost something infinitely precious.

Her one true friend.

Wondering why she should even be thinking such depressing thoughts, Audra leaned back her head, closing her eyes. She was weary enough that she might have dozed off for a few moments, but Mrs. McGuiness stepped into the parlor to announce she had a caller.

"Tell whoever it is that I am not at home." Audra said.

"But 'tis your uncle, the Reverend Mr. Masters."

Audra's eyes flew open. What had brought him out to Meadow Lane so early in the day? She winced. Perhaps the old man had justifiably a few questions regarding what had happened at the ball last night. She had never thought the time would come when she would be so reluctant to see her favorite relative, but she wished Uncle Matthew would have given her a few days, nay perhaps weeks, to recuperate before facing him.

As it stood, she was not even given a few seconds, for he found his own way into the parlor. Somberly attired in black, somehow even his clerical collar failed to dispel his air of roguishness. The white waves of his hair were as ever neatly bound into a queue, the nip of autumn reddening his plump cheeks and nose. The familiar spring to his step caused Audra to eye him with some resentment.

No man of his years should be looking so bustling after having lingered into the wee hours at a ball. Especially not when she was feeling so dragged out herself. She roused herself enough to stand and greet him with a kiss.

"Good morrow, Uncle Matt."

"So the gel remembers who I am," the old man groaned. "I was beginning to wonder after being abandoned at the castle like a forgotten parasol or some other frippery to be fetched later."

"I am sorry, sir. Did not Jack Coachman explain how Cecily had been taken ill? I instructed him to do so."

"Humph!" He eyed Audra in a penetrating manner she found most uncomfortable.

"Truly, sir, she was. I have been up half the night with her. I don't know what could have come over her so suddenly. A touch of influenza perhaps."

"More like a touch too much of champagne," Uncle Matthew said as he made himself at home, settling into Audra's armchair.

"Champagne!" Audra exclaimed. "Muffin was drinking champagne? She has never taken anything stronger than lemonade."

"A girl must have her first sips sometime. Everyone must eventually learn to deal with the fruit of the vine." Uncle Matthew raised his eyes piously. "I, myself, have devoted half my life to the study of the brew."

But Audra only shook her head, this new information lashing her with remorse, adding to her burden of guilt. "I should have watched Cecily more closely last night. I should have taken better care of her."

"Nonsense. The girl had plenty of care. That Coleby woman was there, wasn't she? And Lady Augusta was most gracious and attentive to the child, introducing her to eligible partners."

"Did she do so? I-I fear I didn't notice." No, Audra scolded herself, because you were far too taken up with noticing the lady's brother.

"For my part," Uncle Matt said, pausing to help himself to a pinch of snuff, "I was glad to see you less absorbed in hovering over your sister and more bent on enjoying yourself. You did enjoy the ball, did you not?"

"It was . . . tolerable." She hated the shrewd look the rector gave her.

He heaved a deep sigh. "I wish I could say I thought that the duke found it so. But he looked quite glum, poor fellow. Especially at the supper hour."

"Oh, no! Did he?" Audra cried. Feeling a self-conscious blush about to steal into her cheeks, she turned abruptly to face the window. "I mean, I am sure that is a deal too bad."

"I never saw any man appear so pulled down," her uncle continued mournfully. "However, his spirits seemed somewhat improved when he called upon me this morning."

"He what?" Audra whipped about, gaping at her great-uncle. Her uncle took an unmercifully long time about responding, being more absorbed in his snuff. Audra thought she would dump the entire contents of the box over his head if he didn't continue.

"The duke visited you?" she prompted. "Why?"

"Why not, my dear? Though the Raeburn family never attended my church, I've known His Grace since the days he was in short coats, although it has been many years since I had set eyes upon him." Uncle Matthew chuckled. "I believe he was agreeably surprised yestereve to discover me still alive."

"That does not explain what His Grace wanted of you this morning."

"Merely to talk."

Audra regarded her uncle as suspiciously as a general might one of his aides suspected of entertaining the enemy.

"Talk? Talk about what?"

"Many things. The scriptures, moral tracts. His Grace is a most learned man."

"And I don't doubt that he's every bit as pious as you are. Don't tease, Uncle. What did that man really want? Did it have anything to do with—"

She never had the opportunity to complete the question, for at that moment the housekeeper bustled into the parlor, to announce that another carriage had arrived.

"Tell whoever it is that I am not at home," Audra said tersely.

"But this time, it is your aunt, miss."

Audra felt as though she were already up to her eyebrows with vexing relatives. "That's impossible," she snapped. "I haven't got an aunt within a hundred miles of here."

"Well, there's one whose maid is piling up bandboxes in the front hall this very moment, miss," Mrs. McGuiness said dourly. "Come all the way from London, so she says. But if you think the woman is an imposter—" The housekeeper shrugged, preparing to retreat.

"Wait!" Audra cried. "From London? N-not Aunt Saunders?"

"The very same, miss." Mrs. McGuiness smirked. Audra sometimes wondered if her housekeeper would announce even the beginning of Armageddon with such grim satisfaction.

Audra braced herself against Uncle Matt's chair for support. She could not have been more astounded and dismayed than if a bolt of lightning had rent her house asunder. Mrs. Prudence Saunders, here at Meadow Lane? Audra had little time to collect herself, only exchange a startled glance with Uncle Matthew before the lady was ushered into the room.

It had been many years since Audra's disastrous Season in London when she had parted from her aunt upon such bad terms. But her mother's elder sister still appeared as spare and austere as Audra remembered her, a veritable icicle of a woman, her fine-boned frame garbed in silvery gray.

Audra often thought nature had divided her gifts most unfairly between Lady Arabella and Mrs. Saunders. While Mama had got all the dimpled prettiness and too much of a zest for life, Aunt Prudence received more than her share of common sense and rigid propriety. So much so that it rendered the woman rather joyless.

Her eyes were so pale a blue as to be almost mild, insignificant. Aunt Saunders remedied this defect by frequent use of a lorgnette, which device she now trained upon Audra, subjecting her to a critical inspection.

It was absurd, but Audra suddenly felt all of nineteen again, gawky and hopelessly inadequate. She tugged nervously at her lace spinster's cap, smoothing back a stray curl.

"Well, miss," Mrs. Saunders rapped out. "I have had a long and disagreeable journey from London. Do you mean to stand there forever gaping at me?"

"N-no, Aunt, I . . ." Audra managed to sink into an awkward curtsy. " 'Tis only what a shock . . . I mean, what a surprise to see you here."

Embracing Aunt Saunders was out of the question, but the woman did deign to offer Audra two fingers to clasp.

"Did you not send me a letter full of the most extraordinary supplication on your sister's behalf?" her aunt asked.

"Well, yes, I did." Audra refrained from saying that she had thought it likely her aunt had consigned her appeal to the fireplace grate. Certainly she had never expected Aunt Saunders to come swooping all the way down from London like one of the Furies of legend.

All the way from London? Of a sudden, the full import of her aunt's visit dawned upon Audra, what Mrs. Saunders's purpose must be. A wild hope stirred within her.

"Oh, Aunt, then you *have* decided to bring Cecily out this Season. You have come to fetch her to London. I shall go tell my sister at once. She will be overjoyed."

"Not so fast, miss," Aunt Saunders said before Audra could dash from the room. "I have not entirely forgotten certain past disasters. Although I fully appreciate my duty toward my nieces, I am much more careful *these* days whom I take on as a protégée. I shall have to inspect the girl first."

Audra wanted to retort that Cecily was not a horse, but she

managed to curb her tongue. She took a deep breath, reminding herself that Mrs. Saunders was Cecily's best, perhaps her only chance of a Season in London.

"Of course, Aunt," she agreed. "But I am sure you will find my sister quite charming. Not in the least like me."

"I hope so," Mrs. Saunders said frostily. She then leveled her lorgnette at the parlor, subjecting the comfortable room to her disapproving gaze. She drew up short, nearly dropping her glass when she came to the old gentleman ensconced by the hearth.

Audra had all but forgotten Uncle Matthew's presence herself. Usually so quick to greet any feminine company, sweeping his most courtly bow, the Reverend Mr. Masters had not stirred at the sight of Mrs. Saunders. Now he rose stiffly to his feet, made the barest nod instead of his usual magnificent leg.

"Aunt Saunders," Audra began. "This is my—"

"I know who it is." Mrs. Saunders gave a shudder of distaste. "We met before, at the time of your sister's christening."

"Indeed," Audra murmured nervously. She had heard some tale passed through the family of some unpleasantness between Mrs. Saunders and the Reverend Mr. Masters, but she had never credited it. Surely not even such an old rogue as her uncle would ever have been tempted to pinch Aunt Saunders.

"Madam," he said. "I would *like* to say I am pleased to make your acquaintance again."

But I am not. Her uncle might as well have added the words. His manner proclaimed it. After clasping Mrs. Saunders's hand, he actually returned to the fire, holding out his fingers to the blaze as if he had been nipped by frostbite.

Aunt Saunders turned away from him with a scornful sniff. "And where is Cecily? I should like to see the child at once."

"Oh, no!" Audra protested, her mind filling with a vision of Cecily with her bloodshot eyes, abovestairs recovering from a bout of too much champagne. "That is, I fear my sister is still abed."

"At this hour! I hope she is not of a frail nature. I despise sickly people."

"No, truly, Cecily blooms with good health. She is . . . merely being fashionable. She has heard that in London all proper young ladies spend their morning abed, and . . . and Cecily always tries to be proper."

"That sounds promising. Very well. Then show me to your guest room so that I may rid myself of the dust of the road. I shall expect the child to put in her appearance by teatime."

"Certainly, Aunt."

Audra held open the door herself, eager to escape from the room especially as she could tell that Uncle Matthew was seething with indignation, ready to burst from the desire to vent his opinion of Mrs. Saunders's introduction into the household.

As soon as she saw her aunt settled into the cottage's one spare bedchamber, Audra instructed Mrs. McGuiness to fetch her uncle some port, hoping that it would put the old gentleman in a more mellow frame of mind so that he would do or say nothing to affront Mrs. Saunders.

Feeling rather harried, Audra rushed to Cecily's bedchamber. Flinging back her curtains to let in the light, Audra called out, "Hurry, Muffin, you must get up."

The only response was a moan. Cecily's muffled voice came from beneath the lacy white counterpane. "Please don't shout, Audra. I am dying."

Audra darted over to Cecily's wardrobe, rapidly inspecting her array of dresses. "Now what must you wear?" she muttered. "Something demure, but quite elegant, I think."

"All I need is a winding sheet," Cecily said. "You may have my best brooch, Audra. And give Uncle Matthew my miniature to remember me by."

Audra paused, long enough to give the mound upon the bed an impatient glance. "You must rouse yourself, Cecily. Aunt Saunders has arrived from London to see you."

"Upon my death bed?"

"No, you goose. To see if you are in fit state to be conveyed to London and gotten ready for your coming out."

"What!" Cecily emerged from beneath the bedclothes, sitting bolt upright.

"I suppose I must tell Aunt Saunders she has arrived too late, only in time to witness your demise—"

But Cecily scarce heeded her. With a tiny shriek, she bolted off the bed. "Oh, Audra, you must send Heloise to me at once with the curling iron. I've got to do something with my hair, and where are my sandals?"

As Cecily darted frantically about the room, Audra retreated with a wry smile. Never had a dying woman made so miraculous a recovery.

The wine Mrs. McGuiness served the Reverend Mr. Masters must have been soured, for the first thing the old man did when Audra returned to the drawing room was to demand when she intended to send "that woman" packing.

"Mrs. McGuiness?" Audra said lightly. "Well, I grant she is not always the most cheerful creature but—"

"You know who I mean, miss. That winged harpy from London. That Medusa who must have you already turned to stone. Meekly accepting all her insults, behaving like some milk-and-water miss!"

Audra stiffened defensively. "But you must see what an opportunity this is for Cecily, Uncle. You yourself said this reclusive lifestyle was bad for the child. If my aunt takes her to London, Cecily's future will be assured."

"And yours?" he thundered.

"Then I will not be obliged to attend balls anymore. I may actually find time to read again."

"That was not what I had in mind!" Fair quivering with indignation, her uncle strode to the bellpull and rang for the housekeeper to demand his hat and cloak.

"You won't be staying for tea, Uncle?" Audra asked, ashamed for feeling slightly relieved.

"In the company of that woman? No, thank you. I prefer my afternoon tea a little on the sweet side and not with curdled milk."

Barely pausing to shrug into his cloak, Uncle Matthew jammed his tricorne upon his head and exited from the lodge in a state of high dudgeon.

107

Audra sighed, regret at seeing her favorite uncle driven from her door mingling with a foreboding of the hours that stretched ahead of her.

But somehow she managed to scrape through the rest of the afternoon. Aunt Saunders, unaccustomed to country hours, was not pleased to hear how early they supped at Meadow Lane.

"And you employ a female to cook for you, Audra?" she complained. "I would have thought the time you spent with me in London would have given you some better notion of how to conduct a household. But there—" Aunt Saunders gave a shrug of resignation, that martyred expression Audra remembered too well.

Cecily had retired to change again for dinner. As Audra and her aunt waited for the girl in the parlor, watching the sun set over the garden, neither woman had much to say, which Audra feared was just as well.

She was relieved when Cecily finally did join them. The girl was looking particularly sweet with a ribbon catching back her blond curls, her dainty form garbed in tawny-pink taffeta. She had even tied an absurd little bow onto Frou-frou's collar.

The vision of such a perfect young lady should have pleased Aunt Saunders, but she merely pursed her lips, staring through her lorgnette.

"I have never approved of a dog being brought into the parlor, Cecily."

"It's not a dog, Aunt," Audra said. "It's a pug."

Although Cecily looked a little crestfallen at her aunt's disapproval, she hastened to say, "Frou-frou is very well behaved, Aunt Saunders, but I shall make sure you won't be bothered. I will make her stay over here in her basket quite out of the way."

Muffin was trying so hard to please. It would not have hurt that poker-faced old witch to offer her one encouraging smile.

It was worse somehow watching Cecily pinned beneath her aunt's critical eye than any agonies Audra had ever endured when herself a victim of that infernal lorgnette. But she struggled to curb her resentment.

Her aunt summoned Cecily to sit beside her on the settee.

"So, child," Mrs. Saunders said. "You have grown a great deal since I last saw you, but happily not so tall as your sister. You have been living mostly with Audra then? A rather odd arrangement, I must say, but then I understand your late father was singularly without relatives and as for your mama . . . Well!" Aunt Saunders gave an expressive shrug. "So I suppose Audra has had a great deal of influence over your education?"

"Oh, yes, Aunt," Cecily began, innocently unaware of the danger lurking beneath the question. "Audra always made sure that I could ride well and—"

"But for the last two years," Audra hastily interposed, "Cecily has been attending Miss Hudson's Academy."

"Indeed? I am relieved to hear it. And what accomplishments have you acquired, child?"

While poor Cecily stammered on through this inquisition, Audra found herself virtually ignored. She drifted toward the window to peer out at the garden. Not even the moon was out tonight, leaving the landscape beyond a black rustling void. It was the sort of chilly evening best spent alone, curled before the fire with a good book. Or if not alone, at least with someone more congenial than Aunt Saunders, someone less given to the fidgets than Muffin. A someone also disposed to read, or to talk about something besides ladies' hats, to jest a little or merely to sit and watch the fire crackle in companionable silence.

A someone Audra had never been able to imagine clearly until now. But the night itself seemed alive with raven-black hair and dark eyes, a heavy scowl that when it did lighten to a smile, was capable of warming nights far colder than this one.

Audra rubbed her eyes as if to dispel the image, appalled by her own thoughts. The shock of Aunt Saunders's arrival must have unsettled her more than she knew. Or perhaps she had been reading too many romantic novels this past year. She should get back to the more acerbic wit of a Swift or Pope.

Trying to snap herself out of this peculiar dreamy mood, she was aided by her aunt's frigid tones. Mrs. Saunders said, "Audra! What *is* that uproar coming from your front hall?"

"Uproar?" Audra straightened, listening, for the first time

109

becoming aware of doors slamming, the tread of heavy footsteps.

"Surely, even in these barbaric regions you do not receive callers this close to the supper hour?" Mrs. Saunders asked.

"No, Aunt," Audra said wearily. She did not even trouble turning around when she heard the parlor door swing open.

"Tell whoever it is that I am not at home, Mrs. McGuiness," she called out.

"Why don't you tell him yourself?" a familiar gruff voice replied.

Raeburn.

Audra's pulse gave a violent leap. She whipped about so suddenly she bumped up against a Greek statuette upon the parlor table and barely grabbed it before it crashed to the ground. Pressing her hands to still her thudding heart, she could only stare at the tall, dark man who seemed to fill her doorway. But she didn't know why she should be so surprised. His Grace seemed possessed of an evil genius for springing up when she least expected him. It was small comfort to know that she was not the only one so startled. Cecily gave a tiny shriek, and even Aunt Saunders dropped her lorgnette.

Swept in from the night, Raeburn presented a rather alarming picture, the black wind-tossed hair, the heavy drawn brows, the harsh complexion, the fierce, burning eyes. Despite the immaculate cut of his Garrick, he had more the look of a wandering brigand than a member of the peerage.

"Forgive me, ladies," he drawled. "I didn't mean to startle you. Your housekeeper seemed rather distracted by a mishap in the kitchens, some small excitement over a mouse caught nibbling at the Rhenish tarts, so I told her I could show myself in."

Aunt Saunders was the first to recover, seizing up her lorgnette, spluttering. "Upon my word, Audra. Is it your habit to have strange men running tame in your parlor?"

"Madam," Raeburn said. "I never run *tame* anywhere."

At this juncture, Audra managed to find her voice and rush forward to intervene before her aunt had a seizure. She stammered out introductions, but Mrs. Saunders appeared only partly mollified at the mention of Raeburn's name. In her rigid social code, not even dukes burst into ladies' parlors unannounced.

Lest her aunt believe this sort of thing occurred at Meadow Lane all the time, Audra added, "Of course, this is all such a surprise, His Grace never having honored us with a visit before."

She might well have saved her breath, for at that moment Cecily's treacherous pug leaped forward, panting, rolling her eyes with adoration, and scrabbling at Raeburn's boots as if he were a familiar and frequent visitor. When Aunt Saunders stared at Audra, she could only smile weakly, before turning her embarrassed anger upon Frou-frou.

"Get down! Down I say," she said, commands which, of course, the pug utterly ignored.

"Sit!" Raeburn thundered.

It was the outside of enough when that infernal dog obeyed him at once. Although Raeburn grimaced at the sight of the pug's bow, he bent down to scratch the dog behind its ear.

Cecily recovered enough from her terror to suggest, "She likes it better beneath the chin, Your Grace." She scooted closer to show Raeburn the exact spot.

"I doubt His Grace came here tonight to pet your dog, Cecily," Aunt Saunders said.

"No more, I did, madam." As Raeburn slowly straightened, Audra wished her aunt had left the man alone, to fuss over the dog all evening if he pleased. For now his attention focused on her.

Audra took a skittish step back, although all he did was look at her, one of his quick, appraising stares. She had wondered if they ever met again if he would be angry or merely icily distant. But he looked so confounded . . . affable, except for that wicked glint in his eye. Raeburn was never so dangerous as when he behaved with an excess of civility, and Audra had a strong urge to place a chair in between them.

"In fact, Miss Masters, I felt obliged to call upon you, owing to your unseasonably quick departure last evening."

"I can explain that—" Audra began.

111

"No need for explanations, my dear Miss Masters. I only came to return something that I believe belongs to you."

Audra stared at him, but her incomprehension swift turned to horror when from beneath his Garrick, he produced her dancing slippers, a little the worse for having been tossed into the dirt last night. An outraged gasp escaped Aunt Saunders, as His Grace calmly set the shoes upon the parlor table.

A moment of the most awful silence ensued. Audra moistened her lips, a wild denial almost springing to her lips, a declaration that they weren't hers. They were far too small.

But Cecily was already piping up, "Why, Audra. Those are your dancing shoes."

The next time anyone came to call, Audra thought she would lock both Cecily and her dog in a closet. She felt a hot tide of color wash over her cheeks.

"Why, why, yes, so they are," Audra said, unable to meet her aunt's shocked and accusing stare. "You see I-I was obliged to take them off when I was at the Castle Raeburn last night. . . ."

That sounded perfectly dreadful. Audra swallowed and tried again, "I am sure His Grace could tell you, Aunt. It was he who first suggested I should be rid of the shoes. . . ."

No, that sounded infinitely worse. Audra cast an appealing glance at Raeburn, but the cursed man just stood there, his arms folded, a most interested look of inquiry upon his face.

"Cecily and I attended a ball at Castle Raeburn last night," Audra floundered.

"Alone?" her aunt asked icily.

"No, I was there, too," the irrepressible Raeburn put in.

Audra glowered at him. "My aunt doesn't mean that, you fool, er, ah, Your Grace. Sh-she . . . It was all perfectly proper, Aunt Saunders. We were escorted by my uncle, the Reverend Mr. Masters."

Her aunt shuddered at mere mention of the name, and Audra could see she was making bad worse. At that welcome moment, the parlor door opened. Never did Audra expect to be so thankful for one of Mrs. McGuiness's interruptions. The housekeeper came to inform her that the dinner was ready to be served.

112

"Is His Grace also expected to dine?" Mrs. McGuiness asked somewhat dubiously. "Shall I lay covers for four?"

"No," Audra choked out, at the same time Raeburn drawled, "How kind."

Audra's gaze locked with his for a moment. Twin demons seemed to dance into those tormenting dark eyes for all his expression of assumed meekness.

"Of course, I have lingered from home so long, I fear my own sister will have dined without me. But I have no wish to intrude. I am sure my chef can always send me up a bit of cold beef from the larder." Raeburn heaved a deep wistful sigh. "I shall bid you ladies good evening. Of course, there is no need to thank me, Miss Masters, for riding so far out of my way to return your property."

Thank him! In another second, Audra thought she was going to give him a mighty shove through the parlor doors, but with a soft cry, Cecily sprang to her feet.

"Oh, no, Your Grace. You would not be intruding at all. We should all be delighted to have you dine with us, wouldn't we, Audra? Aunt Saunders?"

Mrs. Saunders maintained a rigid silence. As for Audra, she muttered an oath under her breath.

"With so many charming entreaties, how could a man refuse?" Raeburn said, sweeping a mocking bow.

Audra half feared that her aunt might take umbrage, but years of proper breeding came to Mrs. Saunders's rescue. Although she clearly showed her disapproval of Raeburn in every rigid line of her frame, when the time came for him to lead her in to supper she permitted him to take her arm.

As the duke and her aunt disappeared through the parlor doors, Audra held Cecily back, hissing in her ear. "Muffin, whatever possessed you to invite that man to dine?"

"Why, Audra, he looked so very sad at the thought of having cold beef."

"The man is a duke, you little widgeon. His staff would serve him a seventeen-course meal at two in the morning if he desired it."

Cecily's rosebud lips set into a mulish line. "Well, I don't care, Audra. It was still the proper thing to do. Miss Hudson always said that a lady should behave graciously to all her guests, even the unexpected ones."

"Miss Hudson never had to deal with the Duke of Raeburn."

"He is terrifying, even when he is being polite. I suppose it is going to be rather uncomfortable sitting down to dine with both him and Aunt Saunders."

"Uncomfortable!" Audra snorted, for once forgetting her younger sister's delicate ears. "A banquet in hell would be as nothing to it."

But ignoring Cecily's shocked cry, she propelled her sister along, down to the dining chamber where her aunt and the devil were waiting.

Chapter 8

The tension in the dining room was by far thicker than the herring soup. Audra had never been troubled by indigestion before, but every bite she took seemed to settle into her stomach like a lump of cold lead. Perched on the edge of her chair, she kept stealing glances past the gleaming crockery and silverplate to where Raeburn sat at the head of the table. With each spoonful he took, she experienced a brief moment of relief. At least with his mouth full he couldn't talk, and she lived in dread of what he might say next.

To either side of her, Cecily and Mrs. Saunders sipped at their own soup in complete silence. Cecily's usual bright chatter had been stilled by nervousness. As for Aunt Saunders, she was too caught up in grimacing as she stirred her soup, inspecting it.

At last she pursed her lips, declaring, "This soup is too watery, Audra. If you persist in setting up your own household, an arrangement of which I have never approved, at least you could engage proper servants. You should dismiss your cook at once."

Audra didn't trouble to explain that usually she was so absorbed in her reading, she never noticed what she ate. Her cook's shortcomings had never troubled her before, but she flinched when her aunt continued to criticize.

"This stuff is perfectly dreadful. Really, Audra, to be setting out such food for your guests! I cannot imagine what His Grace must be thinking, or what you should say to him."

Raeburn's lips twitched. "Knowing Miss Masters, she will tell me that since I invited myself to dine here, if I don't like the soup, I may go be hanged."

He read her thoughts so well, Audra nearly choked. But when Aunt Saunders stiffened with indignation, Audra hastened to disclaim, "Of course, I would not say anything so rude, Your Grace."

"Wouldn't you? Then you are obviously not yourself this evening, m'dear."

Audra's legs were long, but not long enough to afford her the pleasure of kicking Raeburn under the table. She had to content herself with looking daggers at him, an expression he serenely ignored.

Although he screwed up his face with every mouthful he took, he said, "For my part, I find the soup delicious. The best I ever ate."

"Do you think so?" Audra asked. "I shall be certain to have my cook send yours the recipe so Your Grace may have it every day."

"How considerate of you, Miss Masters. Just be sure the recipe is exact with nothing extra added. Like hemlock."

Audra bit back a retort. She could almost have enjoyed this exchange but for her aunt's outraged expression. Mrs. Saunders never made jests nor understood them. Although it took a great deal of effort, Audra fixed her attention upon her plate, pretending she had not heard Raeburn's last comment.

To her mortification, the rest of the meal was not much of an

115

improvement upon the first course. Mrs. Saunders was quick to point this out, Raeburn just as swift to disagree with her. She found the mutton too tough. The duke said it melted in his mouth. Mrs. Saunders found Audra's choice of china a little garish. Raeburn declared the bright border so charming it even made the ragout of artichoke bottoms taste better. Her aunt insisted the roast of beef was overdone. Raeburn liked his meat a little burned.

By the dessert course, even her aunt had lost some of her rigid composure. Audra half feared to see Mrs. Saunders fling down her napkin at any moment and declare she was going to pack up her things. Audra scarce waited for the dishes to be cleared away before rising and suggesting that the ladies retire to the parlor.

She took great pains to assure Raeburn there was no need for him to rush on their account. "Enjoy your port, sir," she said through gritted teeth. "Take as long as you like."

" 'Til hell ices over, in fact," he murmured, quizzing her with those tormenting dark eyes.

Audra could have told him that it was in a fair way to being frozen already. One look at her aunt's pokerlike expression was enough to assure anyone of that. But she contented herself with a stiff curtsy, following the other two women out of the room.

No sooner had Audra entered the parlor, than Mrs. Saunders informed Cecily that the girl should retire.

"I am sure His Grace will excuse you, child. You need your rest, and I need a few moments *alone* with your sister."

Audra grimaced at the ominous sound of that, but she made no protest, for Cecily appeared quite glad to escape. After bidding a cheery good night, she forgot all of her ladylike graces and scampered out of the room, much after the fashion she had done as a little girl. Except that Muffin had never retired to bed before with such eagerness, Audra recalled with a rueful smile.

Watching the girl depart, Audra keenly envied her, being in no humor to listen to one of Mrs. Saunders's tirades. The door had scarce closed on Cecily, when her aunt commenced at once to tear the Duke of Raeburn's character to shreds.

116

"I declare that man must be quite mad. So disagreeable and such odd manners. He seems to possess no notion of his own consequence."

Audra thought that was one of Raeburn's greatest charms, but it would hardly serve to point that out to Mrs. Saunders. As vexed as she was herself with His Grace, Audra had to curb a sudden and fierce desire to defend him against this attack.

Her aunt continued to scold, "And your own manner toward him, Audra! Far too free and easy. Most unbecoming. Do not think me a fool. I quite see what you are about with him."

"You do?" Audra didn't think she was "about" anything with Raeburn, but astonishingly, she felt a hot blush creep up her cheeks.

"I don't entirely blame you."

"You don't?" Audra echoed, wishing she knew what the deuce they were talking about.

"The duke is, after all, possessed of an ancient title, extensive estates, a handsome fortune. He must seem an ideal match for Cecily."

"For Muffin?" Audra nearly laughed in her aunt's face. "She is quite terrified of the man. Raeburn would make a meal of her. He needs the sort of wife who will box his ears occasionally."

"No lady ever strikes a gentleman. She finds some more genteel way of expressing her displeasure."

"I suppose a swift kick to the shins would also serve the purpose."

"You always did possess a most unseemly sense of humor, Audra," her aunt said severely. "However, I am relieved to see that you at least realize the absurdity of your matchmaking efforts."

"But I wasn't . . . I haven't—"

"Besides being quite mad," Mrs. Saunders said, "I have never heard that His Grace has shown any inclination to be married."

"That is where you are quite out, Aunt," Audra said, smiling at the memory of poor Raeburn besieged at the ball by eager ladies. "He has been searching most strenuously for a bride."

"Has he?" Mrs. Saunders appeared skeptical, then thoughtful. "I suppose he is thinking of the succession. He is getting on in years."

"Oh, quite in his dotage."

Though her aunt froze her with a look, she ignored Audra's interruption. "That changes things entirely. If he is indeed marriage-minded, perhaps you did right to court his interest."

"I see. A half-mad duke dangling for a wife is more acceptable than an insane one who wishes to remain unwed."

"Don't be pert, miss. Small wonder that the duke treats you with such shocking familiarity. Your own improper attitude has encouraged him. I am sure you don't want him thinking that you are like your mother."

No, Audra didn't want that. But why did it sting so to hear Aunt Saunders say it?

"At least one thing can be said for my mama," Audra snapped back, without thinking. "She never wanted for offers."

Audra immediately regretted the remark. She had long ago sensed that Aunt Saunders, for all her criticism of Lady Arabella with her multiplicity of husbands, had envied her sister as well. Her aunt, who longed to be elevated to the peerage, had to content herself with being plain Mrs. Saunders, the only proposal she had ever received.

As Audra saw a hint of red creep into her aunt's pale cheeks, her heart sank. Now she'd done it. Whistled Cecily's London Season down the wind.

The hand holding the lorgnette quivered, but her aunt replied in a controlled voice. "To be sure, Arabella did have many offers, but not all of them were respectable. I am sure we both want far different for Cecily."

"Yes, Aunt. I am sorry."

"Then we must strive to correct His Grace's impression that he may make so free in this house. You shall send Mrs. McGuiness to him, with our regrets. Inform him that we have all retired, but he may return tomorrow and call in more proper fashion. He will understand this subtle reproof that we found his conduct tonight unacceptable."

Audra rolled her eyes. "I fear Raeburn is not given to accepting subtle reproofs, Aunt. If you have anything to say to him, you'd best do it more roundly."

"I trust I know better than you, Audra. See that my instructions are carried out. Being still wearied from my journey, I am going up to bed. You would not want me to feel obliged to return to London so soon."

Their eyes met, and Audra understood the implied threat. She must do as she was told or her aunt would depart at once. Audra didn't enjoy subtle reproofs any more than Raeburn would. But for Cecily's sake, she managed to swallow her pride and bid her aunt good night.

After Mrs. Saunders had gone, Audra had no other vent for her anger than thrusting the poker savagely at the logs on the fire. She raised a flurry of crackles and sparks that disturbed Frou-frou, still dozing nearby in her basket. The dog regarded Audra through one jaundiced eye, then went back to sleep.

"Lazy little bitch," Audra muttered. "If you had any spirit at all, you would have bitten that woman."

But then if Audra had had any, so would she, or at least she would have sent Mrs. Saunders back to London. Audra stared balefully at the peaceful-looking pug. That foolish dog was still wearing the ribbon Cecily had put there. Why did all her sister's girlish dreams seemed tied up in that silly little bow?

"Oh, the devil!" Audra said, feeling frustrated beyond endurance.

"Were you summoning me?" Raeburn's deep voice startled her. As before she had not realized that he had come into the parlor. Did that man never make a normal entrance into a room?

Audra straightened abruptly, the poker still in her hand. She might not be able to say all she wanted to Aunt Saunders, but that did not apply to Raeburn. Never mind her aunt's orders. She would send Raeburn away herself with a flea in his ear and take great satisfaction in doing so.

Mustering all her pent-up wrath, she prepared to begin, but he wasn't even looking at her. He glanced around the empty parlor, saying, "What? I am to be deprived of becoming better acquainted with Aunt Saunders? And I was even prepared to fetch my cloak to ward off the chill."

His gaze came to rest upon Audra, the poker grasped in her fingers. "On the other hand, it promises to be a trifle warm in here."

Her temper sizzling as much as the flames, Audra slammed the poker back into its position on the grate. "Your Grace—" she began wrathfully.

"I know it is improper, but I would prefer it if you would call me Simon."

"There are many things I would like to call you at this moment, but that is not one of them."

When Raeburn laughed, she clenched her teeth and strove to begin again, but he interrupted once more, demanding, "What's that thing on your head?"

"Your Grace, I—" She broke off, raising one hand self-consciously to her temple. "What thing?"

"That lacy nonsense covering your hair."

"It's a cap."

"I hate it."

"Could we ever discuss something besides the way I arrange my hair—"

"Whatever you please," he said affably.

"Such as why you are behaving like such a confounded blackguard this evening."

"At least I, Miss Masters, am running true to my character. I wish I could say the same for you. If I had heard you mew 'Yes, Aunt Saunders' one more time, I think I would have been ill from something besides that dinner you served up to me."

"I thought you said it was perfect." Audra gave an angry laugh. "Listening to you this evening, apparently everything I do is perfect."

"Alas, no. But I'll be hanged if I ever let anyone else say so, especially not that . . . that old, gray crow." He frowned. "What the deuce has gotten into you, Audra? I never expected to see you truckle to anyone."

Audra was not so angry that she failed to note his disconcerting but somehow delightful use of her name. "I wasn't truckling. Merely being respectful. Though it is none of your concern, I have need of my aunt's good opinion. She has a house in town, to say nothing of all manner of connections with the ton."

"What the devil does that matter?"

"It matters a great deal if one goes to London for the Season."

Though Raeburn's eyes were snapping with annoyance, his voice sounded more subdued as he asked, "You are going away? You plan to accompany that woman back to the city?"

"Not me. Cecily."

Was it her imagination or did Raeburn seem relieved?

"Poor child," he said.

"She desires it above all things," Audra said. "And neither you nor anyone else is going to deprive her of this chance. So I am warning you—"

"Hold! Softly, my girl." Raeburn's tone was gently chiding. "I would never try to stop *Cecily* from going."

"You nearly did, the way you came waltzing in here, bringing back those dratted shoes. All your jests, the way you have been tormenting my aunt. You have given her the impression that I run an improper household. Th-that I must be a bad influence on my sister."

To Audra's horror, her voice broke. She was both appalled and astonished to discover herself near to tears. Raeburn muttered an oath, but she caught enough of it to realize he was damning himself, not her.

She scarce knew whether it was better or worse when he took her hand, roughly imprisoning it between his own massive ones. "I am sorry, Audra. I will admit I was annoyed at the way you left me in the lurch last night, and I resolved to have my revenge. I fear I carried my teasing too far."

"I suppose there was no real harm done." Audra tugged her hand free. She turned away to take a hasty swipe at her eyes. "Even without you, I would have run afoul of Aunt Saunders sooner or later. I always do. I never seem to do anything right, but for Cecily, I was trying so hard to impress her this time, to

121

show her I had made quite a respectable home here at the lodge."

"And so you have. The place is charming. I have always been fond of it. It was once my older brother's retreat, you know." Having made this confession, Raeburn lapsed into silence.

When Audra dared look at him, she saw those harsh features stilled into lines more vulnerable, and in his eyes, a look of rare sweet melancholy.

"Was that the same brother who . . . who died in the hunting accident?" Audra asked hesitantly.

Raeburn nodded. "Robert often used this lodge. Like me, he seemed to feel the need to escape from the burdens of being the duke for a while. Of course, the place was more austere then. I can't even remember if Robert had draperies."

"You must not care for all the changes I have made."

"No, you gave it just the touches it needed. I was wrong to let it remain so neglected and gloomy after Robert's death." Raeburn gave her a half-sheepish look. "You will think me quite mad, but whenever I passed by on horseback, I always had the impression the cottage was frowning. You seem to have made it smile again. I thank you for that. I believe Robert would have liked very much to have you living here."

Fully aware of the enormity of this compliment, Audra was too overcome to speak.

Raeburn appeared to give himself a brisk shake. "But enough of these foolish reminiscences. I appear to have distracted you from what you meant to say to me."

"Which you know only too well how to do," Audra retorted with a tiny smile. "I am under strict orders from my aunt to send you on your way, not to let you return until you promise to behave better."

"I should not like to have to stay away, that *long*. It seems a pity I should have to leave so soon. The evening is quite young yet, with the others gone," Raeburn murmured, regarding her through half-lowered lids, "That leaves the two of us quite alone. I thought that we might . . ."

When he hesitated, Audra's pulse skipped a beat. Her hand fluttered nervously to her collar.

"Play a little chess. Your uncle says you are quite good at the game."

Audra did not know whether she felt more disappointed or relieved by this unexpected suggestion. But it reminded her of another grievance. "Yes, I gather you had quite a long talk with my uncle. I should think the pair of you might have better things to do than gossip about me."

"That was not my intent at all. I was merely, er, seeking spiritual advice." As he uttered this plumper, Raeburn concealed his face from her by bending over her chessboard. "Do you prefer the black or white pieces, m'dear?"

Although she was sorely tempted, Audra said firmly, "Neither. You know it is quite impossible for you to remain here when there is no one else present."

"Why? I promise I won't attempt to ravish you, not after seeing the way you can wield that poker."

"Of course I am not afraid that you would attempt anything so mutton-headed as that," Audra said scornfully. "But I have explained to you why I must behave with the strictest propriety."

"Your aunt must be sound asleep by now. How would she know? Your grim-faced housekeeper scarce seems the sort to indulge in a bit of backstairs gossip."

"No, she isn't. I don't think she likes Aunt Saunders above half." To her dismay, Audra watched Raeburn pull up a stool, settling behind the board. She made one last desperate effort to excuse herself. "I never play chess with any other gentlemen besides Uncle."

"Why is that?"

"Because most men sulk when they lose, and if I have to let you win, what's the point in playing?"

"Why, you arrogant little witch. Sit down at once," Raeburn barked.

Audra hesitated a moment more, but inclination won out. She drew up the opposite stool, saying, "Very well. But only one game, then you positively must go. Fortunately this shouldn't take that long."

But when Audra reached for a pawn to make her first move, his hand closed over hers, arresting the gesture.

"Wait a minute." His eyes were dark with suspicion. "After what you said, even if I win, how will I know that you did not throw the game on purpose?"

Audra smiled sweetly. "I fear you never will, sir."

"That won't do. There must be some wager, something that will make it so disagreeable for you to lose, I will be certain that you have to play your best."

"Name any amount you like, Your Grace, short of ten thousand pounds."

"I wasn't thinking of money." The gleam that came into his eyes made her wary. "If I win, you have to give me a kiss."

"What!" Audra drew back so sharply she nearly upset the whole chessboard. "H-how ridiculous. I won't agree to any such thing."

"Of course, if you lack that much confidence in your skill . . ."

He was goading her. Any prudent and proper young lady would have risen indignantly and pointed him toward the door. Finding herself sadly lacking in either of those virtues, Audra remained where she was.

Raising her chin in defiance, she demanded, "And just what do I get if . . . *when* I win?"

"Whatever you like."

Audra thought a minute, but it did not take her long to come up with an answer. "I want the freedom to pillage your library anytime I like."

Raeburn's lips twitched, but he extended his hand solemnly to her across the table.

"Done," he said.

He didn't even smile as they shook on it, but something lurked in his eyes that made Audra feel curiously like a lamb being led to the fleecing.

She settled back to make her first move. But her confidence felt restored as she observed Raeburn's manner of play. He took his turns quickly, shifting his pieces with appalling carelessness. Resolving not to be lulled into a feeling of false security, Audra played with more than her usual care.

While she debated at length between inching forward a knight or her bishop, Raeburn's voice broke in unexpectedly upon her thoughts.

"Do you mind if I ask you something?"

"Mmmm?" she replied.

"Why *did* you leave so suddenly last night?"

The question was asked in the softest of accents, but she was still considerably startled. Looking up, she stammered, "Didn't I ever explain? Cecily was taken ill."

"So ill that you couldn't even pause to say good-bye to me?"

"I-I am sorry. I know it was frightfully rude. You must have been quite angry."

"Not angry so much as disappointed. Supper, without you, proved a most tedious affair."

It pleased her, perhaps far too much, to hear him say so.

"My leaving was very likely all for the best," she said. She regretted she had not returned some more noncommittal answer, for Raeburn immediately took her up on it.

"Why would you say a thing like that?" he asked.

"People get the most absurd notions. Th-they . . ." No longer able to meet his gaze, Audra fiddled with the carved ivory knight, hoping he didn't notice the way her fingers trembled. "They might begin to think foolish things l-like that it was me you were fixing your interest upon. Utterly ridiculous, I know."

She waited for him to agree that indeed, it was absurd. She was further flustered when he didn't.

"I see," was all he said gravely. "And you would find such gossip disturbing?"

"No." She was too quick to disclaim. "Usually gossip doesn't bother me in the least. Unless . . . well, I don't like to be accused of flinging myself at men, being thought like my mother."

"My dear, foolish Audra. No one who knows you could ever think that."

125

His voice became suddenly so warm, it was like a caress, brushing along her skin.

"D-do you mind not talking anymore?" she faltered. "You are distracting me from the game."

He lapsed into an obliging silence, but that was somehow worse. His eyes never left her face. Dark, mesmerizing, they seemed to trace every curve, the line of her cheekbones, her jaw, coming to linger upon her lips. The parlor began to seem unaccountably warm. Audra could feel her brow go damp with perspiration, her heart thudding so hard she could scarce think.

She didn't realize how much her concentration had been broken, how much His Grace's own playing had improved, until he said quietly, "Check."

Too late did Audra see the peril to her queen. Raeburn had maneuvered her into a position almost impossible to escape. If she could give herself time to clear her head, to think, she might yet find a way to win. But Audra no longer seemed capable of doing so. She could focus on nothing but how near Raeburn was, only the small table between them, the army of felled pawns and knights a most fragile line of defense.

On impulse, Audra reached out, making one last desperate move—the wrong one.

"Checkmate." In a flash, her queen was gone.

Her eyes flew up to meet his. The heat in the room became nigh unbearable. Audra pushed away from the table and stalked to the window, pressing her hands to her cheeks in an effort to cool them. Her heart pounded as she heard the scrape of another stool, Raeburn's footstep behind her. She sensed how close he stood, even without turning around.

"I don't like to dun a lady, Miss Masters," he said. "But there is the small matter of a wager to be settled."

"It . . . it doesn't count. It wasn't fair," she blurted out. "You did things."

"Are you accusing me of cheating?"

"You deliberately broke my concentration. You . . . you kept *looking* at me."

He placed his hands upon her shoulders and brought her around to face him. "What a great deal of fuss you are making.

I fear that is why I never play with ladies anymore. They take losing so hard." His teasing smile coaxed no response from her.

"It's not the losing," she said. "It's that ridiculous wager."

"Is one kiss such a high price then?" He lowered his hands, releasing her. "Very well, though I would have thought you to have more honor than to renege on a bet."

He started to turn away from her. Although Audra gave vent to an exasperated sigh, she caught him by the sleeve, stopping him.

"Blast you, I never said I was reneging. The whole thing is so extraordinarily foolish, but . . . but take your kiss if you want it. It's not going to be anything so wonderful. I haven't had much practice."

"Well, don't poker up that way. It's not going to hurt, I promise you."

Yet as he stepped closer, Audra could not seem to help tensing her hands into fists in front of her, holding her shoulders as stiff as the backboard of a wagon. Raeburn paused, frowning.

"Do you mind if I take off that lace thing? I can't bring myself to kiss a woman who is trying so hard to look like my maiden aunt."

Before she could even gasp out her protest, he tugged off the lace cap. Her curls at once tumbled free, despite her best effort to smooth them.

"There is a reason I wear that thing, you know," she said. "My hair is heavy, and the cap helps keep it pinned up."

"Yes, forever hidden away." Raeburn plucked ruthlessly at the remaining hairpins until all the strands cascaded about her shoulders in wild disarray.

He brushed it back, his fingers snagging on the silken strands. "Did you know," he said, "that by candlelight, your hair shines with traces of a most remarkable burnished red?"

"You mean like dead leaves," she said hoarsely.

"No, I mean like flames," he murmured. Burrowing beneath her hair, his hand covered the nape of her neck. Gently, but inexorably, he pulled her forward.

As his face drew near, Audra closed her eyes, bracing herself.

127

But his lips merely brushed across hers in a feather-light whisper. The contact was so light, so fleeting, it tantalized her somehow. Almost involuntarily, she uttered a soft protest when he drew back.

Her eyes fluttered open. That was a mistake, for she found herself staring directly into his. She could almost feel herself slipping into the silence of his eyes. Her knees threatened to buckle, and it was a most fortunate thing that Raeburn was strong enough to hold her up.

For she became suddenly aware that he *was* holding her, his arms banding tight about her, crushing her close. His mouth descended upon hers again, this time hard enough to make her aware of his heat, ruthless enough to set the whole room to spinning. Long, lingering moments later, he pulled back. Neither of them scarce daring to draw breath, they stared at each other.

The sensations that coursed through her were wondrous enough, but seeing her own roiling emotions mirrored back in his eyes was like a miracle, almost more than she could bear. Still caught within the circle of his arms, she could not have moved if she had wanted to.

"Th-that felt more like two kisses," she whispered. "I only owed you one."

"Sorry," he said huskily. "I'll return one at once."

This time she didn't wait for him to bend to her, but raised slightly on her toes, her own mouth pliant, eager. She wound her arms about him, twining her fingers in the shagged lengths of his hair. Raeburn's lips moved over hers with such passion it was as if he meant to devour her. Far from being frightened, she embraced him in a manner equally as fierce.

Never had she kissed any man with such wild abandon. In fact, never had she kissed any. What was she doing? The thought, vague as it was, drove a sliver of sanity into her mind. And with the return of sanity came a kind of blind panic. She broke off the kiss, panting, mounting a desperate struggle to be free.

Although his face was flushed with desire, Raeburn permitted her to wrench away, his eyes hazy with confusion.

"Audra?" he said, reaching out to her. Even the way he said her name was enough to prove her undoing.

She backed away. "N-no. Please." Her cheeks burned with doubt and embarrassment. What the devil had gotten into her to be casting herself at Raeburn that way?

More important, what should she do now? She racked her brain for something in one of her books that might help her, some clue as to how she could beat a graceful retreat from this unnerving episode. But at the moment she could not even remember if she knew how to read.

Skittering away from Raeburn, bartering for a little time to regain her composure, she began to pick up the chessmen for want of anything better to do. She almost cursed him when he came to help her.

Although his hair straggled a bit over his brow, he appeared more calm than she. "Did you want to play again?"

Audra vigorously shook her head. "I never dreamed chess could become such a dangerous pastime. Perhaps you had better go."

"Audra."

Her thudding heart seemed to go still as he reached out as if to caress her cheek. It appeared to cost him great effort, but he wrenched his hand away, leaving her untouched.

"Perhaps you are right," he said. He gave her a rueful smile. "I am sorry. It would appear I am not to be trusted without a chaperon after all."

"Nor I," Audra said with chagrin. She could scarce credit the mad way her blood had raced, how she had pulsed with sudden desire in Raeburn's arms, a desire she had never even realized she was capable of. Perhaps she was more her mother's daughter than she had ever been willing to admit.

It was a most dismaying thought and she felt relieved when Raeburn moved toward the door. She offered to have his horse brought round, but he refused.

"I know where the stables are," he said. He paused upon the threshold to glance back at her with a thoughtful frown. "Audra, I hope that what happened here tonight . . . well, it was only a few kisses. Neither of us should react so strongly that we let it spoil our continued acquaintance."

"Oh, no, of course not," Audra said too brightly. She had no intention of overreacting. She was merely going to give up the lease on Meadow Lane and become a Catholic so she could retire to a nunnery and never have to face Raeburn again.

But apparently he read none of this in her face, for he gave a sigh of relief. "You and Miss Cecily should call at the castle tomorrow. My sister would be delighted to receive you. You can even bring your aunt. I promise not to toss her into the moat."

Audra nodded, only wanting him to be gone, to give her poor heart a chance to thud at a normal pace, her cheeks opportunity to assume some other hue besides fiery red.

"Good night, m'dear," he said. "Even if you didn't win the chess game, you are welcome to come pillage my castle anytime you like."

He upturned her palm, planting a brusque kiss there, then turned to stalk away before she had time to react. Still feeling his warmth upon her flesh, her heart a whirl of conflicting emotions, she closed the door. It was not until long moments later she was able to consider his parting invitation.

Come pillage my castle anytime you like. Recalling the intensity in his eyes when he had spoken, it suddenly occurred to her that he might mean far more than the library.

Dismayed, she pressed her hands to her face. Never had she felt so exhilarated and terrified at the same time. Far from accepting his invitation, she intended to flee as far from the Castle Raeburn as a coach and four would take her.

Chapter 9

The Duke of Raeburn was considered to be unapproachable before he had had his morning ride. For that reason none of his household were eager to knock upon the library door to inform him of the latest disaster. The new laundry maid had managed somehow to dye nearly every last one of His Grace's crisp white linen shirts a rather dingy shade of brown.

Rundel, the butler, loftily declared the care of His Grace's wardrobe did not fall within his province. Bartleby, the duke's valet, suggested they all draw lots. In the end, Mrs. Bede, the housekeeper, was despatched to be the bearer of bad tidings. His Grace had never been known to hit a female.

When the trembling woman vanished into the library, Bartleby and Mr. Rundel were not above placing their ears to the door. The oak portal was thick, but His Grace's bellow had a habit of carrying, even through solid stone.

The two menservants were considerably bemused when the housekeeper had been gone long minutes and no explosion of wrath followed. They stumbled back as the door opened much quicker than expected. Mrs. Bede emerged looking pale and a little dazed.

Bartleby, well-accustomed himself to the razor-sharp edge of his master's tongue, inquired sympathetically, "Well, was it very bad, Mrs. Bede? What did His Grace say?"

For a moment, the poor woman seemed unable to find her voice. "H-he said it didn't matter, th-that no doubt there would be a fashion for brown this year and . . . and then . . ."

The butler and valet both leaned forward eagerly.

"And then His Grace *smiled* at me."

Bartleby and Rundel exchanged a startled glance.

"It's perfectly true," she cried. "And such a shock as you well may imagine. My poor nerves will never be the same."

Rundel shook his head solemnly. "When Betty carried in the breakfast dishes, she said His Grace was behaving queerly. The duke bid her good morning before he had even tasted one drop of his coffee. Of course, I didn't believe the girl."

"There is worse," Bartleby said. "I am never one to gossip about the master, but," he lowered his voice to a conspiratorial whisper, "this morning I fancied I heard His Grace *singing* in the bath."

The butler smothered an oath, and Mrs. Bede gave a soft moan. After which dreadful confidences, there seemed nothing more for the two men to do than lead the shaken housekeeper away to the kitchens to be fortified with a cup of tea.

Completely unaware of having raised any consternation among his staff, Simon had already dismissed Mrs. Bede's laundry report from his mind. Whistling a tuneless song, he returned to his task of rummaging his own library shelves.

Although fond of reading, he had never regarded his collection with such eager interest as he did this morning. He pulled out volume after volume, giving each book due consideration, thrusting some back into place, setting others aside.

Richardson? Simon frowned. No, he'd wager his last groat Audra would not care for that author. Too mawkishly sentimental. Ah, but Fielding and Smollett. That was more likely. But no Goldsmith. Simon thrust *The Vicar of Wakefield* farther back on the shelf.

He paused in his perusal only long enough to feel slightly amused at himself. He should have been long gone on his ride by now, not spending his morning rearranging the library for Audra's benefit. It was rather a presumption on his part, this deciding what she would like and what she wouldn't. He had met with the woman fewer times than he could count upon his fingers. How could he claim to know her tastes?

And yet he felt he did, knew her well as if she had been spending every evening here, curled up in that armchair where he had found her the night of the ball, plundering his books, the firelight caught in her hair, the mists of imaginary worlds hazing her eyes.

It was a most agreeable image, and he had to bring himself up short. He was already behaving like something of an idiot. He had set aside enough volumes to keep Audra busy until her hair turned as snowy white as those idiotic caps she wore. And he wanted her to occasionally turn to some other occupation besides reading.

Like chess. He suppressed a grin. He should have been ashamed of himself for his behavior of last night. The wager had only started out as jest. But it seemed the jest was on him. Audra had kissed him back in a manner to steal his reason, and it didn't appear likely to ever be returned.

And yet he held no regrets, only a memory of how warm and sweet her lips had been. Audra consumed his thoughts, leaving him damn near useless for anything. He could not even seem to concentrate on the book sorting for any length of time, and he caught himself staring out the window instead.

If he lingered much longer, he would probably be riding in the rain. The heavens appeared so overcast, a downpour seemed imminent, but somehow even that didn't daunt him. He liked the pearl gray sky. It was the same misty shade as her eyes.

Staring, his thoughts miles away, he was scarce aware of the knock at the library door until his sister burst unceremoniously in upon him. He had breakfasted so early Gus had been still abed. Lady Augusta was already charmingly attired in a cherry-striped morning gown, her hair done up in a cluster of ringlets.

Before she could say anything, he strode forward and kissed her cheek. "Good morning, Augusta. You are looking fresh and pretty this morning with your hair all done up in those . . . those bouncy things."

It was a handsome compliment to pay, especially to one's sister. She should have been pleased instead of staring at him open-mouthed. "Simon, are you feeling all right?"

"Never better. Why?"

" 'Tis only that most mornings you scarce notice that I still have a head, let alone how my hair is arranged. And what have you been doing to set the entire household by its ears already?"

He arched his brows in mild surprise. "Nothing. In fact, I flatter myself that I have been particularly amiable."

"That's precisely what I mean. Your staff is not accustomed to it this early in the day. Poor Betty's hands were trembling as she poured out my chocolate. And as for Mrs. Bede, I think she is lying down, with Bartleby burning feathers beneath her nose. You will be the death of these good people."

"I never realized being in a good mood was a hanging offense," Simon said. "If it will mend matters, I will contrive to glower at Farley when he brings my horse round."

Augusta earnestly suggested that he do so. "All this cheerfulness is beginning to even disconcert me. You have been behaving very oddly since the night of the ball. I don't think I'll ever help you plan another."

"I won't ever need another. I have already met the only— that is, all the ladies that I care to become acquainted with."

She stared at him, her nose crinkling in a slight frown. "Oh? Have you given up seeking a wife, or is there something you are not telling me?"

"If there is, it is no fault of yours, m'dear. I always said the army should engage you to interrogate captured spies. You'd soon worm all their secrets out of them."

But she was not about to be put off by his teasing. When he moved back to the desk to rearrange a stack of books in danger of toppling over, she followed him. She studied him through narrowed eyes.

"You missed dinner last night, owing to some mysterious errand, and according to Betty, you took little for breakfast. If it were anyone else but you, Simon, I would hazard you had fallen in love. Can't eat, can't sleep . . ."

"It so happens I slept quite soundly," he said, trying not to look self-conscious. He had slept well, but only after thoroughly dousing himself with water to cool all heated thoughts of Audra.

"And you have not even gone yet for your morning ride," Augusta accused.

"You can see for yourself how threatening the sky is."

"Since when did that ever stop you? I've seen you ride in downpours that would set more prudent men to building an ark."

He didn't answer. He realized that he was behaving in a manner most unlike himself, but he didn't relish having it pointed out to him. Plunking into the armchair, he grabbed up the nearest book and affected to read. But Augusta leaned over his chair with the most annoying smile.

"If you are going to pretend to read, Simon, you had best select something else. You will never convince me you are interested in *Mrs. Pierson's Hints to a Lady on Household Management.*"

Startled, Simon glanced at the title, then slammed the book closed in disgust.

"Your present state of distraction," his sister murmured. "It wouldn't have anything to do with Miss Masters, would it?"

"Miss Masters?" he repeated. "Why would you think that?"

"Oh, no particular reason. Only the way you nearly flung yourself beneath her coach wheels to prevent her departure from the ball. And you kept her shoes for a token of remembrance."

"I did no such thing. I returned those blasted slippers when I went to see her last—" He broke off, but it was too late. Lady Augusta regarded him with a triumphant gleam.

He shot to his feet, pacing off a few agitated steps. "For heaven's sake, Gus. Don't start letting your imagination run wild. I've known Miss Masters less than a month. We quarrel every time we meet. I've only danced with her once, called upon her once, dined with her once and . . ." He expelled his breath in a sigh, heavy with resignation. "And I think I have damn well gone and fallen in love with her."

Augusta let out a trill of delighted laughter.

"Aye, go ahead and laugh," he said glumly. "I daresay Robert would have, too, seeing me so properly dished. Me, who always scoffed at fairy-tale romances, who could not stomach sitting through a performance of Romeo and Juliet. Now, here I am, behaving like such a veritable mooncalf,

135

young Montague would seem like a pattern card of good sense by comparison."

"My poor Simon," Augusta mocked. But as she extended both hands to him, her eyes were brimming over with happiness.

He squeezed her fingers in a rough grasp, his mouth tipping in a rueful smile. "So, how big a fool does that make me, Gus? I think I must have loved that woman from the first moment I saw her chasing after that fool dog. Is such a thing possible?"

"Only your own heart can tell you that, but I should not be at all surprised. My dear brother, most things in your life you have done in a manner straightforward and direct. Why should falling in love be any different?"

She cast herself into his arms, giving him a fierce hug. "It was so horrid when I thought you meant to marry any female merely to have a duchess. But now, I am so thankful, so happy for you."

Moved and a little embarrassed by this display of sisterly affection, Simon patted her back. "Well, don't go wishing me joy yet, Gus. My lady is as likely to cuff my ears as to offer me a shy kiss when I propose to her."

Augusta drew back with a tiny frown. "Surely you don't think Miss Masters would refuse you?"

Simon was hard put to answer. Audra could be remarkably skittish at times, but she, too, was obviously given to approaching life in a direct manner. He was not a vain man, but as to her feelings for him, he had read much in those speaking gray eyes last night, to say nothing of the message she had conveyed to him with her kiss. Lost in his memories, Simon had no notion how much his expression gave him away until Augusta laughed and said, "Odious man. I can see you are not worried. You are wearing that obnoxiously smug smile gentlemen have when they are quite sure of themselves. So when will you bring your Miss Masters round to see me? I am dying to better make her acquaintance."

"I already invited her to call today, along with her aunt and sister."

"You what!" His sister fairly shrieked. "And here I am with

136

my best afternoon frock wanting mending and scarce a scrap of decent pastry to be found in the kitchens. Men!" After which dark and incomprehensible utterance, Augusta bolted from the library, leaving Simon shaking his head.

He was at liberty then to gather up his crop and take his ride, but still he lingered, finding himself strangely without ambition. He returned to the window, the minutes slipping by as he watched the wind swirling leaves into the moat.

He possessed enough humor to laugh at himself, behaving like a starry-eyed fool, counting the seconds until Audra's carriage was likely to be seen approaching the drawbridge. At least he was not so far gone as to be seeing rainbows or hearing skyrockets bursting.

He was finding love a far quieter emotion, like the warmth of a fire blazing upon the hearth on a chill winter's day or the sparkling glass of some fine, old wine. Although impatient for Audra's arrival, Simon's mellow humor continued far into the afternoon.

His household had even grown a little accustomed to this startling change in his demeanor. When Mr. Wylie, the estate agent, a thin nervous man, approached the duke, he tripped into the library with an air of rare confidence.

To be sure, His Grace did not look as if he heeded Mr. Wylie's report on the tenant farms with his usual strict attention. The duke sat behind his desk, fiddling with the feathered end of his quill pen, but he listened with the most remarkable patience and condescension. That is, until Mr. Wylie reached the matter of Meadow Lane Lodge.

"And Miss Masters said she regrets giving such short notice, but she desires to give up the lease upon the lodge and intends to move out before the end of the month."

"She what?" His Grace thundered in much his old manner. His new-found confidence evaporated, Mr. Wylie fought an urge to dive beneath his chair.

"Well, I-I did not think Your Grace would mind. The lodge is so pleasant, it will not be difficult to find another tenant."

"The lodge be damned. If that woman is planning to go haring off again, I'll—" The grim threat left unfinished, the duke

137

bolted to his feet. Wylie flattened himself against one of the bookcases as His Grace strode past.

His bellow ringing quite clearly through the stone walls, the duke could be heard demanding his horse be brought round at once. Trembling, Wylie cursed himself for ever believing Mrs. Bede's foolish story of the master's recent acquired affability. He hoped that Miss Masters was a young woman possessed of strong nerves. She was going to need them.

Audra's heart felt heavier than the parcel she carried as she wended her way back from the village. The lane seemed to stretch out ahead of her interminably, snaking past harvested fields and tall hedgerows. She had perhaps another two miles to cover before she reached the shelter of the lodge, and the sky above her waxed most threatening.

Yet she paid little heed to the gathering clouds, the relentless gray a perfect complement to her mood. Rather than quickening her stride, she trudged along, shifting the weight of the brown wrapped parcels to her other arm. She had had no real excuse for venturing into the village that morning. Cecily had no pressing need of more ells of lace and rosewater. Audra certainly had need of no more books. She hadn't even finished *Ivanhoe*.

What she had possessed was a need to escape from the lodge for a while, the clatter of her aunt's tongue, Cecily's innocent questions about the duke's departure, time to be alone to think. Uncle Matthew was certain to be cross with Audra when he heard she had come into town without even calling at the parsonage. But she couldn't have faced the old man's penetrating gaze, not after what had happened last night. . . .

Audra had slept badly, but she had hoped upon awakening to find that her sanity had been restored. It hadn't. From the first fluttering open of her eyes, images of Raeburn had danced before her, filling her with strange yearnings, quicksilver flashes of panic.

When she had chanced upon the duke's estate agent riding down High Street, Audra hadn't thought twice. She had impulsively informed Mr. Wylie of her decision to quit the lodge.

But now with the village left far behind her, balancing the unwieldy parcel of books, lace, and scent, Audra began to have doubts as to the wisdom of her action. Although she didn't quite regret it, she was more than a little ashamed. She knew she was running away. Absurd! Just because the Duke of Raeburn had kissed her. His Grace had no reputation for being a lecherous fiend. Despite his unconventional manner, his gruff ways, he was still a gentleman. She was not sure what his intentions were, only that they could not be dishonorable.

What truly alarmed her was that when she had been in his arms, she would not have cared if his thoughts had been a trifle wicked. She had only wanted his kiss to go on forever, and good sense, reputation, the world itself could all spin away and be damned.

She had sometimes wondered what it would be like to fancy oneself in love. It was every bit as giddy and feverish as she had imagined. She was behaving as badly as Lady Arabella ever had.

Audra winced at that reflection. She couldn't help remembering the time she had caught Mama planning to elope, run off from her fourth husband, poor dull Sir Claude Skeffington. Mama had been infatuated with an army captain, a dazzling individual with his bristling mustache and bright red regimentals. None of Audra's pleadings had been capable of bringing Lady Arabella to her senses.

Mama would have created the most dreadful scandal, but luckily, the captain had failed to keep the appointed rendezvous. Lady Arabella had been heartbroken until the end of the week when she had fallen violently in love with that poet she'd met at the Countess Lievens's drum.

The entire incident had been far more wearying to Audra than to her mama. It had taught her quite early on that sudden outbreaks of love were to be treated as highly suspect, given no more consideration than a severe case of the measles.

As for her own recent brush with what Mama had always called the "grande passion," Audra told herself she would recover. When she had left Meadow Lane, she would forget this disconcerting interlude with the Duke of Raeburn. She would return to the peace and solitary existence she had always desired.

Yet far from offering her consolation, this reassurance only caused a cold lump to settle in the bottom of her heart. Never had peace and quiet seemed such a dismal and lonely prospect.

She attempted to shake off this lowering feeling and quicken her footsteps. It would be as well if she could make it back to the lodge before the rain commenced. She would have to endure another of her aunt's scoldings if she returned soaked. Mrs. Saunders was likely to be vexed enough when she discovered that Audra had gone into the village unaccompanied by her maid.

Bent upon hastening her steps, Audra scarce heeded what lay ahead of her as she rounded a curving in the lane. She was considerably startled when a blur of russet streaked across her path from the shelter of the nearby field.

Audra dropped her packages and emitted a gasp, more of surprise than alarm. The animal froze in its tracks. It was a small fox with a white chest, glossy red coat, and black-tipped brush. For a brief instant, Audra found herself staring into liquid gold eyes with a canny intelligence that was almost human.

"You little beauty," she murmured, catching her breath at the sight of the animal, but the cub was already scrambling beneath the hedges opposite. Before Audra had time to recover, she caught another sound above the rustle of leaves. From a great distance across the fields, she heard the "ta-tum" of a horn and the faint baying of hounds.

"Entwhistle," Audra muttered. She gazed anxiously in the direction the fox had disappeared, trying to gauge the animal's chances of escape. Beyond the hedgerow was naught but more open field. It was a long way to the distant outline of the woods. Unless the cub had a burrow nearby, it was likely to be overtaken. Of course on such a windy day, there was always a chance that Entwhistle's hounds would lose the scent.

But as Audra's gaze fell upon the parcels she had dropped, an idea came to her. She didn't intend to leave the matter to chance. Seizing the smallest package, she ripped it open, revealing the bottle of rosewater she had purchased for Cecily.

Racing to the spot in the lane where the fox had first appeared, she uncorked the bottle and began spattering the contents.

The cry of the hounds was closer now. Audra could spot the outline of riders tearing across the field, hard. She had just enough time to grab up the remains of her packages and dart down the lane to find a hiding place behind the hedgerows.

Crouching low behind the thorny branches, she could soon hear in the road beyond a thunder of activity. Peering between the leaves, some fifty yards away, she could see Entwhistle's hounds, blundering along the lane, their din of baying petering out in confusion.

With breathless satisfaction, Audra watched the black-and-white dogs coming to a halt. Tails thrust in the air, noses bent to the ground, they snuffled the place where Cecily's rosewater had sunk into the dirt.

It was not long before the field of riders rushed up, Sir Ralph in the lead. His huntsman shouted out, "Hold hard." Audra winced at the way Entwhistle sawed back on his reins, pulling around his switch-tail bay.

While the whipper-in ran forward to take charge of the dogs, Sir Ralph was already cursing. "Damned curs! They've lost 'im." Not even giving the hounds time to cast, Entwhistle began to lay about with his whip.

When one of the dogs yelped, Audra bit down upon her lip, almost sorry for the trick she had served. Quivering with indignation, she started to rise from her hiding place, about to tell Sir Ralph she would take that whip to him in another moment.

But she was stopped by the sound of an excited bray. One of the dogs had sniffed its way past the rosewater and was setting up a terrific howl.

The huntsman seized Sir Ralph's arm, stopping him in mid-slash. "That's Flyaway, sir. He's recovered the scent."

"Then don't dawdle, you fool. Sound the horn."

To Audra's dismay, she saw the other hounds joining Flyaway and a mad scramble through the hedge commenced. As they erupted into the field, only a stone's throw from where she crouched, Audra tried to shrink down lower.

The huntsman was blowing out the notes of "gone away,"

while the whipper-in shouted encouragement. "Huic, huic, eu at him, my beauties. Foror-or-orrard."

"Oh, no," Audra moaned, already realizing what would follow. She shoved herself as far under the hedge as she could, the thorns tearing at her hands and bonnet. The ground beneath her seemed to tremble as the riders, hard after the dogs, began to jump the hedge. Flying hooves tossed up chunks of dirt coming dangerously near her. She covered her head with her arms, closing her eyes, holding her breath lest one of the horses fail to clear the hedge.

The thundering seemed to rage forever, but in what could have been no more than seconds, the fearful din began to recede. Much shaken, Audra opened her eyes to see the dogs and riders vanishing across the field without a backward glance.

Exhaling a tremulous breath, she struggled to a standing position and brushed herself off. Straightening her bonnet, she regarded the scratches stinging her hands. Well, that little episode had not turned out quite the way she had planned. But she had not been trampled, and perhaps she had bought the cub a little more time to make its escape.

Though still shaky, she fought her way back through the hedge to the lane, only to realize she had quit her hiding place too soon. Another rider, straggling behind the rest of the hunt, galloped toward her down the lane.

Audra thought of diving for cover but felt far too bruised to go through that again. It didn't matter in any case, for the approaching rider had already seen her and bellowed out her name.

Audra winced at the familiar voice. Raeburn. But she was more resigned than surprised. Of course it would be him. Was it not the man's mission in life to come upon her when she least desired or expected him?

As he reined in his powerful black gelding, Audra stared up into the duke's fierce dark eyes. Despite how dazed she felt from her own narrow escape, her heart did a foolish flutter. Raeburn made a much more impressive figure on horseback than Sir Ralph. So tall, the wind riffling the ends of his black hair, the storm clouds themselves seemed to cling to the broad outline of his shoulders.

"Audra!" he snapped. "Are you all right?"

She managed to nod as he slid from the back of his horse.

"Are you sure? You haven't broken anything?" He ran his hands lightly over her arms. Even through the layer of her cloak and gown, she was too conscious of his touch. None of her bones had been broken, but they stood in danger of melting if he pulled her any closer.

Thrusting his hands away, she breathed, "I am fine, truly."

His concern dissolved into a furious glower. "You damned little fool. What have you been about now? I crested the rise of the hill a moment ago, and I saw some idiot female darting behind the hedges, right in the path of where the hunt would go through. I never imagined it would be you."

"I didn't think I could be seen. I am fortunate Sir Ralph didn't notice me."

"Fortunate! Was it your wish to be trampled by that buffoon and his infernal pack?"

"No, of course not." Although a flush of embarrassment stole over her cheeks, Audra felt obliged to explain what she had done with the rosewater, her futile attempt to divert the dogs.

Raeburn's scowl only deepened as he listened to her halting explanation. "You were following Sir Ralph about the countryside to sabotage his hunt?"

"No, it was merely an impulse." She stiffened defensively. "I know it sounds foolish, but I cannot bear to see any creature harmed, not even a fox. Just another of my eccentricities, I suppose. You wouldn't understand."

"I understand perfectly."

That was the devil of it. He did, perhaps more than any other person she had ever known. Those dark eyes of his glowed with such empathy, they seemed to reach out and embrace her, although he scolded, "I don't want to ever catch you taking such a risk again. If you did not already look so thoroughly shaken, I'd box your ears, my girl."

The possessiveness in those gruff tones should have offended

143

her. Instead she felt her knees go weak. She backed away, stammering, "The danger is quite past now, so you need not concern yourself. I dropped my parcels behind the hedge. I'd best fetch them."

"Just one moment, Audra. I must speak with you." He caught hold of her arm and brought her around to face him. "There are some other things going on that I do not understand. What's this nonsense about your leaving Meadow Lane?"

She caught her lip between her teeth. "So Mr. Wylie has already been to see you. He didn't waste any time." There was no reason she should feel so guilty, but she couldn't bring herself to meet Raeburn's eyes. "I hope my decision to give up the lease doesn't inconvenience Your Grace."

"I find it damnably inconvenient. I suppose this latest ill-judged start has something to do with what happened last night—"

"I would as soon forget last night. That has nothing to do with my decision. It is only that once Cecily has gone to London, the lodge will seem so empty. Even Uncle Matthew has spoken of giving up his living, retiring to Bath."

"That rascal? Spending the rest of his days sipping medicinal waters with a parcel of elderly dowagers? You'd best come up with a better tale than that, m'dear."

"In any case, I see no reason for me to remain here."

"Don't you?" Raeburn's voice took on a dangerous note. A wave of panic washed over her, and she backed away from him.

"You'd best ride on, sir. It will rain soon. I must make haste myself, or my aunt and sister will wonder what has become of me."

Spinning on her heel, she set off down the road at a breathless pace. But it was utterly to no avail. She heard him coming after her. Short of running, there was no way she could outdistance his lengthy strides.

Leading his horse by the reins, he fell into step beside her. When she dared risk a glance at him, she noticed he was scowling, though more out of confusion than anger.

"Audra, what is troubling you?" he asked.

She wasn't prepared for him to speak to her that way, not in that quiet, almost tender tone of voice.

"N-nothing."

"Then why are you running away again?"

"I-I am not."

He gave a low mirthless laugh. "My dear girl, if I was prepared to let you, you would hike up your skirts and go bolting away from me faster than that poor fox fled Entwhistle's dogs."

She made no attempt to deny it, only hung her head, wishing she'd worn a bonnet with a larger poke to conceal more of her face.

"I realize my behavior last night was abominable," he said. "I am not very good at declaring myself. In fact, I suppose I haven't done so at all. But when I kissed you, you cannot be thinking that I meant anything dishonorable."

"Oh, n-no. I don't think you meant anything at all. It was merely a wager, a foolish jest. Pray, let us say no more about it."

"It was no jest then, and I am not jesting now. I want to marry you."

"Oh." Her hands flew to her face. Bonnet be damned. She needed a very large hat with a heavy veil. "That is very honorable of Your Grace, to be sure, but a little excessive. It was only one kiss. There is no need for you to feel obliged to offer me, as if you had compromised me."

"Compromised!" he roared, stopping dead in his tracks. "If you don't stop talking such fustian, I'll show you compromise. Damn it woman, I am in love with you."

His words sent a shaft of almost delirious joy through her, but she firmly quelled it. "That's not possible, Your Grace. You hardly know me. It's unlikely you could be in love upon such short acquaintance."

"It's unlikely to be struck by lightning, too, but we both know it happens. I am as fully aware as you how mad this all sounds, but I cannot help it. *I love you.*"

"Then I think you should go home and have a long lie down, Your Grace. Until you are more yourself again."

"Is this your way of refusing me?" He cupped her chin,

forcing her to look up at him as he demanded, "Are you telling me you feel nothing for me?"

Audra thought it would have been much easier if she could tell him exactly that, but it was impossible, not when she was being held hostage by his eyes. "I admit I was also swept away last night, but no one knows better than I to mistrust such sudden emotions."

"Indeed? And exactly how many other times has such a thing happened to you?"

"None," she was forced to admit. She bristled defensively. "But I watched my mother fall in and out of love twice a week."

"You are not your mother, Audra."

"No? I'm beginning to have my doubts."

His sudden sharp intake of breath warned her that he had reached the end of his patience. But she did not have time to react before he seized her by both shoulders. As he hauled her roughly against him, her protest was muffled by his mouth coming down hard upon hers.

She struggled against his ruthless kiss, but it was to no avail. She was no match against his iron strength. And after a time, her struggles became so feeble as to be nonexistent. Even when his lips released hers, she could seem to do no more than murmur, "Please . . ."

"Now," he said hoarsely. "Now what of your doubts, Audra? I'm no rake, but I've kissed enough women to assure you this is no fleeting passion between us. I'm not asking you to marry me tomorrow or even next month. Just stay on at the lodge. Give us a chance to become better acquainted and then—"

"I c-can't," she cried. "I won't. I never wanted anything like this to happen to me. I have always been content as a spinster, to live quietly with my books, alone. Can you not understand?"

"No, I don't."

But this time when she struggled to be free, he released her. "I am not the sort to take a bride by force, but go ahead and run away if you feel you must. I can only tell you this from bitter experience. A book doesn't make a very warm companion on a cold winter's night, Miss Masters."

146

He turned upon his heel. Raeburn's gelding had used the interlude to wander away, cropping some grass. The duke covered the distance to his mount in long strides. Audra had a wild urge to call him back, but proudly, stubbornly, she pressed her lips together.

Seizing the reins, he swung into the saddle and brought the horse around to face her. "I suppose this is farewell, then? I could always tell Wylie to hold off seeking another tenant for the lodge . . . in case you should change your mind."

"I fear that I won't."

He stared down at her and slowly shook his head, but the gesture was more rife with disappointment than anger. "Strange, but I would have wagered most handsomely that you would never be afraid to throw your heart over. It appears that I did not know you as well as I thought."

With a final salute, he urged his horse into a gallop and was gone. Long after he had vanished, Audra stood in the middle of the lane, not knowing whether to cry or curse him. His parting words stung. He had practically called her a coward.

"It doesn't matter," she said fiercely. "It is as well I am blessed with good sense, Your Grace, since you have clearly taken leave of yours."

Her mind yet reeled with the shock of it. The Duke of Raeburn in love with her, asking her to marry him. It was mad, ridiculous, impossible.

"A proper duchess I would make." She sniffed scornfully. And if Raeburn were in his right mind, he would realize the absurdity of it. Someday when he recovered his wits, he would thank her for being so prudent as to remove herself from his proximity, before they were both tempted to embark upon some foolish course they would regret forever.

Buoyed up by these convictions, Audra returned to gather up the parcels she had left scattered behind the hedge. But as she recommenced her weary trudge homeward, such a mood of self-righteousness did not last for long.

This is farewell, then. . . . Simon's voice kept echoing through her mind until she almost wished she could weep as easily as Cecily did. It might have done her a great deal of good

147

to be able to sob her heart out. But being herself, there was nothing she could do but keep walking. Numb at heart, she didn't even notice when it began to rain.

Chapter 10

The Duke of Raeburn was true to his word. He made no further effort to force his suit upon Audra. Nor did he attempt to see her again. By the end of the week, she was recovered enough not to start at the mention of his name or be tempted to fly to the window each time she heard the approach of hoofbeats in the lane.

As for the dull ache that seemed to have settled in her heart, she supposed that, too, would disappear given enough time and distance. At least her decision to leave Meadow Lane met with unqualified approval from one quarter.

Mrs. Saunders nearly smiled when Audra informed her that she had given up the lease. "At last, you are being sensible," her aunt said. "Now you may find some property more suitable than a hunting lodge; this time with a respectable widow to bear you company. Perhaps when Cecily finally weds, you could make your home with her. An elder unmarried sister can be most useful when one begins to have children."

Aunt Saunders proceeded to offer several other helpful suggestions regarding Audra's future, until Audra felt if she received much more of this bracing advice, she would have her first megrim. She was relieved when her aunt turned the conversation to Cecily's prospects instead, more relieved still to discover Mrs. Saunders had finally made up her mind. She would take Cecily to London with her.

Their imminent departure obliged Audra to set aside any

plans for arranging her own removal from Meadow Lane. Wellington had managed to deploy his entire army with far less difficulty than seemed required to send one slip of a girl off to London for the Season.

Two days before Mrs. Saunders and Cecily were scheduled to leave, Audra entered her sister's bedchamber to find it a scene of complete confusion. Unpacked trunks stood open, while the bed was littered with hair ribbons, bonnets, gloves, muslin frocks fairly tumbling to the carpet. And neither Cecily nor her maid were anywhere to be found.

Sighing, Audra proceeded to fold some of the garments herself, laying them away in the bottom of one of the trunks. Although Cecily would be acquiring a new wardrobe in London, she insisted upon taking practically everything with her.

To Audra's astonishment, she discovered an old nightgown that Cecily surely must have outgrown. Setting it aside, her fingers snagged on the delicate lace trim, her heart snagging on a memory. Of a sudden, she could picture so clearly those times when Cecily used to bound into her chamber, a pale blond ghost in her white nightgown as she leaped upon Audra's bed to escape the terror of some nightmare or to demand to hear a story. Muffin's feet would be ice cold because the child never could remember to slip on her mules.

An unexpected wave of melancholy washed over Audra at the recollection. She fought to dispel it, briskly folding up the nightgown, telling herself not to be a wet goose. She would miss Cecily, but it was not the first time she had parted with her sister.

And yet . . . Audra could not delude herself. When Cecily had departed for boarding school, Audra had always known the girl was coming back. But this time was different. Aunt Saunders's remark had given Audra much pause for reflection.

When Cecily finally weds . . . And, of course, Cecily would. It was the natural outcome of a Season in London for a girl like Cecily—pretty, of good family, possessed of a respectable dowry. Audra had no doubt Muffin would soon be betrothed, swept away by some dashing young man to a home of her own. Which was quite right, the way it *should* be.

149

Why, then, did it make the prospects for her own future seem so dreadfully bleak? Audra had always been so certain that she knew what she wanted. After all those years of chaos with Lady Arabella, Audra had desired nothing more than peace, the solitude in which to enjoy her books.

It had never occurred to her until recently that solitude might also mean loneliness. She had never given a thought to marriage until the Duke of Raeburn had stormed across her path. She began to wonder if she had been wrong to refuse him. If not his offer of marriage, at least his request that she remain at Meadow Lane. He had only asked that she give him a little more time, the leisure to court her, but the truth was she had been afraid to grant him even that. Unlike Mama, she had never been able to take risks in matters of the heart. Perhaps it was wrong of her, but she had always flattered herself in being so much more sensible than her parent. She was no longer so sure.

The packing forgotten, Audra sagged down on the edge of her sister's bed, propping her chin on her hand. She had never felt so confused in her entire life. Lady Arabella had been more like a flighty younger sister to her. Audra had always told herself that she was independent enough, she had never felt the lack of a mother . . . until now. But today, she thought she would have given much for the counsel of some older and wiser female.

Lost in these dismal reflections, she scarce noticed when the bedchamber door opened, until Cecily breezed in, slamming it behind her. Ashamed to be caught wool-gathering in this morose fashion, Audra bolted to her feet, briskly resuming the task of folding garments into the trunk.

"Oh! Audra, there you are," Cecily said. Her eyes and cheeks bright from some brisk outdoor exercise, she swept a fur-trimmed pelisse from her shoulders and added it to the pile on the bed. "Whatever are you doing packing my things? Heloise will take care of it."

"I don't mind," Audra said. "And as for your maid, her head is so far in the clouds these days, if the packing were left to her, you would arrive in London with nothing but a toothbrush."

"Indeed. Poor Heloise. Being but a country-bred girl, she is quite overwhelmed at the prospect of our journey."

"Unlike yourself. So sophisticated and entirely blasé about the whole thing."

Cecily pulled a face at Audra before turning away to her mirror. Her face flushed pink with excitement, she removed her bonnet and, humming, she snatched up a brush to smooth out her golden curls.

"I finished my last fitting at the dressmaker's," she said. "So I will at least have one decent traveling frock. Oh, and Audra, don't pack my lilac silk. I will be needing it when we go out to pay calls this afternoon."

"Not again," Audra muttered. It was but another of the disagreeable aspects of having Mrs. Saunders at Meadow Lane. Her aunt had wasted no time in receiving the ladies in the neighborhood whom she felt worthy of her notice and accepting invitations from them.

"I hope it is not the Colebys again," Audra said.

"N-no." Cecily paused in her brushing, long enough to steal an uneasy glance at Audra. "I-I fear Aunt means for us to take tea at Grayhawk Manor."

"Grayhawk Manor? That's where the Entwhistles live!"

"I know. I told Aunt you would not care for it, but Sir Ralph's sisters have been pressing us to call forever. Aunt Saunders feels that we should. Since Sir Ralph is a baronet and the local master of the hunt, that makes him rather an important personage. Pray, Audra, I-I hope you will not make too great a fuss about it."

Audra merely shrugged, saying she supposed she could endure it. Hopefully Sir Ralph would be out riding instead of there to sicken her with his hunt stories. It scarce mattered in any case. She seemed to lack the spirit of late to raise a great fuss about anything.

As she commenced the task of sorting through Cecily's fans, her sister cried out, "Oh, don't throw that one out, Audra. 'Tis my favorite." At which point Audra tartly suggested that Cecily might leave off fussing with her curls and do a little herself toward preparing for the journey to London.

151

"I have!" Cecily said indignantly. "I have only just returned from taking Frou-frou for a walk, to accustom her to what it will be like in London, the streets so full of traffic."

"And what traffic did you possibly find in our quiet little lane?"

"A great deal. The farrier's cart passed us and Lady Coleby's carriage. Frou-frou did quite well until her barking frightened the Duke of Raeburn's horse."

Audra steeled herself not to start at the mention of the duke, but she could not control the quickening of her heart.

"He has acquired a new mount," Cecily said. "Rather skittish."

Half a dozen foolish questions rose to Audra's mind. How had he looked? What had he said? But she gave voice to none of them, merely bending over the trunk, packing fans as though her life depended upon it.

But Cecily required no prodding to keep talking about the encounter. "I was afraid His Grace would be furious with Frou-frou. And you know how terrified I get when he scowls. But when he regained control of his horse, he spoke most kindly to me. He hoped I have a pleasant sojourn in London, and he even asked after you. I told him you had not been feeling quite the thing of late and were probably suffering from a touch of biliousness."

"You what!" Audra straightened so suddenly she banged her knee up against the corner of the trunk. Biting off a curse, she rubbed the afflicted member. "Cecily! You know I am never ill. Whatever possessed you to tell His Grace such a thing?"

"Because it is quite true. You have been so pale and quiet of late. You never even bellowed at Frou-frou the day she chewed up the binding of your Wivenhoe book."

"That's *Ivanhoe*, and it wasn't important. I daresay I would never have gotten around to finishing the book anyway."

"That is precisely what I mean. You have not been reading much, so you must be ill."

"But there is no need for you to go telling Raeburn all of that, Cecily. He might think that I—"

She broke off, flushing with discomfort, forcing herself to

remember it didn't matter what Raeburn might think. She concluded lamely, "I am sure His Grace could not have been much interested in the state of my health."

"But indeed he was. He seemed dreadfully concerned. I think he would have called here this afternoon except that I was obliged to tell him we were going to Grayhawk Manor."

"Thank heaven for that," Audra muttered, never thinking that she would feel grateful for an engagement at the Entwhistles'.

"I have been wondering, Audra," Cecily continued. "Do you know . . . I believe Aunt Saunders must have been wrong about the duke."

"Wrong? In what fashion?"

Cecily did not answer immediately, being more concerned with taming one wayward curl. Satisfied with her hair at last, she left off primping and came to curl up on the bed. She leaned forward in a confiding posture. "When Aunt first came here, do you remember that night His Grace dined with us?"

Audra grimaced and nodded. How could she ever forget it?

"Well, Aunt Saunders entertained some notion that the duke found me attractive, but I have been giving the matter a great deal of thought." Cecily wrinkled her small pert nose.

"Now, don't eat me, Audra," she said. "But I did just begin to wonder if maybe it was not you that the duke might be trying to fix his interest with."

"Me?" Audra croaked, fighting a telltale blush. "H-how absurd."

"I thought so, too, at first, but the more one considers it, it becomes plain that you and His Grace are monstrously well suited."

"We are?"

"Yes, you both make the same sort of odd little jests. He clearly detests large parties, and so do you. I daresay he would never object about your bringing a book to the table, nor mind your being so clever. In fact, I think he rather likes it, and you would never be daunted by his awful scowl or his surly tempers."

She concluded with a little sigh, "I think it would be just

perfect if he were to make you his duchess and sweep you off to his castle to live happily ever after."

"What romantic nonsense, Cecily," Audra said. She forced a smile that was a little tremulous. "Happily-ever-afters are only for heroines in books."

"I might have known you would say something like that. Perhaps I have been foolish, weaving daydreams about you and the duke, but I do worry so about you."

"About me?" Audra echoed, considerably startled by this confession.

"Who will take care of you after I am gone? I mean make sure you are not forever straining your eyes, with your nose in one of those fusty books, reading so much you forget to eat your breakfast."

Audra was hard pressed not to laugh, but Cecily looked so serious, she felt deeply touched at the same time. "I shall contrive not to starve, Muffin," she assured her sister solemnly.

To her dismay, Cecily's eyes clouded with sudden tears. "I almost wish I was not going."

"Why, Cecily, you have talked about nothing but London for months. I thought you were so excited, so happy when Aunt Saunders finally made up her mind."

"I was. I still am, but I am frightened, too."

Audra wrapped her arm about Cecily's shoulders. "What is there for you to be frightened of, pet? You will have a wonderful time. If anyone was ever born to grace Almack's, it is you. I predict you will be the belle of the Season."

"I am not dreading any of that part of it. You know how much I love balls and waltzing and becoming acquainted with new people." Cecily fretted her lower lip. " 'Tis only that I have suddenly realized. I am quite grown up now, am I not? By this time next year, I could be betrothed, even married."

She blushed deeply. "It is a wondrous prospect, but a little terrifying, too, to be trusting the care of one's heart, one's life into the keeping of one man. Do you not think so?"

"Well, I-I . . ." Audra stammered.

Although Cecily snuggled closer, she said, "Oh, I know what you must be thinking, and perhaps you are right. I am a goose. I did not expect you to understand, Audra. You have never been afraid of anything."

Audra found herself unable to reply or even meet her sister's eyes. She gave Cecily a rough squeeze and drew away. "Never mind, Muffin. You are but having a last-minute attack of nerves. Your only fear just now should be that you will break poor Jack Coachman's back when he attempts to lift these trunks of yours."

This sally elicited a watery chuckle from Cecily. By dint of more teasing, Audra soon had her sister smiling and cheerful. By the time Audra left the chamber to attire herself for the ordeal of calling on the Entwhistles, Cecily was quite restored, waltzing about the room as she decided what bracelets to wear, all her doubts and fears banished.

Although Audra smiled, she closed the door behind her with a heavy sigh. If only she had managed to do as much for herself.

Audra expected to derive little pleasure from the afternoon ahead of her. By the time she crossed the threshold of Grayhawk Manor, she had begun to wish she had not been so lethargic, that she had taken the pains to manufacture some excuse to spare herself the ordeal of taking tea with Sir Ralph's sisters.

Her first glimpse of the towering main hall did little to rouse her enthusiasm. What once must have been a respectable Georgian manor had been turned into a veritable chamber of horrors, the walls crammed with hunting prints, deer antlers, and other mounted objects too dreadful to contemplate. Audra stole a closer glimpse at one such and was appalled to realize it must be a fox nose hammered in place with a brass nail. She averted her eyes, trying not to examine any other such trophies more closely.

Fortunately, the drawing room in which the Misses Entwhistle elected to receive their guests boasted a more innocuous decor—a few stiff family portraits and a collection of Wedgwood figurines on an étagère. At one end of the long room stood both a pianoforte and a harp.

Audra devoutly hoped that neither of her hostesses would

be tempted to favor them with a selection that afternoon. Both Sir Ralph's sisters had weak voices. Although they were not twins, they were both pale and colorless creatures, and Audra frequently had difficulty telling them apart.

When they came forward to make their curtsies, Audra was still not sure if she was addressing the elder Miss Entwhistle or Miss Georgianna. It scarce mattered, for Audra was content to let her aunt and Cecily take over the conversation. Ensconcing herself upon the settee with a cup of weak tea, Audra occupied herself with counting the minutes until this ordeal was likely to be over.

The visit was only enlivened when Sir Ralph popped his head in the door for a few moments. He had several of his unruly hunting dogs at his heels, but neither of his meek sisters seemed the least disconcerted at having these beasts running tame through the house, not even when the largest one gulped several biscuits off the tea tray.

After greeting Cecily and Mrs. Saunders, Sir Ralph wrung Audra's hand in hearty fashion, his bristling red hair standing on end like a wild red flame.

"B'gawd, Miss Masters, when my sisters told me you were coming, I could scarce believe it. Coaxed you away from your books at last, eh?" He gave one of his loud braying laughs. "You must have Georgy or Sophy show you over the house. One doesn't like to boast, but quite a place, Grayhawk Manor. Mentioned in all the guidebooks."

Audra managed to return some politely noncommittal answer. If the rest of the manor at all resembled the front hall, she felt she had seen quite enough of it.

But Mrs. Saunders professed herself deeply interested. She was quite fond of touring great houses, although Audra oft thought she only did so to catch the housekeepers out in acts of negligence, examining famous antiques merely to see if they were dusted properly.

The elder Miss Entwhistle kindly offered to escort Mrs. Saunders and Cecily over the manor's finest chambers. Sir Ralph held the door open for the three women, also excusing himself.

"I am expecting something to be delivered soon," he said, giving Audra a broad wink. "But I shan't tell even you what it is, Miss Masters. Quite a surprise. If it arrives soon, I may let you have a peek at it."

After this remark, which was clearly intended to tantalize her, Sir Ralph grinned and quit the room, his dogs galumphing after him.

Far from being intrigued, Audra supposed he must be talking about some new hunter or hound. In either case, she was not interested in viewing any animal that soon would suffer from Sir Ralph's careless handling.

As odious as she found Sir Ralph's presence, she almost regretted his going. She was now left entirely alone with Miss Georgianna Entwhistle, a painfully shy young woman. Holding a conversation with her was next to impossible. Audra felt something akin to a toothdrawer, extracting sentences from the girl syllable by syllable.

She was glad of any interruption, even when it was only the Entwhistle butler come to announce the arrival of another caller. That was, until the manservant made his stiff bow and said, "The Duke of Raeburn awaits in the hall, miss."

In the act of sipping her tea, Audra choked. Miss Georgianna's reaction was no less spectacular. Dropping her slice of bread buttered side down on her frock, she cried out, "The duke! Oh, dear, oh dear. What should I do, Miss Masters? If only Sophia was here. Should I receive His Grace myself?"

It was all Audra could do to refrain from shouting out a resounding, "No." It would have been to no avail in any case for the flustered Georgianna did not wait for her answer. She bade the butler to show His Grace in.

Wringing her hands, Miss Georgianna gave Audra a nervous smile. "S-such an unlooked-for honor. His Grace has never before . . . Well, he does have a way of appearing in the most unexpected fashion, does he not?"

"Like the very devil," Audra murmured. "In another day, he would have been burned at the stake for sorcery."

Georgianna looked considerably startled by this remark, but

157

Audra was spared the trouble of trying to explain it by the arrival of Raeburn himself.

Of a sudden, he seemed to loom in the doorway, like the brooding dark wizard that he was. Audra stiffened. If there was anyplace in the shire she should have been safe from such a chance encounter, it was here at Grayhawk Manor, the home of a man Raeburn held in contempt.

But then, Audra could not help entertaining the suspicion it was none of the Entwhistles the duke had come to see. After all, Cecily had informed His Grace exactly where she would be that afternoon.

Audra's suspicion only deepened when Raeburn strode into the room. He bent over Miss Georgianna's hand, terrifying her with his gruff, "How do you do, madam." But it was at Audra he stared, one brow arched in inquiry, his eyes dark with challenge.

It was a challenge Audra felt unequal to meeting. Her heart thumping madly, she wished she had time to compose herself. How did a woman go about calmly greeting a rejected suitor? She was constantly finding herself pitchforked into these situations the deportment books never covered.

In an agony of embarrassment, she managed to get out little more than a curt, "Good afternoon, Your Grace."

When the other three women returned from touring the house, Audra took the first available opportunity to escape to the other end of the room, pretending to be deeply absorbed by the view out the window, although through the haze of her turbulent emotions, she saw nothing.

Neither the Misses Entwhistle nor Cecily were forceful enough to keep Raeburn engaged in conversation, but Audra assumed that her aunt would be. She was wrong. On the pretext of bringing her another cup of tea, Raeburn joined her at the window.

"Attempting to cut my acquaintance, Miss Masters?" he drawled softly.

"N-no," she stammered. "I was merely admiring the view. There is the most charming . . ." She paused, squinting past the curtains. Exactly what was out there?

"Stables, Miss Masters. They are called stables. It is where the horses are kept." With a wry half-smile, he offered her the cup and saucer, but she shook her head. Her hands were trembling so badly, she did not dare accept it.

He set the china down while she played nervously with the lace at the throat of her gown. She could not bring herself to look at him, but she was all too aware of his presence, how close he stood. It was an idiotic thing to be realizing at this particular moment, but how much she had missed the wretched man these past days, the gruff sound of his voice.

"How astonishing to see *you* here this afternoon," she said to cover her own confusion. "I know Sir Ralph is not exactly a favorite of yours."

"Nor yours either," he reminded her. "Myself, I felt the need of a little company. It is rather dull at the castle. My sister returned to Hampstead yesterday, you know."

"No, I had not heard."

"I fear Gus left rather disheartened. All that effort she put into hostessing that ball to see me leg-shackled to some proper young lady, and now, not a prospective duchess to show for it."

"Lady Augusta can scarce blame you for that. I am sure you did your best to . . . to find a bride."

"Did I? I am beginning to think I might have given up far too easily. You look very pale, Audra. Your sister tells me you have been ill."

"Cecily is a goose!" she said with a fierce blush, then admitted reluctantly, "Perhaps I have been feeling a little strange of late. But 'tis nothing fatal, I assure you. I will recover."

"Likely you will, m'dear. But why do you want to?"

Glancing up, her eyes locked with his, and for a moment, Audra could not recollect the reason herself. The conversation seemed to have slipped into very dangerous channels. Wrenching her gaze away, she took a step back murmuring, "Perhaps we should both return to our seats, Your Grace. I fear my aunt is staring at us."

This was perfectly true. Mrs. Saunders had trained her lorgnette upon their tête-à-tête with a disapproving frown.

Skirting past Raeburn, Audra resumed her place among the other ladies.

Simon made no immediate effort to follow suit. Silently cursing himself for a fool, he thought that he should never have come to Grayhawk Manor. He had only decided to do so earlier that day after he had spoken with Cecily in the lane. The girl's innocent prattle had let slip the interesting fact that Audra had been behaving in ways most unlike herself of late.

Indeed she must be to ever consider crossing Sir Ralph's threshold, a man she quite detested. Since Audra's rejection of his suit, stubborn pride had kept Simon from pursuing her any further. But Cecily's report of her sister's listless manner had intrigued him, given him cause for hope. Enough so that he felt he must see Audra again.

One look into her eyes had told him she'd been as miserable as he these past days. But at his gentle probing, he had watched the familiar alarm chase across her features, making her once more ready to bolt.

Perhaps he had turned out to be a very poor dragon after all, so easily turned aside by her wall of thorns. But he knew he could be as fierce and demanding as he pleased, but to no avail. There were some fears the lady could only conquer herself.

He had accomplished nothing by coming here except perhaps to stir the embers of his own frustration and disappointment. Consequently, he prepared to take his leave when the parlor door opened to admit Sir Ralph.

The baronet's portly features were flushed red with excitement. "B'gawd, it has arrived. You must all come out at once."

Simon did not have the damnedest notion what *it* was, nor much interest in finding out. But Sir Ralph clearly meant to give none of them any peace until they had all trooped outside to view his latest acquisition.

While the ladies gathered up their shawls, Simon retrieved his own Garrick and high-crowned hat from the butler. Sir Ralph led them out to the front of the house. Simon perceived nothing remarkable, only a horse and cart pulled to on the gravel drive. Sir Ralph's huntsman was unloading what appeared to be a small cage from the back of the cart.

160

Upon closer inspection, Simon realized that cowering behind the wire mesh was a small silver-gray fox, the cub's large liquid eyes wide with terror.

"Oh, how sweet," cooed Cecily.

"Vermin!" Mrs. Saunders shuddered.

"No, a *vixen*," Sir Ralph said. "Confiscated it from one of my tenants. The demned fool had found an entire litter of foxes abandoned and never told me. This is the only one survived and he was letting his daughter keep it as a pet. Of all the nonsense."

The baronet chuckled, giving Simon a nudge. "After this beauty's raised to be a mite bigger, the little vixen should provide my hounds with some good sport, eh, Your Grace?"

Raeburn vouchsafed no answer, merely glowering in disgust at Entwhistle's notion of sport. But disgust was too mild a word to apply to Audra's reaction. She turned quite pale, the stricken look in her eyes not much different from the vixen trapped within the cage.

Shivering in the chill November air, the other ladies soon lost interest and returned to the drawing room. Sir Ralph had stepped round to the front of the cart to deliver some instructions regarding the disposition of the fox to his huntsman.

But Audra bit down upon her lip, seeming unable to tear herself away. As her head came slowly up, never had she appeared so vulnerable, her gaze meeting Simon's in mute appeal.

He swore under his breath, knowing he was about to make a great cake of himself. He would be lucky if that fool Entwhistle did not have a fit of apoplexy, but he hunkered down anyway and began to undo the latch of the cage.

The fox crouched away from him in fear. Simon proceeded with caution. Even if the vixen had been raised as a pet, it was still a thing of the wilds.

"Oh, be careful. She might bite you," Audra said, bending down beside him. "Here, take my shawl."

Whipping it from her shoulders, she handed him the soft length of wool. Simon managed to catch the vixen up in the bright folds. Although the animal trembled and shivered, it offered no resistance.

161

As he placed the bundled cub into Audra's eager out-stretched hands, Simon had his reward. For the first time since she had rejected his proposal, she smiled at him.

Raeburn was not given long to bask in the moment, for Sir Ralph had become aware that some mischief was afoot.

"What the deuce!" he shouted, coming round the side of the cart. Simon prepared to head him off, but he saw Audra straighten, the spark of fire coming into her eyes and knew that Entwhistle was about to receive the trimming of his life.

"What the blazes are you planning to do with my fox, Miss Masters?" Sir Ralph demanded with a scowl.

"Run," she gasped out.

This strange answer was not the furious response that Raeburn had expected, any more than the look of panic that overtook her. But he fast saw the reason for this sudden change in expression. It was not inspired by fear of Entwhistle but of three large hounds that came loping up from the stableyard.

On such a cold, cloudy day, the scent of fox carried quite clearly. The dogs would have no difficulty locating their prey, even if the terrified vixen had not been peeking out from the folds of the shawl.

With a loud baying, the hounds charged in Audra's direction. She turned to flee, attempting to hold the cub high out of reach. Raeburn managed to collar one of the dogs, but Sir Ralph's cursing and kicking out with his thick boots only made the situation worse.

Audra feared the wisest course might have been to return the fox to the safety of its cage, but it was too late for that now. One of the dogs was already leaping at her skirts. Her only escape seemed to lie in the direction of the house.

Stumbling up the steps, beneath the portico of the gray stone Georgian manor, she heard Raeburn's shouts behind her above the din of the dogs and Sir Ralph's bellows. But the undisciplined hounds heeded neither of the two men.

With a mighty jump, the largest dog caught the end of the shawl in its powerful jaws. Audra shoved frantically at the manor's heavy oak door, stumbling inside. As she sought to bar the dogs entry, the terrified vixen sank its teeth into Audra's hand.

She cried out at the sharp pain, dropping both shawl and fox, letting the door swing wide. The animal streaked across the hall in a blur of gray, the dogs hard after it. It was unfortunate that Mrs. Saunders chose that particular moment to fling open the drawing room door, demanding, "What is this unseemly—"

Her sentence trailed off in a gasp as the fox shot past her skirts. She had no time to recover before the two dogs rushed forward, knocking her over in their frantic haste.

The pandemonium that followed would remain forever a merciful blur in Audra's mind. She would recollect nothing but a scene of confusion, shrieking women, shattering china, barking dogs.

How long the chaos might have continued she did not know, except that Raeburn had the presence of mind to fling open a window, offering the fox an avenue of escape. With the aid of Sir Ralph's huntsman, he got the dogs under control and removed from the parlor.

Only then did Audra fully realize what a fright she had had. She sank down into an armchair, trembling, clutching her injured hand. Grimacing, she surveyed the disaster that was the drawing room. Bits of broken saucers were strewn everywhere, tables overturned, tea soaking a stain into the carpet. The elder Miss Entwhistle lay moaning upon the settee while Cecily and Georgianna strove to revive her with smelling salts. Aunt Saunders pursed her lips, staring at the muddied paw prints on her gown.

The only one who appeared calm was Raeburn. He produced his handkerchief and stanched the trickle of blood escaping from Audra's wound.

"Fetch me some brandy, Entwhistle," he snapped.

But Sir Ralph was too preoccupied lamenting the loss of his fox. "B'gawd, sir," he bawled. "You've cost me one of the likeliest little vixens I ever saw. I should call you out for this. So I should."

But one black look from Raeburn put a stop to the baronet's

bluster. Unfortunately Mrs. Saunders was not so easily silenced. As soon as she had recovered from her shock, she rounded upon Audra in an icy fury.

"You! You are to blame for this vulgar incident."

"The fault lies more with me, madam," Raeburn began, but Mrs. Saunders took no heed of him, continuing to lash out at Audra.

"This was all a malicious jest, another example of your coarse sense of humor. You set those dogs in here on purpose."

"Of course, I did not, Aunt," Audra said wearily.

"I thought you had finally changed, abandoned your odd ways, acquired some notion of proper conduct. But you still have no more notion how to be a lady than the veriest trollop. Any more so than your mama ever had. I completely wash my hands of you this time. I never intend to set foot beneath any roof that harbors you again."

Audra heard Raeburn draw in an angry breath, but before he could say anything, she placed her hand firmly on his, giving a warning squeeze.

"I quite understand, Aunt Saunders," she faltered. "But you will not hold this against Cecily? You will still take her to London?"

"Of course. If for no other reason than to remove the child from your deplorable sphere of influence."

"Well, I won't go!" Cecily's sudden passionate declaration startled them all, rendering even Mrs. Saunders momentarily speechless. The girl straightened from bending over Miss Entwhistle. Cecily's delicate features were flushed.

"Muffin . . ." Audra tried to caution her, but she had never seen her younger sister tremble with such indignation.

Tears stinging her blue eyes, Cecily stomped her small foot. "You have done nothing but insult my sister ever since you came to Meadow Lane, Aunt Saunders, and I am wearied of it. If you are going to be this mean to Audra, I wish that you had never come to visit us, never invited me to your house."

Mrs. Saunders's lips thinned, her eyes turning to slivers of ice. "Your wish is easily granted, child."

In a state of high dudgeon, she stalked from the room. Raeburn whistled softly under his breath, eying Cecily with admiration. Audra had to swallow past a lump in her throat. Although she was deeply moved by her sister's unexpected championship, she could not help exclaiming, "Oh, Muffin! What *have* you done?"

Cecily gave a shrug that was a shade too careless. " 'Tis of no consequence, Audra. Who wanted to go to dull old London anyway?"

After which heroic declaration, she burst into tears and sank down, burying her face in Audra's lap.

Chapter 11

Upon her return to Meadow Lane Lodge, Mrs. Saunders wasted no time in gathering up her maid and her belongings. She would not spend so much as another night in the company of such ungrateful hoydens as both her nieces had shown themselves to be. Drained herself by the day's events, Audra made no effort to dissuade her.

She was far too preoccupied with soothing Cecily. Suffering from a state of overexcitement and keen disappointment, the girl had wept herself into a megrim. After administering some hartshorn to her sister, Audra felt relieved when Cecily drifted off to sleep.

She was not on hand to witness Mrs. Saunders's departure. The sky had just darkened to a shade of deep purple when that outraged lady flounced out to her carriage. Audra very civilly accompanied her, waiting until she saw her aunt safely bestowed inside the coach, although Mrs. Saunders refused to even bid her farewell.

Audra stepped back as the coachman whipped up the team.

The carriage had not even reached the bend in the lane when the Duke of Raeburn's mount galloped into sight. Raeburn cheerfully tipped his hat to the passing coach, a gesture that, Audra was certain, went quite unacknowledged.

She lingered on her doorstep, watching the duke's approach, for once not surprised to see him. Somehow she had known he would come to her this evening.

He drew rein in front of the cottage, the wind whipping at the ends of his riding cape. As he stared down at her, his half smile glinted in the gathering dusk.

"I take it you are at home this time, Miss Masters?"

"I believe so, Your Grace," she said demurely.

Dismounting, he consigned his horse to the care of one of her grooms, then followed Audra inside. Mrs. McGuiness sniffed with disapproval to discover that Audra had usurped her prerogative of admitting visitors, but she bustled away to fetch refreshments to the parlor.

Still chilled from being out of doors without her shawl, Audra stepped near the fire, holding out her hands to the blaze to warm them. Although very conscious of Raeburn's nearness, she felt strangely calm.

"I saw your aunt leaving posthaste," the duke remarked. "Such dire consequences of our little adventure this afternoon. Do you know that Sir Ralph has vowed never to invite either of us to tea again?"

A wry smile escaped Audra. "I think we shall manage to survive."

"How is your hand?" he asked, stepping closer. "You must take care not to let it become infected. Does it still hurt?"

Audra shook her head. Her calm threatened to desert her at the prospect of his touch. But she made no movement to pull away when he took her hand, examining the bandagings wrapped about her wrist.

Raeburn swore softly. "I am sorry, Audra. The entire disaster was all my doing. If I had not removed that blasted fox from its cage—"

"You only did so to please me. I doubt one man in a hundred would understand my foolish tenderheartedness toward ani-

166

mals. And you are the only one I know who would have acted upon it."

"I suppose that makes us both quite mad."

"Perhaps we are. Cecily says—" She broke off, blushing a little.

"Yes?" he prompted.

"She says that we are well matched."

"What a wise child."

"A most unhappy one. That is my one regret about what happened today. I don't care a fig for the Entwhistles or my aunt's goodwill. But I do feel so wretched about being the cause of Cecily's losing her London Season."

"There is a solution to the problem."

"Don't suggest that I write to my mother. You must know as well as I how futile—"

"I was thinking more about my sister."

"Lady Augusta?"

"You have no notion how fond Gus is of playing match-maker. It would give her the greatest delight to sponsor your sister. Such a treat might even make up to her for all the torment I have put her through these past weeks."

"If you truly think so," Audra said doubtfully. "It would be a wonderful thing for Cecily. The greatest of favors. I have no idea how I would ever repay you for such a kindness."

"Do not look so uneasy about it. I would not demand anything unreasonable such as your marrying me, though I still think that would be a very good notion."

"Perhaps it would be, especially when I need to ask you another favor."

He eyed her questioningly.

"I wondered if it is too late . . . That is, could you instruct your estate agent, Mr. Wylie, not to look out for another tenant. I find I am not so eager to . . . to run away as I thought."

Another man might have required more, but Raeburn would never be the sort to need lengthy explanations. He merely held his arms wide, tenderly pronouncing her name.

"Audra."

She stepped into them, burying her face against his shoulder. He held her close, brushing his lips against her hair.

"You must still be patient with me, Raeburn. I have been a spinster for a long time. After watching Mama so often make a fool of herself, I still find the prospect of being in love quite terrifying."

"You think I do not?" he said, pulling her closer. Gazing down at her tenderly, he said, "We shall take all the time that you need. Even after the banns are cried, you will have three weeks to cry off."

He bent to kiss her, when something dropped from his pocket. She was astonished to see that it was a copy of *Ivanhoe*.

"Your sister told me what her dog had done to yours," he said. "I thought I would lend you mine."

Audra seized it eagerly. "I thought I should never know what became of Ivanhoe and his lady at the end of the book."

"If you like," Raeburn said. "I would be only too happy to demonstrate." Yanking her hard against him, his mouth sought hers in a long, lingering kiss.

The hazy thought crossed Audra's mind. In many ways, Raeburn was far superior to anything in her library. As she tightened her arms about him, the book slipped from her grasp entirely unnoticed.

THE BISHOP'S
DAUGHTER

Chapter 1

Lord Harcourt Arundel never expected a hero's welcome, even though he had been wounded at Waterloo. As he trudged along the lane, leading his dun-colored gelding by the reins, his portmanteau strapped back of the saddle, he felt neither particularly lordly nor heroic. His top boots, buckskins, and frock coat caked with dust, his sun-bronzed features streaked with sweat, what Lord Harry felt was tired.

Still, after a year's absence from his Northamptonshire estate, he would have thought there might be at least one face to smile upon him, someone to bob a curtsy by way of greeting to the returning Earl of Lytton. Yet the only soul stirring was a mongrel dog panting in the shade of the hedgerows, too affected by the heat radiating from the August sun to even bark.

Shading eyes the hue of hunter's green, Lord Harry peered across the empty expanse of his fields, the tall waves of rye but half-cut, the grain corded in neat bundles waiting to be loaded upon the wagons.

Harry frowned, his thick brows as startlingly black as the lustrous waves of his hair. "Where the deuce is everyone?" he muttered.

He had never paid half the attention that he should have to the farming operations on his own land, but even he knew how crucial it was to bring in the rye as soon as it had ripened. Yet the fields bore that tranquil Sunday kind of stillness, although it was near noon of a Saturday.

" 'Twould seem they all heard Hellfire Harry was coming back and took to their heels, eh Ramses?" Lord Harry said, reaching up to pat his horse's neck. Though still puzzled, the frown that was so foreign to Harry's countenance faded to his customary easy smile as he reflected that the only one likely to retreat at his approach would be his stepmother.

His unheralded return would undoubtedly give Sybil a megrim. His presence had been doing so ever since he was seven and first introduced to his new mama, and the condition had not abated a jot these past twenty years.

"Oh, Harry," the Dowager Countess of Lytton would be sure to exclaim, reaching for her smelling salts with a shudder. "You—you look so hale. So robust."

How or why his unfailing good health invariably made his stepmother feel ill, Harry had never been able to fathom. He merely accepted the fact with the philosophical cheerfulness he treated all his fellow creatures' foibles.

The same spirit of tolerance caused him to spare only one more glance for his deserted fields, the obvious evidence of his steward's neglect. Then with a shrug of his broad shoulders, he tugged at Ramses's reins and marched on. The movement, slight as it was, caused a pain to shoot along Harry's left arm.

That shoulder but two months ago had played host to a chunk of shrapnel from a mortar exploding near him in the very thick of battle. The army surgeon had said the wound had healed remarkably well, but he had warned Harry to take the journey home in easy stages.

Harry never did anything in easy stages. Even now he felt more concern for his horse than himself. Ramses had picked up a stone just outside the village of Lytton's Dene. Although Harry had managed to remove it, the soft portion of Ramses's hoof remained bruised and tender.

As he led the halting animal, he murmured words of encouragement, "Not much further now, old fellow. We'll soon have a poultice slapped on that hoof and after a few days' rest, you'll be fit to go."

Harry hoped he would not have to lead the horse the entire way round the park to the drive winding up to Mapleshade Hall, his principal country seat. The stone fence at the back of the park had ever been a crumbling ruin, and Harry trusted that no one would have seen fit to repair it in his absence.

His trust was not misplaced. As the fields sloped away to become woodland, Harry saw that the stonework, far from being repaired, had eroded a little further. There was no difficulty about leading Ramses through the break, thus shortening the journey to the stable by at least half a mile.

And it was not as if anyone up at the hall would be looking out eagerly for Harry's return. Not with his own father dead these past six years. There would be no one to reproach him for not making haste to enter the house. It might have been entirely another matter if Miss Kathryn Towers had returned him a different answer to a certain question. . . .

Harry expelled a faint sigh as he led his horse deeper into the shadows of the timberland. He had not meant to think of Kate. The dappled light filtering through the trees' foliage faded as memory misted before his eyes. Two years had passed since that spring, yet he could still envision Kate so clearly, the warm breeze teasing the dusky locks of her hair, the fragile flowers being unconsciously plucked apart by her slender white fingers as she stood with her back to him. She had looked so soft, so vulnerable, all of a woman with none of the primness of the Bishop of Chillingsworth's daughter about her.

"I don't expect you to understand, Harry," she had said in that low musical voice of hers, "any of the reasons why I cannot marry you."

It was then he should have summoned up all the eloquence and persuasiveness at his command. God knows he could be glib enough upon all other occasions. Why, when he wanted to be tender, did the words seem to form a lump at the base of his throat? He had swallowed that lump and said in teasing tones, "It will do you no good, Kate, to stand there, wreaking havoc upon those poor flowers. I shan't take no for an answer. You shall never be rid of me until you can look me in the eye and tell me you don't love me."

Gripping her shoulders, he had forced her to come about and face him, intending to express all that he could not say with the warmth of his kiss. But she had stiffened and he had felt a tremor pass through her. After a heartbeat of hesitation, she had gazed upon him, her eyes so steady, so clear, the same vivid shade as the violets tumbling heedlessly from her hands. His Kate was gone. It was the bishop's daughter who answered him.

"I don't love you, my lord."

Remembrance of those words pierced Harry with a sharp ache, but no bitterness. Never had he ever felt any bitterness toward Kate, only a sense of longing, a melancholy that sometimes he could shrug off with a quick laugh and sometimes he couldn't.

As he tromped through the woods, each step taking him closer to the empty grandeur of Mapleshade, he felt more than usually prey to gloom and was glad when a diversion occurred to banish Kate's image from his mind.

The sharp crackling of a twig alerted Harry that he was no longer alone. He glanced up eagerly. After the unnatural quiet of the fields, he thought that he would be glad of the sight of any familiar face, even if it should prove to be only Jergens, his dour gameskeeper.

But the sprightly little man who came slipping through the bracken was not Jergens. Balancing a wriggling brown sack upon his shoulder, the shrewd-featured fellow paused to glance over his shoulder, the hairs of his thick red beard seeming to bristle like the fur of a fox scenting pursuit.

Harry's mouth widened to a grin as he recognized Tim Keegan. An itinerant Irish laborer hired on for the extra work at the harvest every summer, the rogue had a habit of "borrowing" hares from his lordship's coveys. Judging from the movement of the sack, Keegan must have snared himself a plump one this time.

Intent upon peering behind him for any sign of the gameskeeper, Keegan took no note of Lord Harry. Regarding the little man's furtive movements with amusement, Harry folded his arms across his chest and waited until Keegan had all but backed into Ramses.

"Halloo, Keegan," Harry said.

The soft greeting nearly caused the Irishman to shoot out of his boots. As his startled gaze fell upon Harry, Keegan's eyes bulged. All color drained from his florid features. He dropped the sack and crossed himself with a loud wail. "Sweet holy Mary, Mother of God defend me."

"Steady on, old man. I never intended to give you that much of a fright." Harry gave Keegan a bracing clap on the shoulder, but far from reassuring the man, it caused Keegan to shrink away, flinging up one hand as though to ward off a blow.

"Saints above! I'll be after putting the rabbit back straightaway, that I will. Just don't be a-haunting me, yer lardship."

Haunting him? What was the fool talking about? Keegan took a sidestep, preparing to bolt. Harry prevented him by catching hold of his coattails.

"What is the matter with you, Keegan?" Securing a firm grip on the man's trembling arm, Harry brought him about, demanding, "Now when have I ever cut up stiff over a plaguey rabbit? I only want to ask you a few questions."

"Questions!" From Keegan's terrified howl, he might have been about to face the Spanish Inquisition.

"Why aren't you at work in the fields? And where is everyone else? I have not seen a soul since passing by the crossroads to the village."

"They—they all be gived the ar'ternoon off to have a look at the memorial an' it please yer worship."

"Memorial? What memorial? Who has died?"

"Why . . . why, *yerself,* me lard."

Keegan's doleful reply startled Harry so much, he released the Irishman.

"Myself?" Harry repeated. Keegan had either had a spot too much of the sun or had been tippling the usquebaugh again. Harry chuckled. "I suppose at the moment I do look like something that has just crept from the grave, and I am nigh dead with fatigue, but—"

"Oh, no. Beggin' yer lardship's pardon," Keegan interrupted tremulously. "Ye must have forgotten. It wasn't fatigue as took yer lardship off, but a great nasty cannonball as smashed off yer head."

His words carried such conviction that Harry had to suppress an urge to touch his own head to make certain it was still affixed to his shoulders.

"Where did you come by such a rum tale as that?" he asked.

" 'Twas yer good vicar Thorpe, me lard."

The vicar? Harry grimaced. That, at least, explained Timothy Keegan's belief that he must be seeing a shade from the other world. Any utterance made by Harry's cousin, the most holy Reverend Adolphus Thorpe, was regarded in the village as being a pronouncement from God, even by a Catholic like Keegan.

"You can plainly see that I am not dead," Harry said. "You must have misunderstood what Reverend Thorpe told you."

"Did I indeed, soor?" Keegan asked, keeping a wary distance between himself and Harry. "Then what about the memorial and the deddycashun this ar-ternoon?"

"The deddy-what?"

"Deddycashun. 'Tis my understandin' 'tis to be sort of a wake for yer lardship, only without the food and drink, which doesn't make it much of a wake a'tall to my way of thinkin'." Keegan fixed Harry with a pitying gaze. "Shabby, I calls it. Ye might as well not even have died."

"But I didn't——" Harry broke off, torn between amusement and exasperation at the absurdity of the conversation. Exhausted as he was and eager to get Ramses to the stable, he did not know why he was stopping to bandy words with this madman. Perhaps it was because the mystery of his empty fields yet remained, and Keegan was so adamant about the memorial.

Was it possible that some ridiculous mistake had occurred and everyone else at Mapleshade also presumed Harry to be— No, impossible!

True, he had taken no pains to communicate with his family since Waterloo, but plenty of his returning comrades knew he was not dead. And the British Army certainly knew it had been no ghost captain who had recently sold his commission. There was no reason that any false report could have been carried back to his home.

Having convinced himself that this was so, Harry could not say why he still felt uneasy. Nor why, instead of pursuing his course toward the stables, he turned to Keegan and said, "Perhaps you had better be showing me this memorial."

The superstitious Keegan did not evince much enthusiasm for accompanying one he persisted in viewing as a ghost. But after Harry had pressed a guinea into his hand and told him he might keep the rabbit besides, Keegan cheerfully declared he would be willing to guide the devil himself under such terms.

"Yer ever as generous a man dead as ye were alive, me lard." Keegan beamed, retrieving the sack. "The memorial be right this way, atop the Hill."

Biting back a smile, Harry followed him, although with this information, he scarce had need of Keegan any longer. In this gently rolling section of Northamptonshire, there was only one slope hereabouts that merited the name, the Hill, being a part of Harry's own parklands. It had ever been Harry's favorite spot those rare times he desired solitude. From the summit, he could gaze down upon his own woods, the lily-bedecked pond, the grassy expanse where deer often grazed, even the distant chimneys of the hall itself. It had been to the Hill that he had retreated as a lad when his favorite pony had broken its leg and had to be destroyed; there, as a man, that he had gone when his father had died; there that he had brought Kate to ask her to be his bride; there that she had refused.

As the tree line thinned and he and Keegan emerged from the shelter of the trees, Harry expected to find his Hill as ever, green, quiet, undisturbed.

He was brought up short by the mass of humanity swarming over it. Only yards ahead of him were his missing farm laborers, mingling with what appeared to be the better part of the villagers from Lytton's Dene. Heavy boots trampled the daisies underfoot, while homespun skirts brushed the grass. This group kept a respectful distance from the denizens of Mapleshade, those servants who staffed Harry's stables and the massive hall itself. At the head of these, Harry could make out the forms of some silk-clad ladies and gentlemen, among them, his nearest neighbors, the portly Squire Gresham and his lady; his own stepmother garbed in deepest mourning; and his cousins, the stately, beautiful Julia Thorpe and her brother, the vicar.

The sunlight gleamed off Adolphus's fair hair as, like an anxious shepherd, that reverend gentleman assembled this rather mixed flock at the Hill's summit where stood some massive, mysterious object draped with canvas.

"Good God!" Harry breathed, no longer able to deny the significance of the scene before him. "It would seem you are right, Mr. Keegan," he said dryly. "I *am* dead."

"Wasn't I after tellin' yer lardship so."

Harry could only shake his head, still unable to fathom how such a ridiculous misunderstanding could have happened. Nor how this gathering on the hillside had come about.

"Why didn't they just hold the service down in the church?" he mused aloud. "I know Adolphus always thought I was paving hell with a vengeance. But I can't believe that even he would refuse me the last rites."

"Oh, nay, me lard. They had you a proper church service, so they did. But this memorial, I heerd tell, was your stepmama's notion, herself wantin' all to remember what a hero ye were."

Harry felt both surprised and touched by this gesture on Sybil's part until Keegan added, "An' it gave her a wonderful chance to throw a dab of work in the way of her friend, Mr. Crosbie."

Harry stiffened at the mention of Lucillus Crosbie, a would-be sculptor. Man-milliner and fortune hunter were two of the kinder epithets Harry had bestowed upon the man. The last time he had been home, a year ago, he had caught Crosbie making sheep's eyes at his stepmother and had introduced the impertinent fellow to the fish at the bottom of Mapleshade's pond. Harry had thought to have seen the last of him. Apparently Lucillus had wasted little time reinstating himself into Sybil's graces when Harry had been reported dead.

Thrusting Ramses's reins at Keegan, Harry bade him look after the horse. "Much as I hate to disappoint everyone," he said. "I am afraid I must announce that I am so inconsiderate as to still be alive."

With that, Harry strode forward from the shelter of the trees and began to mount the Hill. He did not check his step until he reached the fringes of the crowd. It suddenly occurred to him that he might be about to cause consternation to others as he had Keegan by thus announcing his return from the dead. Yet glancing at the rapt expressions about him, Harry believed he could have dressed in a bedsheet and howled like a banshee without attracting attention. All eyes were riveted on Reverend Thorpe.

Harry suspected that most of those about him had attended less to pay final respects than out of curiosity. Harry certainly did not blame them for that. He was curious as hell himself as to what monstrosity of Crosbie's lay concealed beneath that canvas.

As he skirted the crowd, advancing ever higher up the Hill, the sound of the vicar's piercing voice began to carry to him in snatches. His cousin appeared to be delivering some sort of eulogy.

"And I trust that our dear Lord Lytton is at this moment enjoying all the blisses of heaven."

Harry grinned, for he knew full well that the righteous Adolphus was mentally consigning his wicked cousin to the hottest of flames. Reverend Thorpe's speech became even more disjointed as he tried to enumerate Harry's many virtues and was apparently having difficulty thinking of any.

At last the Reverend blurted out, "Er—a most godly man, an example to the entire community."

Harry, who by this time had arrived behind the squire, within a stone's throw of the monument, nearly choked. *Godly?* He, who had never seen the inside of a church since his christening day? And even then he had been carried screaming into the vestibule.

Harry saw that he had best step forward at once and save his cousin the embarrassment of coming out with any more such plumpers. But before he could edge past the squire's bulky frame, the vicar turned, stretching up one hand toward the canvas.

The crowd collectively held its breath as the vicar intoned, "This solemn edifice has been erected by a grieving mother to the memory of the most generous and affectionate of sons, a brave and bold hero whose life has been so tragically cut short. But with this likeness mounted upon the Hill, Lord Harcourt

179

Andrew Stephen Arundel, the fifth Earl of Lytton, will dwell among us forever."

As the canvas came away, Harry expected to see some awful representation of himself in stone, garbed in full military dress in one of those stiff, unnatural poses. As he gazed upward, he was as confounded as the rest of the assemblage. Mounted upon a plinth, rising to a full seven feet of glory, stood the muscular figure of man carved in Classical fashion, his tightly curling hair in nowise resembling Harry's own straight locks. But no one paid much heed to the head for the statue had been carved stark naked. Only the modest manner in which the figure held a sword before him prevented the full disclosure of his manhood.

A stunned hush fell over the crowd, then many of the women present let out shocked and delighted shrieks, while the men exclaimed.

"Damnation," the squire roared.

"Abomination!" The outraged vicar staggered back as though he had uncovered the devil himself.

"Exquisite," the Dowager Lady Lytton cooed, dabbing at her plump face with a black-edged handkerchief, taking pains not to mar the layering of paint meant to conceal her fifty-odd years.

"Ridiculous!" said the squire's thin wife. "It looks nothing like Lord Harry. He was never so thick about the waist, and I am sure he had a much finer set of legs—"

"Upon my word, madam." The squire leveled his wife an awful stare. "You seem to have made a thorough study of the matter."

Mrs. Gresham colored. "It is nothing that any woman . . . er . . . that is— *Anyone* who knew his lordship would say the same."

By this time, Harry feared the only mourner present with tears glistening in his eyes was himself as he struggled to contain his mirth. But as his gaze chanced upon his cousin Julia, affecting to look so prim, so disapproving, all the while she kept stealing glances upward at the statue's firmly muscled buttocks, it became entirely too much for Harry's self-control.

He burst into a roar of laughter that seemed to ring all the more loudly amid the astonished silence of the crowd.

Indignant faces turned toward him only to go pale with recognition. Through his peals of mirth he heard the gasps, his name rippling through the crowd like a rush of wind through the willows. His stepmother let out a piercing cry and clutched at her heart. The Reverend Thorpe so far forgot himself as to take the name of the Lord in vain.

Harry tried to speak, but couldn't. He could only glance helplessly about him, wishing he could find at least one other kindred spirit to share this moment, someone else who could see the humor of the situation.

Instead he encountered a face that drove the laughter from his lips, the last face in the world he had expected to encounter. Standing close to his shoulder was a solemn-looking lady garbed in pearl gray, so close that he wondered how he could have missed her before.

Harry experienced a shock not unlike the one he had felt when blasted from his saddle at Waterloo. He stared into violet eyes that registered a mingling of disbelief, joy, and reproach.

"Kate!" Harry cried hoarsely.

Kate's lips attempted to form his name as what little color she possessed drained from her cheeks. Harry retained just enough presence of mind to open his arms wide and catch her as she swayed into a dead faint.

Chapter 2

Miss Kathryn Towers had nearly decided not to attend the dedication of Lord Lytton's memorial. An hour before the ceremony was scheduled to begin, she had lingered in the parlor window seat of the cottage orné she shared with her mother in the village of Lytton's Dene.

It was unusual for Kate to sit idle for so long, staring vacantly out the window, but that is what she had been doing, her gaze fixing upon the elder bushes growing just beneath the latticed panes, their white blossoms thick among the greenery like a scattering of summer snow.

Snow . . . Would she ever be able to think of it again without also thinking of Harry? It had been winter when he had first come crashing, quite literally into her life, that last winter when Papa had still been alive. A sad, half smile tipped Kate's lips.

She had been bundled up in a fur-lined cloak, strolling in the garden of the Episcopal Palace at Chillingsworth, watching the deep blue of twilight fade to darkness. The full moon rose, shining a silvery glow over the snow-shrouded landscape, making the garden sparkle like crystal. The blanket of white had cast a hush over everything, an aura of enchantment, of expectancy as though something was about to happen. Or was that now only her imagination in looking back? For something *had* happened. . . .

A curricle had come smashing through the low-lying hedge, finishing up by knocking over the statue of John the Apostle. One wheel of the carriage broke, flinging its driver into what remained of the rose bed.

With a cry of alarm, Kate rushed forward, but the man was already climbing from the wreckage quite unperturbed, dusting snow from the torn capes of his garrick. As he went round to quiet his horse, he said, "Sorry, miss, but it was either your statue or a little urchin who slipped into the road."

"It—it was John the Apostle," Kate stammered.

"Who? The urchin?"

"No, the statue," she said solemnly.

For some reason, that made the stranger laugh. "Rather odd place to keep an apostle."

Secretly Kate agreed with him. She had always said the statue was placed far too close to the hedge, although she would not have expressed her opinion in quite the same manner.

182

As the moonlight outlined his profile, the thick waves of coal dark hair, the strong, stubborn jawline, she recognized who he was. Kate felt a tingling of alarm as she realized it was a most dangerous man who had invaded her garden. Even she had heard of Hellfire Harry, the wild young Earl of Lytton who frequently drove in from his estates to Chillingsworth. Not to attend services in the cathedral either, but to engage in such vulgar pursuits as attending race meets and prize fights or to carouse with his friends in one of the taverns.

But when she noticed his forehead was bleeding, all thoughts of Harry's dubious reputation had been swept from her mind. As the bishop's daughter, she had no choice but to invite him into the palace, even though the bishop was gone to read the services at evensong and her mother was away attending the confinement of one of her dearest friends.

Nor had she any choice but to see to his wound, although he would only permit her to do so after he had made sure that his horse was well cared for. As she had prepared to place sticking plaster on the cut, she found herself studying his lordship's face. He was perhaps more handsome at close range than he had appeared those times she had glimpsed him from a distance, his features, even in the winter, bearing the rugged, healthy appearance of a man who spends most of his time out of doors. Kathryn had always supposed that one as reportedly wicked as Lord Lytton would bear some signs of it in his countenance, a hinting of dissipation.

But there was naught of the hardened roué about Harry's face, only a clean strength in the angular line of his jaw, an almost boyishness in the jet black strand of hair that tumbled across his forehead, mischief lurking in the most vivid green eyes Kate had ever seen.

With her parents gone, she should never have encouraged him to stay, but how could she turn an injured man from her doorstep? She asked him to partake of tea.

She could still remember how awkward his large hands had looked balancing the dainty Sevres cup, heroically screwing up his face with each sip he took. She sat upon the settee, mending the tear in his garrick, the snow softly falling outside the tall windows, the fire blazing on the hearth, the deep sound of Harry's voice rumbling pleasantly in her ears. She could not remember exactly what outrageous things he had said, only that she had never smiled and blushed so much in her life.

From time to time she peeked up from her work to steal glances at him. Her father had raised her to be wary, to place no value on mere handsomeness. It was the beauties of a man's character that mattered.

But why had not the bishop seen fit to warn her how dangerous green eyes could be, eyes that crinkled at the corners when a man laughed and a smile that came so warm, so ready, so utterly disarming?

A smile that Kate could scarce bring herself to believe she would never see again. . . .

"Kate?" Her mother's voice had cut through Kate's haze of memories. Rather reluctantly, she turned to face the tiny wisp of a woman who stood regarding her. Although it had been two years since Papa's death, her mother still wore her simple black gowns, the white lace of her widow's cap most becoming to her silvery blond hair and the soft contours of her face. Maisie Towers's plain countenance bore the lines of her years, but her eyes remained the same deep violet shade as Kate's, although Kate often felt that her mother's held more of a sweetness of expression than her own.

"It is nearly past noon. You have decided not to attend the dedication after all?" Mrs. Towers asked, a hint of relief in her tones.

At that moment, with Harry's memory so fresh, so poignant in her mind, Kate wished she could cry out, no, she did not wish to go. Her mourning for Harry had ever been a private matter. Indeed, she almost felt as though she was not entitled to any grief, having turned Harry away. She didn't want to attend the dedication, be expected to admire some horrid memorial. Harry had not been the kind of man whose image could be captured in cold, unfeeling stone.

When Kate took so long about answering, her mother sank down beside her on the window seat. Rather diffidently, she covered one of Kate's hands with her own.

"You don't have to go if you don't want to, Kate," Mrs. Towers said. "I could offer some excuse to the vicar's sister when she comes to call for you."

Gazing into her mother's eyes, Kate found an unexpected amount of sympathy. She wanted to cast herself into her mother's arms and burst into tears. But Mrs. Towers's health had ever been delicate. Even as a child, Kate had known she must not distress Mama with her own miseries. And indeed how could anyone as gentle and uncomplicated as her mother possibly understand the bewildering conflict of Kate's emotions about Harry? She scarce understood them herself.

Suppressing a sigh, Kate drew her hand back from her mother's comforting warmth.

"Of course, I must attend the dedication, Mama," she said. "It is my duty."

Mentally, Kate scolded herself for forgetting that. She was still the bishop's daughter, and no one knew better than Kate what was expected of one in that role.

"I realize that someone of our family should attend," her mother murmured, "but perhaps I should go instead."

"Oh, no, Mama. *You* out in this heat? Unthinkable."

"I am not so fragile as you would suppose, Kate. I should gladly do it to spare you—" Her mother broke off, looking uncomfortable. "Even though we never discussed it, I could not help noticing what passed between you and Lord Harry that winter. I thought you had developed a tendre for—"

"No!" Kate cried. Appalled by her own outburst, she rose to her feet and took a nervous turn about the small, cramped parlor. Forcing a smile to her lips, she said, "You are so romantical, Mama. How could I possibly have fallen in love with a man I knew Papa would strongly disapprove of?"

"I don't suppose you could, Kate." Mrs. Towers sighed. "You were ever the most sensible girl."

Why that pronouncement should make her mother look so melancholy, Kate did not understand. She felt rather relieved when they were interrupted by a light rap on the door. The plump, pretty maid, Mollie, came bouncing into the room, nearly knocking her father's bust of Thomas à Becket from its perch atop the pianoforte.

After the spaciousness of the palace, the Towers family belongings were crowded within the cottage. Kate's pianoforte abutted so close to the bookcase containing the bishop's religious tomes that the glass doors with their elegant tracery could scarce be opened.

As Kate rushed forward in time to save Becket, Mollie dipped into a curtsy, her cap ribbons fluttering saucily behind her.

"Mollie, I have told you to take more care when entering a room," Kate said.

"Sorry, Miss Kate. I was in that much of a hurry to tell you that Miss Thorpe be waiting outside with her carriage."

"Why didn't you show her in?"

Mollie thrust her nose upward in imitation of the vicar's sister. "Miss Thorpe did not *deign* to come inside, miss."

Kate frowned. But before she could rebuke the girl, Mrs. Towers said gently, "Thank you, Mollie. That will do."

With an unrepentant grin, Mollie ducked back out of the room. Sensing that her mother intended to make one final appeal to change her mind, and fearing that she might be weak enough to be persuaded, Kate also made haste. Gathering up her gloves from the window seat, she briskly put them on. Kissing her mother's cheek, she said, "I shall not be gone long, Mama. You must not worry about me."

Her mother's only reply had been a sad, wistful kind of smile.

Bustling out of the parlor, Kate paused before the pier glass in the tiny front vestibule only long enough to don her bonnet. Primping and fussing over one's appearance was the worst sort of vanity.

And it was not as though she had a great deal to fuss about, Kate thought wryly as she began to tie the satin ribbons beneath her chin in a modest bow. She was just passably pretty. Only Harry had ever said she was beautiful, but it had been one of those rare times he had not been teasing her. . . .

Kate's hands had stilled upon the ribbon. Staring at her reflection, she could find no beauty, only a quiet despair in eyes that seemed far too large for the pale oval of her face.

Averting her gaze, Kate forced her fingers back into brisk movement, finishing the bow, smoothing the tendrils of her dark ringlets already damp and curling overmuch from the heat. There was nothing wrong, she assured herself. She had been ill of late . . . the influenza. That was why she had no color.

Strange that this bout of influenza should have come upon you a month ago, a voice inside her jabbed. *About the same time you heard that Harry had been killed.*

But Kate chose to ignore the voice. With hands that trembled slightly, she retrieved her parasol from the hall stand and stepped out of the cottage's cool shelter into a hot flood of sunlight.

As she trudged down the path toward the garden gate, she stole one glance behind her. Never had the cottage with its ivy-covered walls and roof of bright green Colleystone tile seemed like such a place of refuge. If only Lady Lytton had not insisted that memorial be erected upon that same hill where she had last seen Harry. How was she ever to face the ordeal ahead of her, the rush of painful memories?

With all the dignity to be expected of the late Bishop of Chillingsworth's daughter, Kate adjured herself sternly. Squaring her shoulders, she turned, marching onward through the creaking wooden gate.

The Thorpes' barouche awaited her in the lane, the coachman patiently standing at the head of the team of bays. Kate had often heard the more spiteful among the villagers wondering why a country vicar should possess such an equipage, but as Julia Thorpe loftily reminded everyone, she and her brother *were* first cousins to an earl.

The coachman stepped forward to greet Kate and hand her into the carriage. As Kate blinked, adjusting her eyes to the coach's dark blue velvet interior, she discerned the figure of Miss Julia Thorpe in the opposite corner.

A tall, fair-haired woman, Miss Thorpe's blue gray eyes

187

showed signs of annoyance. However, at Kate's entrance, she abandoned the hard expression and summoned a frostly smile.

"Ah, there you are at last, Kathryn." To the coachman, Julia snapped, "Don't dawdle, Smythe. We are already likely to be late."

"Yes, miss."

As the coach door slammed closed, Kate sank down upon the seat opposite Julia. "I am sorry," she said. "I should have been ready when you called. I seem to have spent too much of the morning wool-gathering."

"My dear Kathryn, I perfectly understand. Quite frequently, it takes me longer to attire myself than I ever would have anticipated, but the end result is worth it. You look quite charming."

The compliment lost much of its force as Julia arched one pencil-thin brow and eyed Kate's gown in a dubious manner.

But Kate's serenity remained unruffled. She apologized to no one for the old-fashioned cut of her gowns. The pearl gray frock suited her with its low waist and soft flowing skirt, a lace-trimmed fichu draped about the shoulders, crossing modestly in the front. Her only ornament was a single red rose pinned at the valley of her breasts. Such a style was far more proper for a bishop's daughter than the latest fashions that clung so shockingly to the figure, leaving little to the imagination. It was Kate's pride that she had never had a gown from a fashionable modiste, all her clothing orders going to an impecunious widow with four children to support. By contrast, Julia's mourning garb of black silk was of the first stare of elegance, the skirt cut on severe straight lines, the matching spencer held closed by braided frogs. The ensemble was set off tastefully by a costly set of pearls and made an excellent foil for Julia's fair-haired beauty.

As the coach lurched into movement, an awkward silence settled over the interior. Kate frequently found herself not knowing what to say to Julia, which was odd, because since Kate had moved to Lytton's Dene six months ago, Miss Thorpe had proclaimed herself to be Kate's dearest friend.

Kate had never had a "dearest friend," but she had difficulty envisioning Julia in the role. Such a cool, elegant woman, nearly seven years Kate's senior, so clever it was almost alarming. Kate wondered why Julia chose to seek out such a dull companion as herself. Yet it seemed ungrateful, almost wicked to question a friendship so freely offered. Perhaps Julia was lonely, too.

But feeling as low as Kate did this morning, she would have preferred to have walked to Mapleshade, seeking a little solitude in which to compose her thoughts.

As the carriage lumbered along, Kate stared out the window to avoid Julia's penetrating gaze. The main road through Lytton's Dene passed by in a swirling haze of dust. The village was no more than a small collection of thatch-covered houses, a handful of tiny shops, and a little blue-and-white post office all set around the village green opposite the Tudor-style inn, named the Arundel Arms in honor of Harry's family.

The barouche rattled through the village in a flash. By the time they crossed the hump-backed bridge set over a trickle of stream, the spire of St. Benedict's Church came into view, and Kate became aware that Miss Thorpe was speaking of her brother.

"And Adolphus asked me to convey his apologies. He would so liked to have accompanied you. Lady Lytton expects him to deliver some sort of address at this sorry affair, extolling the virtues of my late cousin. Poor Adolphus was still scrambling to finish it when I left him.

"Rather a task." Julia essayed a laugh. "One does not like to speak ill of the dead, but it is sometimes difficult to speak good of them either."

Kate tensed as though she had received a sharp kick. "I beg your pardon?"

"Ah, I see I have shocked you. Don't misunderstand me. I was fond of Lytton. But it is difficult to eulogize a man whose best points were that he was an excellent whip and a hard rider to hounds."

"I am sure that Ha— I mean Lord Lytton had many other amiable qualities," Kate said stiffly.

"But then you did not know him very well, did you?"

Kate swallowed the urge to hotly refute that. Papa had once said nearly the same thing to her when he had feared she might be considering Harry's suit.

"Truly," Julia said, her voice filled with amusement. "What will poor Adolphus say? He can scarcely declare that Lytton was a god-fearing man."

No, Kate reluctantly had to agree. Harry had once remarked that even drawing too near the doors of a church was likely to make him break out in hives.

"And one certainly cannot acclaim Lytton as a scholar. I doubt he ever touched a book in his life."

Yes, he had. Despite her mounting irritation, Kate bit back a smile, remembering the rainy afternoon, she had been blue-deviled, and Harry had entertained her by demonstrating what a remarkable tower could be built from her father's heavy religious tomes.

"And," the relentless Julia continued, "neither can Lytton be praised as a good landlord. One only has to glance out the window for proof of that."

She nodded toward a distant farm building they were passing, the thatched roof of which showed signs of caving in at one section. Kate recognized the structure as belonging to one of his lordship's tenants.

That she could not deny any of Julia's charges only added to Kate's misery and roused an anger within her bosom such as she rarely felt. She suppressed an impulse to snap out in Harry's defense. At least he had been unfailingly tolerant and kind, which was more than could be said of a certain sharp-tongued vicar's sister.

Kate had swallowed the remark, clenching her gloved hands in her lap, more than a little appalled by her own ill-nature. She had hailed with relief the carriage turning toward the great iron gates of the lodge that led into Mapleshade Park. Hitherto luke-warm in her feelings toward Julia, she had the notion that a moment more spent in her company and Kate would quite learn to hate her "dearest friend."

* * *

Kate had not stood more than five minutes upon the hillside when she wished she had listened to her mother. She should not have come. The sun beat down ruthlessly upon her head, yet she did not think to open her parasol. She stood gripping the ivory carved handle, standing a little apart from the others in isolated misery. A hum of bright chatter filled the air as the other ladies and gentlemen present speculated what lay beneath that mysterious mountain of canvas.

Kate realized this was not a funeral service. That had been held in the church for Harry weeks ago. This was only the dedication of his memorial, but still—! Everyone did not have to act as though this were some sort of Hyde Park fête, as though Harry had died years ago.

The only one displaying any grief was Harry's stepmama. The Dowager Lady Lytton sniffed in her black-edged handkerchief as she stood conversing with Julia. Kate, who found the old lady with her brassy curls and painted cheeks rather shocking, had been unable to do more than murmur a few polite words to her.

If such a thing had been possible, Kate thought she would far rather have stepped back a few paces and mingled with Harry's servants. From the youngest chambermaid to the stately old butler, Mr. Gravshaw, they remained somberly quiet, their faces a reflection of sorrowful respect. To Kate, there seemed to be more honest emotion in the way one of the stable lads surreptitiously wiped his eyes on his sleeve than all of Lady Lytton's elegant dabbings.

Even more did Kate wish herself far away when she drew too close to Squire Gresham and chanced to overhear some of the remarks he was making to his wife.

"You don't think it'd be considered too f'rard, do you, Sophy," he mumbled, "if I was just to drop a word in Lady Lytton's ear? There's a couple of prime hunters of Harry's I've always had my eye on and I wouldn't want anyone else stealing a march on me."

"I doubt it would do you a particle of good, Squire," said Mrs. Gresham. "Those horses would rightfully be the property of the new earl, his to dispose of."

"That dour cousin of Harry's from up north?" the squire growled. "A penny-pinching Scot who will drive a hard bargain. Rot the luck!"

Her heart firing with indignation, Kate moved back so she did not have to hear any more. She had scolded Harry herself for his preoccupation with his horses, but somehow the squire scheming over Harry's grave to have his favorite hunters inspired Kate with a most unchristian desire to break her parasol over Gresham's head.

It was a relief when Reverend Thorpe commanded everyone to silence and began his speech. After the first few words, Kate blotted out the sound of his voice. She did not want to hear the vicar damning Harry with faint praise.

Her head thumped unpleasantly as she brushed her damp brow with the back of her glove. It was so hot. Was it only her fancy or had the breezes here been much more warm and gentle when Harry had been alive?

She could not say. She had only been to this hillside the one time before, and that had been spring. Harry had driven her out here to ask her to be his bride. If her answer had been different, she, too, would be wearing black, but she would have had nearly two years with Harry. Nay if she had married him, perhaps he would never have gone away. She would have dissuaded him from rushing off to fight Bonaparte. Harry might still be—

Kate squeezed her eyes tight. No, she could not think such things as that. She had given Harry the only possible answer she could. Never could she have married him. If she had ever been the least unsure, matters had been made clear to her that morning Papa had called her into his study.

The bishop's silvery halo of hair had been bent over his desk, as ever spread with pages of some scholarly text he was working upon. His stern eyes softened as he invited Kate to be seated.

He came directly to the point. Lord Lytton was being most particular in his attentions to Kate. Papa trusted that even such a reckless young man as he would not trifle with the daughter of a bishop.

"Oh, no, Papa," Kate said. Harry, after his own fashion, had ever behaved like a gentleman.

"You have developed a preference for this young man?" the bishop asked.

Kate blushed. "I—I enjoy his company." It had been a mild way to express the whirlwind effect that Harry frequently had upon her heart.

But even that admission was enough to bring a worried frown to Papa's brow, which Kate hated to see. The bishop had looked tired and ill so much of late.

Papa settled back in his chair, trying to suspend his judgment, waiting for Kate to explain what qualifications Harry possessed to make him suitable as a husband.

Kate knew her father well enough to realize he did not mean worldly possessions such as title or fortune. She stared down at the floor, embarrassed. What could she say, that Harry was like rays of sun streaking through a gray sky, that he could always make her laugh, that being with him was like waltzing through a world that was all holiday? Such fanciful considerations would not weigh with Papa, even as Kate knew she must not allow them to weigh with herself.

When she remained silent, her father began to patiently point out his own reservations. The bishop was never one to visit the sins of the father upon the child, but it was well known that old Lord Lytton, Harry's father, had been a man of great wickedness, steeped in vice. He had led his son down the same path, gaming, hard drinking, indulging every wild sport while all duty had been set aside.

But Papa said nothing that Kate's own sensible mind had not already told her. Yes, indeed, Lord Harry was too irresponsible and too reckless to make a proper mate for a bishop's daughter. She and Harry were too unlike, coming from two very different worlds.

To have accepted Harry would have been to disappoint and worry her father, at a time when he was already seriously ill. She had tried to explain all that to Harry, but he would not understand. His comprehension was limited to one question. Did she love him or not?

Kate had made up her mind that she could not possibly love Harry, but she never realized what self-possession it would take to look him in the eye and tell him so.

I don't love you, my lord.

Could she have ever pronounced those words if she had not distanced herself from him by using his title? Even now Kate was not sure. Harry had not noticed her avoidance of his name. There had only been a flicker of something in his eyes. Pain? Disappointment?

He had not behaved as though his heart was broken. If anything he had been more talkative, more teasing than ever escorting her back to the carriage. It had been the last time she had ever seen him. Perhaps Harry had been relieved himself by her refusal, finally realizing how wise she had been.

Then why didn't she feel wise? Kate thought bleakly, standing here on Harry's hillside, waiting for his memorial to be unveiled, her throat burning with unshed tears.

She scarce noticed when a tall broad-shouldered man edged past her to stand behind the squire. The sound of the vicar's voice droned on as though from a great distance. Would Adolphus Thorpe never make an end? Kate swayed on her feet, only wanting this ordeal to be over before she utterly disgraced herself.

When the memorial was unveiled at last, Kate spared the statue one brief glance. A hot blush stole into her cheeks as she averted her gaze. What an outrage! What an affront to Harry's memory.

But suddenly, so clearly in her mind, she could hear the echo of Harry's teasing voice, almost feel him chucking her playfully under the chin as he had been wont to do. "Come, Kate, smile. You take things much too seriously."

The recollection was so vivid, it nearly brought the tears spilling over at last. The statue was horrid. But how Harry would have laughed. She could almost hear him. . . .

It took Kate a few seconds to realize the deep booming sound was not a product of her mind. Someone actually was laughing, roaring with it—the tall man who had brushed past her earlier.

Kate turned to gaze up at him reproachfully. She froze, encountering a pair of twinkling green eyes, the roguish smile that had haunted her dreams.

"Kate," Harry said, his smile fading.

She stared at him, her heart racing, the blood thundering in her ears. Her head swam as her eyes tried to convince her stubborn mind that the man standing before her was no chimera, no figment of her overwrought imagination.

Her lips attempted to form his name. Harry . . . Harry still alive, standing so close she had but to reach out and touch him, the answer to a prayer kept so silent, so deep within her heart, she had not even been aware of making it.

She took a faltering step toward Lord Lytton. Then, for the first time in her life, the self-possessed Miss Kathryn Towers sank down into a swoon.

Chapter 3

The world in which Kate floated was cool, dark, and soothing. She wanted to linger there as long as she could, but part of her strained toward the faraway sound of a voice calling her name.

"Kate? Kate . . . can you not hear me? Gravshaw! Hasn't anyone located those blasted smelling salts? What? Hurry, man. Hand them over."

The next instant, Kate's peace-filled darkness was disrupted by something strong and pungent being shoved beneath her nose. Moaning softly, she rolled her head to one side, trying to escape the vile odor.

"Thank God. She's coming round. Kate!" The voice came sharper, more insistent this time. Strong fingers ruthlessly chafed her wrists. "Gravshaw, go see if Sam has left to fetch the doctor. And for God's sake, keep that flock of clucking women out of here. ..."

The voice faded as Kate fluttered her eyes open. Her first feeling was one of bewilderment. She had the vague notion that she had been napping and expected to find herself in the tiny parlor of the cottage. She blinked, her dazed eyes instead taking in the dimensions of a lofty room with tall French windows, the chamber's rich oak paneling bestrewn with paintings of the hunt. She was stretched out upon a sofa of rich brocade, a mound of cushions beneath her head.

Before she could begin to fathom where she might be, her view of the room was cut off when a tall, masculine figure loomed over her.

It was Harry. Kate had an idea that she should have been surprised to see him, yet all she felt was an unspeakable happiness at his presence.

"Kate? Are you all right?" he asked, laying his hand against her brow.

Kate experienced a childlike feeling of disappointment that his lips were not quirked in that familiar smile she so longed to see. His eyes were somber with concern, almost an element of fear lurking in them. His face had an unnatural pallor beneath his layering of tan. An absurd thought flitted through Kate's mind. He could have been a ghost.

Could have been? He *should* have been. Harry was supposed to be dead. Remembrance slapped Kate like an icy wave, dashing away the remnants of confusion as the recent scene on the hillside came back to her. Harry's monument had just been unveiled. She had heard someone laughing and turned to rebuke him only to find . . . Harry. *Alive!*

She still could not believe it. As he knelt down beside the sofa, she extended her fingers to retouch his cheek. He immediately caught her hand, encasing it in the warm strength of his own.

"Kate, darling, you will unman me if you look at me that way," he murmured. He turned his hand and pressed a kiss against her palm. "I assure you I am not some dread specter come back to haunt you."

"Harry?" she whispered. "You are alive? Truly?"

"So I have always believed, my love, but I have never been so glad of it as at this moment."

Kate choked on a joyful sob and struggled to rise, her head yet reeling.

"Nay, gently, Kate." Harry slipped one arm behind her shoulders to support her. With the other hand, he produced a tumbler of brandy that had been resting nearby on a tripod table.

But such nearness to the man she had thought dead, lost forever, was having a strange effect on Kate. Impelled by a rush of feeling such as she had never known, she startled Harry by flinging her arms about his neck, dashing the crystal glass to the floor.

Harry made a weak attempt to remonstrate, to ease her back among the cushions. He cradled her in his arms, brushing a reverent kiss upon her brow. But in the delirium of her joy, Kate quite forgot that she was a bishop's daughter. She tipped back her head, eagerly seeking his lips. Harry's eyes widened, but his noble resistance lasted no more than a second.

The warmth of Harry's lips against her own was a novel sensation to Kate. She had never kissed a man before, never daring as much even in her dreams.

She felt as though her heart stood quite still and raced madly all at the same time. She tightened her arms about him, passionately melding her mouth to his, the fire spreading more quickly through her veins than any brandy could have accomplished.

It was Harry who broke the contact, easing her away with a long, shuddering sigh.

"Damme!" He breathed, then gave a shaky laugh. "If I had any notion this was the sort of reception awaiting me, I would have despatched the French Army and come back much sooner."

A tender light came into his eyes, as he stroked a stray curl back from her brow. "But what a fright you gave me, Kate, collapsing in my arms that way."

A watery chuckle escaped Kate. What a fright she had given him! What about the way he had sprung up from nowhere after all those tormenting days when she had believed him dead? It was only now that she could acknowledge to herself exactly how much she had grieved, how much she had longed to hear the delightful peal of Harry's laughter.

Harry's laughter ... the thought somehow disturbed her glow of happiness like a pebble breaking the serene surface of a pond. Yes, Harry had been laughing, while she had been near to bursting into tears.

Kate's smile slowly faded.

Harry failed to note the change in her expression. He was trying to reconcile his memory of the prim girl who had turned down his marriage proposal with this woman who had cast herself so passionately into his arms. He did not waste too much effort in doing so. There was no surer way to destroy a miracle than to question it too closely.

If he was dreaming, he thought, leaning over Kate for another kiss, he did not want to be awakened. Too late did he see the unaccustomed flash of fire in her eyes, the blur of her hand as she struck out, soundly boxing his ears.

He had been bending over Kate in such a manner that the blow knocked him off balance and sent him sprawling back onto the carpet. Harry gaped up at the wrathful goddess who leaped to her feet, towering over him, her dark hair tumbling about her shoulders, her eyes the hue of a summer storm. If she had had any lightning bolts at her disposal, Harry sensed that he would have been done for.

"You—you heartless beast," Kate cried. "You unfeeling monster."

There was no doubt these bewildering epithets were directed at himself. She doubled up her fists as though she would fly at him again. Harry braced himself, but she merely flounced past him and took to pacing before the windows with short, furious steps, drawing in deep breaths as though trying to regain her self-control.

198

Harry sat up slowly, rubbing his stinging ear. He stared at Kate in astonishment. The kiss had been startling enough, but this! Kate was the last woman in the world to offer a man violence. And what an incomprehensible shift in mood. None of this was in the least like his well-bred, even-tempered Kate. What could have possibly come over her?

Harry could think of only one explanation. He made no move to rise from the carpet, but sat dangling his hands over his knees, a beatific smile spreading over his features.

"You lied to me, Kathryn Towers," he announced triumphantly.

She paused long enough in her pacing to direct a killing glare at him. "I lied! How dare you, sir. You the most infamous liar of them all—"

"You lied to me that day on the Hill. You do love me, have done so all along."

"I do not! I quite detest you. When I think of how all this time—"

"The kiss made me a little suspicious," Harry continued unperturbed. "But the slap confirms it. You would never be so angry now if you were not head over ears in love."

Kate caught her breath in a furious hiss. She snatched up a Sevres vase from the mantle as though she would fling it at his head.

Harry grinned. "Do go ahead and throw it, Kate, and I will know you completely adore me."

For one second he thought she meant to take him up on that. But with a small frustrated cry, she replaced the vase, trembling with the effort it cost her.

Harry sprang to his feet. Thinking that all would be well if he could only get her back into his arms, Harry attempted to cross the room to her. But she ducked behind a Hepplewhite chair, using the fragile piece of furniture as a barrier.

"Don't you come near me," she said, through clenched teeth.

Harry stopped, but he said in aggrieved tones, "You need not act as though I was some sort of a Bluebeard. It was you who kissed me; then I got slapped for it."

"Don't you dare mention that kiss to me! You knew I was not myself. If you had been a gentleman, you would not have encouraged me."

"It would have taken more than being a gentleman," Harry retorted. "I would have had to have been dead."

"You could pretend you were," she flung back bitterly. "You seem to be remarkably good at it."

Comprehension dawned upon Harry at last as to the true source of her anger. But he was not in the least disturbed to discover that his beloved believed him capable of perpetrating such a dreadful jest. Truthfully when the devil of mischief was upon him, there were some people upon whom he would not have minded playing such a joke. But never his Kate.

That she was so enraged by her belief only afforded Harry further proof that she did care for him very deeply, more so than she was willing to admit. It was all he could do to control the ebullience of his own spirits and say to her soothingly, "Come, Kate. You are far too overexcited. Come back and sit beside me and we'll—"

She vehemently shook her head. Harry felt at an extreme disadvantage, trying to offer explanations with the chair between them, but he did not wish to upset her further. At least some of the color had come back into her cheeks.

"I did not pretend to be dead, Kate. I don't know how this infernal misunderstanding came about. I just arrived home today."

She gave a scornful sniff. "How convenient that you should have arrived just in time to attend your own dedication."

"Yes, it was convenient—I mean, it was the most dashed coincidence." Harry studied her stony profile with a sinking heart and realized she did not believe him. He could scarce blame her. "I don't pretend that in the past I might not have been capable of serving up such a trick, but never to you, Kate. Good Lord, what are you even doing here in Lytton's Dene? I had heard that after your father . . . that you had gone to live with your grandmother near Lewes."

"I moved to Lytton's Dene six months ago."

"To be closer to me?" Harry asked coaxingly.

"No! Mama admired a cottage in the village. After our period of mourning was at an end, I thought it would be good for her to still be near her old friends from Chillingsworth."

"Then why not just stay in Chillingsworth?"

When she compressed her lips together, refusing to answer, Harry smiled. "After that kiss and that slap, are you still going to deny you love me?"

"I don't intend to deny anything, because I don't ever intend to speak to you again." Kate drew herself rigidly upright. "Now if you will excuse me, my lord, I am going home."

"Kate . . ."

"What have you done with my gloves and bonnet?" She came from behind the chair to search the room in a distracted, ineffectual manner.

Harry had some vague recollection of having taken off her bonnet and flung it down upon the hillside during his first effort to rouse her from her faint. One of her gloves lay discarded by the sofa's claw leg. Harry grabbed it up.

When Kate stretched out her hand for it, he held it just out of her reach.

"Even the cruelest of ladies will let her knight have some token of remembrance," he said, hoping to wheedle a smile from her.

"A knight, certainly, but not a knave." She refused to come any closer to retrieve the article. With a stiff shrug, she said, "You may as well keep it. You appear to have lost the other one."

Turning up her heel, she stalked away. But when she reached the door, the brass knob refused to yield beneath her grasp. She rattled it, then looked accusingly at Harry.

He held up the key with an apologetic glance. "I had to do something to keep away that pack of henwitted females. When you first fainted, Julia and the rest of 'em nigh suffocated you beneath a pile of silk fans."

"Unlock this door at once, sir."

He crossed his arms over his chest. "I don't think I shall," he said, "until you listen to what I have to say."

"You open that door right now!" She stamped her foot, then turned and tugged at the knob. "You open it or I . . . I will—"

In frustration, she struck her palm against the unmoving barrier of oak. Her shoulders sagged, and she rested her forehead against the grain, the tears beginning to trickle down her cheeks.

"Oh, Lord," Harry exclaimed in horror. "No, here now, Kate. Don't do that." He rushed to her side. "I would rather face a field of bayonets all over again than make you cry."

Peering down at her, he slapped futilely at his waistcoat. He never seemed to have a damned handkerchief about him. He attempted to check the flow of crystal drops with his fingers, but she averted her face and produced her own pristine square of lace-edged linen.

Harry rested his hands on her shoulders. "Please don't cry, Kate. You know I was only teasing you. I'll unlock the blasted door at once if that's what you really want."

"I want to go home!"

"And so you shall. In my own carriage."

"No, I don't need—I came with—" But Kate appeared to think twice about what she had been about to say. Dabbing furiously at her eyes, she said with as much dignity as she could muster, "Th-thank you, my lord. I am most grateful for your offer. I should like to ride in your coach . . .

"Alone," she added pointedly.

Harry sighed. How had she guessed that he fully planned on accompanying her, continuing to plead his case in the privacy of the carriage? He started to argue with her, but one glance at her tear-swollen eyes, the genuine distress marring the serenity of her features, and Harry held his tongue.

He was being a selfish brute. Kate had received a dreadful shock whether it had been of his making or not. She was clearly overwrought. Although it took all of his self-restraint, he realized the best course would be to send her home, allow her some time to compose herself. Kate was a most fair-minded woman. When she was more herself, she would be willing to listen to him. He hoped.

As she dried the last of her tears, Harry unlocked the door.

202

When he swung the barrier open, he was considerably startled when his cousin Julia all but tumbled across the threshold.

Julia's gaze flicked from Kate's reddened eyes to Harry. His cousin subjected him to a basilisk stare. "What have you been doing to this poor girl, Lytton?"

"You ought to know," Harry said dryly.. "Or did the thickness of the door prove too much for you?"

Another woman might have blushed at the implication she had been eavesdropping, but it was not so easy to discompose Julia. Ignoring Harry, she descended upon Kate.

"My dearest Kathryn, I have been so anxious about you. I would have been at your side, but between Lytton and his odious butler, I was not permitted to get near you."

Harry raised his brows in frowning surprise. When had Miss Towers become Julia's "dearest Kathryn"? He half feared that Kate would cast herself beneath Julia's protection, closing ranks in that manner women had when they feel they have been much abused by the male sex.

But Kate only murmured something indistinguishable and shrank back, showing no pleasure in Julia's solicitude. Julia rounded on Harry.

"I see that your behavior has not improved in the time you have been away, Lytton. You still have no more notion of propriety than the kitchen cat. Did it not occur to you that you could have utterly ruined Miss Tower's reputation, keeping her closeted with you in that fashion?"

As Kate blanched with dismay, Harry could have wrung his cousin's neck.

"Fortunately," Julia continued, "I had the foresight to direct the squire and his wife and all your other guests into the front salon where they are having refreshment. No one is aware of how long you and Kathryn have been alone together."

"Thank you, Julia," Harry said grimly. "It is such a relief to have you so busy upon my behalf."

She peered down the length of her nose at him. "I did not do it for you, cousin. I fear nothing will save you from the consequences of your folly this time. The latest prank of yours, appearing at your own memorial, is bound to raise such a scandal that—"

"Later, Julia," Harry broke in, observing Kate wearily touch a hand to her brow. "You can ring a peal over me as much as you please, but now I must fetch my carriage round for Kate. You can see she is still not well."

"Your carriage!" Julia said. "Kathryn came with me."

But Harry had already tucked Kate's arm beneath his own to lead her toward the curving oak stair descending into the main hall. Although Kate did not lean on him for support, neither did she attempt to pull away. Harry had the feeling that she was as relieved as he was to be escaping Julia's clacking tongue.

But Miss Thorpe was not so easily vanquished. She trailed after them, insisting she would take Kathryn home. Harry, however, had had long experience in fobbing off Julia's attempts to order him about, and he prevented her from riding roughshod over Kate as well since she seemed in no state to defend herself.

By the time Harry led her out to the gravel drive circling Mapleshade's front lawn, Kate looked exhausted from Julia's badgering. He handed her into the recesses of his most comfortable and well-sprung coach. At the last second, one of the gardeners came rushing up with Kate's bonnet.

Leaning in through the carriage's open door, Harry passed it up to her, the garment much the worse from his previous rough handling of it, the poke front crushed beyond redemption.

Kate took the bonnet from him without a word.

"I shall come to call upon you soon, Kate," he said.

Kate stared stonily straight in front of her. "I fear I shall not be at home, my lord."

"What! At two in the morning?"

This sally did not produce so much as the quiver of a response. Harry sighed. He hated letting her go this way. Swallowed up in the vastness of the coach, she looked so small, so prim and obstinate, so completely adorable, he longed for nothing more than to gather her up in his arms.

"I don't suppose this is a good moment to ask you again to marry me?" he said wistfully. At her reproachful glare, he

204

threw up one hand in a peacemaking gesture. "One cannot hang a man for asking, Kate."

Making her his best leg, he closed the door and stepped back, giving the coachman the signal to whip up the horses.

"And now that I am convinced you love me," Harry muttered. "I *will* ask you, Kate. Again and again, until one of these days you are going to forget yourself and say yes."

Shading his eyes, he followed the coach's progress down the long drive until it disappeared into the line of trees fronting the park. Sighing, Harry turned back toward the house. Despite the unsatisfactory nature of his reunion with Kate, he moved with a lighthearted spring to his step, feeling far different from the man who only a matter of a few hours ago had trudged past his empty fields.

Hope was a heady draught, and Harry felt nigh drunk with it. With his hands on his hips, he paused to stare up at his home, feeling somehow that he had never fully appreciated the old hall. At one time a medieval manor house, two projecting wings had been added after the Restoration, along with hipped roofs and a balustrade. But the original brickwork, although now considered unfashionable, remained untouched, and Harry vowed that it would continue to be so during his lifetime. It gave the hall a much warmer glow than those modern facing tiles of silvery white.

Imagining the day when he would bring Kate across the threshold as his bride, Harry doted upon every brick of the old place. He doted upon the huge stone lions that stood guarding the forecourt, upon the unspoiled expanse of lawn.

But his present rush of good humor did not quite extend to doting upon the tall fair-haired man who awaited him in the manor's open doorway.

Although not fond of Reverend Thorpe, Harry did not dislike his cousin either. At times he even thought Adolphus was not a bad sort, except when he appeared to be half choking on his clerical collar.

As Harry strode up the steps to join the vicar beneath the portico, he noted with half-humorous dismay the way Reverend

Thorpe tugged at his starched neckband as though to draw attention to the badge of his authority.

"Cousin Harry," he said sternly.

"Cousin Adolphus," Harry replied pleasantly.

"My lord, I scarce know what to say to you—"

Being familiar with Adolphus, Harry was damned sure he was going to think of something. "Whatever it is, I am sure it can keep till later. I am done in. It has been, saving your presence, one hell of a day."

"Others might say the same. You should go to your stepmother at once and beg her pardon for the distress you have brought her. She is prostrate, my lord, completely prostrate."

"A man is only entitled to have one female swoon in his arms per day, Adolphus. I have already had mine. You may feel quite free to take on the next one."

"My lord!" the vicar exclaimed in outraged accents.

"Believe me, Adolphus," Harry said. "I am not being totally unfeeling. For me to go to Sybil would be like exposing an already sick woman to a case of the pox. She will be much more ready to receive me when she has recovered a little."

Harry managed to edge past the vicar, slipping inside the hall, only to run dead into Julia. He was not surprised this time. Julia was frequently to be found hovering at her brother's elbow.

She glowered at Harry, apparently still annoyed with him for having whisked Kate out of her clutches.

"Lytton, I must speak to you. Your conduct—"

Harry stopped her with an upraised hand. "My dear Julia, I know I promised you the pleasure of giving me a setdown, but I fear it must once again be deferred. I must have a word with all those guests you so obligingly herded into the front salon, perhaps even raise a glass with the squire. Timothy Keegan informs me that English memorial services are sadly wanting, and I feel I should do something to raise our reputation."

Having effectively rendered both of the Thorpes speechless with indignation, Harry strolled on his way, whistling cheerfully.

* * *

Although the gathering in the salon never reached the proportions of what Keegan would have termed a passable wake, the atmosphere became much more convivial with Harry's entrance. The ladies fussed over him and called him a naughty rogue, the squire swearing that by gawd, even if his lordship did keep refusing to sell those hunters, the squire was damned glad to see the lad home safe again.

The only ones of the party to leave early were the Thorpes. The vicar's barouche rumbled down the drive at a great speed as though eager to distance itself from the hall and the return of its incorrigible master.

Julia stared out the coach window, her flawless profile as hard and unyielding as if carved of marble. She bore the dubious distinction of being acclaimed the loveliest spinster in the shire. Her beauty had never been enough to compensate for her lack of fortune or her fixed belief that she could improve the character of any man she met.

She even felt that she could have redeemed her cousin Harry if he had ever asked her to be his wife. But as his lordship had never shown the good sense to make her an offer, Julia had long ago washed her hands of him. She was not so ill-natured as to wish that Lord Lytton *had* died at Waterloo, but his return promised to be a great nuisance, especially from what Julia had already observed of his attentions toward Kate.

It was not that Julia was in the least jealous on her own account. No, the chief source of her vexation was that she had already marked Miss Kathryn Towers down for her own brother.

As the carriage rattled past the park gates, Julia turned to the vicar seated opposite her and broke the rigid silence they had maintained since leaving the hall.

"Well! Now that Lytton has returned, you may be assured, he will be stirring up some mischief."

"There is nothing new in that, my dear," Adolphus said wearily.

"I fear he may have already begun . . . with Kathryn Towers." Julia observed her brother closely for his reaction.

Adolphus's eyes widened. "Why, I thought that was one of

207

Lord Harry's more commendable actions today, his solicitude for Miss Towers."

Solicitude! Julia pressed her hand to her eyes, the degree of her brother's naïveté as ever confounding her. Only a blind man would have mistaken the loverlike way Lytton had swooped up Kathryn in his arms and charged back to the house with her as being mere solicitude. His lordship had appeared suitably distraught and heroic enough to set several more young ladies off into a swoon.

"Lytton's attentions to Kathryn were most improper," Julia said. "As her friend he should have allowed me to take care of her. He actually thrust me aside. I could not hear all that he said to her when they were alone in the Hunt parlor but—"

"Julia! You were never eavesdropping."

"It was my moral obligation to do so. Lytton was practically holding the poor girl a prisoner in that room."

"I cannot believe that even Lytton would seek to molest a respectable young woman beneath the roof of his ancestral home."

"He was not molesting her. I think he is trying to fix his interest with her."

"What! On such brief acquaintance?"

"He had met her before," Julia explained with strained patience. "Two years ago in Chillingsworth. There were even rumors that Lytton wished to marry Kathryn, but the bishop would have none of it."

"Oh." Adolphus blinked.

Julia found the single syllable as a reply most unsatisfactory.

"Is that all you have to say?" she demanded, "when I have just told you that your ne'er-do-well cousin may be planning to steal your intended bride."

Adolphus's lips curved in a deprecating smile. "I would scarce dare call Miss Towers so. We are not on such terms as that."

"You could be, if you would make the slightest push. Have I not told you that she is perfect for you, Adolphus? Absolutely perfect?"

"Yes, you have, my dear. Upon many occasions." Adolphus

squirmed. "Miss Towers is a most amiable young woman, but—"

"Amiable! She is modest, well-favored, bred to be a clergyman's wife and ... and simply perfect," Julia finished by breaking off what she had actually been about to say. It would do no good to point out to one as lacking in ambition as Adolphus Kathryn's other charms. Although only possessed of a respectable competence, Kathryn's chief fortune lay in her connections. She had one uncle highly placed in the cabinet of the present ministry, to say nothing of her circle of acquaintances within the cathedral close at Chillingsworth. It was most unfortunate that her father, the bishop, should be dead, but Kate still retained enough influential friends to be certain that her future husband would not be left to languish as parson of some obscure country vicarage. Julia intended to see her brother become a dean or at least an archdeacon with several livings at his disposal.

Adolphus should see for himself what a good match Kathryn would be, but instead his handsome brow furrowed into a troubled frown.

"You may be right, Julia—I mean, of course you are right," he hastily amended. "Miss Towers is perfect, but if, as you believe, Lord Harry should have some notion of settling down and wishes to wed the young lady, I do not feel it would be right to set myself up as rival to him."

As Julia fixed him with a cold stare, her brother stammered, "Y-you tend to forget my position here. Although he is our cousin, Harry is also lord of the manor. I can never provoke his lordship while I owe him such a debt of gratitude. It was he who presented me with the living—"

"Lytton would have presented St. Benedict's to the first tinker coming down the lane," Julia said scornfully, "if only to spare himself further responsibility in the matter."

Thus dismissing her brother's obligations to Lord Lytton, Julia proceeded to inform Adolphus how he should call upon Kathryn at once to see how she fared, perhaps even take her a small nosegay from the parsonage garden. But neither coaxing or insisting could move him to do so.

"I have a sermon to finish for the morrow," Adolphus said, his jaw cutting in stubborn fashion.

Julia saw that nothing she could say would convince him and, although considerably annoyed, was obliged to give over for the moment. Adolphus could be led to a certain point, but when he waxed obstinate, it was best to let be or she would only have more difficulty reopening the subject of his court-ship later.

Julia had realized a long time ago that she was much more clever than her younger brother. She would never have been so unmaidenly as to admit being discontent with her lot, a frustra-tion that her sex barred her from the education that seemed to have been wasted upon Adolphus. Instead, she found her so-lace by managing his life for him.

It distressed her when she thought that perhaps Adolphus might truly be content to be no more than the vicar of Lytton's Dene. She had far greater plans for him, and neither his mod-esty nor Lytton's interference were going to ruin these schemes.

When they arrived at the vicarage, Adolphus's last word on the subject was to pat her kindly on the shoulder and tell her not to fret. "I am sure the Almighty will decide whom your good friend Kathryn should marry."

Although Julia bowed her head in pious acquiescence, she realized that the Almighty frequently had a way of arranging things not to her satisfaction. But not this time, she thought, her lips thinning dangerously. Not if she had anything to say in the matter.

Come what may, Julia vowed, Lord Lytton would not have Kate.

Chapter 4

Maisie Towers settled herself upon the window seat and stole one glance through the sun-glazed panes, hoping for some sign of a carriage billowing in a dusty cloud along the lane. Surely Kate should have been home by now, Mrs. Towers began to fret, then adjured herself not to be a fool. Kate was not likely to break any bones attending a dedication service upon a hillside.

No, not any bones, Mrs. Towers thought, suppressing a worried sigh, *only a heart.* She forced her gaze away from the window and summoned an attentive smile for her guests, all the while wishing them at Jericho.

Mrs. Prangle, the archdeacon's wife, had been ensconced upon the settee for over half an hour, her inquisitive eyes taking in every detail of the cottage, her sharp, unlovely voice rasping at Mrs. Towers's nerves. Seated upon either side of Mrs. Prangle were her two red-haired daughters. Doubtless in a few years they would grow to be most sensible girls, but now they showed a distressing tendency to giggle.

"And I told archdeacon," Mrs. Prangle trilled on, "that I was going out this way to visit my sister in any case, so I must stop and call upon Maisie Towers and dear Kathryn. Such a pity she should be away from home."

Mrs. Towers smiled, nodded, and wished she had accompanied her daughter.

Mrs. Prangle arched her neck, glancing about her. "This is a charming house, although rather small. Have you got but the one parlor? And such a tiny dining room. Rather a change for you, my dear, after the splendor of the bishop's palace."

The Misses Prangle giggled their agreement.

"The cottage is large enough for Kate and me," Mrs. Towers said mildly. She liked the coziness of her small house, although at the moment she wished it were located at the tip of Wales, too far for Mrs. Prangle and the other gossipy ladies of Chillingsworth to call. Dear Kate had meant to be so kind, arranging it that her mother should be near her old acquaintances. Mrs. Towers had been quite unable to tell the poor child she had no desire to see most of those prying women again.

"The late bishop, rest his soul, was such a saintly man," Mrs. Prangle said, her bonnet feathers nodding as she mounted a fresh attack. "He never used his position to amass a fortune as some might have done, did he?"

This was such a bald-faced attempt to discover how Mrs. Towers and Kate had been left circumstanced, that Mrs. Towers stiffened. She had never known how to depress such impertinence. Kate would have known how to answer Mrs. Prangle. Kate had always known, far better than her retiring mother, how to deal with the never-ending stream of canons' wives, prebendaries' daughters and vicars' nieces who had trickled through the drawing rooms of the bishop's palace.

But Kate was not here, and Mrs. Towers did the best she could. She succeeded in changing the subject by inquiring after the archdeacon's son at Eton.

As Mrs. Prangle boasted how young George had become the boon companion of a duke's son, the china clock upon the mantel chimed three. Mrs. Towers noted with alarm that Mrs. Prangle might linger until tea time and that Kate still had not returned home.

Her anxious gaze traveled to the window once more. She had never been able to divine the true extent of Kate's feelings for the late Lord Lytton, but all her motherly instincts told her that her daughter was hiding a great deal of pain.

She should have put her foot down, duty be hanged, and not permitted Kate to go through the ordeal of attending that dedication. But she never had been able to take a firm line with Kate. Sometimes she stood a little in awe of her own daughter, so reserved, so self-possessed, so much like her father—

"Ooh!"

Mrs. Towers was startled from her thoughts by a squeal of delight from the youngest Miss Prangle. "Can that be Miss Towers coming home now? What an elegant coach!"

Mrs. Towers had allowed her mind to wander so far that she had been unaware that a conveyance had pulled up before the gate, but not the one she looked for. Before she could obtain a clearer view, the other three women joined her at the window, and she was nigh suffocated by a profusion of bouncing curls and muslin gowns.

Managing to peer past Mrs. Prangle's feathers, Mrs. Towers determined that it was not the vicar's smart barouche, but a much more impressive coach, fit to have been a state carriage for royalty.

"Look at the coat of arms on the door," Miss Prangle exclaimed. "Would that be the Arundel family crest?"

"No," Mrs. Towers said, a chill of recognition coursing through her. "It-it is . . ." The Prangles regarded her breathlessly. "It is . . . my mother-in-law," Mrs. Towers said.

The sight of the grande dame being handed from the coach by a bewigged footman in scarlet and gold livery caused the Prangles to shiver with excitement, but Mrs. Towers's heart sank in dismay.

Winifred Aldarcie Towers, the Lady Dane, had been widowed for many years now. One of her chief forms of amusement was to descend unexpectedly upon the families of her numerous offspring. With the bishop in his grave, Mrs. Towers had considered herself safe from any more such visitations. How disconcerting to discover she was wrong.

As Mrs. Prangle and her tittering daughters fussed, smoothing out their gowns and hair, Mrs. Towers rose to her feet with all the resignation of a condemned prisoner.

All too soon the door to the parlor opened, the pert Mollie entering the room in subdued fashion.

"Lady Dane," Mollie announced in awed accents.

She flattened herself against the door as her ladyship swept past. Lady Dane stalked into the parlor with all the majesty of a queen, leaning upon a silver-handled cane she in nowise needed, her bearing still upright, her step unhampered despite her advancing years. Her figure had lost none of its statuesque proportions, her eye none of its keenness. The only signs of age were the lovely waves of white hair flowing back from her brow, the feathering of lines upon her skin, which only seemed to draw attention to the aristocratic fineness of her bone structure.

Even in her youth something in Winifred Towers's countenance had made all the young men tremble in her presence, address her as madam. Only one had ever been privileged to see the softness of her smiles and that had been the bandy-legged little Baron of Dane whom she had chosen to marry.

No hint of that smile now transformed Lady Dane's features as she crossed the threshold of the tiny parlor, her hawklike gaze taking in both the chamber and its occupants. Mrs. Towers forced herself forward to greet her ladyship.

"Mother Towers. What a surprise."

"Maisie." Lady Dane unbent enough to offer her cheek, which Mrs. Towers dutifully saluted. She had then no choice but to present Mrs. Prangle and her daughters, who embarked upon a frenzied round of curtsying.

After subjecting the Prangles to a glacial stare, Lady Dane condescended to extend two fingers by way of greeting.

"I had the privilege of meeting your ladyship before at Chillingsworth," Mrs. Prangle gushed, "though I daresay my lady has forgotten."

"I daresay that I have," Lady Dane said. Her ladyship had a most royally impressive habit of rolling her *r*'s.

As abashed as Mrs. Prangle appeared, she was fully prepared to renew the acquaintance and made a movement to herd her daughters back to the settee.

"You must not think of staying upon my account," Lady Dane said in arctic accents. "I fear Maisie has already kept you beyond the time considered civil for an afternoon call."

Mrs. Prangle flushed a bright red but for once appeared unable to find anything to say. With scarce more than the raising of an eyebrow, Lady Dane sent the archdeacon's wife and daughters bustling toward the door.

This high-handed maneuver almost put Mrs. Towers in charity with her ladyship. Returning from seeing the Prangles to their coach, a gentle laugh escaped her as she asked Lady Dane, "However did you guess that woman had outstayed her welcome?"

"It required no great perspicacity. A most vulgar female," her ladyship pronounced. "*I* should have told my maid to deny that I was at home."

Mrs. Towers felt certain that her ladyship would, but she was not made of such stern stuff. Despite Lady Dane's masterly disposal of the Prangles, Mrs. Towers's smile vanished when she saw the footman dragging into the hall several large trunks to say nothing of a dressing case, her ladyship's maid following, her arms full of a supply of her ladyship's own bed linens. "I trust you have a chamber available for me?" Lady Dane asked. "Yes, of course," Mrs. Towers said, considerably dismayed by this invasion. She retained presence of mind to direct the footman and lady's maid upstairs to the proper bedchamber before inviting Lady Dane to be seated in the parlor.

"I shall have Mollie bring in some tea."

"I prefer lemonade," said her ladyship.

Mrs. Towers did not believe they had lemons in the kitchen, but she knew her small household held Lady Dane in such awe that her housekeeper would procure some forthwith.

Having given her instructions, by the time Mrs. Towers returned to the parlor, she discovered that Lady Dane had eschewed the settee vacated by the Prangles and had enthroned herself upon a stiff-backed chair.

Seating herself upon the settee, Mrs. Towers nervously inquired after her ladyship's health. She had heard that Lady Dane had gone to take the waters in Bath. Had her ladyship just returned from there?

Lady Dane returned a brief answer. Never one to engage in idle chatter, she demanded abruptly, "Where is Kathryn?"

"She is gone to attend the dedication of poor Lord Lytton's memorial. I expect her home at any time."

Her ladyship offered no comment, merely scowling at the

information. "I saw Kathryn briefly in London a fortnight ago. Did she tell you?"

"She mentioned it." Mrs. Towers had encouraged Kate to visit her cousin in the hopes that a little varied society might improve her spirits. "Kate only stayed a week. I suppose summer is not the best time to be in the city."

"The child looked positively haggard," Lady Dane said.

"She had been ill with a severe bout of influenza."

"Stuff! She is pining away for that young man, Lord Harry."

"I fear you are mistaken, my lady," Mrs. Towers said quietly. "Kate insists she did not love him."

Lady Dane gave her that look that always made Mrs. Towers feel like a perfect widgeon.

"Humpfh! The girl might be able to throw dust in your eyes, Maisie, but—"

Her ladyship broke off at the sound of another carriage arriving. Mrs. Towers glanced toward the window and saw her daughter alighting and coming up the walk at last. She thought she would have done anything to spare Kate her ladyship's overwhelming presence at this moment. She wished that Lady Dane would be kind enough not to mention Lord Harry, but one could scarce tell her ladyship to mind her tongue. Mrs. Towers took a hesitant step forward, thinking that at least she might warn Kate of her grandmother's arrival.

But it was already too late, for the parlor door came flying open. Mrs. Towers was not prepared for the flushed young woman who bolted into the chamber, her bonnet missing, her eyes sparkling with indignation.

"Mama, you will never guess what—" Kate stopped in midsentence at the sight of Lady Dane. "Grandmother!" Kate's greeting betokened surprise and a hint of wariness.

She recovered enough to kiss her ladyship's upturned cheek in the approved manner. Kate cast a doubtful glance toward her mother as though seeking an explanation for Lady Dane's presence. Miss Towers could only respond by a bewildered shake of her head.

Lady Dane rapped her cane upon the carpet. "Don't keep us in suspense, miss. I gather something untoward happened at the dedication? Likely Sybil Arundel made a spectacle of herself as usual."

Lady Dane's remark snapped Kate's attention back to the original source of her agitation. She remained silent a moment, then burst out, "It has nothing to do with Lady Lytton. It's Lord Harry. He's still alive."

"What!" Mrs. Towers exclaimed in the same breath as Lady Dane.

"He arrived at his own dedication," Kate cried. "He had just been pretending to be dead all this time."

Mrs. Towers was as shocked and aggrieved by such conduct as her daughter, but Lady Dane broke into one of her rare trills of laughter.

"The rogue! I wish I had been there to see it. He must have made you all look like a parcel of fools, standing about in this blazing heat to gape at some ridiculous memorial."

"I didn't find it so amusing, Grandmama," Kate said in a taut voice.

"Of course. *You* wouldn't." Although still chuckling, her ladyship's eyes held a gleam of sympathy. " 'Tis most understandable you should be somewhat distressed, considering you are not exactly indifferent to the young man."

Somewhat distressed! This seemed such a callous way of describing Kate's distraught state that Mrs. Towers cast a reproachful glance at her mother-in-law. She moved closer to Kate, intending to slip a comforting arm about her daughter's waist, but Kate scarce seemed to notice the gesture.

"I *was* indifferent to Lord Lytton before, Grandmama," Kate said, drawing herself up proudly, "but now I quite despise the man. If you will excuse me, I must go and change before tea."

"Kate!" But Mrs. Towers's gentle protest was lost as Kate dashed out of the room. She longed to go after her daughter, but past experience had taught her it would do little good. Sagging down upon the settee, her head spun with the shock of the tidings. Lord Lytton still alive . . .

Only Lady Dane appeared quite unperturbed.

"I told you the girl was in love with him."

* * *

Kate fled upstairs. She had been longing for the sanctuary of her own room ever since her flustered exit from Mapleshade Hall and Harry's disturbing presence. Stepping inside the small bedchamber, Kate closed the door behind her and leaned against it with a tremulous sigh.

The room's walls were painted green, a soothing shade that captured the softer hues of the forest. The only furnishings were the four-poster bed, the wardrobe, a washstand, a dressing table, and a chair, all carved of satinwood, all of the utmost simplicity appropriate to a clergyman's daughter, except for a few touches of lace here and there that her feminine heart *would* crave.

Yet for once the room's sylvan peacefulness was little balm to Kate's troubled spirits. She stalked away from the door, trying to draw rein upon her emotions, flattering herself that in some measure she had begun to do so.

The delusion lasted until she got a glimpse of herself in the mirror affixed to the dressing table. She all but shrank from the bonnetless hoyden staring back at her, a hectic flush coloring her face, her dark curls in a tangle. Kate pressed her hands to her cheeks in dismay. She looked like a wild woman, and to think that she had appeared thus before Lady Dane of all people. Kate had the feeling her grandmother did not approve of her in any case—a most novel and disturbing sensation to one accustomed to always meeting with approbation.

Lowering herself onto the chair, Kate started to snatch up a pearl-handled brush, then froze. Leaning closer to the mirror, her eyes widened in horror. Her mouth! She touched one trembling fingertip to lips that to her mind appeared swollen and bruised. She groaned. All the world must guess how she had been kissing Harry Arundel.

Kate's gaze strayed to the miniature of her father upon the dressing table, the bishop's stern eyes regarding her from the silver frame. With a guilty start, Kate laid the portrait face down.

Bad enough that she had embraced Harry in such wanton fashion, but she had actually struck him in a fit of temper like some brawling tavern wench. She had had every provocation to do so, but it was not the icily bred reaction to be expected of a lady, let alone the propriety demanded of a bishop's daughter.

Utterly sunk in her own esteem, Kate rested her arms upon the dressing table. Laying her head down, she finally gave vent to the stormy bout of tears that had been brewing for hours. She cried like an overtired child who had too many events crammed in one day, weeping out her shame over her own conduct.

It was some time before her sobs ceased. When she at last raised her head, she felt drained but somehow the better for it. She trudged over to the washstand and poured water from the pitcher into the basin. Splashing the cold liquid over her face, she cleansed away the ravages of her tears.

Drawing in a steadying breath, she straightened, feeling more able to face the future . . . a future that now had to include Harry very much alive, who had come crashing back into her life once more. Whatever was she going to do?

For a moment, she harbored a cowardly wish to be far from Lytton's Dene. It would not be easy to confront Harry again, especially knowing his feelings toward her remained the same. He still wanted her. As gratifying as that was, she could no more accept Harry now than two years ago. If anything the case was more impossible now that the bishop was dead. It would be as though she had waited until poor Papa was in his grave to seek out the man he would not have wished her to marry.

This mad prank of Harry's, pretending to be dead, only served to reinforce Kate's own doubts about him. She required a more serious turn of mind in the man she would deem suitable as a husband. No, she was as resolved as ever. She and Harry would not suit.

Yet in making this resolution, Kate knew she was reckoning with one powerful force. Harry, himself. That wretched kiss! Whatever had possessed her? She had just been coming out of a swoon. She hadn't in the least known what she was doing, but she would never be able to convince Harry of that. Never would he give her any peace.

She could refuse to see him as she had threatened, but she

knew Harry far too well. He would not be turned away by a tale of her not being at home. He was perfectly capable of coming round at two in the morning and chucking pebbles at her window.

She would have to see him again, but where would she find the composure to do so? Seeking strength, she turned to the one source she had been taught to trust since a child.

Dropping to her knees by the bed, she folded her hands and raised her eyes earnestly to the chamber's scrolled ceiling.

"Dear Father in Heaven," she prayed, "give me the wisdom to deal with Harry. Help me to keep him at arm's length."

But even God did not seem to be heeding Kate today. Instead of any comforting feeling of assurance, she was visited by an image of Harry so strong her breath snagged in her throat. Not the Harry of the wicked grin, but the way he looked those sweet, rare times, his eye darkening in that fashion that made her heart pound harder, his lips curving so tenderly.

Kate sighed. Somehow her prayer for deliverance turned into a grateful flow of thanksgiving at finding Harry so very much alive.

And that prayer, she had the strangest notion, God had heard.

Kate's own resolves about Lord Harry notwithstanding, her future conduct to the Earl of Lytton was already being decided upon by her formidable grandmother.

From her throne in the parlor, Lady Dane sipped her lemonade and informed Mrs. Towers, "This entirely changes everything. The purpose of my visit here was to persuade you to allow me to take Kate abroad, try to restore some life back into the girl. With the young man dead, this is the worst place she could be, but with Lytton alive . . . ah, that is entirely another matter. She must stay put until the marriage is all arranged."

Mrs. Towers thought her mother-in-law was marching a deal too fast. "But you heard what Kate said—"

"I heard." Her ladyship's mouth hooked into a fleeting smile.

"Even before Lord Lytton's outrageous prank," Mrs. Towers

220

said, "Kate would not have thought of marrying him. The bishop never approved of him."

"That doesn't surprise me," her ladyship sniffed. She stared up at the three-quarter length portrait of her son mounted above the mantel. A most handsome man garbed in the full glory of the robes of his divine calling, it should have been a sight calculated to bring pride to any mother's heart. That it did not find great favor with Lady Dane scarcely surprised Mrs. Towers. Her late husband and his mother had never dealt well together. It was something she had never understood—how without shouting, never once raising their well-modulated voices, the pair of them could make the tension in a room thicker than the puddings served with the Sunday beef. Even with her son dead, Lady Dane made no odds about her feelings.

"Dylan was never my favorite child. Too stiff-necked by half. I always feared that Kate was cut from the same cloth. But when I saw her with Lord Harry that last winter, the girl had become almost human. I should have taken a hand in the matter then. But I am determined to rectify my negligence now. Kate is going to marry the Earl of Lytton."

Mrs. Towers heard this pronouncement with dismay, fearing her ladyship's interference was only bound to make the situation worse. Although she knew trying to turn Lady Dane aside from her determined course would be like attempting to stop a tidal wave, Mrs. Towers made one last desperate appeal.

"I fear it won't do, my lady. In many ways, Kate is like her papa. She is a most serious-minded girl. Charming as Lord Lytton is, I fear he will never be respectable enough for her."

"He shall be made respectable enough," Lady Dane announced. "I shall see to it."

Mrs. Towers was hard pressed to stifle a groan. Her heart filled with dread, foreseeing that the peace of their days at Lytton's Dene were quite coming to an end. Much as she, too, wished to see Kate happily wed, she felt a pang of sympathy for Lord Lytton, who could have no notion of the storm about to descend upon him. Mrs. Towers had a strong desire to despatch a note of warning to that unfortunate young man.

Chapter 5

The master bedchamber at Mapleshade Hall stretched out with the vastness of a ballroom, the walls hung with sixteenth-century Flemish tapestries, the massive fireplace carved of white marble. The chamber had originally been designed by the first Earl of Lytton for the entertainment of his king, the monogram of Charles Stuart still to be found upon the elaborately carved ceiling.

After the death of the Merry Monarch and the succession of dour James, royalty ceased to visit Mapleshade, and the next generation of Arundels gradually appropriated the magnificent chamber for their own use.

To the present earl, tucked away behind the heavy gold damask bedcurtains, the chamber spoke not of any glorious past or imposing grandeur. Lord Harry was conscious only of how good it felt to be back in his own bed.

As fatigued as he had been, the night passed in a deep sleep of oblivion. Only as the hours of morning began to sift by, did dreamings overtake him.

"Kate," he murmured, caught in that pleasing semistate between dozing and waking. Nestling his face deeper among the pillows, he imagined her removing her bonnet, shaking loose her fall of dusky curls, the tresses tumbling all silken over his fingers. Her eyes were shy and inviting, her mouth warm and eager.

He heaved a contented sigh at the vision he had conjured. Somehow he had always known that beneath the prim facade of the bishop's daughter beat the heart of a most passionate woman. With a muzzy smile, he clutched at his pillow, recalling the sensation of Kate in his arms, all soft and yielding.

His fantasy was rudely disrupted by a sharp rap upon the bedchamber door. Harry ignored the brisk summons. It had to be a mistake. His servants knew better than to disturb him at this hour of a Sunday.

He tried to drift back into his dream, concentrating on the carnelian outline of Kate's lips. But his imagined kiss was again interrupted by a second knock, louder than the first. Harry responded with a snarl.

The fool in the hall beyond must have taken it for encouragement to enter. Harry heard the door creaking open.

"My lord?"

"He's not here," Harry mumbled, then cursed at the footfall on the carpet. Someone drew open the bedcurtains a crack, allowing a sliver of light to fall across his face. "What the devil—"

Harry focused on the upright form of his butler. Gravshaw's face was screwed up into the most peculiar expression. It took Harry a full minute to realize that the impassive manservant was actually in a state of some agitation.

Harry regarded him through bleary eyes. "Whatever has happened, this time I am not responsible."

"Oh, my lord. There—there is this woman belowstairs."

"Miss Towers?" Harry shot up onto one elbow, the absurd hope stirring him more fully awake.

"No, my lord. She says she—"

"Then send the wench packing," Harry said, losing interest. He rolled over, drawing the coverlet up to his ears, adding with a yawn, "In the future send away all applicants for my hand. Tell them the post has been filled."

"My lord!" Gravshaw persisted, "It is an elderly female. She says—"

"She must be here to see Sybil. Direct her to my stepmother and leave me in peace."

Harry put an end to the conversation by stuffing his head under the pillow. As though from a great distance, he heard

Gravshaw's despairing, "Very good, my lord," and then the muffled sound of the door closing again.

Harry emerged from beneath the pillow, believing he had heard the last of the incident. He had just succeeded in recapturing his drowsy state, embarking upon another delicious dream of Kate, when the chamber door slammed open again, this time accompanied by the sound of bickering voices, the stentorian tones of his butler and the militant accent of some unknown female.

"Madam, I beg you. His lordship does not receive callers—"

"Stand out of my way, you gibbering fool."

"My lady, this is most unseemly."

"Idiot. I am old enough to be his grandmother."

"But my lady," Gravshaw implored. "Think of your own reputation."

"At my time of life," came the tart reply, "if there be any who think scandal of my being in a young man's bedchamber, the more fool they."

Harry had the feeling that Gravshaw was getting the worst of this exchange, a notion that was reinforced when he detected the rustle of skirts advancing upon the bed. The next Harry knew, his bedcurtains were wrenched open. He winced at the sudden flaring of light.

"Madam!" He heard Gravshaw huff.

Harry struggled to a sitting position, flinging one hand across his eyes. "Gravshaw. What the deuce!"

"My lord. I tried to keep her out," Gravshaw moaned. "But it was impossible short of offering her ladyship bodily harm."

"It would have been worse for you, my man, if you had tried it." The apparition standing over Harry's bed pounded a cane against the floor. Harry's dazed eyes took in the figure of a most regal lady with a countenance stern enough to have daunted the entire French line.

"Off with you, sirrah," this strange woman commanded Gravshaw. "Fetch Lord Lytton his breakfast."

Gravshaw glanced at Harry, clearly appealing for his intervention. Harry shoved back the strands of hair tumbling into

224

his eyes, trying to convince himself that he was awake and not strayed into the midst of some mad nightmare.

"Begging your pardon, madam," he said, "but I think you must be in the wrong house. I don't believe I have had the pleasure—"

"I am Lady Dane," the woman ripped out.

Harry, who slept in the state nature intended, dragged the counterpane higher across the dark hairs matting his bared chest. "I trust your ladyship will forgive me if I don't make you my leg, but—"

"Impertinent rogue! I am Kathryn's grandmother."

Harry's jaw dropped open. Kate's grandma? Oh, Lord! The reason for this rather unorthodox morning call seemed to become abundantly clear to him. His gaze skated uneasily to the rigid form of his butler.

"Perhaps you *had* better go, Gravshaw."

"Very good, my lord," Gravshaw said at his most wooden. It was his pride that he had never permitted any unbidden guests to enter the house, let alone the master's bedchamber. With a somewhat crestfallen air, he retired from the field.

Harry's attention swept back to the woman who had bested his indomitable butler. Lady Dane's stance was unyielding as iron, and Harry took to the defensive.

"I don't know all that Kate might have told you about yesterday. I expect you have every right to be angry with me, but I don't intend to apologize for that kiss. It was the first time I have ever been that bold with Kate and—"

"Hold a moment, sir." The first hinting of amusement crossed Lady Dane's stern features. "You don't know Kate very well if you imagine she came talebearing to me. The girl didn't get all that color in her face just from the sun. But if you think that I am here to scold you, my lord, you are far off the mark."

"Then why are you here?" Harry asked.

"I shall tell you when you are more suitably attired to receive a lady."

Turning away from him, she stalked down the length of the room, flinging back over her shoulder, "And don't dawdle."

225

Harry stared after her a moment in a dumbfounded silence. But curiosity soon roused him to action. Obviously Lady Dane hadn't come to rip up at him over some fancied insult toward Kate. So what did she want of him?

Pushing the bedcovers aside, Harry scrambled for the door that led to the adjoining dressing room. He shrugged into a pair of breeches and white shirt, then donned a satin dressing gown, belting it with a sash. Pausing to peek in the mirror, he ran his hand thoughtfully over his jaw, but he sensed that her ladyship was not the sort to take offense at the sight of an unshaven male. She was more likely to be annoyed if he kept her waiting. Swiftly combing his hair, he dashed some water on his face and returned to the bedchamber.

Gravshaw had just entered, bearing the tray with the breakfast Lady Dane had ordered for Harry. She directed the butler to place it upon a table before the empty fireplace, the hearth swept clean for the summer. Gravshaw was then dismissed. He exited from the room, the picture of affronted dignity.

Harry watched as Lady Dane settled herself into the depths of a wing-back chair and proceeded to pour out the coffee. His lips twitched. He had small experience of grandmothers, but he suspected that her ladyship was not of the usual variety. She behaved as though it were an everyday occurrence to invade a man's bedchamber, which for her, perhaps it was. Harry had a notion the lady did as she damned well pleased.

Strolling forward, he drew up a chair opposite her. He had always felt more comfortable with people who behaved in outrageous fashion than those who punctiliously observed all the rigors of a social code.

Lady Dane removed the covers of the silver breakfast service and thrust at Harry a plate laden with muffins, dry toast, eggs, crispy bits of bacon, and deviled kidneys.

"Won't you be joining me?" he asked.

"I breakfasted *hours* ago," she told him loftily.

Harry grinned, but bent over his plate with assumed meekness. As he ate, he was aware of her ladyship studying him over the rim of her coffee cup.

"You have a look of your mother about you," she pro-

226

nounced. "She came out the same year as my eldest daughter. I knew her ladyship quite well."

"I fear I didn't," Harry said. His mother had died before his third birthday. It saddened him to think he bore not even the most vague memory of her.

"More's the pity," Lady Dane said, some of her sternness melting. "Nan Thorpe was a magnificent girl. The best horsewoman I ever knew. She could manage her men with the same skill as she did her horses. You and your father would have been the better for it if she had lived."

"I am sure we would have." He set his plate aside and waited for her ladyship to come to the point of her visit. She did so with an alarming bluntness.

"Do you love my granddaughter, sir?"

"Yes," Harry replied, equally forthright.

"You still wish to marry her?"

"Very much so."

"Then you have an odd way of going about it. I suppose you thought to pique her interest by pretending to be dead?"

"That was not of my devising." Harry frowned. Yesterday afternoon, he had finally managed to uncover an explanation for his "demise." His death had been reported on the basis of a saber found engraved with his name near a body blackened beyond recognition, the same saber he had tossed to a friend before making that final, fatal charge. Charles had become unarmed, and Harry had still had his pistol.

Leaning back in his chair, Harry briefly closed his eyes, his heart heavy with the memory of that grim moment. He had heard much talk of the glories of battle, but all he recollected was choking on gunsmoke, the terrifying sense of confusion, the thunderous explosions, the screams of the wounded, the searing pain in his shoulder, his horse going down beneath him.

"It must have been Charlie they found with my sword," Harry said wearily, opening his eyes. "When I came to, I had been taken to a convent where some nuns looked after me. I didn't make much effort to communicate to anyone that I was safe, but I never deliberately set out to deceive anyone either."

He paused, glancing toward Lady Dane. "Do you think Kate will ever believe me?"

Her ladyship's features had remained noncommittal during his account. She said slowly, "Kate is not an unreasonable girl, but I am not sure it will make much difference whether she believes you or not."

"But she loves me. She could not hide that from me yesterday." Unable to ever keep still for long, Harry rose and leaned upon the back of his chair. "She fainted in my arms, kissed me, gave me a clout upon the ears that was like to take my head off."

"That sounds like a young woman in love," Lady Dane said dryly. "But that doesn't alter the fact that you and my granddaughter are a strangely mismatched pair. I should have never thought to put the two of you in harness together."

A brief laugh escaped Harry. "I wouldn't have either. I must have passed Kate at least a dozen times upon the streets of Chillingsworth and never particularly noticed her. And then one winter evening . . ." Harry sighed. He stalked restlessly toward the chamber's tall windows and stared out at the sunwashed morning. Over the tops of the trees in his park, one could just make out the distant spire of St. Benedict's. But the greenery of summer blurred before Harry's eyes, and he was once more seeing a world blanketed in white, Kate settled before the fire, her dark curls spilling about her face as she bent over his garrick, her eyes shining with a soft light as though all the serenity of the world was to be found centered there.

He had felt like a weary traveler, descending from the windblasted heights of some mountain peak and coming across a quiet vale whose stillness had touched his heart.

"As I sat watching her," Harry murmured, "it slowly came to me that . . . that she was beautiful. I think it must have been at that precise moment that I fell in love with her, that I knew my life was never going to mean anything without her."

Harry did not realize he voiced his thoughts aloud until Lady Dane asked, "And so, sir. Did you ever explain all this to her?"

He flushed, forced a smile, and shrugged. "Not in so many words."

Her ladyship nodded with understanding. "Aye, I know. My husband was never a one for making pretty speeches either. But women, foolish creatures that we are, occasionally like to hear them."

"Do you think that pretty speeches would win me Kate?"

"Frankly, no. Is that how you are planning to go about it?"

Harry didn't answer. His chief plan of campaign was to gather up Kate in his arms, capture her lips ruthlessly until she responded in kind, melting against him, but he could scarce confess that to her grandmother.

He didn't have to. The old lady was too shrewd by half.

"That won't answer either, attempting to make love to her all day long," she said, raking him with her keen gaze. "Though I imagine you could make quite a satisfactory job of it. But it will always come down to this. Kate possesses a rock-hard bottom of sobriety. She gets it from her father, though where he came by it, the Lord only knows."

Harry heaved a frustrated sigh. "Then what do you suggest I do? I don't intend to let her slip away from me this time."

"Your only hope, young man, is to acquire an image of respectability. That absurd memorial out there can be put to some use. Let it commemorate the demise of Hellfire Harry."

"Hellfire Harry has been dead for some time," he said bitterly. "Do you think I would have ever presumed to ask Kate to marry me if I had not meant to put my wild days behind me?"

"Apparently you failed to convince her of that." Leaning on her cane, her ladyship rose majestically to her feet. "You may begin this morning by making your appearance in St. Benedict's."

"St. Benedict's!"

"It is a church, my lord, not a debtor's prison."

"I know but—but to try to make Kate believe I have turned into some sort of psalm singer! It seems the worst sort of hypocrisy."

"Not a psalm singer, but a man who understands his duty to God and sets a good example for his people. You cannot expect a bishop's daughter to marry an irreligious dog."

"I would do anything for Kate," Harry said, "slay any dragon but—"

"She doesn't need any dragons slain. She will be more impressed by the sight of you cracking open a prayer book."

Harry opened his mouth to voice another protest, but he felt caught on the crest of a wave, propelling him irresistibly forward. Before he knew where he was at, her ladyship had pulled the bell and summoned his valet to help him dress.

"You have not much time. Services begin in twenty minutes," Lady Dane said, gliding toward the door.

Harry made one last effort to save himself from what he anticipated was going to be an embarrassing and likely futile ordeal. He called after Lady Dane, "You know there is a belief in the village that if Hellfire Harry sets foot inside St. Benedict's, the roof will come tumbling down."

"I am prepared to take the risk," said Lady Dane, calmly closing the door behind her.

The bell in St. Benedict's tower had long since rung its final warning knell as Harry sprinted up the steps. He paused beneath the eight-column portico to catch his breath, leaning one gloved hand up against the church's mottled stonework.

"Hang it all," Harry muttered. Nothing had ever looked more forbidding than the set of massive wooden doors closed in his face. He whipped off his high-crowned beaver hat and brushed back the dark strands of hair from his brow in frustration.

Now what the deuce was he supposed to do? His father had opened many doors to him in his life, the exclusive gaming club at White's, Gentleman Jackson's prizefighting salon, the discreet chambers of many lovely opera dancers. But the governor had never seen fit to initiate Harry as to the doings behind St. Benedict's mysterious portals.

He guessed that those inside must already be deep into the service. Harry grimaced. He would cause enough of a stir simply by entering St. Benedict's without creeping in late as well. Despite what his cousin Julia might think, Harry did not enjoy setting the world by the ears.

He was tempted to turn and slip quietly away again, only held back by a single thought . . . Kate. She was behind that barrier, her face likely stilled into solemn lines as she prayed. For him? Harry doubted it, remembering how they had parted yesterday, the cruel trick she believed he had played. Lady Dane was right. Kisses alone would not be enough to erase such bad impressions.

Harry sighed and took one last self-conscious inventory of his appearance. He was immaculately (and to him, most uncomfortably) attired in biscuit-colored breeches that clung to the outline of his muscular thighs, the forest green coat straining across his shoulders, unbuttoned to reveal the shirt frills peeking beneath a striped waistcoat. The starched cravat with all its intricate folds felt like it was choking him.

Drawing in a deep breath, Harry eased one of the church doors open a crack, enough to peer inside, his eyes adjusting to the dark stone of the interior. The lancet windows let in not so much as a whisper of breeze on this hot, summer morning. The scent of the flowers adorning the altar hung in the breathless air like a heavy perfume, the rise and fall of the vicar's voice as sonorous as the drone of bees outside the window.

The benches and pews, scarred and venerable with age, held most of the citizens of Lytton's Dene, some of Harry's servants from the hall, and the gentry from the surrounding countryside, like Squire Gresham's boisterous family.

Adolphus made an impressive sight in his vestments, mounted high above the congregation upon the elaborately carved pulpit Harry had heard acclaimed as the pride of St. Benedict's. Harry craned his neck, scanning the pews, but he could not see Kate.

Easing the door open further to slip inside, Harry winced. The ancient hinges groaned so loudly that all the coffins in the graveyard might well have been creaking open to offer up their dead.

No matter how careful Harry tried to be, the door banged closed behind him with a loud thud. Those on the rear benches were already shifting to see what sinner dared to sneak in after the service had begun. The inevitable astonished whispers followed, and Harry could see some of the good folk actually casting anxious glances toward the roof.

At any other time he might have been amused, but his sense of humor seemed to fail him. Giving a nervous tug to his cravat, he started forward, but no matter how quietly he attempted to walk, his Hessians clattered on the stone floor. Those in the front were now also turning to stare, including his cousin Julia, who cast him a look of blistering reproach.

Harry was beginning to feel like the devil invading the sanctuary of some holy shrine when he spied Kate. She sat three rows from the front, near the aisle, by her mother and Lady Dane. Kate alone appeared unaware of any disturbance, although by this time the astounded Adolphus had floundered, losing his place in the text.

Serenely bent over her prayer book, Kate was wearing one of those old-fashioned gowns that became her so well, a white muslin embroidered with dainty flowers. A cluster of ebony curls peeked from beneath a bonnet trimmed with pink rosettes and a satin ribbon was tied in a demure bow beneath the delicate curve of her chin. Never, Harry thought wistfully, had she looked more like an angel.

She did not glance up until his shadow fell across the pages of her book. Kate emitted a tiny gasp, the volume tumbling from her grasp to land at his feet. Harry bent to retrieve it, handing it back to her with a rueful smile. Two bright spots of color appeared in her cheeks as Harry edged himself beside her on the pew.

"You are in the wrong seat, my lord," she whispered, staring rigidly toward the altar.

Harry spared a glance toward the pew at the very front reserved for the Arundel family, the coat of arms carved on the end. It was unoccupied this morning, for as usual his stepmother had one of her megrims.

"It looks too lonely over there," Harry murmured.

Kate said nothing more, diving behind the protection of her prayer book. Much to Harry's relief, the commotion he had caused died away, all eyes turned back to the front as Adolphus coughed, then shuffled the pages, resuming his place in the service.

But Harry continued to be aware of the stiffness in Kate's frame, noticing how she shrank from brushing up against him. Lady Dane had been wrong, Harry thought, suppressing a sigh. His coming here today had only caused Kate unhappiness and embarrassment.

For her part, Kate could concentrate neither on the pages of her book nor upon what Reverend Thorpe was saying. St. Benedict's was the one place she felt safe from Harry's pursuit. Whatever was he doing here? She knew she had threatened not to be at home when he would call, but surely not even he would seek to foist his attention upon her in church.

She risked one indignant glance at him and was startled to note he appeared as ill at ease as she. Perhaps more so. She tried to remember she had resolved to harden her heart against this man, keep him at a distance. But it touched something deep inside her to see Harry, so strong, so self-assured, looking humbled like an outcast in the very church his ancestors had built.

She nudged his arm. With a mute gesture, she offered to share her prayer book. He flashed a grateful smile that tugged at her heart, although she blushed more deeply when he removed the book from her grasp and gently returned it to her, right side up.

With Harry's sun-bronzed features bent so close to her own, it made an end to any prospect of her deriving benefit from the vicar's sermon. She caught but one word in ten, her gaze straying to the way Harry's dark lashes shadowed his eyes, the sweet, sensitive curve of his mouth, the square, wholly masculine line of his jaw. She felt her pulse quicken. Would she ever be able to study Harry's face again without being drawn to his lips, the memory of his kiss . . . ?

Kate flushed with shame, scandalized by the direction she had allowed her thoughts to take—and in church of all places! When the last amen sounded, she echoed it with relief, feeling the need to put some distance between herself and Harry.

Harry stepped back to allow her to pass by him into the aisle.

233

She was aware of his low-murmured greeting to her mother and grandmother, but Kate kept walking, following the other parishioners crowding toward the door.

Only when she had stepped out into the sunlight of the churchyard did she pause to take a steadying breath. She knew Harry would be hard on her heels, and she turned over in her mind the speeches she had lain awake half the night rehearsing.

My lord, I must insist that we be no more than mere acquaintances. It will be the better for both of us.

Kate nodded. That had a noble ring to it, kind but firm. *My lord . . .* she repeated to herself again, certain that Harry would be joining her at any moment.

But as she glanced back to the church doors, she saw that Harry had been cut off from her by a sea of people. The squire was clapping him on the back and roaring out that St. Benedict's had not known such excitement since the invasion of the Roundhead army. Others . . . mostly ladies, Kate noted with a frown, were wringing Harry's hand and exclaiming over him.

Of course Kate had always been aware how attractive Harry was to the ladies, so handsome in the raffish way most women adored, his smile so winning. But not until that moment did she realize that ever since the night he had crashed into her garden, she was accustomed to his attention being fixed solely upon her.

Not that she was in the least jealous. No, how absurd, she thought, nearly ruining the toe of her sandal by digging it into the dirt. She didn't even have the right to be jealous, having so thoroughly thrust Harry out of her life. And in fact—she crushed several blades of grass beneath her foot—she was relieved Harry was too preoccupied to rush to her side.

Turning her back upon him, she stalked up the steps of the church portico to where Reverend Thorpe lingered. The poor man looked a little forlorn, being accustomed after the service to have most of his flock gathered about him.

"Today's sermon was most . . . most enlightening," Kate said, wincing a little at this polite lie, unable to recall one word of the discourse.

"Thank you," the vicar said, "You are most kind, Miss Towers—"

He was interrupted by Julia bustling up to join them, in time to hear these last remarks. "The sermon would have gone much better without the disturbance," she said, her lovely face marred by a peevish expression. "Whatever possessed Lytton to come here this morning?"

As Julia asked the question, her eyes seemed to bore into Kate. Kate felt her color heighten.

"He likely came to pray," Kate said, struggling to keep the acid tones out of her own voice. "Surely there is nothing so remarkable in that."

"For Lytton, it would be," Julia said flatly.

Reverend Thorpe hastened to interpose. "I was most gratified that Lord Harry came. It seems our cousin has taken heed of my admonishments at last."

Julia shot her brother such a look, Kate half feared she meant to call the vicar a fool. But she merely grated, "You are much too good, Adolphus."

Kate had always thought so herself, that the vicar was virtuous to the point of being a little priggish. But she had been much ashamed of herself for harboring such an unbecoming opinion. As a bishop's daughter, she should have taken more pleasure in the worthy Mr. Thorpe's company. Yet she felt nothing but dismay when Julia extended an invitation for her to dine at the parsonage.

"We could spend a nice quiet afternoon together, just you, I, and Adolphus—"

"Oh, thank you," Kate said, but made haste to stammer out her excuses. She had so many pressing duties, with her grandmama arrived but yesterday. Her mother would be wanting her. Indeed she should have not kept Mama standing about in the heat even this long. Murmuring her farewells, Kate bolted back down the steps. She all but blundered into the squire's hoydenish daughter, Becky.

"Isn't it grand, Miss Towers, having Lord Harry back?" the girl cried happily. "He's such a great gun."

Kate resisted the impulse to glance to where Harry was

235

surrounded by an admiring throng. "It is most pleasant," she agreed with Becky. "But I doubt your mama would care to hear you use such unladylike expressions."

Becky ignored the reproof. The lively redhead had a knack for hearing only what she wished. She chattered on, "Lord Harry looks ever so smart today. In prime twig. I am glad, for he appeared terribly blue-deviled yesterday when he realized his friend must be dead."

"I-I beg your pardon?" Kate asked.

"His friend, Charles Masters. You know, the one his lordship lent his sword to during the battle. That's why everyone thought Lord Harry had been killed, and here the poor fellow himself knew nothing about it."

"What—" Kate began hoarsely. She forced Becky to go through the entire story over again, not an easy task, for the girl expected herself to be immediately understood even though she never related any tale in logical sequence.

By the time Becky sauntered off to greet another acquaintance, Kate had pieced enough of the facts together to feel herself go pale. So Harry had not been responsible for the rumor of his own death. He had been as much a victim of the grievous error as anyone else.

And to think how horridly she had treated him ... Kate pressed one hand to her cheek. But why hadn't Harry told her the truth at once, she wailed inwardly. *He tried to. You wouldn't listen,* her merciless conscience replied.

Kate hung her head. She should go to Harry, apologize to him at once. But if Kate had one failing, her Papa had often admonished her, it was her pride. The bishop had always been so understanding because he bore the same sin himself. It was most difficult to admit when one had been wrong.

She stole a glance toward Harry. He had managed to escape the flock of females but had fallen into the squire's clutches. Gresham was obviously badgering his lordship about selling those hunters. Harry was laughing but firmly shaking his head.

Kate flushed with shame. Overcome with remorse, she felt she could not face Harry at that moment. Quickening her steps,

236

she hastened to where her mother already waited by the gig drawn up in the lane by their sole male servant, John.

To her dismay, Kate discovered that a problem had arisen regarding their transportation. Her grandmother, who had come to church on her own after some mysterious errand, had imperiously dismissed her coach back to the stables.

Lady Dane raised strenuous objections to riding crushed between Kate and her mother in the gig. "Far too crowded for three on a hot day," her ladyship declared.

Kate sighed but offered to walk. She truly did not mind, it being her favorite form of exercise, but Lady Dane also objected to that.

"Nonsense. Your mother would never want you walking in this heat. Would you, Maisie?"

"Well, I—" Mrs. Towers began.

"That settles it." To Kate's horror, Lady Dane turned about and snapped, "Lytton!"

"Oh, no, Grandmama, pray don't," Kate faltered, guessing Lady Dane's intent. She hoped Harry might not have heard. But she did not know how it was—Lady Dane never actually raised her voice, yet it had such carrying power.

Across the churchyard, Harry's head snapped up eagerly. Bowing, he managed to escape Gresham, even the squire forced to give way before a summons from Lady Dane.

In several quick strides, Harry crossed over to the gig. Kate averted her face, scarcely knowing where to look. Although Harry addressed her grandmother, Kate sensed his eyes were upon herself.

"My lady?"

"I cannot abide being crowded upon such a hot day. Perhaps you would be so obliging as to fetch Kate home, my lord."

"With pleasure."

"No, I-I must not impose," Kate said. "That is, I must call upon . . . upon Mrs. Hudderston. I promised to bring her a recipe for our housekeeper's honey syrup. Little Tom has developed the most distressing cough."

"Then Lytton may take you there as well," Lady Dane said, disposing of his lordship as though he operated a hackney cab.

Kate half turned to her mother for support, but she knew it would not be the least use expecting the gentle Mrs. Towers to resist Lady Dane's ruthless maneuvers.

In her flustered state, Kate was never quite certain how she got there, but she found herself being handed up into Lord Harry's curricle. At least, she noted with some relief, he was not driving the high-perch phaeton that Harry knew made her nervous.

It was not until Harry leaped up beside her to take the reins that Kate realized his lordship had somehow dispensed with his groom. If she had not known better, it would almost seem as though Lady Dane and his lordship were linked in a conspiracy to get her alone with Lord Harry. Kate dismissed the notion at once as being foolish, born out of the butterflies that seemed to have taken up residence inside her.

Harry whipped up his team, setting the chestnuts with their flowing manes into motion. The reins looped about his gloved hands with an easy grace, Harry expertly maneuvered his vehicle past the press of other carriages and wagons exiting from the churchyard.

A silence that seemed more heavy than the still summer air settled over them, until Harry sent the team into a smart trot down the dusty lane. Harry cleared his throat.

"Er—cracking good sermon we had this morning."

"Yes," Kate said faintly. She removed her fan from her reticule, applying it with more vigor than was necessary.

"I always did like that tale about the prodigal son returning. How everyone forgave him no matter how wicked he had been. . . ." Harry's voice trailed off suggestively.

Kate knew this was a perfect opening for her to beg his pardon. She glanced down at her clenched hands, her throat tightening.

Harry startled her by suddenly drawing rein, bringing the horses to a dead halt. A large oak spread its shade over the road, protecting them somewhat from the scorching sun. A mournful-looking cow peered at them over a fence.

"Kate." Harry turned to her. She could not bring herself to look at him. "I am sorry . . . about this morning, I mean."

He was apologizing to her? Kate's remorse deepened until she felt ready to sink.

"I never intended to interrupt the service."

"You don't have to beg pardon for coming to church, my lord," Kate said. "I thought it was wonderful—"

"No, it wasn't," Harry replied glumly. He started to reach for her hand, barely checking the movement. "I can't deceive you about motives. I only came because of you, because of wanting to see you, hoping you might think better of me. Perhaps you might even like to have me there beside you."

The constriction in Kate's throat tightened so she could scarce breathe. It occurred to her that she had indeed liked having Harry there, too much. As the bishop's daughter, she knew she ought to tell him the only reason for attending church should be his own soul, but she found herself too deeply touched to think that he had altered the pattern of a lifetime simply for her sake.

Swallowing her pride at last, she said in a low voice, " 'Tis I who should apologize to you, my lord. I heard how the report of your death came about, that it was none of your doing."

"Well! That's a great relief." Harry heaved a cheerful sigh. "Though there's nothing for you to be sorry about."

"All those terrible names I called you!"

"Oh, I am sure I deserved them for something or other." Harry peered down at her, hating the distress he saw gathering in her eyes. Plague take it, he would rather he had done what she had wrongly accused him of, than see Kate looking so wretched with guilt.

"But—but you were wounded," she faltered.

"Only a trifle."

"And I hit you. So hard."

"True. You have a most impressive bunch of fives. But I really need to teach you not to lead with your right."

Kate's conscience appeared too stern to allow even one smile to escape her.

"If you are feeling that guilty," Harry said, leaning his face closer, "You may kiss me and make it feel better. Then I shall be only too happy to turn the other cheek."

Kate shrank back. She wasn't feeling that stricken with remorse. "It was partly your fault, my lord," she said, biting
down upon her lip. "Why did you never write to tell anyone
what had become of you?"

Harry raised his shoulders in a shrug that was perhaps a
shade too nonchalant. "I didn't suppose anyone would much
care."

"There are a great many people who do." She swallowed.
"I-I am quite fond of you, my lord."

"Kate!"

"And I trust we shall always be friends," she added primly.

Harry moved closer, stealing his arm about her waist. "I
hope so, too. I know I am considered hopelessly unfashionable, but I think it much better when married people can
remain friends."

He saw the flash of alarm in her eyes and knew he was rushing his fences. Though it took a great effort of will on his part,
he withdrew his arm. "No need to look so panicked," he said.
"That wasn't the beginning of another proposal. I never ask
girls to marry me on Sunday."

When she cast him a doubtful glance, he drew himself up
with feigned sternness. "It's supposed to be a day of rest, Miss
Towers. As a bishop's daughter, you should know that."

An indignant gasp escaped her that turned into a most
unwilling gurgle of laughter. "Oh, Harry, you really are
abominable."

"That's better," he approved, turning his attention back to
his restive horses, giving them the office to start up again. "I
thought you were going to 'my lord' me to death."

The team set off down the road, a jauntiness in their step that
was reflected in the lifting of Harry's own spirits. True, Kate's
response had not been all that he had hoped. She was not ready
to cast herself into his arms, but at least he had got her to smile.
And Harry had learned to be . . . oh, just a trifle more patient
than he had been two years ago.

Kate struggled to school her face into a more prim expression, but it was a losing battle. Harry had ever been able to
make her laugh when she tried too hard to be serious. He

grinned at her and tossed the reins in her lap. Kate caught them in a gesture that was almost reflexive.

"Do you still remember?" he asked.

"Of course I do," Kate said, taking up the challenge, gathering up the leather in a firm, but graceful grip. It was Harry himself who had taught her to handle a team. He watched her critically for a moment, then relaxed back against the seat appearing satisfied with her performance.

It was not an accomplishment of which her Papa would ever have approved, but Kate could not help a glow of pride creeping into her cheeks. Harry did not permit just *anyone* to drive his chestnuts.

As the team followed the winding lane, sweeping past the hedgerows and fields, Kate sensed another distance being closed as well—the span of two years. The constraint she had expected to feel with Harry simply did not exist. It was as though all those lonely, empty days, weeks, months had never been.

She sensed that Harry felt it, too. He loosened his cravat, heaving a contented sigh.

"Lord, it's good to be home. I had nigh forgotten how green it all is here. . . . Nothing has changed," he added softly, looking toward her. She knew from the warmth in his eyes he was speaking of more than his lands.

Her heart gave an answering flutter and she half started to agree with him. But memory intruded. Something indeed had changed since that spring. There was a freshly laid stone among all the other aged memorials in the vast cold halls of Chillingsworth Cathedral.

Kate's shoulders sagged beneath a mixed weight of sorrow and guilt. Harry read the change in her expression all too well.

"I was sorry to hear about your father," he said.

He spoke with a quiet simplicity, and Kate knew that, despite the differences that had existed between himself and the late bishop, Harry meant it.

"Thank you," she murmured. Although Harry had been away in London at the time of her father's death, a spray of flowers had found its way to her door. The enclosed card had borne but one word, *Harry*. Yet somehow that had brought her more consolation than all the scriptural outpourings of her father's ecclesiastical friends.

It had not been long after that she had received the tidings that Harry had bought his commission. Kate had been deeply troubled by this rash action, and she ventured to mention it to him.

"I was worried about you when I heard you joined the army. I was afraid that perhaps it was all my doing—that I was to blame."

"Because I was nursing a broken heart? Nonsense, Kate. You know I have a tougher hide than that. No, it was simply that London was becoming a dead bore and, in any event, it's family tradition. All the Lytton men at sometime or other seem to have gotten a mad hankering to run off to be a soldier." After a pause, Harry said reflectively, "Though I don't know why. Rum business soldiering."

Despite the offhand nature of the comment, something in Harry's tone caused Kate to glance at him. His features had stilled into somber lines, a darkness gathered in the wells of his eyes that Kate had never seen there before. In that instant Kate realized Harry had sustained more wounds at Waterloo than just his arm. So full of life himself, he was not the sort of man to take pleasure in death, not even of his enemies.

She longed to reach out to him, comfort him, but as ever Harry was quick to toss off his own somber mood with a jest. He proceeded to assure her with mock solemnity, "You see me returned home, my Kate, content to live the rest of my life as a sober country gentleman. I intend to become so stuffed with respectability, my tailor shall have to let out my waistcoats."

Kate could not quite prevent her brow from quirking in dubious fashion. Harry began to make all sort of outrageous promises that ranged from attending church every Sunday to never engaging in any sport more dangerous than whist for a penny a point.

Although he had her laughing as they drew near the turning to Hudderston farm, Kate could not forbear remarking, "I hope all this newfound respectability includes showing a greater interest in your estates."

"Oh, indubitably," Harry said, taking the reins from her, guiding the curricle past the stile.

The Hudderstons were some of Harry's best tenants. The wide, welcoming barnyard was as well noted for its flock of speckled hens as for its brood of lively, sandy-haired children. The only thing that marred the appearance of the snug, solidly built stone farmhouse was that one end of the thatched roof had through time and neglect begun to sag.

"Lord!" Harry exclaimed in shock as he reined in his team.

Kate half turned to him, not wishing Harry to be too distraught with remorse. After all, he had been away so long, but any reassurance she had been about to give was cut off when Harry emitted a low whistle.

"Damme! But those children have grown several hands since I saw them last. Even little Jack."

So saying, Harry was quick to alight. He handed down Kate and was soon swallowed in a sea of freckled faces. Despite the passage of time, he was somehow still able to identify all the little Hudderstons by name.

Kate could only gape at him as she realized that Harry didn't seem to notice the roof was about to cave in on their heads. She could have shaken him, but it would have taken a far more hard-hearted female not to melt at the sight of Harry tossing a small girl up onto his shoulders, her braids flying amid squeals of delight.

"Oh, Harry." Kate sighed, shaking her head ruefully.

So charming . . . but so irresponsible, just as the bishop had always said.

And even though Kate could not help smiling as she followed Harry toward the house, a string of little ones hanging on to his coattails, she could feel the shadow of her father once more passing between them.

Chapter 6

Dawn broke over Mapleshade, a fine mist shrouding the distant majesty of the towering trees, golden light spilling across the dewy green lawn until it resembled some lush carpet scattered with pearls. Harry peered out the study window, rubbing eyes gritty from lack of sleep.

It was not the first time he had watched the sun come up over his parklands. He had often witnessed this magnificent spectacle after one of those grueling all-night card sessions with his father, or riding home in the wee hours, his head splitting from carousing at one of the inns in Chillingsworth.

This time, however, it was a far different reason that found him out of his bed at daybreak. Wearily, Harry's gaze tracked to the oak desk littered with sheets of rumpled parchment, the candle that was no more than a charred wick protruding from a lump of dried wax. The scene bore mute testimony to his nightlong labors, going over the condition of his estate—a most dismaying and unrewarding task.

Massaging some of the stiffness from his neck, Harry turned back to the far more agreeable prospect that lay just outside his window. He had never been given much to flights of fancy, but his lands, beneath the sun's first rays, bore an aura of enchantment, the mists and soft light conjuring up images of days gone by.

Harry could well imagine the first earl, that dashing cavalier, charging across the lawn toward the Hill, the plumes of his hat waving, his sword drawn in defiance against Cromwell's soldiers, his bold deeds winning for him the heart of his lady fair.

Aye, Harry envied that ancient lord. How easy he had had

things. Merely rattle his saber, hold Mapleshade against a score or so of Roundheads, mayhap endure a wound or two, and the woman of his dreamings had melted into his embrace.

"But I'll wager the woman in question was not a bishop's daughter," Harry murmured with a wry smile. Quite the reverse. He had not seen Kate since he had driven her home from church five days ago, and their parting had been far from warm.

He had sensed the change in her immediately after, what had been for him, a most delightful visit to Hudderston's farm. But as he had handed Kate back into the curricle, she had been distant, taking refuge behind the prim demeanor he knew far too well.

When he had set her down at her own gate, she had attempted to fob him off with a stiff handshake. But he had held her fast, summoning up his most engaging grin.

"*Now* what have I done wrong, Kate?"

She refused to answer him, merely looking flustered. Finally he did manage to goad her into saying, "It is not so much what you have done, my lord, as *what you have not.*"

As Harry tried to figure out what the devil that meant, Kate disengaged her hand, blushing deeply. "Forgive me, my lord. I should not— It is not my place to say— Good afternoon and thank you so much for bringing me home."

She had given him a look, at once so sad and somehow filled with disappointment, before fleeing into the sanctuary of her cottage, leaving Harry standing at the gate, feeling more confused than ever.

It was then that he had discovered the advantage of having an ally within Kate's stronghold. Kate might continue to try to avoid him, but not so her grandmama. When he had asked Lady Dane if she knew what had gone awry, that formidable dame did not mince words.

"It's the state of your tenants' farms, you young cawker. Kate feels you haven't been doing your duty by 'em and the heavens forfend! If there was one word that girl *was* taught the meaning of before she could even say 'mama,' it was 'duty.' "

At first, Harry had waxed indignant against the charge. He

might not be the best of landlords, but as for neglect! He frequently passed by his tenants' farms on horseback, enjoyed tousling the curls of the babes, jesting with the men, playfully flirting with their good wives, listening to the grandfathers spin tales of their youth.

But he took enough heed of what Lady Dane had told him to ride back to the Hudderston place and study it through more critical eyes. What he saw caused his face to burn with shame. The plaguey roof was all but coming down upon their heads.

As in turn he examined his other properties, he made discoveries equally as mortifying. To think that Kate must also have noticed all this. No wonder she thought him such a frippery fellow.

Hence his midnight session, trying to sort out the problems of the estate, poring over accounts until his head ached, wondering what was to be done, not quite knowing where to begin. As he had paced before the study window, watching the sun rise, he had at last in desperation sent for his steward.

A soft knock at the door alerted him of Warburton's approach. Harry hastened to settle himself behind the desk, attempting to arrange the papers into a more tidy heap.

"Come in," he called.

The steward crept into the room. Warburton was a thin man, as dry as the parchment sheets of ancient ledgers, his eyes the color of faded ink.

"You sent for me, my lord?" he asked in a hesitant tone.

"Yes, I did."

Warburton looked utterly confounded. Harry supposed he could understand why. In truth, he had scarce ever paid more heed to Warburton than to one of the books in the library, devoting his interest to the advice of his head groom or his gameskeeper.

"Come and sit down," Harry said.

Warburton did so, but he perched on the very edge of his seat as though yet expecting to find that the request for his presence had all been a mistake. His dull eyes drooped from the weight of skin bagging beneath them. Harry experienced a twinge of guilt as it occurred to him that he had dragged the old man from his bed at a most unreasonable hour.

But when Harry apologized, the steward protested, "Nay, my lord, I was awake. It has been a lifelong habit of mine to be up at first light of day."

"Mine as well." Harry grimaced, then moved on to the purpose of the interview. "I have been making a tour of the estate."

Warburton's eyes rounded with even greater astonishment.

Harry tapped a piece of parchment laid before him. "I have compiled a rather long list of matters that need attention."

Warburton stiffened. "I have done my best, my lord, as I have always done—"

"I am not blaming you," Harry interrupted soothingly. "Even a good servant cannot make up for a bad master. I know that in the past I have given you short shrift when you attempted to discuss estate business. The truth is . . ."

Harry trailed off. The truth was that although his father had taught him many things, to ride like the devil, to drive to an inch, to fire a pistol with creditable accuracy, the governor had never done much by way of teaching Harry how to look after the estate. Although he now regretted that circumstance, Harry was far too honest to lay all the blame at the old earl's door.

"I have been an idle and ignorant fellow," Harry concluded instead. "But now I want to take more of a hand with Mapleshade, but I must rely on you for instruction, Warburton. Do you think you could contrive to teach a dull dog like me?"

Mr. Warburton gaped at him for a moment, then said, looking both flattered and disconcerted, "C-certainly, my lord. That is not that I think you are a dull dog, but that if you really mean it, I would be most happy to assist you."

Harry bit back a smile at this flustered speech and assured Warburton he would be most grateful. But in the next few minutes, Harry was not quite so sure. Never would he have guessed the dour Warburton could be so voluble.

With an eagerness that bordered on pathos, the steward proceeded to barrage Harry with a stream of facts about land taxes, farm leases, and crop rotation until Harry was laughingly obliged to fling up one hand.

"My dear fellow, I don't think I can quite master the whole of it in one morning. Perhaps we could deal with the most immediate problem. I am concerned about the state of some of my tenants' farm buildings."

Warburton's face fell. As Harry proceeded to outline his plan for repairs to the Hudderston roof, the steward looked downright uncomfortable.

"That would be wonderful, my lord, and I should have seen to it myself long ago." Warburton paused and coughed delicately against his hand. "But for one small problem—the funds."

Harry felt his face wash a dull red. He did not require any further explanation from the steward. His estates had been encumbered with debt when he had inherited them, due mostly to his father's penchant for gaming. Harry had never acquired the governor's taste for the dice and cards, but with a stab of conscience, he realized he had never been good at practicing economies himself, his own particular vices being his horses and an openhanded policy about lending money to friends.

He sighed. "Surely there must be at least enough income to thatch the Hudderston roof."

Warburton said nothing, merely reached for the quill pen and sketched out some estimated figures for Harry.

"That much for a wretched pile of straw?"

"The war caused a shortage, my lord. Perhaps if this year's crops do well and none of the money is drained out of the estate, by next spring—"

"By next spring, the Hudderstons will be using their roof for rushes. There must be some quicker way."

"I suppose you could sell off some of the timber."

Harry thought of the ancient fell of trees that was the crowning glory of his lands. No, he would not figure in the history of Mapleshade as the earl who had cut the timber. Neither did he find Warburton's next suggestion any more palatable.

"Raise the farm rents? That would be worse than a window tax, and a little like asking the Hudderstons to pay for the privilege of having a hole in their roof."

Warburton spread his hands in a helpless gesture. "Then I don't know what other remedy remains, my lord."

Unfortunately, Harry did. The thought came to him with the swiftness of a sword thrust and just as piercing. He tried to resist the notion, but he feared the longer he dwelled on the prospect, the less likely he would be able to act upon it.

"I know of another way to obtain the necessary money," he said quietly. He offered Warburton no explanation, but reached for the quill with grim purpose. He scrawled out a note which he sanded, folded, sealed, and handed to Warburton.

"See that this is delivered to Squire Gresham."

"Oh, my lord. Not your hunters!"

Harry attempted a careless shrug, but could not quite manage it. "No sense having a pack of horses eating me out of house and stable. I daresay I shan't have much time for hunting in any case."

Warburton accepted the note, but he regarded Harry with a new light of respect in his eyes and a sympathy that made Harry uncomfortable. Harry turned away, adding gruffly, "I suppose if one means to do a thing, there is no sense of going at it by halves. The chestnuts may go as well. I am meeting my old friend, Sam Ffolliot in the village this afternoon. I am sure he would offer a fair price."

"Mr. Ffolliot!" Warburton choked in dismay.

When Harry regarded the steward from beneath upraised brows, Warburton flushed.

"That is, I have heard tell the Honorable Mr. Ffolliot is a most amiable gentleman. . . ."

Harry grinned. "Folly is a complete ass, but he takes good care of his horses."

Within days of his return, Harry had been besieged by an invitation from the honorable Samuel. Folly meant to race his footman against Lord Erwin's, laying a monkey on the outcome. Even if Harry did not wish to place a wager, he might just want to come along and crack a bottle or two with the fellows.

But such pleasures had long ago begun to pall for Harry. All too frequently he had found himself yawning behind his hand

and checking his watch. Somehow he seemed to have out-grown his former companions. Perhaps falling in love with Kate had done that. His stint as a soldier had surely finished it.

Yet he could not bring himself to completely snub his old friend. Of a certainty, Folly had far more hair than wit and Harry had hauled the man out of more than one scrape. But there was no real harm in him, no trace of that streak of mean-ness that characterized Harry's other erstwhile companion, Lord Erwin. Thus Harry had agreed to pass at least the after-noon with Folly at the Arundel Arms in the village. The meet-ing would serve a double purpose if he could persuade Folly to buy the chestnuts.

Having reached his decision, Harry refused to dwell on the sale of his horses any further, wanting neither pity nor praise. Instead he engaged Warburton in a discussion of how the money thus raised could best be spent, a talk that moved on to some schemes the steward had been perishing to set into mo-tion for many a day that would improve the future income of the estate.

Harry could not say that the morning sped by. When he arose from the desk, he felt curiously more drained than after a hard day on the hunting field. But he carried away with him a satisfied feeling of having accomplished something.

It did not surprise him when he received a reply from Squire Gresham as early as that same afternoon. In his eagerness to close the deal, the squire had sent along not only the necessary bank notes, but a groom to fetch away the horses.

Harry had reconciled himself to the loss of the hunters, but he did not feel particularly enthusiastic about watching them being led away. Directing the squire's man toward the stables, Harry betook himself to another part of the house to change into his riding clothes for the meeting with Folly.

Before he departed, he thought he might as well see to an-other grim duty and be done with it—that of his daily inquiry after the state of his stepmother's health. Ever since his return, Sybil had kept to her rooms. Their initial reunion had proved disastrous, Harry's continued refusal to receive Lucillus Crosbie causing Sybil to collapse in tears. Although he remained adamant, Harry did his best to make it up to her in other ways.

As he passed through the long gallery that contained the portraits of his ancestors, he half fancied that from within their gilt frames those raffish gentlemen regarded him with amused sympathy, from the first bold cavalier to that bewigged rogue who had been Harry's grandfather.

The line of portraits stretched unending until recent times, where naught but a bare panel remained. The spot where the last earl should have been was empty. It filled Harry with regret that his father had ever been too restless even to sit for his own painting, leaving Harry with nothing more to remember him by than recollections of some rollicking good times.

And Sybil.

Harry drew up outside the door to his stepmother's sitting room. Squaring his shoulders, he knocked, but not too loudly, lest Sybil accuse him of giving her a headache before he even set foot in the room.

He waited for the familiar quavery response, but nothing but a heavy silence greeted him from the opposite side of the portal. After a moment, he thought he detected a hushed whispering and then a scuffling sound.

Harry knocked again. "My lady?"

More scuffling and then renewed silence.

Harry frowned. Headaches be damned. He knocked louder this time. "My lady, is anything—"

"Ohhh." He was cut off by a low groan. A weak voice bade him enter, an unnecessary command, for Harry was already pushing the door open.

He paused on the threshold, half fearing he might find Sybil going off into one of her swoons. She was indeed reclining on a gilt Egyptian-style sofa, her usual posture, but not in her usual attire. Even by this time of day it was nothing to find Sybil still in curl papers, her dressing gown draped about her ample form.

But although she lay upon the sofa, one hand flung over her eyes, her brassy curls were arranged neatly beneath a lace cap,

251

and she was attired in a sprigged muslin gown that would have looked quite charming on someone thirty years younger.

"Oh, Harcourt," she said. "What are you doing here? I thought you had gone out riding."

Was it his imagination or did Sybil seem even more dismayed than usual to see him? Harry started to answer her, then recalled Sybil did not like anyone "shouting" across the room.

Closing the door as softly as he could, he inched forward, taking care to avoid an étagère crammed with bric-a-brac. Ever since he was a lad, his stepmother's sitting room had always made him edgy, every available surface cluttered with fragile china objects. He never failed to break a piece of it, sending Sybil off into paroxysms of tears, while he slunk guiltily away, the evidence of his crime clutched in his hands.

"I came to see how you are getting on today," he said, "before I ride into the village. If there is anything that I can do for you—"

"No, nothing. Nothing at all." Sybil stunned him by the brightness of her smile. She fidgeted nervously with the gold filigree bracelet banding one plump wrist. "Do run along, my dear boy. You are looking positively piqued. I am sure you must be wanting some fresh air."

Never could Harry recall being Sybil's "dear boy" or her showing solicitude for the state of his health. Harry eyed her dubiously and wondered what might be in the latest medicine she was quacking herself with. He moved to examine the small table at her elbow, only to be brought up short. The familiar tray with its array of smelling salts, headache powders, and assorted strange bottles was missing.

In its place was a teapot, cups, and saucers—two sets of them to be precise. At that same moment, Harry caught a whiff of a familiar, cloying odor. Lavender water. Sybil had many faults but dousing herself with scents wasn't one of them.

Harry's eyes narrowed dangerously, but he concealed his suspicion and sudden flare of anger behind a tight-lipped smile.

"It is good of you to be so concerned about me," he said, strolling about the room with forced casualness, his gaze dart-

252

ing here and there. Most of the furniture in the room was as dainty as Sybil's china, with elegant scrolled arms and legs. The only area of the parlor that afforded any place of concealment was . . .

Harry glanced toward the open window, the brocade drapery billowing ever so slightly with the summer breeze. At the curtain's hemline Harry could just make out the toe of a boot.

"But fresh air does not seem to be my problem," Harry continued. "In fact, I think I am taking a chill. If you don't mind, I'll just close the window."

"No," Sybil shrieked, sitting bolt upright. But Harry was already striding toward the casement. In another second, he had collared the slender young man hiding behind the draperies, dragging Lucillus Crosbie from his place of concealment.

Crosbie was a good-looking youth, his waves of light brown hair flowing past his ridiculously high shirt points. His dreamy eyes, which most of the ladies declared so poetic, now bulged with alarm.

"L-lord Lytton," he gasped, struggling to free himself from Harry's grasp. "Please don't do anything hasty. I can explain—"

"No explanations are necessary. I thought, upon one other occasion, I had made my feelings about your calling upon her ladyship perfectly clear."

"You did, sir, but—" Crosbie paled as Harry tightened his grip. "Oh, pray, not the pond again!"

"Nay, I wouldn't dream of so disturbing the fish."

Before Crosbie could say another word, Harry hefted him off his feet and tossed the fellow out the window. Crosbie's own startled howl was only eclipsed by Sybil's scream.

As Harry slammed the window closed, she flung herself across the room, pressing both her hands and face against the glass.

"Oh, Harcourt. You—you ruffian. You have dropped poor Mr. Crosbie into the rose bushes."

"Blasted careless of me. Roses are so damned hard to grow."

Harry glared out the window himself, watching Crosbie struggle painfully to his feet. Although he risked a longing glance at Lady Lytton, the fellow possessed enough sense to limp away from the house.

Striding into the hall, Harry shouted for one of the footmen to make certain Crosbie found his way off the property, also snapping out, "Tell Gravshaw I want a word with him."

His once redoubtable manservant was getting confoundedly careless about whom he let through the front door. It would be much easier to vent his exasperation with Gravshaw than return to deal with Sybil.

Harry did not relish having to preach propriety to anyone. Considering his own past, it made him feel ridiculous. But damn it all, Sybil was his stepmother. No matter how foolish the woman was, he couldn't stand idly by and let a jackanapes like Crosbie make a cake of her.

When he returned to the sitting room, he half feared to find Sybil already sunk into hysterics. Instead she stood silhouetted by the window, drawn up into a dramatic pose that would have done credit to a Sarah Siddons.

"Harcourt! You are entirely too cruel."

"I don't call it cruel to try to protect you from the havey-cavey intentions of Lucillus Crosbie."

"Lucillus is a gentleman. He wants to marry me."

"He's a dashed—"

"Don't shout!" Lady Lytton pressed one hand to her brow. "Your voice goes right through my poor head." She staggered to the sofa and began searching behind the pillow for her smelling salts.

Harry had not realized he was shouting. It was amazing how Sybil always found his voice too loud when he was saying something she did not care to hear. He continued doggedly, "Crosbie is a dashed fortune hunter—"

"He is not! You don't know him. He has the sweetest nature imaginable." Sybil paused long enough to uncork the bottle of sal volatile and take a fortifying sniff. "He is willing to consign my widow's jointure to perdition if that is what it would take to convince you of his good intent."

"Is he indeed? And what the deuce would the pair of you live upon?"

"Lucillus has prospects. He is a brilliant sculptor."

Harry rolled his eyes.

Sybil thumped her plump fist angrily against the sofa. "Even you said the statue for your memorial was well executed."

"Yes," Harry grudgingly conceded, "but in questionable taste."

"That wasn't Lucillus's fault. He was obliged to use a statue of Apollo he had already designed. He merely changed the head and substituted a sword for the lyre. It was remarkably clever of Lucillus and a great savings as well."

"You mean you obtained my memorial secondhand?" Harry asked in a slightly unsteady voice.

Lady Lytton bristled defensively. "The tidings of your death came at very short notice, Harcourt. I managed the best I could."

"S-so you did." Harry's lively sense of the ridiculous overcame him. Despite how hard he tried to control it, a bark of laughter escaped him.

Her ladyship eyed him reproachfully. "I never thought even you could be this unfeeling, Harcourt. When you were named as trustee of my jointure, I never said a word, though I did think it most odd, that a child should be given such control over the parent. But I trusted you to behave reasonably. Never did I think . . ." Both of Sybil's chins quivered. "You wish to see me a human sacrifice. Buried alive with your father."

Harry sobered immediately. "No, I don't. Believe me," he added with great feeling. "*No one* wants to see you remarried more than I. But not to a court card like Crosbie. Damn! For you to be setting up a fool like that in my father's place. It's an insult to his memory."

Sybil's face colored, her cheeks turning the same bright red as her rouge. "No one respects your father's memory more than I. I have been a good widow, but I am far too young to go on . . . I hate black and Lucillus is not a fool. . . ." Her tangled speech trailed off into incoherency, the inevitable flood of tears commencing.

As she sobbed tragically into her handkerchief, Harry watched her in acute discomfort. He hated making anyone so

255

miserable, and there was nothing more odious than being told that something was being done for one's own good.

But any temptation he might have felt to yield was checked by the memory of those final hours he had spent at the old earl's bedside. His father had known he was dying, but he wanted no clergyman about him, only Harry and his pack of hunting dogs. The governor had no fear of death and no regrets about the way he had lived his life save one.

"I should have never married again," his father had confessed to Harry. "There was only ever one woman for me, my boy, and that was your mother. Poor Sybil. I've been the very devil of a husband to her. The foolish creature has not a whit of sense or she never would have had me. It's going to be up to you to look after her when I'm gone, Harry."

Harry's throat tightened at the memory. It was the only thing the old earl had ever asked of him, the only responsibility he had ever laid upon Harry's shoulders. There might be little else in his life he had ever done right. Surely he could manage to fulfill his father's one simple request.

Harry's conscience pricked him just a little, for he knew it was not only the old earl he was thinking of, but Kate. Good Lord, what would she think of him if he was so careless of his duty as to permit his stepmother to wed some silly chubb half her age?

Nay, even though he was disturbed by Sybil's gusty weeping, Harry remained resolved. He made one more effort to console his stepmama, patting her awkwardly on her shoulder.

"I tell you what I will do, my lady. At the end of the summer, I will convey you to Bath. You've always enjoyed taking the waters, and the town would be full of more eligible suitors."

"Old men with the gout!" was Sybil's wailing response to his hopeful suggestion. Recognizing the beginning of some strong hysterics, Harry prudently backed toward the door. He suddenly realized that this was the first time he had entered Sybil's room without breaking any china, but he did not expect his stepmother to take much consolation in that at the moment.

Wearily, Harry turned and let himself out.

* * *

Julia Thorpe unfurled her parasol, shortening her longer stride to match Kate's as they strolled through the village of Lytton's Dene. Miss Thorpe, as ever, managed to present a crisp, fresh appearance, despite the heat and dust coating the lane.

Kate could not help recalling a laughing remark Harry had once made about his cousin's cool elegance. "Aye, icebergs don't easily melt."

As for herself, Kate could already feel her curls damp with perspiration beneath her bonnet, and her muslin gown clung to her as shockingly as though she had deliberately dampened her petticoats. She wondered what possessed her to be ranging abroad on such a hot afternoon, except that she had decided she had been keeping too close to the house of late. She had been nowhere since last Sunday and was beginning to feel quite out of touch with the world.

With the world? a voice inside her jeered. *Or with Harry Arundel?* It was quite true she had neither seen nor heard from Harry since their abrupt parting at her gate. Her manner had not been such as to encourage his lordship to call again. Perhaps she had convinced him at last to abandon his pursuit of her. Perhaps he had simply found something more interesting to occupy his time.

In either event, she told herself, she felt relieved that Harry had ceased to plague her, although her relief had taken on a most strange form, leaving her feeling restless, starting at every knock upon the cottage door, flying to the window to gaze out at every passing rider.

Such nervousness, however, Kate had convinced herself, had nothing to do with Harry's absence. No, more likely it was to be blamed upon the vicar's sister, for although she had seen nothing of his lordship, she had seen far too much of Julia these past days.

Even now as they skirted past Mr. Rising's carpentry shop, the smell of wood shavings and the clang of hammers heavy in the air, Julia seemed all too oppressively close to Kate's side.

"It is far too hot to be out walking," Julia complained. "I declare we both must be quite mad."

257

Kate forbore to remind Julia that she had not been invited along upon this expedition. It had been Julia who had insisted upon accompanying her.

"If you are feeling unwell," Kate began hopefully, "and wish to return to the vicarage, I would quite understand—"

"Nonsense. My dear Kate, I would not think of abandoning you." Julia gave her one of her arctic smiles, and linked her arm through Kate's in a possessive manner Kate found nigh suffocating. The thought flashed through her mind that now she knew how prisoners in gaol must feel, so closely guarded. She dismissed the notion at once as mere peevishness, born out of the heat and irritation of nerves.

"So where is it that you wish to go?" Julia asked after the manner of an adult humoring a tiresome child.

"I had thought of calling in at Miss Lethbridge's." Kate indicated a small pink-and-white brick shop with some bonnets displayed in a bow-front window.

"Why ever would you want to go in there? That wretched woman trades in nothing but gossip."

Kate had to agree, and as a bishop's daughter, of course, she had no use for gossip. All the same she heard herself replying, "Miss Lethbridge has acquired a length of brown merino that I am thinking of purchasing to have done up into a winter cloak."

Julia made no comment, but her opinion was expressed clearly by the supercilious fashion in which she arched her brows. But she followed Kate to the shop across the lane without further demur.

The interior of Miss Lethbridge's shop was small and close, the narrow shelves crammed with an odd assortment of fripperies, laces, ribbons, gloves, bonnets, and stockings that comprised the elderly spinster's stock in trade. The establishment was empty when Kate and Julia entered, Miss Lethbridge folding up the silk fringe she had failed to sell to her last customer.

The diminutive woman summoned up a polite smile for the vicar's sister, but she bustled out from behind the counter to greet Kate with enthusiasm.

"The brown merino, Miss Towers? Bless you, my dear, I shall fetch it in a trice."

Hurrying to one of the lower shelves, Miss Lethbridge dragged out a bolt of cloth that she displayed to Kate upon the counter.

"A good serviceable fabric, my dear," the shopkeeper said.

Kate half-heartedly examined the ugly fabric that was the exact shade of the mud that filled the lane after a hard rain. She was aware of Julia close at her elbow, the lines of her face taut with a kind of bored impatience. It roused a rare streak of perversity in Kate, and she took her time about studying the fabric, although she wondered herself why she persisted in lingering when she had no intention of making a purchase.

As usual, Miss Lethbridge's tongue ran on at such a breathless rate of speed, she was oft unintelligible. Kate listened in desultory fashion, having no interest in the latest prank of the squire's hoydenish daughter or how the butcher's boy had been caught stealing a slab of bacon.

But the shopkeeper's next remark caused her to glance up eagerly in spite of herself. "I beg your pardon, Miss Lethbridge. What did you say about Lord Lytton?"

Miss Lethbridge blinked, her bright inquisitive eyes rounding in surprise. "Why, nothing, my dear. I merely remarked that if you did wish to buy the cloth, I would have it sent to your cottage. On such a hot day, you surely wouldn't be wanting to *carry* it."

"Oh," Kate said faintly, a rush of embarrassment flooding into her cheeks. Beneath Julia's sharp stare and Miss Lethbridge's look of motherly amusement, Kate felt ready to sink beneath the floorboards.

It only made matters worse when Miss Lethbridge patted her arm. "Bless you, child, there's no need for you to color up so. I am sure all the young ladies hereabouts are fair starved for some word of Lord Harry. I have been telling everyone—"

"I assure you," Julia interrupted icily, "neither Miss Towers nor I is prey to any such vulgar curiosity."

Kate knew she should agree with Julia, but she felt more like stuffing a kerchief in Miss Thorpe's mouth. Miss Lethbridge appeared affronted.

"I do not consider it vulgar to show a friendly concern for one's neighbors," she huffed. "But far be it from me to be burdening you with any tales of his lordship. The poor lamb." Miss Lethbridge heaved a deep sigh before briskly setting about to refold the bolt of brown cloth.

It was entirely too much for Kate. Despite Julia's look of disgust, Kate put her hand timidly over Miss Lethbridge's to still the woman's movements.

"Oh, pray, Miss Lethbridge. Whatever did you mean? Why did you call the earl a poor lamb?"

Miss Lethbridge's lips were compressed in a taut line, but when she glanced up at Kate's face, her expression softened.

"Why, only that I think there must be something gravely amiss with his lordship since he's come back. He's done naught but a little gentle riding over his own estates, nothing at all in his usual dashing style. There's some as have been saying that Lord Harry was wounded more badly at Waterloo than any of us know."

"Surely not," Kate faltered.

Miss Lethbridge nodded solemnly. "Why else would the earl sell off all his best hunters? 'Tis obvious the poor gentleman must not be able to ever hunt or jump again."

"Harry sold his hunters?" Kate cried, aghast.

"What utter nonsense," Julia broke in, abandoning her pose of disdainful disinterest. "Lytton prizes his precious beasts above rubies. Never would he part with them."

"That is where you are quite out, Miss Thorpe," Miss Lethbridge said, her thin features flushing with triumph. "For not an hour since, I saw the squire's groom leading those horses through the village. Paid a wicked high price for them, the squire did. I cannot imagine what Mrs. Gresham will say to him." She added slyly, "Though I am surprised that any of this is news to you, Miss Thorpe. You being his lordship's cousin and so thick with him as you are forever telling everyone."

Julia sucked in her breath with a sharp hiss. Turning a cold shoulder upon Miss Lethbridge, she said to Kate, "If you are quite finished here, Kate, I should like to go."

"Yes, I am ready," Kate said, although she wanted nothing more than to remain and ply Miss Lethbridge with a dozen more questions, even with Julia's critical gaze fixed upon her. But it was obvious the shopkeeper had already told her all she knew about Harry.

But why would Harry sell off his most prized possessions? Harry had never given a fig for the consequence of his title, his vast estates, or acquiring great riches. But his horses! Kate had seen him care as tenderly for their well-being as a father would his babes. She could not imagine what dire circumstances would have induced Harry to part with them.

So unsettled was she by these unexpected tidings that Kate ended by purchasing the ugly brown cloth, though she scarce realized what she did. She quit the shop with a worried frown creasing her brow, all but forgetting Julia's presence.

Miss Thorpe was quick to remind her. "That insufferable gossiping creature," Julia said as soon as they had gained the street outside. "But there! She is typical of the incivility and lack of gentility to be found in this wretched village. I am only astonished that you should have encouraged her, Kathryn."

"I only wanted to know—" Ruefully, Kate bit down upon her lip, for once feeling far too disturbed to be guarded in Miss Thorpe's presence. "Julia, why do you think Harry has sold his horses?"

"Heaven only knows. Lytton is forever in some sort of scrape."

Kate found this reply far from reassuring.

"I am far more concerned about you, Kathryn," Julia continued.

"Me? Why?"

"You display a most unseemingly interest in Lytton's doings." Julia regarded her through narrowed eyes. "You have not been so foolish as to fall in love with my cousin, I hope?"

Kate glanced quickly away, willing her color not to rise. "Of course not."

"I am glad to hear it. Lytton is a sad rake, you know."

261

"He is not!"

Julia's eyebrows rose. With great effort, Kate lowered her voice. "That—that is, I know Lord Harry can be a shocking flirt, but there is such a kindness in him. He would never set out to break any lady's heart."

"He is my cousin, and I believe I know him far better than you," Julia began angrily, then checked herself. She forced a smile to her lips. "But, my dear Kate, let us not fall into a quarrel over him. It is far more attention than Lytton deserves, I promise you. It is only the heat that is making us both so cross and—" Julia broke off with a look of extreme annoyance. "I have left my parasol in that wretched woman's shop. If I do not retrieve it at once, I would not put it beyond her to sell it to her next customer."

Julia clearly expected Kate to return with her, but Kate made no move to do so. After muttering in vexed tones that she would catch up to Kate, Julia strode back toward Miss Lethbridge's. Kate had to suppress a strong urge to bolt along the lane and thus escape Julia's oppressive presence. She was growing weary of Miss Thorpe's sharp tongue, her repeated attacks upon Harry.

It seemed to Kate that she displayed little cousinly regard for his lordship, rather callously dismissing Miss Lethbridge's speculations that something was gravely amiss with Harry. Could the shopkeeper be right in her surmise about the severity of Harry's wound? It would be just like him to conceal such a thing from everyone.

Scarce heeding where she walked, Kate strained to remember every detail of her outing with Harry the previous Sunday, every expression upon his face. Never had he seemed more hale and yet . . . Upon further recollection, had his movements seemed not quite so quick as usual? And yes, Kate was certain that she recalled him turning away when he had lifted her down from the curricle. To conceal a grimace of pain perhaps?

With such alarming thoughts chasing through her mind, Kate did not realize she had wandered too far out into the lane until she was alerted by the thunder of hooves, a blast of a horn.

Blowing upon his yard of tin, a coachman was urging the afternoon stage toward the inn yard of the Arundel Arms.

The team of four sweating horses was bearing down upon her. Kate froze in momentary panic. Her heart leapt into her throat, but before she could make a move, she felt strong arms dragging her to safety.

Kate spun about, colliding with the hard wall of Harry's chest as the stage rattled past. His arms banded about her, crushing her so tightly she could feel his heart thudding as hard as her own. He swore at her.

"Damn it, Kate. What on earth did you think you were doing?"

She shook her head, unable to answer him at first. She had no notion whence Harry had sprung, only feeling grateful that he was there, even if he did huskily call her "a little fool" and hold her far too close.

For a moment all Kate could do was lean weakly against him, soothed by the comforting feel of his arms about her. But as her fright subsided, she became all too conscious of her position, being embraced by Lord Harry for all the village to see.

Drawing in a steadying breath, she pulled away from him, gazing up at his face. All thoughts of her own near calamity fled, her mind returning to the worries that had so troubled her earlier.

She scrutinized his features more earnestly than she had ever done before. He looked haggard, deep lines of exhaustion carved about his eyes, stealing away the smile from his lips. She feared it was owing to far more than his recent concern for her safety.

"Are you all right, my lord?" she asked.

Harry's grim expression vanished. For a second he appeared nonplussed, then his features broke into his familiar irrepressible grin.

"Am I all right?" he laughed. "The woman nearly flings herself beneath a coach and then asks if I am all right?"

"I mean . . . are you quite well?"

"Well enough, although I would be a dashed sight better if

you did not choose to wander about in the midst of the road. What the devil possessed you, Kate?"

"I fear I was woolgathering."

Harry arched one brow wickedly. "Daydreaming about me?"

"It so happens that I was. . . ." Kate started to confess, then stopped, beginning to feel a little foolish. She was not about to admit to Harry how she had permitted her imagination to run away with her. For it was patently obvious she had done so. Harry might bear an appearance of fatigue, but his swift rescue of her and a quick perusal of his hard muscular frame demonstrated there was naught in the least amiss with his body. Kate wrenched her eyes away, heat stealing into her cheeks. She longed to simply ask Harry about the hunters, but how could she do so without revealing she had been gossiping about him with Miss Lethbridge?

"I was admiring the bonnet," she finished lamely, "in the window across the way and not watching where I was going. I but came into the village to do a little shopping."

"For your bride clothes, I hope." Roguish lights danced to Harry's green eyes as he caught her hand, brushing a playful kiss against her fingertips.

Kate tried to summon a reproving frown, but could not quite manage it. Even that fleeting contact of Harry's lips sent a breathless, tingling kind of rush through her.

"It isn't Sunday anymore," he reminded her. The rogue's light vanished, the warmth in his eyes becoming more intense. "Will you marry me, Kate?"

"N-no. Oh, Harry, please." She made a weak protest as he upturned her hand and placed a not so chaste kiss upon her wrist, the heated contact seeming to sear her flesh.

"M-my lord, you mustn't," Kate cried, attempting to disengage her hand, casting a flustered glance about her. Her distress must have been evident enough, for Harry released her at once.

"I am sorry, Kate," he said. "I had no intentions of trying to make love to you in the middle of the road. 'Tis only that you cannot imagine how much I have been missing you these past few days."

So where have you been, she had an urge to demand. But to

do so would be to admit, even to herself, how much she had been missing him.

Kate fussed with her bonnet, straightening it, attempting to regain her composure. "And what brings you to the village this afternoon, my lord?"

Harry's lips twitched, and Kate suspected that he regarded her with a kind of tender amusement. But he replied solemnly enough, "Well, besides keeping damsels from straying beneath coach wheels, I have come to meet an old friend, Miss Towers."

Kate saw no sign of a mount or Harry's curricle. Dear heavens! Had he sold all his horses?

"You came on foot?" she asked.

Harry looked rather surprised. "Of course not. I rode Ramses."

Kate sighed with relief, which only caused Harry's expression of puzzlement to deepen.

"I left Ramses at the stable over at the inn where I was to meet Folly," he explained. "But the dratted fellow is never on time."

"Folly?"

"Yes, have you never met him? He lives not far from Chillingsworth and I am sure—Ah, well, never mind, I shall introduce you, for here he comes at last."

Turning, Harry raised his arm and proceeded to hail the driver of a gig who was tooling into the village at a spanking pace. He was on the point of sweeping past, but at Harry's call, the gentleman sharply drew rein. Kate stepped back to avoid the spray of dust, waving her hand before her eyes.

"Folly, you idiot," Harry choked.

It took Kate's vision a moment to clear before she could make out the form of Harry's friend. Her first impression was of a dapper young man wearing a curly brimmed beaver, his clothing protected by a riding cloak with a multiplicity of capes. He was, Kate supposed, what she had heard vulgarly referred to as a "buck of the first stare."

It was only when Harry began to perform the introductions and the man swept the hat from his glossy waves, that Kate obtained a clear view of an amiable and familiar countenance. She stiffened with the recognition.

"The Honorable Samuel Ffolliot," Harry was saying. "And this is—"

"Mr. Ffolliot and I have met before," Kate said in clipped tones.

"I daresay not," Mr. Ffolliot replied jovially. "Not likely I should forget such a pretty lady."

"It was at the episcopal palace in Chillingsworth. My father was the late bishop of that diocese."

Mr. Ffolliot regarded her with polite bewilderment, his wide innocent eyes appealing to Harry for enlightenment, but Harry was obviously equally at a loss.

A hard knot burned in Kate's throat. To think that this fool did not even remember the incident that had nigh broken her father's heart.

"It was upon the occasion that your pistol shot shattered the stained glass in the Blessed Lady chapel."

"Oh, Lord!" Kate thought she heard Harry mutter under his breath, but she was too caught up in the painful remembrance to take much heed. She could still see her father's shoulders bent with grief as he stood surveying the colorful shards that had once been a magnificent representation of the Madonna and child, one of the few examples of fourteenth-century stained glass to have survived both the ravages of Henry the Eighth and later, the Puritan army.

Mr. Ffolliot scratched his head, then a shading of guilt pinkened his cheeks. "Oh, yes, now that you mention it, I do remember something of the sort." He offered Kate a deprecating smile. "But truly, I meant no harm. I suppose I must have been fox—er that is, I was having a little trouble with my vision that day—and it was only a wager."

Kate set her face into grim lines, offering him no hope of pardon, so he appealed to Harry. "I did pay to have the window replaced—with some nice new glass, you know, which I am sure would have been much better than that old stuff that had to have been there for ages."

"Four centuries, to be exact," Kate said tersely.

Mr. Ffolliot beamed. "There! That is just what I meant—"

"Oh, do be quiet, Folly." Harry grimaced, casting an uneasy glance at Kate. "What's done is done. There is hardly anything to be gained by raking over old coals."

Her entire frame rigid with reproach, Kate did not agree with him. Such wanton destruction as Mr. Ffolliot had caused could not be so easily forgiven or forgotten. What gave her more pain than anything else was to discover that Harry could be friends with such a man.

An uncomfortable silence settled over the three of them, only to be broken as Julia at last came down the lane seeking Kate. Never had Harry shown such relief to see his cousin.

Vaulting up beside Mr. Ffolliot, he strongly suggested that the ladies be left to pursue their shopping, his haste to get Samuel away quite evident. With a final tip of his hat to Kate and Julia, Mr. Ffolliot started up his mare, heading toward the inn yard.

Kate turned away immediately, ignoring the rather anxious smile that Harry offered her in parting. Julia fell into step beside her.

"I am sorry that I took so long, Kathryn," she said. "But that foolish woman had already put my parasol in a 'safe place' and then the creature could not recollect what she had done with it. But I daresay Lytton and his friend kept you agreeably entertained?"

Kate made no reply to this rather barbed question, quickening her pace. She only wanted to return to the peaceful sanctuary that was her cottage and indeed was wishing she had never left it.

"Lytton seems to have wasted little time in seeking out the old set."

Kate knew she should simply let Julia's remark go unquestioned. If Miss Thorpe had anything to say about Harry, it was generally unkind. But Kate could not seem to help herself.

"Old set?" she asked.

"His old circle of friends, Ffolliot, Lord Erwin, and the others. All of them quite wild and quite foolish. Did you never hear of them?"

"No," Kate said, feeling quite numb with misery.

"I daresay even Lytton would not have brought such disreputable company with him when he visited the bishop's palace." Julia added, on a note of almost malicious amusement, "In any event, now we know why Lytton was obliged to sell off his hunters."

"We do?"

"It is obvious. He had to pay off gaming debts."

"No!"

"My dear Kate, what do you think Lytton and his friends do of nights for entertainment? They scarcely sit about, reading scripture to each other."

"I-I . . ." Kate faltered, feeling herself go pale. But she managed to rally. "I am sure I scarce gave the matter any thought, being no concern of mine. Now let us make haste. It is almost teatime, and I am suddenly feeling most fatigued."

She set off at a brisk pace, but Julia, with her longer legs, had no difficulty in keeping doggedly at her side.

Julia experienced a mild sensation of triumph. Ever since she had seen Lytton drive off with Kate last Sunday, she had been experiencing all manner of alarm, the apprehension that her own scheme for marrying Kate to Adolphus would come to naught. She had attempted to keep as close a watch as she could over Kate these past few days, subtly pointing out his lordship's defects whenever opportunity availed.

But never had she felt that she had delivered a master stroke until now. She pressed home her advantage, now bringing up the subject of her brother, praising all his manifold virtues.

"And he is so shy," she said as she and Kate turned in at the cottage gate. "I fear he has developed a tendre for you, yet his modesty prevents him from speaking. Of course, you know that nothing would give me greater joy than to have you as my sister."

"Indeed," Kate murmured wearily.

It vexed Julia to realize Kate had likely not heard a word she had been saying. A rebuke sprang to her lips, only to be stilled as she studied Kate's face. In her eyes lurked an expression of such deep-set misery that Julia was moved to a rare stirring of pity.

She had become fond of Kate, as much as she was capable of being fond of anyone. She was shrewd enough to guess that Kate was indeed in love with Lord Lytton, and it caused Kate great unhappiness to believe that he could be a hardened gamester.

Guilt niggled at Julia, for she was aware that despite all his other inequities, Harry had no taste for gaming.

Yet he could have changed, she argued with herself. Besides, he had enough other faults to make him unsuitable as a husband for Kate. And as for love, Julia had never experienced such a tender emotion herself, but with a little fortitude on Kate's part, it could be easily dismissed.

Thus quieting her conscience, Julia followed Kate in to tea. Before she had passed into the cottage, she had suppressed the twinge of sympathy and convinced herself that she was acting in the girl's best interests. By the time she had done with Kate, not only would she abandon all tender feelings for Lord Lytton, Kate would quite sensibly learn to despise the man.

Chapter 7

The shadows had lengthened across the parlor by the time Miss Thorpe took her leave of Kate. Mrs. Towers was glad to see the cottage door close behind that icily bred young woman. She did not know what the vicar's sister had been whispering to Kate, only that Kate listened with little pleasure.

In point of fact, Mrs. Towers could scarce recall having seen Kate look more dejected and miserable, not even in those days following the bishop's death. She had appeared serene enough when setting out for her walk earlier. Mrs. Towers strongly suspected that something had gone awry during that little expedition to the village, and that something most likely had to do with Lord Harry.

But when she ventured to ask Kate if anything troubled her, Mrs. Towers received the usual reply.

"You must not worry about me, Mama," Kate was quick to answer, following it up with a brisk hug. The affection was there, Mrs. Towers thought sadly, but so were the protective walls forever closing her out.

Supper proved a dismal affair with Kate saying too little and Lady Dane saying too much. Her ladyship appeared in none the best of humors either, scolding Kate for getting too much sun "traipsing about all afternoon with that Thorpe chit."

By the time the meal had ended, Kate pleaded a headache and tried to escape to her room, but Lady Dane insisted they all retire to the parlor. Mrs. Towers tried to intervene on her daughter's behalf, but as usual her gentle objections were swept aside.

"I have a gift I wish to present to Kate," her ladyship insisted.

Kate had no choice but to precede Lady Dane into the parlor. She sat stiffly upon the settee, regarding with lackluster eyes the elegantly trimmed bandbox that her ladyship presented to her.

"I did not have that sent all the way from London merely for you to stare at it," Lady Dane said, nudging the box closer to Kate with the tip of her cane. "Open it."

Sighing, Kate slipped off the ribbon and removed the lid to reveal a ball gown cut on the latest and most fashionable lines. As she shook out the folds of white India gauze shot through with silver and delicate pink silk appliqué, Mrs. Towers exclaimed with delight, but Kate regarded the gift with no more than dutiful politeness.

"Thank you, Grandmama," she said in wooden accents.

"I ordered that frock for you from my own modiste," Lady Dane said with great satisfaction, seemingly oblivious to Kate's lack of enthusiasm. "I daresay it will require a few alterations, but my maid Hortense can see to that. She is clever with a needle, as all these Frenchwomen are. I am sure she can have it finished in time for the assembly tomorrow night."

"I never attend the local assembly, Grandmama." Kate folded the gown carefully and returned it to the box.

"Then 'tis high time that you did."

"My papa would never have approved. He did not think it seemly for the bishop's daughter to be seen at a public dance."

"But you are no longer the bishop's daughter."

Although Kate flinched at this tart reminder, her lips set into that expression of prim obstinacy that Mrs. Towers knew all too well. She stole a glance at Lady Dane's equally determined features.

"Oh dear," Mrs. Towers thought with a sinking heart. She reached nervously for her embroidery from her needlework basket, making a timid effort to change the subject that was ignored.

"There is no reason why you should not attend the assembly under my chaperonage," Lady Dane continued.

"That is very good of you, Grandmama, but I do not *wish* to go."

"Nonsense. A little dancing would do you good. You should see to it that the girl gets out more, Maisie."

"Why, I-I . . ." Mrs. Towers began, quite disconcerted by this unexpected attack. But she had no need to proceed before Kate leapt to her defense.

"It is not in the least Mama's fault. I have been too busy for such frivolous pursuits as dancing."

"Busy!" Lady Dane was far too elegant to snort, but the sound that she made came perilously close to it. "Busy with what may I ask? Exactly what have you been doing with yourself, child, buried here in this dismal village for the past year?"

"Many things." Kate lifted her chin proudly. "Receiving callers and . . . and visiting the sick of the parish—"

"That task should rather fall to that Thorpe female," Lady Dane said. "She is the vicar's sister, is she not?"

"Julia is not always . . . disposed to such work. As a matter of Christian charity, I felt that I—"

271

"Charity is all well enough," her ladyship interrupted. "But one bears a duty to one's own family."

"I have always looked after Mama," Kate cried.

"Indeed! Kate is a most attentive daughter." But Mrs. Tower's faint interjection went unheeded.

"You have other duties, my girl," Lady Dane said. "The foremost being not to saddle your mother with the care of you till the end of her days. 'Tis time you thought of marriage."

"Oh, pray, don't," Mrs. Towers protested. Kate looked so stricken by her grandmother's harsh words that for once Mrs. Towers actually thought of telling Lady Dane to be silent. Instead she said, " 'Tis not as though Kate . . . she is scarcely yet on the shelf."

"She will be if she continues to dillydally," was her ladyship's inexorable reply. "The child is no longer in mourning. It is time Kate met some eligible young men. If there is not any particular one hereabouts she wishes to marry, then I shall insist that she comes to London for the Season."

"That will hardly be necessary, Grandmama." Kate rose from the settee, the color flying in her cheeks, her eyes overbright. "I shall attend the assembly if that is what you wish. I never intend to be a burden to my family. I hope that I will always know my duty."

With that noble speech, Kate gathered up the bandbox with the air of an ancient Christian martyr going to face the lions and fled from the room.

As soon as her daughter had gone, Mrs. Towers shot to her feet, gripping the back of an armchair with trembling hands. Rarely had she ever dared contradict her mother-in-law, but her umbrage at Lady Dane's callous treatment of Kate could not be contained.

"You were far too hard upon her." Mrs. Towers quivered with indignation. "How could you make her feel as though she were no longer wanted in her own home?"

"Do sit down, Maisie. I have no patience for such sentimental piffle." When Mrs. Towers did not immediately comply, Lady Dane fixed her with her eagle's eye and sharply rapped her cane. "Sit down if you please!"

Mrs. Towers didn't please, but she sank back into the chair, despising herself for a faint heart.

"Some sternness with the girl seems wanted. My other tactics have not worked thus far." Lady Dane scowled. "I shall have to have another word with Lytton. Whatever can the boy be about? He should be more attentive, nosegays and that sort of thing, not leaving Kate alone for days on end."

Mrs. Towers wished Lady Dane would leave both Lord Harry and Kate alone, wished even more for the courage to tell her so. She said, "I still fail to see how being cruel to Kate can remedy the situation."

"It is not cruel to appeal to the only thing the child comprehends, her sense of duty. You know she loves the boy. We simply have to find the way to overcome her ridiculous scruples."

Mrs. Towers did not find bullying Kate a proper method, but Lady Dane talked heedlessly on, weaving her own plans. "I shall make sure Lytton attends that assembly as well." Her ladyship chuckled. "A little waltzing in the arms of that handsome young man and, you mark my words, Kate will leap forward most eagerly to embrace her 'duty.' "

"Kate doesn't waltz."

"Then I shall find her a dancing master."

Mrs. Towers stifled a groan, sagging back against her chair.

Lady Dane unbent enough to offer a consoling nod. "You must not fret so, my dear Maisie. I have raised four daughters, all of them as muddleheaded as your Kate, and I guided every last one of them into successful marriages. Depend upon it, I'll wager Kate is even now coming to her senses and deciding that she will have Lord Harry."

Long after the rest of the household had lapsed into the peaceful stillness of night, Kate tossed and turned upon her feather tick pillows. Sleep was impossible with the events of the day crowding forward into her mind—that disastrous encounter with Harry in the village, Julia's acid whisperings about him, but most especially the disturbing conversation she had had with her grandmother.

You are no longer the bishop's daughter . . . what have you been doing with yourself . . . your duty to marry.

Kate rolled over, stuffing her head beneath the pillow, but she could not seem to shut out that insistent voice. At last, despairing of finding any repose, Kate rose from her bed and slipped on her wrapper. Lighting a candle, she left her bedchamber and made her way through the silent house.

Kate scarce knew what drew her toward the tiny front parlor. Perhaps because it was the one room in the cottage that retained an aura of her father's presence. Sadly, she trailed her fingers over his marble busts, the bookcase that housed all the bishop's ponderous texts.

Never had she missed her father so keenly as she did tonight; never did she feel in such want of his wisdom. Setting her candle upon the mantel, she gazed upward, trying to draw some consolation from the portrait of the serene and saintly looking man mounted so far above her, but disturbingly, the bishop seemed to stare back at her with Lady Dane's eyes, full of stern reproach.

What have you been doing with yourself this past year?

Kate averted her head, as though to avoid that too piercing gaze. Aye, she had been quick to justify herself to her grandmother earlier, but standing before her own merciless conscience, Kate could find no satisfactory answer. The months all seemed to have evaporated like the mists of a dream. She vaguely recalled those numb, empty days after her father had died, packing away their belongings in the palace, moving to the cottage at Lytton's Dene.

And after that, her hours had fallen into a routine of . . . of . . . Kate winced, seeing clearly now all the little tasks she had manufactured, tasks to give herself some sense of importance, something to do while she waited. . . . She sagged down upon the settee, her struggles against the realization no longer of any avail.

She had spent the last year of her life waiting for Harry to come home.

"No! No, I didn't," Kate said, but the whisper sounded feeble in the room's unrelenting silence. She hugged one of the

274

settee cushions to her breasts as though that soft silk could somehow shield her from the truth.

Aye, she had flattered herself that she had been so sensible, sending Harry away, avowing that she could never be his bride. Yet had her foolish heart not always kept on hoping that someday, somehow, she would be able to give Harry a different answer?

What had she expected? Kate wondered bitterly. Some sort of a miracle? Harry's return from the dead had indeed seemed like one, but the fates conspired again most cruelly to show her that the bishop's daughter and Hellfire Harry were worlds apart. The neglect of his lands, seeing him in the company of that dreadful Ffolliot man, hearing the tale of how he had gamed his horses away—all of that should have been more than enough to convince Kate that her Papa's warnings against Harry had been justified.

And *still* she did not want to believe anything bad of Harry. Still she feared that if he gave her that smile that seemed to draw her straight to his heart, if he asked her again to wed him, she would want to fling herself into his arms with a resounding yes.

"What am I going to do, Papa?" Kate murmured. How could she end this torment? Even if she went away from Lytton's Dene, Harry could always follow her. How could she put herself forever beyond temptation?

The answer came to her unbidden with the memory of Lady Dane's harsh words, '*Tis your duty to marry.*

If she were betrothed to another man, Harry could no longer continue to tease her. He could not keep proposing to a woman who was pledged to another.

The thought seemed to settle in her stomach like a lump of cold lead, but Kate had never been shy about embracing her duty, no matter how painful the prospect.

However, Lady Dane's suggestion of repairing to London for the Season would not do at all. No, Papa would never have approved of that. He had always said that the city was filled with naught but rackety young men like Har—

Kate was quick to suppress the unhappy thought, concentrating on the sort of man the bishop would have wished her to wed. A scholar, a man of sound moral principle, sober, steady, a man very like . . .

Adolphus Thorpe.

The mere notion of the solemn vicar made Kate quail and long to dive back to her bedchamber, pull the covers up over head. She promptly felt ashamed of herself for this reaction.

Why not Mr. Thorpe? she adjured herself. Had not Julia strongly hinted that the vicar harbored an affection for Kate? Kate had never glimpsed any sign of such emotion upon Mr. Thorpe's impassive face, but Julia likely knew her own brother's heart far better than Kate.

Adolphus was so handsome, so virtuous, so . . . so *worthy*. As the vicar's wife, her life would be filled with peace and respectability, fraught with useful purpose.

But no love, no laughter, no breathless expectation of something delightful waiting just—

Kate pressed a hand to her brow as though to quell this dampening reflection. She must put all such nonsense out of her head. Her consolation must be that she was at last acting with wisdom.

She knew that Julia and her brother would attend the assembly tomorrow night. Kate would also go, just as she had promised her grandmother. If she discerned any evidence of partiality in Adolphus Thorpe, Kate meant to offer the bashful clergyman every encouragement to ask for her hand.

The resolution brought her little comfort, but at least she now felt exhausted enough to return to her bed. Back within the confines of her room, she snuffed out the candle and burrowed wearily beneath the coverlet.

Yet no sooner had she closed her eyes than Harry's face appeared to her with haunting clarity. He seemed to stare at her, but with no reproach, his laughing green eyes merely sad.

"I have made the wisest decision for both of us. Indeed I have," Kate nearly cried aloud. She rolled over and managed to dispel Harry's image from her mind. But it took her much longer to banish the feeling that her "wisdom" was somehow betraying them both.

Chapter 8

The night seemed spun from black velvet, the moon a silver disk suspended in the sky. The heady scent of the last of the summer roses drifted through the open windows of the assembly rooms that adjoined the Arundel Arms.

Scarcely large enough to afford space for more than a dozen couples to stand up in comfort, the hall was thronged with its subscribers, mostly the gentry of the surrounding countryside.

The candlelit scene bore none of the dazzling grandeur of a London ballroom, the gowns worn more often of muslin than silk, wreaths of flowers taking the place of flashing gemstones. Yet what was lacking in grandeur was made up for in enthusiasm as the orchestra began to tune their instruments.

Only Kate was able to keep her toes from tapping at the first scrape of the violins. Never had she felt less like dancing, her dainty kid slippers seeming weighted with lead.

"Smile, child," Lady Dane chided her. "You've come here to enjoy yourself, not pay a visit to the tooth-drawer."

Kate made an effort to appear more light of heart, all the while wishing herself at home snug in her bed. It had been one thing to form her noble resolve regarding Adolphus Thorpe in the security of her own parlor, quite another to actually prepare to act upon it.

She felt shamefully relieved to note that the vicar and his sister were not yet present. Kate's gaze constantly strayed toward the arched doorway, her pulses fluttering with trepidation. But it was not the Thorpes' arrival that comprised her chief dread, but the possibility of a certain other gentleman's appearance. She had no reason to suppose Harry ever frequented the assembly, but he had a penchant for doing the unexpected, scattering her best-formed intentions like a hurtling ball toppling ninepins. One smile, one laugh, one touch of his hand and all her wisdom had a way of flying out the window.

But not tonight, Kate promised herself. Even if Harry did come, she would greet him with the distance and decorum Papa would have expected of his daughter. Unconsciously she stiffened her shoulders. As she did so, she caught a glimpse of her reflection in the window's night-darkened panes.

Who was that strange young woman that hovered like some unhappy phantom behind the glass? Kate scarce knew herself. Her grandmother's French maid had fussed and primped, decking Kate out in the new gown with its high waistline emphasizing the soft curve of her breasts. Instead of the simple flowers Kate was accustomed to wear for adornment, Lady Dane's diamond necklet glittered about her throat. Hortense had caught up Kate's hair from its loose-flowing style and arranged it in a mass of curls pinned up to form a chignon, a gold diadem banding her forehead after the Greek fashion.

Never had she looked so elegant, so stylish. Never had she felt so miserably self-conscious. But she did her best to smile at the young gentlemen who flocked to her side, begging to lead her into the dance.

Other young ladies might have preened themselves at being so sought after, but Kate accepted the situation with gravity. She was not unused to such attention. She had never wanted for a partner at any of the sedate parties she had attended. But she had oft suspected that all those eager young clergymen had stood up with her out of duty or ambition to please her father. Now she supposed it was her fashionable new gown that attracted the gentlemen.

Only Harry had ever sought her out for herself alone. To him she had not been the bishop's daughter, but simply Kate. And when he had danced with her, the world had seemed to fall by the wayside. Caught up by the night and music—

Kate's fingers tightened about the fan, nearly crushing the delicate silk as she fought off the poignant memory. She needed no such recollections to haunt her for she would not, *must not* dance with Harry tonight. As though he had indeed risen up before her, reaching for her with that too beguiling smile, Kate began to promise her dances with a recklessness that bordered on panic, even engaging to waltz with Lieutenant Porter, a newly commissioned naval officer she scarcely knew. Should Harry arrive, he would find Kate with every dance already pledged.

Feeling as though she had erected somewhat of a defense, Kate breathed out a deep sigh. She had actually begun to relax when the vicar and his sister arrived. Kate recalled her purpose in coming to the assembly, and her tensions coiled anew.

The Thorpes edged forward into the hall, Julia and Adolphus resembling nothing so much as a magnificent pair of Dresden china figurines with their matching fair hair and celestial blue eyes. While Mr. Thorpe paused to greet the squire and several of the important landowners of the district, Julia's gaze swept the crowded room with icy disdain. When she caught sight of Kate, she bore purposefully down upon her.

"Kathryn Towers! Such an agreeable surprise." Julia extended both her hands, catching up Kate's by way of greeting. Miss Thorpe's skin was as cool and smooth as silk, leaving little warmth in her grasp. "You did not tell me you were coming here this evening."

Julia's statement hinted of accusation as though Kate had a duty to keep Miss Thorpe informed of all her movements.

"I did not realize that I would be here myself until the last," Kate said. Carefully she disengaged her hands from Miss Thorpe's possessive grip. Julia's eyes skimmed critically over Kate's attire. For once she nodded with approval.

"You look quite *à la mode*. Such a pleasant change."

Kate thanked her for the rather dubious compliment. She supposed she should respond in kind, but she doubted Julia needed to be told how lovely she looked. She was easily the most beautiful woman present, attired in a gown of mauve and white silk, with a long train that proclaimed she had no intentions of dancing.

"There is nothing more tedious than having one's toes trampled by a parcel of provincial clods," Julia said. "I only attend

279

these dreary assemblies because they seem to amuse Adolphus. I do hope you have saved a dance for him?"

Mindful of her own plans regarding Mr. Thorpe, Kate had done just that, but she felt strangely reluctant to tell Julia so. Yet Julia did not wait for her reply. Miss Thorpe turned and beckoned imperiously to where her brother had lingered by the punch bowl to exchange a few words with the squire. "Adolphus, do come here and tell Kate how well she looks."

Kate thought the vicar appeared a trifle vexed by Julia's summons, but if so, he concealed his annoyance behind a polite smile.

As Mr. Thorpe approached, Kate unfurled her fan. She plied it nervously, wishing it were large enough to hide behind. She had never felt flustered in the vicar's presence before, but neither had she ever considered him as a prospective suitor.

"Good evening, Miss Towers," he said.

"Good evening," Kate murmured, at last daring to look up at him. Her pulses immediately stilled. There was nothing in Mr. Thorpe's mild blue eyes to make even the most giddy maiden feel all of a flutter. If the vicar adored her as Julia claimed, Kate thought dubiously, he certainly did not wear his heart on his sleeve.

"Do say something about Kate's gown," Julia prompted her brother. "Does she not look lovely?"

Mr. Thorpe said all that was required of him and Kate thanked him, her somber manner matching his own. The conversation threatened to lag until Julia said, "Adolphus, you must claim Kate's hand for the next dance before all her other admirers descend upon her."

"Well, I—" Mr. Thorpe began.

"And dearest Kate, you must accept him."

"Well, I—" Kate began.

"How charming. Then that is all settled."

And so it seemed to be, although Kate's mind whirled, scarce sure who actually had made the invitation or who had accepted it. She felt a real sense of relief when Julia moved off to speak to another acquaintance, a relief Kate was astonished to catch reflected in the vicar's own eyes.

They exchanged a half-guilty, half-embarrassed smile that vanished as quickly as the fleeting feeling of kinship. He offered her his arm to lead her to the head of the set that was forming.

The vicar was such a stiff young man, Kate rather expected his movements to be as wooden as a marionette's. To her surprise, he proved quite a graceful dancer, although he was inclined to apologize for his skill.

"I daresay you are thinking the worst of me," he said as they circled each other, "for taking such pleasure in so worldly an activity."

"Not at all," Kate assured him. "Even my father was fond of an occasional quadrille."

Heartened by receiving the late bishop's approval, Mr. Thorpe abandoned some of his formality. Away from Julia, he appeared to have no difficulty in carrying on a conversation. His manners were unaffected and gentlemanlike, his discourse as serious as Kate could require. Kate tried to listen earnestly, but her thoughts kept straying.

She studied the vicar's face and caught herself looking for some resemblance to Harry. But the cousins could not have been more unlike. Kate supposed Adolphus would be judged the more handsome, his skin smooth and unblemished, yet Kate could not help thinking his face might be much improved by some of those fine lines that laughter had carved about Harry's eyes.

Kate quickly dismissed such thoughts as frivolous. As she and Mr. Thorpe came together in the movement of the dance, she realized with dismay he must have asked her a question and patiently awaited her reply.

"I beg your pardon," she said blushing, "but I fear I did not quite hear you."

"It does not matter." Mr. Thorpe heaved a melancholy sigh. "Julia says that I have a habit of forever prosing on."

"Then Miss Thorpe is quite unkind," Kate retorted without thinking. In a flash of insight, it occurred to her that outside of the pulpit Mr. Thorpe was likely not given much encouragement to speak his views by his clever and sharp-tongued sister.

Knowing how discomfited Julia frequently made her feel, Kate experienced a rush of sympathy for the vicar.

"Pray do continue," she urged him. "I am most interested in what you have to say." Quite forgetting the notions of marriage that made her so awkward in his presence, Kate resolved that at least she would accord the poor man some attention. She gazed up at Mr. Thorpe, her smile inspired only by kindness.

But the gentle expression did not escape Julia Thorpe's notice from her vantage point near the doorway. Having snubbed Lieutenant Porter's impertinent offer to dance with her, Julia had stationed herself where she could keep her brother and Kate under constant observation.

Noting the way Kate hung upon Adolphus's every word, Julia's mouth thinned into a smile of triumph. Praise the Lord! Her brother was doing something right at last. She had been admonishing him forever to make an effort to charm Kate, nigh despairing that he would heed her advice.

At this distance, she could not tell what utterances fell from Adolphus's lips, but Kate was clearly captivated. Hereinafter, Julia supposed she must accord her brother a new respect. She had been quite right to believe that the sensible Kathryn needed only a little encouragement to forget her foolish infatuation with Lytton. Although Julia was not given to let her imagination run riot, she could not help calculating how long it might take before the banns of her brother's marriage to the bishop's daughter would be cried. A year perhaps for the wedding to take place, for Kate's powerful relatives to secure Adolphus a better position, for all three of them to be gone from this dreary little village.

These agreeable reflections were disrupted as she was jostled by a latecomer arriving in the assembly hall. Julia turned to haughtily rebuke the oaf who was even now removing his high-crowned beaver hat, revealing familiar waves of glossy, coal dark hair. He flashed one of those lightning quick smiles that could send the most surly of lackeys scurrying to do his bidding.

"Lytton!" Julia exclaimed in the same accents of dismay and bitter loathing she would have said "Lucifer."

Her cousin tossed off his cloak to the porter tending the door before turning back to Julia with his customary infuriating good humor.

"Julia, you must not act so overjoyed to see me. You know how people love to gossip."

"What are you doing here?" she said, her face flushing with disappointment and rage.

"You are forever asking me that," Harry complained. "I begin to think you are surprised to see me anywhere outside the regions of hell."

" 'Tis where you belong—" Julia choked off the retort, groping for the remnants of her frigid dignity.

Harry chucked her lightly under the chin. "Don't put yourself into a taking, my dear coz. I have not come here tonight to dance with *you*."

He smiled at Julia's gasp of outrage and moved on his way, fully aware of her looking such daggers at him, he fancied he could almost feel the sharp points pricking his back. He supposed he ought to be ashamed of himself for ruffling Julia's feathers, but he was surely entitled to a little amusement.

It had been a most unamusing day. More dreary accounts to be gone over with Warburton, more hysterics from Sybil over that Crosbie fellow, and once again no opportunity to see Kate. The only thing that had sustained him had been the missive he received from Lady Dane, commanding him to attend the assembly. Kate would be present, her ladyship assured him, and possibly in "a more receptive mind regarding the subject of marriage." Harry had his doubts on that score. Kate had looked far from receptive at their last parting when he had dragged Folly away before the blasted idiot could say anything more to affront her. Still Harry held enough confidence in Lady Dane that he conjured up an agreeable image of Kate awaiting him, seated demurely at her grandmother's side, refusing all invitations to dance until Harry should arrive. Her hair would be tumbled about her shoulders in those long silky ringlets, her dress one of those sweet flowing frocks that made her look as though she had stepped from a portrait by Gainsborough.

Harry's spirits raised a trifle at these delightful imaginings,

283

and he edged his way through the crowded assembly with impatient step. Taking no heed of the dancers or other acquaintances who greeted him, Harry sought out Lady Dane.

Her ladyship was not difficult to find. Ensconced in one corner like a queen holding court, she kept the local ladies at an awed distance. When she espied Harry, she frowned and summoned him, her gesture rife with a most royal displeasure.

Harry inched his way toward her and made his leg, but before he could speak, Lady Dane hissed at him, "Impudent rascal. Where have you been?"

"I had some difficulty with my horse," Harry began. The old cobbie he had been obliged to employ now that his chestnuts were gone had raised great objection to being hitched to the curricle. As Harry had helped the groom to quiet the vile-tempered beast, the nag had given Harry's arm a savage nip that left him with quite a swelling bruise.

"I am not talking about tonight," Lady Dane said with a rap of the ever-present cane. "I mean all this past week, sirrah!"

"I have been buried up to my eyebrows, trying to set my properties to rights. You did bid me become more respectable."

"I said respectable, not dull!"

Harry felt his good humor slip a notch. It seemed unjust for her ladyship to rake him over the coals when he had simply been doing his best to follow her advice. He decided it might be better to let the subject drop.

"Where is Kate?" he asked instead. "You told me she would be here."

"No," her ladyship said in a voice of withering scorn. "I summoned you here to dance with me. Of course, Kate is here, you young cawker. And you'd best look sharp before she is snatched from under your nose."

Her ladyship's acid remark made little sense to Harry, but when she prodded him with her cane and gestured toward the dancers, Harry turned obediently. He eyed the couples promenading in the center of the room, his gaze flitting from one pretty face to another without interest. He vaguely recognized most of the chits present except for the elegant dasher with the Grecian headdress.

Harry took a closer look, then sucked in his breath like a bunch of fives had delivered a punishing blow to the stomach. Kate! It could not be—but it was, her dark hair done up in that style that was all the rage, the white silk gown clinging revealingly to her sylphlike frame. As lovely as the ensemble was, it robbed Kate of that piquant charm that was all her own, making her look like any of half a dozen other society misses rigged out by the dressmaker's art.

"What have you done to her?" Harry groused at Lady Dane in bitter disappointment.

"What have I done with her?" her ladyship asked in ominous accents. "You might better worry what that yellow-haired dolt dancing with her is now doing."

Harry angled another glance at the dance floor. Amid the swirling dancers, it took him a moment to ascertain which was Kate's partner. When he did, he shrugged.

"Why, 'tis only my cousin, Adolphus."

"The *Reverend* Mr. Thorpe," Lady Dane corrected him. "A perfect match for a bishop's daughter or so I have had to listen to all these old tabbies about me atwittering. If Kate has come to think so, too, it will be all your own fault."

"My fault?" Harry choked.

"For dillydallying. I did my best for you, giving the child a good lecture, telling her it was her duty to marry."

"Saving your ladyship's pardon, but that was a perfectly buffleheaded thing to do," Harry said indignantly. "I don't want Kate casting herself at me out of duty."

"Then you need not worry, because she does not appear to be flinging toward you at all."

Harry thought Lady Dane was raising a dust over nothing, but her remarks were beginning to make him a little uneasy. He made his way closer to the lines of dancers, studying Kate and Adolphus through narrowed eyes.

As the pair met, circled, and parted again, a heavy scowl settled upon Harry's brow. If Kate had been fluttering her fan, outright flirting with his cousin, he could have borne it. But, nay, her eyes raised to the vicar's held no trace of the coquette, only such a gentle expression, her smile so sweet, Harry

285

felt a red-hot brand twist inside of him, searing him with a jealousy such as he had never experienced before.

It was not fair. He could have easily dispatched any other sort of rival. He could outride, outshoot, outfight anyone within the country for Kate. But she did not judge men by such criteria. When it came to the matter of dreary respectability, Harry was painfully aware that, next to Adolphus, he was a lightweight. The vicar would have met the late bishop's approval with a vengeance, and Kate had to be realizing that. Harry's wretched cousin was not exactly hard for a woman to look upon either.

"I should have offered the living at St. Benedict's to that other fellow," Harry muttered beneath his breath. "The one with the wart on his nose."

Damme! It was intolerable. The last of Harry's patience snapped. He had attended church; he had worked on a set of musty books when he would have far rather been kissing Kate; he had given up his most prized horses and then been bitten by a vile-tempered knacker's ware into the bargain. After all that, he'd be damned if he was going to lose Kate to some . . . some *vicar.*

Harry had a strong urge to stride forward and drag her away from Adolphus, but he checked his temper enough to keep from causing an uproar. He waited for the set to finish, grinding his teeth until they ached, his arms locked over his chest.

As the strains of the dance faded to silence, Harry watched his cousin lead Kate from the floor. Was it his imagination or was there already something proprietary in the way Adolphus linked his arm through Kate's?

Pressing his way past the other couples retreating from the floor, Harry followed after Kate. Adolphus was on the point of surrendering her to her next partner, a cheerful young lieutenant whom Harry recognized as Frank Porter.

The vicar was the first to notice Harry's approach. The fellow, damn his eyes, actually had the impudence to hold out his hand and look rather pleased to see Harry.

"Why, Cousin Harry—"

"Lord Lytton to you," Harry grated.

Adolphus's smile faded to one of consternation and bewilderment. "Er-certainly, my lord. This is a most unlooked-for pleasure to see you here this evening."

"Evidently." After delivering this unmistakable snub, Harry rounded on Kate. "Good evening, Miss Towers."

Kate started at the sound of Harry's voice, so deep, so close to her ear, the voice she had been half dreading, half hoping to hear all evening. Her heart skipped a beat. She felt grateful that she had a moment to school her features before she turned to face him.

She managed a rather unsteady, "Good evening, my lord." Risking a glance at him, she stood frozen. She thought herself familiar with every expression of Harry's, from his devil's grin to that warm steady gaze that was always her undoing.

But never before had she seen this unsmiling look that rendered his swarthy features so harsh, the deep furrows by his mouth for once not stemming from laughter.

His voice had a most unsettling edge as he said, "I have come to claim my dance."

"Alas, I—I fear you come too late, my lord. My dances are all bespoken."

"The next dance is mine." Harry reached for her hand, a dangerous glint in his eyes.

A sensation of inexplicable alarm spread through Kate. "Why, Harry, I—I, no, indeed, my lord. You are quite mistaken. I—"

Harry's hand locked about her wrist, tugging her toward the dance floor.

"I say, Lytton, this is the most barefaced piracy I have ever witnessed." But Lieutenant Porter's good-natured protest was lost as Harry pulled Kate out to the center of the floor.

So much for Kate's plan of defense. She might have known Harry would do something this outrageous. The thought of resisting entered her mind, only to be dismissed. People were already turning to stare.

Yet Harry's action bore none of the mark of his usual teasing mischief. She sensed a suppressed anger about him. Although she could not begin to guess its cause, his dark mood frightened her a little.

"You are being most uncivil, my lord," she said in the sternest voice she could muster.

"I have never been noted for my social graces, Miss Towers."

As the strains of a waltz sounded, he yanked her hard into his arms. Kate let out a gasp that was part outrage, part alarm. But she had no choice but to set her feet into motion, following where Harry led.

As he whirled her in a circle, he continued in that sneering tone that was not Harry's and that Kate felt she could rapidly learn to hate. "You seemed less than delighted to see me, my dear."

"You—you took me by surprise. I did not notice you arrive."

"Very likely because you were too busy making calf's eyes at my cousin."

Kate flinched as though he had struck her. Never had she known Harry to say anything so deliberately cruel. Yet it gave her a startling clue to his anger. Was it possible Harry could be jealous? It seemed the most likely answer. Her plan to marry the vicar and put an end to Harry's pursuit had appeared so simple a solution. What a witling she had been to think that Harry would stand idly by while it happened.

She longed to return a sharp answer to Harry's caustic remark, but much to her annoyance, a flood tide of guilty color rushed into her cheeks.

Harry's mouth thinned to a taut, white line. "Ah, so I see there *is* another reason for your continued refusals of my offer of marriage. Do you expect me to wish you joy, Kate? I will see Adolphus planted in his own churchyard first."

"You are being ridiculous, my lord. If you wish me to continue this dance, pray speak of something else."

As though he sensed her urge to break away, Harry tightened his grip upon her hand. She could feel the heat of his other palm against the small of her back, seeming to sear her through the filmy gown. Kate stumbled slightly. She had but learned to waltz only that morning, and dancing with Harry was nothing like her practice with the dancing master her grandmama had produced. The willowy Mr. James had not been so rock hard, nor had he looked ready to eat her alive. Harry's gaze dipped down the front of her gown, and his scowl assumed an even blacker hue.

"Where the devil did you get that frock?"

"Grandmama gave it to me," Kate said, raising her chin with more defiance than she felt.

"I detest it," he growled.

"I did not wear it with any thought of pleasing you, my lord." Kate felt her own temper stir. "I expected you to be seeking some less mild diversion tonight with your *friends*."

"I wondered how long it would take before you flung Folly into my teeth."

"It is you who brought up Mr. Ffolliot's name, sir, not I."

"I would try to defend the poor fellow to you, but I doubt it would do a damned bit of good. And I am not about to try to justify my friendship with the man."

"No one asked you to!" Goaded beyond endurance, it was all Kate could do to keep up the semblance of waltzing. "I am sure I do not care if you choose to sully your good name by associating with such unworthy companions who—who encourage you to play so deep you lose your best horses and—"

"What!" Harry missed a step and another couple nearly crashed into them. His eyes blazed so strangely that she was nigh afraid to speak, but she continued valiantly, "It—it is well known how you had to sell your hunters to meet your gambling debts."

"It is indeed? By whom? Who told you such a thing?"

"Well, I—I . . ." Kate hesitated. Beneath the roilings of Harry's anger, she detected a flash of pain, but not a trace of guilt. And Harry was not the sort of man to dissemble. Kate suddenly felt no longer so sure of herself.

"Never mind. It scarce matters who," Harry said in flat tones. "The important thing is that *you* believed it."

He lapsed into a stony silence, but beneath the grim facade, Kate caught hintings of a deep and abiding hurt. She had the sinking feeling that she had somehow wronged Harry yet again.

The waltz seemed to drag on forever, the lilting music a mockery of the numbing unhappiness and shame Kate felt seeping through her. When the dance ended, Harry no longer looked angry, merely tired, a soul-deep weariness dulling his eyes.

"I will escort you back to your grandmother," he said.

"My lord . . ." She trailed off. Now scarce was the time to be asking him for explanations that she should have sought much sooner instead of being so quick to credit Julia's tale.

He offered her his arm, stiff and unyielding. She rested her fingertips against the crook, feeling the distance widen between them as though they had been separated by miles.

To add to Kate's misery, they had not taken many steps when they were accosted by the squire. He greeted Harry in his usual bluff fashion, and what must the wretched fellow do but go nattering on about what a magnificent run he had enjoyed that morning on Harry's own hunter.

Harry tried for an expression of polite indifference but could not quite manage it.

The squire clapped him on the shoulder. "No need to look so glum, sir. I paid you a handsome price for those horses and from what I have heard tell, you are putting the money to good use. What you invest on your lands you will get back tenfold, to say nothing of making the Hudderstons happy as mudlarks."

Kate felt her heart nigh go still. "The Hudderstons?" she asked hoarsely.

The squire chuckled. "Aye, his lordship's tenants these days are likely to dub him 'Saint Harry.' "

"What a parcel of nonsense," Harry said, appearing both annoyed and embarrassed. He tugged at Kate's arm. "If you will excuse us, Mr. Gresham—"

"The lad has been dropping a great deal of his blunt," the squire continued, ignoring Harry. "Fixing up the Hudderstons' roof and new drains for the old Stratton place . . ."

Kate closed her eyes, the full impact of exactly how wrong she'd been striking her like a thunderclap. Dear God!

290

Not gaming debts. Harry had used the money to fix up his tenants' farms, those self-same tenants she had accused him of neglecting.

The squire rattled on, warming to his subject with great relish until Harry interrupted him. "I don't think Miss Towers is much interested in roofs and drains."

"Isn't she?" The squire peered fiercely at Kate from beneath his bushy brows. "Why, I think you mistake her, my lord. I've always said Miss Kate was a cut above these other mutton-headed females. A most sensible girl."

"Indeed I am not," Kate whispered. "I am the greatest of fools."

Neither of the men seemed to hear her as the music struck up again. The squire declared he must seek out Mrs. Gresham for the next dance. "After all these years, I am still her favorite beau." Giving a broad wink, the burly man moved off in search of his wife.

Without his looming presence, Kate felt as though she had been left entirely alone with Harry. She scarce knew how to face him or what to say. Harry gently disengaged his arm from hers.

"I believe Lieutenant Porter is coming to claim you, Miss Towers. So I will simply bid you good night."

"Harry," she faltered, but by the time she could bring herself to look up, Harry was already gone. She caught a glimpse of him disappearing beneath the archway.

The genial lieutenant was doomed once more to be left without a partner, for Kate plunged after Harry. She paused in the hall's open doorway, the cool night air striking against her heated cheeks. Her heart torn with remorse, Kate watched Harry head for the nearby inn yard. In another moment, he would vanish into the night.

Kate hesitated, biting down hard upon her lip. Bishops' daughters did not race in pursuit of young men beneath the light of the moon. But she simply couldn't allow Harry to leave this way. Hitching up her skirts, she started after him.

Harry cleared the ground with long swift strides, obliging

291

Kate to run to catch up with him. Breathlessly, she planted herself in his path.

"H-harry. Please . . . do wait."

Moonlight sculpted his features, throwing the strong, hard lines of his profile into sharp relief. His eyes registered neither welcome nor censure, only emptiness.

"Go back, Kate," he said dully. "You should not be out here alone with me. Think of your reputation."

Tears gathered at the ends of Kate's lashes. She drew an unsteady breath. "The—the devil with my reputation!"

At least her vehemence produced some reaction, his brows arching upward in astonishment. She laid one hand against his chest as though that light gesture could somehow stay him.

"I—I am sorry," she said. "I didn't mean to hurt you, to . . . to ever believe— 'Tis only when I heard about the sale of your horses I could not imagine—"

"That there could be any good reason for my actions," Harry finished for her. He looked away, his jaw working painfully. "Damn it, Kate. I am well accustomed to the world cheerfully believing the worst of me, but you! When you join them, it tears me to flinders."

Kate's heart constricted, and she was possessed of a reckless impulse to do anything to make him amends, banish the pain she heard threading his voice. Fully realizing it was not the wisest thing to do, she stood on tiptoe and brushed a kiss along his cheek.

"I am sorry," she whispered again.

It was as though she had set a match to tinder. With a low groan, Harry caught her hard against him, burying his face against the pulse beat at her throat. Kate knew she should protest, but somehow her arms wound about his neck and she clung to him.

But moments before, Harry had nearly given in to despair. When Kate had leveled her false accusation, so full of righteous indignation, he had heard the old bishop speaking. Harry's quest to win her seemed impossible. She would ever be her papa's daughter.

Yet no trace of that prim creature now remained in the

woman who so tenderly sought his pardon, the warmth of her arms the gentlest of consolation. Harry meant to do no more than hold her, but the longings of the past two years proved too much for him. The scent of her, the feel of her, all the softness, the sweetness that was Kate drove him nigh to madness.

He began to trail fire-ridden kisses along the column of her neck, the delicate curve of her jaw, her temple, her eyelids. Even if she had resisted, Harry was not sure he could have stopped. But she did not resist, tipping up her face like a rose seeking the warmth of the sun.

"Kate . . . Kate," he murmured between kisses. "I can scarce be patient any longer. *Will* you marry me?"

"I don't know. Oh, I don't know. I feel so . . . confused."

Harry sought to add to that confusion by claiming her lips. He kissed her without mercy, ruthlessly plundering her mouth until she sagged weakly against him.

Papa had warned her, Kate thought muzzily, about the dangers of moonlight and a man like Harry. And Papa had been so right. She shivered with the delicious fiery sensations coursing through her. Caught between despair and rapture, she held Harry tighter, her lips pleading for more.

It was left to Harry to be the one first coming to his senses. Just as his own passion threatened to burst the bounds of reason, he caught the sound of some drunken revelers staggering down the steps of the nearby inn.

In another few moments, he and Kate would be discovered at their moonlight tryst. "The devil with it," Harry thought, bending over her for another kiss, an evil voice seeming to whisper in his ear that if they were caught in a compromising situation, Kate would have to marry him.

But he did not want her that way, any more than he wanted her coming to him out of some misguided notion of duty. With a heavy sigh, he summoned up all his willpower and thrust her from him.

She looked momentarily dazed, then hurt and bewildered. Even within the shadows of darkness, he could see the blush that heated her cheeks. Harry forced a smile, speaking in mock sternness.

"This behavior would be outrageous, Miss Towers, even if we were betrothed. You might be ready to consign your reputation to perdition, but I have turned respectable."

Kate gave an indignant gasp, then one of those unwilling gurgles of laughter that so delighted Harry. He took her by the arm, nudging her back toward the hall.

"For I would as soon not exchange greetings with any of those gentlemen heading toward the stables. And I mistake not, they have already shot the cat."

"No! Truly, Harry?" Kate glanced back with a look of horror.

" 'Tis only an expression, sweetheart. It means they are quite inebriated."

"Oh," Kate said, with such an innocent relief that Harry longed to kiss her all over again. He paused at the steps leading into the assembly hall, hating to take her back inside after all that just passed between them, so much left unsaid.

Kate seemed to feel a reluctance, too, for she rested her hand timidly upon his sleeve. "Harry . . ." She gazed up at him, her violet eyes earnest and troubled. "I have been so unfair to you."

"Nay, Kate. No more apologies—"

"I do not mean just about the horses," she went on quickly. "But also about what I said a while ago when you asked me to marry you. *I don't know.* Such a foolish answer."

"On the contrary, it was a most delightful answer." He caught her hand, kissing her fingertips but only lightly, playfully, lest he once more be carried away. "You give a fellow cause to hope."

Her lashes fluttered down as though she could not meet his gaze. "I thought I had made up my mind, that I knew what I must do when I came here this evening—"

"If you go near Adolphus Thorpe again other than to hear a sermon—" Harry started to growl.

"I won't," Kate promised with a gentle laugh. "I know that I could never marry him *now.*"

"Kate!" Harry nigh forgot everything, starting to pull her toward him again. But a more formidable threat than the drunkards hove into view. He could see Julia making her way toward the open doorway.

"Damn!" Harry swore.

"It is just as well," Kate said. "I need time to reflect, and I have more than a few words to say to Miss Thorpe."

The fierceness of Kate's expression as she took the stairs and marched back into the hall left Harry gaping with astonishment. If she had been a man, Harry thought he would be offering to be her second. Although he had no clear idea of her quarrel with Julia, he hastened after Kate, intrigued to hear what she would say.

But he was doomed to disappointment. He had not got far when he was cornered by Lady Dane.

"Well?" she demanded.

Harry regarded her questioningly in turn, widening his eyes to the fullest extent of innocence. "Well what, my lady?"

"Do not be pert with me, sir. You have had my granddaughter outside beneath the moon long enough, you had best be prepared to give me tidings of your engagement."

Harry grimaced. He might have known nothing would escape her ladyship's eagle eyes.

"Alas, I have no good tidings to give you as yet. But soon, I feel, very soon." He could not refrain from looking a little smug, remembering Kate's response to his kiss. "And I must tell your ladyship, I find that my methods are far more effective than yours."

"Wicked rogue!" Lady Dane gave him a sharp dig with her cane, but she was smiling.

Harry turned to look for Kate, but to his disappointment she had already finished with Julia. Kate was taking her place opposite some callow youth for the next dance. She looked as proper as ever, but the color yet glowed high in her cheeks.

A wry smile escaped Harry. She had not accepted his proposal yet, but this time she had not refused him either. Decidedly this was progress. It put him in such a cheerful frame of mind that he was able to watch with equanimity Kate make her way through a succession of dancing partners.

While Lieutenant Porter at last had his dance with her, Harry made his way toward the punch bowl, nearly walking into the Reverend Thorpe.

Adolphus flattened himself against the wall in an effort to stay out of Harry's path. "M-my lord, I beg your pardon."

"Cousin Harry," Harry gently chided him, then walked on, leaving the poor man thoroughly dumbfounded and bewildered.

As Harry sipped his punch, he was astonished to discover that more than one of his neighboring landowners had remarked on the improvements he had begun making upon his estates. He found himself the center of a great deal of attention and approval, which rendered him somewhat uncomfortable. He was not at all accustomed to being lauded for virtuous behavior.

"Mapleshade has always been a grand estate," Squire Gresham remarked. "I'd stake it against any other in England."

The other men chorused hearty agreement.

"Perhaps Mapleshade once was worthy of such praise." A chill female voice cut through the masculine ones. Harry glanced down to find Julia unexpectedly at his side. Her disposition was as soured as if she had been drinking lemonade instead of punch. What had Kate said to her? Harry would have given the last of his horses to know.

She continued with a sneer, "There certainly were times far more glorious at Mapleshade than the present. The harvests were much more prosperous, the old fête day the event of the season."

"Ah, well, I am not quite as old as you, Julia," Harry drawled. "I don't remember any of that."

As the men chuckled, Julia turned quite red. "Nor does anyone else. Most of Mapleshade's revered and time-honored customs appear to have ended with your father."

Harry knew he should let this spiteful remark go unchallenged. But damn, it was a jab at the governor as well as himself.

"It so happens," he announced loftily, "that I have every intention of reviving the old fête day."

His statement produced a hubbub of excitement and the

squire fairly wrung his hand by way of congratulations. The news spread round the room, and Kate regarded him through eyes glowing with pride.

Harry could not resist raising his punch cup in a mocking salute to his discomfited cousin. That was one in the eye for Julia. It was not until he downed the sticky-sweet liquid that a daunting thought hit him, nigh causing him to choke.

Harry did not have the damnedest notion what the ancient fête day was.

Chapter 9

What on earth had he done? Harry thought the following morning as he lay flat on his back, staring up at the canopy of the bed looming above him. He could scarce believe he had permitted Julia to goad him into such an undertaking—a revival of the old harvest fête. Great heavens, what did he know about playing lord of the manor?

As he reviewed that disastrous moment at the assembly, when he had grandly made his announcement, he still didn't know what had come over him. He couldn't blame it upon that watery punch. Perhaps it had been the far more heady draught of Kate's sweet eyes trained upon him, so expectant. How could he have disappointed her?

And, he admitted as he stretched, locking his arms behind his head, it had been worth it, the way her face had suffused with delight, her glow of pride in him. He had always wondered why those dashed fool knights had rigged themselves out in all that armor, letting some other dolt take a run at them with a lance, risking being knocked head over ears. Such recklessness could only have been inspired by a lady.

Tilting, however, seemed a plagued sight easier than what he had undertaken. Upon his return home last night, he had asked Gravshaw exactly what the deuce was supposed to take place at this fête. The elderly retainer had explained the holiday had always taken place after the harvest, consisting of a dinner for the laborers, the tenants, and the local gentry, to say nothing of the games and the ball held early in the evening. Harry had far rather Gravshaw *had* said nothing of those.

Harry didn't have the damnedest notion of how to arrange any sort of ball or games, at least not respectable ones. And he was not such a muttonhead as to believe Sybil was going to be the least use to him. The event was going to turn out an utter shambles. He would undoubtedly make a fool of himself before most of the countryside. Worse still, he would diminish himself in Kate's eyes just as she was nigh ready to fall into his arms.

With a low groan, Harry rolled over when he heard a discreet knock at the door. He barked a curt command to enter and within moments, Gravshaw stood framed in the bedcurtain openings.

"My lord, Lady Dane is belowstairs," the butler began in long suffering accents, "and she—"

"I am just rising." Harry sat bolt upright in alarm, groping for the sheet. "Tell her ladyship I shall be belowstairs directly!"

"Very good, my lord."

Harry could not quite be certain, but he thought his redoubtable manservant heaved a sigh of relief as he quit the room. Fully acquainted with her ladyship's impatience and her methods, Harry wasted no time in repairing to his dressing room.

He shaved and garbed himself in haste, which in nowise disconcerted his valet. Bardle, by this time, was quite used to the young master's fits and starts. Harry was never as inclined to linger over his toilet as that dapper little man would have liked.

As Harry descended the front hall stairs two at a time, he wondered what brought her ladyship down upon him this time. Of all those present at the assembly, he believed that only she had sensed the unease beneath his smiling good humor after he had promised to revive the fête. She had probably come to tell him what an idiot he was, Harry thought with a wry grin. Her ladyship was most adept at that.

He discovered that Gravshaw had escorted her ladyship into the main salon, the most elaborate and formal in the house, well suited to Lady Dane, but not much favored by Harry. The massive chamber was too dark and solemn by half with the furniture done in mahogany, the marble fireplace overly ostentatious, and the draperies a most regal but forbidding gold-fringed purple.

As Harry entered the drawing room, he found her ladyship settled upon a heavily carved chair, and greatly to his astonishment, on the settee opposite was Sybil. Not only fully dressed, but belowstairs before two of the clock. For once she was not reclining, but sitting erect like a schoolgirl in the presence of a stern governess, an expression of the most civil terror upon her plump features. Her smelling salts were at her elbow, but she appeared half-afraid to reach for them under Lady Dane's disapproving stare.

"There you are at last, Lytton," her ladyship said before he could so much as bow over her hand. "I have just been informing your stepmama of your plans to hold the harvest day fête."

"You must be quite mad, Harcourt." Sybil sneaked a quick sniff of her salts. "My precarious health will never permit—"

"I am fully aware of the delicate state of your health, madam." Lady Dane's obvious contempt reduced Sybil to quaking silence. "That is why we have ridden over this morning to offer you and Lord Lytton our help."

"We?" Harry asked.

Lady Dane nodded toward someone behind him, a quiet presence who had escaped his notice. Harry turned toward the tall windows, the morning light pouring through them dispelling the chamber's gloom.

But to Harry it was not the sun that accomplished this feat so much as the slight figure who stood outlined by its rays, a vision all soft muslin, lace, and ribbons of rose, her dark hair cascading from beneath a demure straw bonnet.

"Kate," Harry breathed.

When she gave him that half-shy smile, he suddenly felt as though he could conquer a dozen harvest fêtes. Aye, and half the world as well.

Grandmama had presented her suggestion to Kate earlier that morning with her customary delicacy. Sybil Arundel had wool for brains, she said roundly, and Lord Harry was a mere man. Between the two of them, there was no hope that the fête could be a success until some more competent female took a hand. It was the only neighborly and *Christian* thing to do.

It sounded to Kate like a rather shocking piece of interference, but before she quite knew where she was at, she was hustled into her grandmother's carriage and on the way to Mapleshade.

The sight of Harry's genuine relief and gratitude at the offer served to end most of Kate's qualms. After the injustice she had done him, she was eager to join Lady Dane in coming to his aid. But in the busy days that ensued, Kate soon discovered Lady Dane gave the term "we" its most royal usage. Her ladyship's notion of helping was to preside over tea in the parlor while commanding Kate and Harry "not to dawdle."

As the Dowager Countess of Lytton took to her bed with a hastily acquired bout of influenza, Kate was obliged to take charge of the proceedings, Harry's household staff coming to her more and more for their instructions regarding the preparations.

Not that Kate actually minded. She had not been so happily occupied since the days she had played hostess for her father at the episcopal palace. She threw herself into the planning with a will, determined to arrange a fête that would do Harry credit and silence forever Julia Thorpe's criticisms of him.

The only aspect of it all that disturbed Kate was that Grandmama was astonishingly lax in her chaperonage, frequently leaving Kate alone in Harry's company. Of course Harry was supposed to be hard at work in his own study, but that room conveniently adjoined the Hunt parlor, which had been assigned to Kate for her use.

More oft than not Harry lounged in the doorway, his gaze

warmer than the fire crackling on the hearth to dispel the early autumn chill. Kate tried to concentrate on such weighty matters as the menu for the fête that Harry's cook had submitted for her approval. But it was difficult to ignore that much masculinity leaning against one's door jamb, the sleeves of Harry's linen shirt rolled up to expose the strength of his bronzed forearms.

"Shall I put another log on the fire?" he asked. "Are you quite warm enough, Kate?"

"Yes, my lord."

"If you want anything, you know you have but to say so."

"Yes, my lord."

The rogue-green eyes became more bold, the deep voice soft and suggestive. "We could simply forget all this fête nonsense and you could elope with me today."

"*No,* my lord."

Harry grinned, preparing to retreat. Kate, who had been wishing him to leave her in peace, suddenly discovered she could not bear for him to do so.

"No, Harry. Wait . . ."

He paused questioningly.

"I—I do need you."

He beamed, taking an eager step forward.

"To—to help me go over the list of names for the invitations."

Harry came to an abrupt halt, his expectant expression fading to a rueful disappointment. But he straightened his waistcoat, rolling his sleeves down into a more decorous attitude. "I am entirely at your disposal, my lady."

The Hunt parlor boasted at least a half dozen of fine Hepplewhite chairs upholstered in striped silk, the legs and arms finely carved by the hand of a master craftsman. Yet it did not surprise Kate in the least that Harry ignored all those elegant creations and settled beside her on the sofa.

She stiffened with immediate wariness. Harry had behaved like a gentleman since that night of the assembly, but Kate oft detected a most disquieting gleam in his eye. She was not sure she entirely trusted him. Even less did she trust the propriety of her own response. The memory of his kisses had the power to

301

fire her blood, urging her to fling sanity to the winds as she had in the dark shadows of the inn yard.

Feeling a quiver run through her at his nearness, Kate moved further into the corner of the sofa. She reached briskly for the quill pen upon the small writing desk set before her.

"Naturally," she said, "all of your laborers and tenants will attend the fête. But you must decide which of your neighbors you mean to have."

Harry edged closer, ostensibly to peer over her shoulder at the list she was compiling, his dark head drawing alarmingly nigh her own.

"Of course, the Greshams and the Thorpes will be invited." Kate heard her own voice rise a shade higher. "And your step-mama asked me to be sure Mr. Crosbie's name is included."

She felt Harry freeze. Although he moved not a muscle, she sensed the tension that coursed through him.

"Completely out of the question," he said harshly.

Kate glanced up, astonished at the forbidding expression darkening the countenance that had been smiling only a moment before.

"But—but what shall I say to Lady Lytton?" Kate asked.

"I shall deal with her. She should have known better than to suggest such a thing to you. Sybil is well aware how I feel about Mr. Crosbie. He is either a fortune hunter or a fool, I care not which. I won't have him hanging about my stepmother. My father left me the responsibility of looking after her, and that is exactly what I intend to do."

Harry snatched the quill from Kate and scratched out Crosbie's name with such energy, he nigh tore the parchment. Noting the hard determination in Harry's face, Kate did not even think of challenging him upon Lady Lytton's behalf. If Mr. Crosbie was indeed that bad, then she believed Harry's feelings did him credit. But it did rather astonish her to see that he could look as stern as her own papa ever had.

Harry relaxed again as Kate moved on down the list. "The Porters, the Truetts." He nodded with disinterested approval at this recital of the names of the most prominent families in the shire.

When Kate had come to the end, she said, "Is there no one whom I have left off—some particular friend you would wish invited?"

Even as she asked, Kate caught herself hesitating, the memory of Mr. Ffolliot not far from her mind, although both she and Harry, as though by mutual agreement, had ever refrained from mentioning that gentleman's name.

Harry shrugged. "I have complete faith in your judgment, Kate. Ask whomever you think proper."

Kate knew she should not accept this carte blanche, but could not help feeling a little relieved. Harry had a perfect right to receive Mr. Ffolliot if he chose, yet Kate did not know if she could have endured that disreputable man's presence.

She had been focusing so hard upon the list, she did not realize that Harry had stolen the opportunity to inch closer. She started, becoming aware that his arm rested behind her along the sofa, those strong tanned fingers dangling tantalizingly near her shoulder.

Kate trembled at the temptation. She knew she would have to but lean back and offer her lips for him to—

Quickly she shot to her feet. "I had better ring for Gravshaw. He will best be able to help us with planning the dining arrangements."

She half feared Harry might tug her back down beside him, but she managed to dart trembling round the desk and cross the room in safety. She tugged vigorously at the bellpull.

When she dared glance at Harry, she saw that he had not made one move to intercept her, his eyes glimmering with amusement and impatience.

"Very well. Have it your own way, Miss Towers. But once we have done with this wretched fête, I assure you it will take far more than a butler to come to your rescue."

The threat sounded only part in jest, but Kate could scarce blame Harry for coming to the end of his forbearance. She had been much more fair to him when she had flatly told him no, kept him at a distance.

Her current state of indecision and confusion filled her with shame. She could scarce deny any longer that she loved Harry, not even to herself. Then what kept holding her back? But one thing—the whisper of a memory. Her father. She could still hear the bishop's voice warning her to proceed with care.

By the time Gravshaw answered her summons, Kate managed to recover her composure. But she avoided the sofa, settling herself primly upon one of the Hepplewhite chairs. Looking rather disgruntled, Harry crossed his arms over his chest. Stretching out his long legs, he propped his boots upon the writing desk, evincing little interest in the arrangements being made for his guests.

Gravshaw, however, entered into the discussion with all the earnest consideration it deserved. Tables would be set up in the fields for the farmhands, a tent provided for the tenants, while the more distinguished guests would be entertained in the hall's magnificent dining room. The difficulty arose with classifying certain individuals such as the Strattons. Although simple farmers the same as the Hudderstons, Mrs. Stratton now kept a carriage and sent her daughter to an exclusive boarding school.

"If you'll pardon my saying so, Miss Towers," Gravshaw remarked, "Mrs. Stratton is getting above herself. There will be a great deal of resentment if she is raised above her neighbors to the honor of dining room."

"That is very true." Kate frowned, thoughtfully whisking the end of the quill against her chin. And she wanted no such bustle created. Harry's fête must be perfect, without even the shading of any ill will or spiteful gossip to spoil it.

She and Gravshaw continued to fret and speculate for several moments more upon the fate of the annoying Mrs. Stratton until Harry broke in, "For heaven's sake, I don't think Wellington gave such consideration to the deployment of his troops at Waterloo. Let everyone fill their plates and sit where they find room. I am sure I shouldn't complain even if I end up next to old Timothy Keegan."

Kate exchanged a pained look with Gravshaw. Harry, bearing so little regard for his own consequence, could not be expected to understand how those of lesser rank might be far more jealous of theirs. Sighing, Kate gently removed Harry's feet from the desk and suggested he might want to consult with Mr. Warburton to see how the construction of the marquee was coming.

"Trying to be rid of me, eh?" Harry chuckled. "What reward will I receive for taking myself off like a good boy?"

Ignoring this pointed question, Kate took him by the arm and escorted him firmly to the door. "And do make sure Mr. Warburton remembers that we require another tent for the ladies to take tea."

Harry went without resisting, but at the threshold he paused to murmur, "I would gladly do all that you require, Kate, for one kiss."

"For one box on the ears, sir." She thrust him out, but Harry still managed to whisper several more wicked suggestions before she closed the door in his face.

Kate fought down a blush before turning to face Gravshaw, dreading lest he had noticed some of this byplay. She thought she detected a hint of a smile, but by the time she resumed her seat the elderly butler had settled his face into lines of nigh painful gravity.

Without further interruption from Harry, they were able to settle the matter of seating before teatime, the socially ambitious Mrs. Stratton firmly relegated to the tent where she belonged.

"The cards of invitation have arrived from the printers," Gravshaw said. "Shall I have them brought in?"

"Yes, but you need not rush." Kate pushed back from the desk, flexing her toes within her soft kid boots. "I am rather stiff from sitting so long and should like to take a turn about the garden."

"Very good, my lady." Gravshaw bowed himself out.

It was not until the door had closed behind him that the import of what the dignified manservant had said struck Kate.

My lady.

Kate pressed her hands to her cheeks in dismay. Whether it had been a slip of the tongue or the title used with deliberation scarce mattered. Either prospect was equally disconcerting.

Her constant presence at Mapleshade had obviously given rise to expectations, even in the servants' quarters.

But were they expectations she intended to fulfill? Most earnestly did Kate seek to probe the depths of her own heart. What answer would she give the next time Harry asked her to marry him, *seriously* asked?

She had to acknowledge how comfortable she had become these past days, even in her temporary role as mistress of Mapleshade. And its earl . . . how much more so dependent upon his presence for her happiness. Odd how the sharing of such simple domestic routines like teatime, dinner, working together on the details of the fête had drawn them into a greater intimacy than ever before. She had observed firsthand how hard Harry strove to be a good master, that combination of humor and firmness with which he treated his dependents.

"He's so different, Papa," Kate murmured, "so different from the wild, heedless young man you believed him to be."

If only her father were there to realize it. If only the bishop were there to give his blessing . . .

The thought brought with it a wave of melancholy. Kate did her best to shake it off. There was no sense repining for what could never be. The decision regarding Harry was as ever hers to make. Instead of moping here, she would do far better to go for her walk as she had planned. Perhaps the brisk air would clarify her thinking.

Scooping up her shawl, Kate let herself out through one of the French doors leading to Mapleshade's formal garden. She felt glad of the warm wool draped about her shoulders, the nip of September in the air despite the sun glinting along the gravel pathways.

Most of the flowers had lost their bloom, the roses dying on the vine, yet Kate still reveled in the orderly layout of the beds, the neat rows of hedges all a delight to her tidy soul. She filled her lungs with the crisp air and wandered toward the summerhouse, a pagodalike structure that stood at the hub of the garden.

She had no intention of going inside, merely skirting past it.

But her plans were abruptly altered when an arm shot out of the shadowy depths and yanked her beneath the arched opening.

Kate let out a squeak of surprise. She could not imagine that it would be other than Harry perpetrating such mischief. It was on the tip of her tongue to scold him for giving her such a fright, when her gaze adjusted to the pagoda's gloom-filled interior. It was not Harry's green eyes that twinkled back at her, but those of a stranger, looking rather nervous and frightened himself.

His cherubic features framed by ridiculously high starched shirt points, the young man appeared harmless enough, but he did not relax his grasp upon her wrist.

Kate's lips parted to cry out.

"Oh, don't scream," a female voice shuddered. " 'Twill go right through my head."

Kate's mouth closed. She glanced down with astonishment to discover Lady Lytton seated on a bench. Apparently she had made a remarkable recovery from her influenza. Despite the chill of the day, her gown sported a shockingly low décolletage. The gooseflesh forming beneath the dusting of pearl powder made an interesting effect, and the glow in her ladyship's cheeks for once owed to more than rouge.

"We didn't mean to alarm you, Miss Towers," the strange young man said. " 'Tis only that we saw you passing by and could not allow such an opportunity for seeing you alone to escape us."

Lady Lytton beamed at him as though he had said something remarkably clever. "Indeed, Miss Towers. I was most desirous to have you make this gentleman's acquaintance. This is Mr. Lucillus Crosbie."

"Mr. Crosbie!" Kate gasped. She wrenched her hand away as though he had suddenly become a snake banding her wrist. *The* Lucillus Crosbie? The same one she had heard Harry denounce with such vehemence only an hour before? Kate backed nervously toward the arched opening.

"Indeed, sir. You should not be here—"

"Of course, he shouldn't," Lady Lytton interrupted petulantly. "Why do you think we are hiding in here?"

"If Lord Harry discovers you . . ." Kate shuddered to think what Harry might do.

Mr. Crosbie visibly shared her sentiments. He paled, saying, "His lordship tossed me out twice, once into the pond, once out the window."

"Did he?" Kate's alarm grew, having no desire to witness Harry inspired to such violence. "Then I think your wisest course would be to leave at once, sir."

"But we must talk to you," her ladyship wailed.

"It will do no good. I already told Lord Harry about your wish that Mr. Crosbie attend the fête and he said—"

"Oh, plague take the fête," Mr. Crosbie exclaimed with great passion. He clasped Lady Lytton's hand to his heart. "Miss Towers, we can bear this separation no longer. We want to be married."

Kate's mouth gaped open and she had to force it closed. Gazing from the pink-cheeked young man to the lady nigh twice his age, she thought she had never been more shocked. She felt much like a swimmer already aware of being in dangerous shallows who suddenly plunges in over her head.

She sagged down onto a bench opposite the duo clutching each other in such dramatic fashion. "I-I doubt Harry will ever permit such a thing."

"I know that." Lady Lytton sniffed, groping for her handkerchief. "He has been behaving like . . . like a regular Capulet."

The image of Harry playing tyrannical parent to Lady Lytton's Juliet was a ludicrous one, but Kate did not feel in the least like laughing. She scarce knew what to say to this pair of ill-assorted lovers, but they apparently mistook her silence for encouragement and began to pour out their hopes and mutual devotion.

"Lord Lytton does not believe I love Sybil, but I do," Mr. Crosbie declared. "He cannot understand. Miss Towers, I have a mama and seven older sisters. Seven! Not a one of them has ever taken my ambition to be a sculptor seriously. They think I should join the army." He paused to direct a speaking glance at her ladyship. "Only Sybil has ever believed in me."

308

"Dear boy!" She squeezed his hand. "You shall rival Michelangelo."

"I am now in a position to support a wife," Mr. Crosbie continued eagerly. "Thanks to Sybil's patronage, I have obtained some commissions in Chillingsworth to work on some tombs in the cathedral."

Recalling the memorial Mr. Crosbie had designed for Harry, Kate had a horrifying vision of the future decor of that ancient and venerable church, but she managed to say, "My . . . my congratulations, Mr. Crosbie, but I do not understand why you chose to confide in me. The proper person to address would be Lord Harry—"

"He will not listen!" Mr. Crosbie said. "At least not to us."

"But to you, my dear—" Lady Sybil began.

"Oh, no. No!" Kate repeated firmly as she realized what they were about to ask her. She started to rise, but this time she was detained by Sybil's plump hand. She angled an arch glance at Mr. Crosbie. "My dear Lucillus, if you could but allow me a moment alone with Miss Towers."

He looked loath to leave her, but he agreed, his eyes so rapt with adoration Kate doubted he would have refused any request of Lady Lytton's. He retreated to the opposite end of the summerhouse, out of earshot.

Kate longed to retreat as well, not sure what was coming next. With her youthful lover gone, Lady Lytton bundled up more sensibly within the folds of her own shawl, abandoning the simper she habitually wore.

"I daresay you think me quite a silly old woman, my dear," she said. Ignoring Kate's mild protest, she rushed on, "But I am not so silly I don't know my own mind. I was quite young when I married the first time, Miss Towers. Harry's papa picked me out of the line of debutantes at Almack's in less time than he spent choosing a horse."

She winced. "Such a great booming voice my lord had, but it was a good match. My parents were pleased." Her ladyship's soft chin stiffened with resolution. "This time I am old enough to marry to please myself, and I shall do so. Lucillus is so gentle, so . . . so sensitive. I don't want to cause poor Harcourt any sort of scandal, but he is making me quite desperate."

Lady Lytton angled a coy and coaxing glance at Kate, reaching out to pat her hand. "You could avert much of this discord, Miss Towers. I am not such a widgeon that I haven't noticed the way Harcourt looks at you. You could talk him round."

Kate started to deny she had any such power over Harry, but she could not quite manage to do so. For she feared she could persuade Harry if she set herself to the task, and strangely enough she was not unsympathetic to Lady Lytton's cause. The world might raise its eyebrows at such a peculiar match, but Kate detected a genuine vein of affection running beneath all of her ladyship's and Mr. Crosbie's melodramatic protestations.

But to agree to use her influence with Harry in their behalf, the sort of influence a wife might exert upon a husband, why that was tantamount to confirming the tie between herself and Harry.

Yet Kate was not proof against the entreaty in Lady Lytton's eyes. "I—I suppose I could try," she murmured with great reluctance.

Even this vague promise was enough to set Lady Lytton into transports of delight. She called over Mr. Crosbie and the pair of them nigh overwhelmed Kate with their expressions of gratitude. Kate nodded weakly, inching toward the arch, at last making good her escape. She left them holding hands, whispering tender vows and all manner of wildly impractical plans.

"Whew!" Kate sighed as she all but fled back to the house. She must have taken complete leave of her senses. Whatever had induced her to become involved in Lady Lytton's romantic tangle when Kate could not even manage to sort out her own? She regretted the pledge she had given, but it was not in Kate to go back on her word.

She entered the house with a feeling of trepidation, not looking forward to broaching the subject with Harry. She had never seen him quite so fierce about anything as his loathing for Mr. Crosbie.

To her relief, she was granted a temporary reprieve. Harry

had ridden out upon some errands and was not expected back until dinner. After the unsettling interview with Harry's step-mama, it was all Kate could do to seat herself at the desk and commence the mundane task of addressing the invitations.

Her promise to Lady Lytton continued to prey upon her mind even as she dipped her quill into the ink. Perhaps with Harry returning so late, she had best wait until tomorrow to approach him. No, tomorrow was Sunday and on Monday, she recalled, he was engaged to attend a horse auction with the squire and after that— By degrees, Kate convinced herself, it might be best to even wait until after the fête.

If the day was the success she hoped, Harry would like be in a most congenial mood and . . . and . . . Kate paused in mid-stroke, recollecting that after the fête, Harry had hinted he had strong designs. Might he not likely counter her plea for Lady Lytton with some tender demands of his own? Demands that sent a shiver of anticipation coursing through Kate.

Blushing at her own imaginings, Kate nearly knocked over the inkstand as she heard the parlor door creaking open. Harry? Her defenses immediately went up; she called out, "I am addressing the invitations, my lord. If you have come to torment me, I shall never—"

The half-playful warning died upon her lips as she glanced up. It was not Harry who paused upon the threshold, but Miss Thorpe, the crisp silk of her frock rustling against the frame.

"Oh. Julia," Kate said in flat tones.

Miss Thorpe gave her a brittle smile. Relations between Kate and the vicar's sister had been less than cordial since the eve of the assembly. Kate had not outright accused Julia of lying, but she had made it quite plain she no longer cared to hear anything from Miss Thorpe regarding Harry.

After an awkward pause, Julia said, "I came to call upon Lady Lytton, but when Gravshaw told me you were in here, I could not resist stopping in. I . . . I trust you are not still angry with me over that unfortunate misunderstanding about Lytton?" This last was pronounced in a hesitant manner far different from Julia's usual forthright speech.

"No, I am not angry," Kate said quietly, "but I fear I am

311

rather occupied." She bent over the invitations again, hoping that Julia would take the hint and just go away.

Instead Julia glided further into the room to peer over Kate's shoulder. "Oh, dear, I did not realize Lytton had pressed you into service as his secretary." She essayed a light laugh, but it was obvious her amusement was forced.

"I don't mind in the least," Kate said. Her quill spattered some ink upon one of the vellum cards. She sought to blot it, stifling an impatient exclamation. It was nigh impossible to proceed with Julia hovering at her elbow, reading the guest list, her gloved fingers fidgeting with the stack of invitations.

"You have been so occupied of late. I have missed you, Kathryn," she said. "There is a scarcity of congenial company to be found in this wretched village."

Kate doubted Julia would succeed in finding "congenial company" wherever she might be, but Miss Thorpe's voice held a threading of real unhappiness. Though she hardly knew why, Kate was moved by a feeling of pity for the beautiful, self-possessed woman.

"I shall have more time to spare after the fête," Kate said.

"Will you? Somehow I doubt that." Julia took a restless turn about the room, a moody expression marring the lovely lines of her profile. "I greatly fear that you will soon have less time for me than ever. One would have to be blind not to see what your constant presence at Mapleshade portends. The entire village is preparing to wish you joy."

Kate supposed she should have been disconcerted by Julia's words. Only days ago, she would have been quick to refute them. But now the phrase seemed to stick in her mind, like a most gentle and beguiling melody. *Wish you joy*—the words conjured up images of church bells and wedding days . . . images of Harry.

A tiny smile curved Kate's lips, soft with all a young girl's dreamings. She had no idea how the expression transformed her features, but Julia noted it—the faraway look that brightened Kate's eyes, the flush that tinted her cheeks.

It was as though Kate hovered on the brink of some great happiness, a happiness and contentment Julia sensed she

312

would never know. She suddenly felt blighted and far older than her twenty-seven years.

Her own plans had turned to ash. Since Lytton's jealous display at the assembly, Adolphus declared he would not go near Kate except to read the service of her marriage to the earl. And Julia's attempts to discredit Lytton had misfired, what with all those fools like the squire fawning over the improvements his lordship was making at Mapleshade.

Even her effort to remind everyone of Lytton's neglect, taunting him over the abandonment of the estate's ancient customs, had proved a dismal failure. Who would have guessed that Lytton would take up the challenge and the reviving of the fête would draw him closer to Kate than ever?

With Kate's help, the fête would be a success. Wasn't that how things had always gone for Lytton? No matter how undeserving he was, her reckless cousin bore a charmed existence, always emerging the winner. But then he was a man, Julia thought with unreasoning anger, able to have whatever he had wanted from life; education, travel, the freedom to do whatever he damned well pleased.

Now Lytton would have the bishop's daughter as well, while Julia remained buried alive to the end of her days in Lytton's Dene with her fool of a brother.

Oh, but Kate would eventually be sorry. Lytton might be a pattern card of behavior now, letting her arrange the fête to her satisfaction, with her proper list of guests, but wait a month or two. The earl's disreputable companions would once more overrun Mapleshade and—

Yet why did it have to take a month or two? A sudden notion caused Julia to suck in her breath, a notion that should never have occurred to a vicar's sister, nor to any other lady.

But Julia Thorpe was a most desperate woman. She half glanced away from Kate, fearing that her guilty intentions must show upon her face, but Kate had gone back to her work with the invitations and was not even looking at Julia.

Concealing her nervousness, Julia sidled toward the desk.

"I suppose I must leave you to your task. If I linger here too long, Adolphus will be wondering where I am. The poor man cannot even order up his own dinner without me."

As she leaned over the writing table to make her farewells, she quickly palmed several of the blank invitation cards and hid them in the folds of her skirts. She held her breath, but Kate did not notice a thing.

Too anxious and relieved to be rid of me, Julia thought with a stab of anger and unexpected hurt. "After all your hard work," she said to Kate with a glinting smile as she let herself out, "I do trust this fête proves a roaring success."

Safely on the other side of the door, she stuffed the stolen cards into her reticule, her mouth pinching with a hard determination.

"Aye, a roaring success," she repeated bitterly. "But not if I can help it."

Chapter 10

The day of the fête, Kate peeked out the cottage door and cast an anxious glance toward the skies. But after a week of intermittent rain, it appeared as though the heavens themselves had decided to cooperate. The deep blue soaring above Kate's head looked as though it had been splashed by a painter's brush, the cottony wisps of clouds placed by an artist's hand. The noontide sun warmed her cheeks, promising one of those delicious days when summer seemed to have strayed back into the midst of autumn.

A perfect day . . . what could possibly go wrong? Unfortunately, Kate could think of nigh half a dozen things. The chef could burn the sauce for the ducklings, the fiddlers for the dance could forget to come, the fieldhands could consume too much ale and begin a drunken brawl, Lady Lytton could take to her bed with a megrim and not even be there to act as Harry's hostess.

Kate fretted her lip, wishing she could be at his side. But that would have been improper in the extreme, giving rise to even more gossip. All she could do was to take her place among the guests, attempt to smile, while inwardly she would be on pins and needles of apprehension.

Kate had to content herself with arriving at Mapleshade as early as possible. With this view in mind, she ducked back into the house to urge her mother and grandmother to make haste.

Despite the warmth of the day, Kate insisted upon seeing her mother bundled into a woolen shawl.

"I am not a hothouse flower," Mrs. Towers protested, then gave a gentle laugh when Kate foisted a parasol upon her as well to keep off the sun.

"You are not used to being so much out of doors, Mama," Kate said. "But if it becomes too much for you, I daresay you can rest in one of the parlors." She gave her mother's hand a reassuring squeeze. "And you need not fret about the company. I know you are shy of greeting a parcel of strangers. But you are acquainted with the squire's wife and, with his lordship's permission, I invited some of the people from Chillingsworth. Your friend Mrs. Prangle and her daughters will be present."

Mrs. Towers winced and for a moment looked so ill, Kate feared that Mama might not be able to attend after all. But she recovered herself and thanked Kate in a tremulous voice.

Suffused with a warm glow of having done her mother a tremendous kindness, Kate bustled off to see what was keeping Lady Dane. But her ladyship was not to be hurried.

She declared, "I have never been so vulgar as to arrive first at any function, and I do not intend to begin at this time of my life."

There was naught Kate could do for the next half hour but pace the front hall in frustration, alternately straightening the brim of her straw hat with its flowing ribbons, and smoothing the folds of her lavender gown, the starch in her white lace tucker already going a little limp.

It was past one of the clock when they finally left the house and mounted into Lady Dane's regal carriage. Kate was in a fever of impatience by the time the coach straggled through the park gates, lumbering down the sweeping drive that led to Mapleshade.

The sun glowed warm off the hall's red brick, the wings of the magnificent old house seeming to extend like welcoming arms. Kate drew some comfort from the fact that others appeared to be fashionably late as well. She could just see the Prangles vanishing into the house to make their curtsies to their host, while liveried footmen in their tricornes sprang to assist the Gresham family from their carriage.

Being nearest to the door, Kate was the first of her own party to alight. As she turned to make certain Mama descended in safety with the footman's aid, Kate caught sight of a startling apparition. An urchin darted past, so small he was not yet in breeches, his stubby legs protruding from beneath his frock. The child's head was all but lost beneath a man's high-crowned beaver hat, the brim of which sagged over his pudgy nose.

Yet somehow the lad found his way across the drive to where a group of other children were shrieking and gleefully clambering over the massive stone lions that graced the forecourt, their fierce dignity somewhat diminished by being ridden like donkeys.

Kate had no difficulty recognizing the sandy-colored hair and freckles of the numerous Hudderston progeny. She gave a soft exclamation of surprise as she had no difficulty recognizing the tall figure in their midst either.

There was no need for any of the guests to hasten within to greet their host, Kate thought wryly, for the lord of the manor stood at this moment laughingly scooping up the same imp who had purloined his hat.

The dark strands of his hair tumbled appealingly across his brow; Harry whirled the small boy in a circle, heeding neither possible damage to his immaculate biscuit-colored breeches or the sapphire blue frock coat straining across his shoulders. His glossy black beaver hat flew from the child's head, spinning across the lawn.

316

"Harry," Kate murmured ruefully. She stalked toward him, retrieving the hat and brushing its brim. But how did one begin to scold a man bringing such happiness to a chubby-cheeked babe, the little one's shrill giggles blending with the deep boom of Harry's own laughter.

"My lord," she began severely.

"Kate!" Harry set the child down at once. His eyes warmed at the sight of her. "Little deserter! There you are at last. How dare you leave me so long at the mercy of these hordes of descending brigands."

The children shrieked with delight at this description, immediately beginning to brandish all sorts of imaginary weapons.

"This—this is scarcely a proper way to greet your guests," Kate said, her voice unsteadied by an unwilling ripple of amusement.

"Indeed it is not." His voice dropped to a husky murmur, "But if I greeted you the way I think I should, your grandmama would whack me with her cane."

Harry captured Kate's hand and raised it to his lips, the warmth of his mouth caressing her fingertips in such a fashion any lady might be pardoned for dealing him a sharp rap. How could Harry make even a kiss upon the hand so wonderfully improper?

Yet Kate had no thought of rebuking him. Her heart thudded out a reckless beat, but she managed to say, "Th—these children should be shooed around to the back. They might hurt themselves and—"

"Nonsense. I always played upon these lions as a boy. I think the old fellows must have got rather lonely over the years. They should have children romping over them."

Despite herself, Kate was beset by a most appealing image of curly-haired moppets, their ringlets Harry's midnight hue, their eyes his laughing green.

"Half a dozen at least," she murmured, then realizing what she had said, felt herself flush scarlet to the roots of her hair.

Harry merely smiled. Their eyes met, and a current seemed to rush between them. Harry started to speak, but little could be

317

said with the children all eager ears and yet another coach arriving down the drive.

Sighing, Harry tucked her arm beneath his, and they headed toward the house. As they walked up the stairs, beneath the ivy-twined pillars, Kate was astonished at how familiar it already seemed to her. In a curious way, it was like being a weary traveler who had at last come home.

Harry escorted Kate, her mother, and Lady Dane into Mapleshade's massive dining chamber where Lady Lytton was stationed to receive guests. Besides affording immediate access to the south lawn where the marquee was erected, the room was one of the most magnificent in the manor, a relict of the original house, the walls hung with priceless seventeenth-century tapestries woven in Belgium.

Lady Lytton made an odd contrast, very modern in her Grecian-style gown, banded so high and tight that it plumped her bosom to a most alarming state of fullness. Her cheeks were berouged, her curls as brassy as ever, but she greeted each new arrival graciously enough, only occasionally wincing at voices shrill with merriment.

As Kate made her curtsy, Lady Lytton wrung her hand and cast her a conspiratorial glance that rendered Kate acutely uncomfortable. Under the cover of all the bright chatter, her ladyship managed to whisper, "You still have not spoken to Harcourt?"

"No," Kate murmured. "But I promise I will attempt it today."

"I do hope so, my dear, for Lucillus grows quite impatient, and I feel ready to perish with longing myself. If we do not obtain Harcourt's consent soon, we will be forced to do something quite *drastic*."

By this time, Kate was accustomed to her ladyship's dramatic utterances. All the same she felt relieved to move on, surrendering her place to the next arrival. Kate yet doubted the wisdom of attempting to interfere on Lady Lytton's behalf, but she had to admit that, today, if any day, Harry might be approachable.

He sparkled with more than his customary good humor as he

circulated the crowded room, herding people out onto the lawn, with a quick smile here, a bit of banter there.

Harry might be slow to notice a collapsing roof unless his attention was drawn to it, but he seemed to never forget a name or a face even among the least of his tenants, nor the smallest details of their existence such as who had recently recovered from a bout of ague, or whose child was due to be christened soon.

It was people, not things, that mattered to Harry, and *that*, Kate was rapidly coming to realize, was one of his most endearing traits. Her heart swelling with pride and love, she could scarce tear her gaze from him, her spirits remaining unruffled even when Julia Thorpe entered the room.

She bid good day to the icy blonde with equanimity, although she did half fear Julia would attach herself to her side as usual. Julia, however, seemed uncommonly distracted herself, her eyes turning so often to the door even Squire Gresham was provoked into commenting upon it.

"Hah, Miss Thorpe, what handsome beau are you expecting?"

Kate rather expected Julia to give the poor man a look of chilling disdain, but instead a faint guilty color stole into her cheeks. It was the first time Kate had ever seen Miss Thorpe blush. She wondered if, amazingly enough, the squire's jest might be true, but Julia recovered herself quickly.

"I am merely breathless with anticipation," she drawled. "I have never attended a party given by my cousin before, and Lord Lytton is always so full of surprises."

"I doubt there will be any today," Kate was quick to snap.

"You may be right." Julia shot one more glance at the door, her mouth drawing down into an expression of disgust and disappointment. She turned abruptly and made her way out onto the lawn.

Kate scarce had much time to wonder at Julia's odd behavior, for she soon exited from the dining chamber herself. Mama, she thought, was looking a little lost, so Kate made sure she found Mrs. Prangle. Kate settled her mother upon a bench beneath one of the towering maples and left her to enjoy the company of her old friend.

Of course, Kate had no need to see to Lady Dane's comfort. Lady Dane strolled across the lawn like a visiting dignitary, inspiring young Becky Gresham and the Misses Prangle to curtsy so low, their muslin frocks seemed in imminent peril of grass stains. With the others of her party suitably entertained, it was herself Kate found at a loss.

She paced the grounds anxiously, but Harry's household staff had executed all her careful plans with great efficiency. Two colorful silk tents had been erected upon the lawn, the smaller a place for the ladies to retire out of the heat, the larger set up with baize-covered benches for the tenantry to dine.

Further into the park, tables had been placed for the laborers, along with a stand to hand out ale in decorous amounts. Space had been cleared for the games, with greased poles for climbing, an area marked off for footraces, a dais built for Harry to hand out the prizes, and a circle where pony rides had been arranged for the tenants' children, this last being Harry's notion.

All progressed as smoothly as though Mapleshade had been the sight of such revelry for years. Left with nothing to do, Kate wandered aimlessly toward the part of the lawn where targets had been mounted and bows and arrows provided. Becky Gresham was demonstrating her prowess at archery while flirting with some nattily dressed stripling in a manner that would have quite shocked her mama.

The sun climbed steadily toward the hottest part of the afternoon. Realizing she had forgotten her parasol, Kate prepared to retreat toward the tent when a hand took her by the elbow.

"Come now, Miss Towers," a teasing male voice scolded. "Wilting so soon? You cannot retire until you have had your turn at the targets."

She glanced up to find Harry smiling down at her. "Do allow me to give you a lesson with the bow."

She was more than glad to see him, but she eased away, demurring. "No, my lord. It would not be right. You should see to your guests."

320

"I have greeted every last one of 'em in the approved lordlike manner. Besides, you are one of my guests. You may as well enjoy it, for next year . . ."

He left the threat unfinished, a challenge in his eye. He half expected Kate to poker up as she often did at such hintings, but instead she acquiesced meekly, holding out her hand for the bow.

"Very well, my lord."

Harry's triumph in having achieved his object, being near to Kate, was only mildly diminished by the fact that he knew next to nothing about archery. The sport had always struck him as a little tame, but he managed to string a bow.

Next came the part he liked best, slipping his arms about Kate to help her take aim at the target. She was not in the least stiff, leaning trustingly against him as he arranged his hands over hers, fitting the arrow into place.

"Now take aim." He lowered his face until it was level with hers, the velvety soft curve of her cheek but a breath away, the wisps of her curls tickling his nose, the sweet, fresh scent of her more seductive than any perfume.

Would this accursed day never come to an end? Plague take the fête! He was beset with an urge to whisper to her right now all the things he had been longing to say, fairly confident of her answer.

Barely he restrained himself. No, by God, this time he would do it right. Later when all the guests were gone, and— No, not the Hill this time. That had proved unlucky.

Harry helped Kate draw back the bow while thinking the garden, perhaps. He would even go down upon one knee, forcing his clumsy tongue to find all the right words, and then she would be in his arms, her lips eager. . . .

Kate released the bow, the shot going wild. It was only then that Harry realized how flushed she was as she stepped out of the circle of his arms. They both glanced to where her arrow now lodged in the trunk of an ancient oak.

"I am sorry," Harry said. "Don't eat me, Kate. But I have a confession to make. I don't know a blamed thing about archery."

"No, but I do," Kate said softly. "I have done it frequently."

Harry could only stare at her, the reason for her deception as patently obvious as his own. She looked so adorably flustered and sheepish that Harry was on the verge of forgetting his guests and his carefully laid plans for the garden when he heard someone calling his name.

"I say, Lytton! Where the deuce are you?"

The amiable voice sounded damnably familiar, but it could not be. Harry turned slowly, then cursed under his breath at the sight of the slender young man approaching, twirling a cane, his hat tipped to a jaunty angle.

Folly! What the deuce was he doing here? And with Lord Erwin trailing in his wake. Harry's lips thinned at the sight of the peer noted chiefly for his doubtful linen and coarse manners. Erwin's bewhiskered jowls put one in mind of a pugnacious bulldog, the expression in his small, dark eyes equally as mean.

Too confounded to react, Harry stood frozen until Folly spotted him and tripped over, beaming.

"Here we are at last, old boy. I nigh forgot the right turning in the lane," he said, just as though he had been expected all along. Harry began to wonder if he was losing his mind.

Before he could say a word, Folly's face lit up and he swooped down on Kate. "Ah, Miss Towers, you here? So delighted to see you again."

Kate had blanched, going rigid with shocked disapproval. But Folly, poor ass, would never be likely to notice that. He bowed over Kate's hand as if she were his oldest and dearest friend.

Erwin made not the slightest effort to greet anyone. He stared about him, scowling. "What the devil is all this, Lytton?"

"I was about to ask you the same thing," Harry muttered. "Why have you come?"

Folly, overhearing the question, released Kate's clenched fingers, his eyes rounding with surprise. "Why, have I got the wrong day again? Nay, I cannot have. It says right here on the

322

invitation." With that he fished a slightly rumpled card from his pocket.

A tiny gasp escaped Kate. Harry was equally confounded. Good Lord! Could Kate possibly have invited . . . No, it was obvious she hadn't, for she was looking at Harry with an expression of utter betrayal. Stumbling about, she gathered up her skirts and fled across the lawn.

"Kate!" Harry cried, taking a distracted step after her, but he could scarce go haring off until he had sorted to the bottom of this.

"What is amiss with her?" Folly asked.

"Starched-up female," Erwin growled. "Where are the Cyprians?"

"And when is the mill to take place?" Folly chimed in. "Have we missed it?"

"What in blazes are you talking about?" Harry thought he was about to run mad.

"It says it all right here in the postscript of your invitation." Folly waved the vellum before Harry's eyes.

Harry seized it, frowning at the inked lines promising all manner of diversions from a prize fight to "young ladies more than willing to play Hunt the Squirrel." Whoever was responsible for this mischief had done a credible job of imitating Harry's own splatterdash style of handwriting.

"This is someone's notion of a very poor jest," he said, crushing the invitation in his fist.

"We rode out nigh ten miles for a jest?" Erwin snarled.

"No mill?" Folly asked, his mouth drooping with disappointment.

"I am afraid not and as you can see, the entertainment here is not at all the sort you would care for—"

"You mean," Folly interrupted, "you didn't even invite us?"

"You would not like such a party. It is mostly to reward my tenants and laborers—"

"I believe my lord is trying to tell us," Erwin said, his eyes narrowing dangerously, "he intends to order us off his grounds."

"I say! Harry!" Folly protested.

Harry sighed. He did not give a damn for any of Erwin's angry bluster. He had never much liked the man, considering him a deplorable influence on weak-minded fellows like Mr. Ffolliot. Harry found it much more difficult to harden his heart against his old friend. Folly was regarding him with a mixture of hurt and chagrin like a small boy being chased off from joining in a game of cricket.

"Of course you are welcome to stay," Harry conceded. "As long as you remain on your best behavior. My guests here today are the like of the squire, the vicar, clergy from Chillingsworth, elderly ladies. I would not have any of them offended."

"Certainly not!" Folly brightened. "You need not lecture me like I was a dashed schoolboy, Harry."

Harry arched one brow in dubious fashion. He would far rather Folly and Erwin had gone, but saw no remedy for the situation. His immediate concern was to find Kate and clear up this misunderstanding. Although uneasy about leaving the pair to wander tame among his staid guests, Harry excused himself.

Watching Harry go, the honorable Mr. Ffolliot shook his head. "Vicars? Clergy? Elderly ladies? What's got into Harry?"

"Heard tell as how he's been dangling after some parson's daughter." Lord Erwin snorted with disgust. "That's enough to be the ruination of any man. Let's get out of here."

"Nay, don't be so hasty, sir. There's oft jolly sport to be found at these fête things, usually some sort of games, I believe. We might get up a wager or two."

Erwin mopped his sweating brow with a soiled handkerchief. "I suppose I could use a drop of something to wet my throat. Let's see what's being dished out in that tent over there."

The two men strode toward the smaller of the two tents, ducking beneath the silk flap. The only one about was a young footman arranging dainty silk-cushioned stools next to a table bearing a silver urn.

Pulling a face, Folly gave the tea service a wide berth, moving toward a promising-looking punch bowl. As he bent over, stirring a ladle through the golden-colored liquid, he sniffed suspiciously, catching the odor of lemon.

"Damnation! You—you don't suppose Harry really means for us to drink this stuff?" Folly exclaimed.

"Wouldn't surprise me. The man's become as priggish as a bleedin' Methodist." Erwin's mouth tipped into a sly leer. "Fortunately, I always come prepared."

Waiting until the footman had left, his lordship reached beneath his frock coat and produced a small flask that he uncorked. He sniffed the contents with appreciation.

"Blue Ruin," he announced and proceeded to tip the flask, dumping the gin into the lemonade.

"Here now!" Folly said. "I don't think you ought to be doing that, Erwin."

"Why not? If Lytton is too big a nipsqueeze to provide proper refreshment, then his guests must perforce look to themselves."

Raising the ladle, Erwin took a sip. "Still too weak." Before Folly's horrified gaze, he produced a second flask that he also poured into the punch bowl. Folly considered himself a two-bottle man, but only the finest Madeira. Gin was—well, damned coarse, fit for naught but the lower orders.

Satisfied with his creation, Erwin was just about to dip himself out a cupful when a stern voice rang out. "Sir! My lord, I beg your pardons."

Folly whipped about as guiltily as if he had been the one plying the gin. Framed in the tent opening, he saw that stiff-necked manservant of Harry's, the butler he believed, name of Gravedigger or some such.

The elderly retainer did not appear to have noticed Erwin's actions for he said with frigid courtesy, "This tent is solely for the use of the ladies, but if you gentlemen would be pleased to follow me, I shall provide you with more suitable refreshments."

For the ladies! Folly stared at Erwin aghast. But his lordship merely shrugged, his mouth splitting into a malicious grin.

It took Harry so long to find Kate, he had begun to fear she had ordered up her carriage and gone home. He located her at last, leaning against the maple near the area where the children were taking their pony rides. She stared at the ground, fidgeting with the handle of her parasol, her face shadowed with unhappiness.

"Kate." Harry hastened to plant himself in front of her. Bracing one hand on either side of her against the tree trunk, he cut off any possibility of escape.

She made no move, except for her initial start of surprise. Paling, she refused to glance up, the thickness of her lashes veiling her eyes.

"I realize how it must appear to you, Kate," Harry said. "But I would not have invited Folly here, knowing how you feel about him. And certainly I would not have asked a peep-of-day boy like Erwin."

"They had a card—" she began.

"How they got it, I have no idea. If you didn't send it—"

"Of course, I didn't," she choked.

"Then someone tried to stir up a nasty piece of mischief. I have no notion of whom, but I shall get to the bottom of it before the day is out."

A seemingly endless silence ensued, in which Harry could do naught but regard her anxiously. Then she raised her head, her earnest gaze probing his. Slowly, she nodded. In that moment, Harry felt much like a general, finally emerging the victor in a hard-fought campaign.

She believed him. She trusted him.

He cupped his fingers gently beneath her chin. "Don't worry, Kate," he said. "I won't let them do anything to spoil our fête."

His reassurance coaxed a smile from her. Her lips were so sweet and inviting, he would have given much to linger, steal a kiss, but despite Folly's assurances, the honorable Samuel had a way of creating disasters and Harry didn't trust Erwin one jot. If he was going to keep his pledge, he need must tear himself away from Kate. He did so with reluctance, his only consolation that before the day's end, he would himself wring a pledge from Kate, one that would bind her to him forever.

Even though she watched Harry depart with regret, Kate's

spirits soared from the misery that had engulfed her but moments before. It had been a jolt to see Mr. Ffolliot and Lord Erwin arrive. It had not hurt her that Harry had asked them, so much as the thought he had done so without warning her. She had not wanted to believe it, but the invitation card had seemed incontrovertible proof.

She was so very glad to know she had been wrong. For all Harry's faults, deceit was not among them. But who could have played such a terrible trick? Kate's mind drifted back to the day she had been addressing invitations, a sudden clear image of Miss Thorpe leaning over the writing desk.

No, surely not! Kate was shocked by her own suspicion. Despite Julia's unreasoning dislike of Harry, Kate could not picture the vicar's sister doing anything so dishonorable, so . . . so deliberately cruel.

Yet the thought persisted to trouble her. It only added to her distress to perceive that Mama was not having a good time, either. It was the most pernicious thing, but Kate observed that every time Mrs. Prangle settled in for a comfortable prose with Mrs. Towers, along would come Lady Dane. Grandmother's icy hauteur quite cowed the archdeacon's wife and frightened her from Mama's side.

Her poor mother retreated at last into the tent that had been erected for the ladies. Scolding herself for not looking after her mother better, Kate hurried to join her.

A few other women had also retired out of the heat, among them Mrs. Gresham and Julia. Kate longed to ask Miss Thorpe if— No, how could she accuse her of anything so terrible? It would be most shameful if Kate were wrong, which she must be.

It did not help Kate's feelings, trying to remain generous and just to Miss Thorpe, to hear Julia in the process of abusing the fête to Mrs. Gresham.

"A dreary affair," she said, "even the lemonade has gone bad." She sniffed with disdain, setting down her cup.

"What utter nonsense." Kate was quick to spring to the defense. "Lemonade going bad? I never heard of such a thing."

"Taste it for yourself," Julia said with a shrug.

Kate stalked over and poured herself a cup. With the first sip, she nigh choked. It did indeed have a most peculiarly bitter flavor, but she would have choked even more before admitting such a thing to Julia.

"There is nothing in the least wrong with it." She forced down another swallow.

Julia's mouth pursed in annoyance. "My dearest Kate, there is something gravely amiss with your sense of taste."

She raised her cup and took another drink. "Ugh, nasty."

In pure defiance, Kate downed the entire contents of her own, if only to prove how mistaken Julia was. Soon the other ladies were drawn into the dispute. After swallowing a glassful, Mrs. Gresham sputtered and ranged herself on Miss Thorpe's side. Mrs. Towers, although she puckered at her first mouthful, agreed quite loyally with Kate. The women continued to sip, argue, refill their cups, and argue some more.

By her third glassful, Kate began to feel rather strange. Her fingers were going numb, but the most delightful tingly sensations rushed through her veins, making her feel quite light in the head. The quarrel started to seem not only downright silly, but the most amusing thing she had ever heard.

When Julia swayed, trying to say "purr-feckitly dretful" and could not get it out, Kate clapped a hand to her mouth.

A high-pitched giggle escaped her that she scarce recognized as her own.

Harry handed out the last of the prizes, a new cloak of gray worsted to the burly youth who had won the final race. He smiled vacantly while he glanced about him. Where was Kate? After all her anxiety, she had not come to watch any of the games. Nor had many of the other ladies. Perhaps the heat was proving too much for them. The sun blazing down on his head was certainly beginning to make him feel a little irritable.

He had not even had a chance to tell Kate that Mr. Ffolliot and Lord Erwin had departed with as much haste as they had arrived. Folly had slunk away, scarce taking time to bid farewell, looking more guilty than a pickpocket caught with his hand inside a lady's reticule. Harry had been too relieved by the departure to wonder overmuch at such odd behavior. He was sorry to see Ffolliot so much in Erwin's company. Perhaps at some later date, he could make an effort to persuade Folly—

A reluctant grin escaped Harry. He was indeed far gone if he planned to begin preaching reformation to others. What would the governor have thought!

So far the fête had been an unqualified success. But as the hour for the supper approached, Harry began to get a little anxious. He never had been much good sorting out ranks or who should be escorting whom into dinner. Where was Kate?

Harry's mind was not eased by the sight of Gravshaw approaching him. The man appeared uncommonly flustered, his coattails flapping behind him in a most unbutlerlike fashion. Harry grimaced. Flying into a pelter was getting to be an infernally bad habit with his once indomitable servant.

"Oh, my lord. You must come at once."

"Now what? Has one of the kitchen boys dropped the custards?"

"No, my lord." Gravshaw bent forward and mumbled something about grave crisis and ladies in the tent.

"What sort of crisis?" Harry drawled. "Are they in danger of bringing the contraption tumbling about their ears?"

"It wouldn't surprise me, sir."

"What?!"

Gravshaw pokered up, refusing to say more, glancing about him as though fearful of being overheard. With an exasperated sigh, Harry motioned him off, falling into step behind, feeling a little impatient of having to deal with another tempest in a teapot. Where the deuce was Kate?

"There, my lord." Gravshaw pointed at the tent flap with a trembling finger. "Never in all my days as—"

"Oh, stubble it, Gravshaw. I get enough high drama from Lady Lytton without . . ."

Harry trailed off, startled by the sound that suddenly rang out from the tent, laughter, but not the well-bred mirth to be expected from ladies of quality. It sounded more like some doxies on a drunken spree.

He darted a questioning look at Gravshaw, who stared

stolidly ahead of him. Harry entered the tent with the butler creeping at his heels. Before Harry had time to so much as blink, a flash of silver came hurtling at him. A lady's sandal glanced off his chest and landed at his feet.

Startled, Harry tracked the missile to its owner. Julia leaned against Mrs. Gresham, the squire's wife providing none too steady support as Julia struggled to remove her other shoe.

"Gravshaw!" she barked. "You rashcal. Dinnit I bid you fetch some champagne?"

Harry's jaw went slack, the flushed blowsy-looking woman scarcely resembling the icy perfection that was Julia Thorpe. Her unfocused blue eyes drifted toward him and she hiccuped.

"Good. Here's Lytton. He'll make that villain obey."

Mrs. Gresham tittered. She ogled Harry and slurred, "I do love this fashion for tight breeches." She whispered something to Kate's mama and both women went off into a fit of that disconcerting laughter.

Damnation! If Harry had not known better, he would have said they were all as well glazed as a parcel of sailors on shore leave. In the midst of this madness, it was a great relief to see Kate seated calmly on a stool. Harry hastened over to her.

"Kate, what's wrong with your mother and Julia?"

She glanced up slowly, a beatific smile spreading over her face.

"Harry!" Kate swayed to her feet, and if Harry had not caught her, she would have tumbled to the ground. She merely giggled, wrapping her arms around his neck. Harry inhaled an unmistakable odor.

"Gin!" he cried, outraged. "Gravshaw, what the devil have you been feeding these women?"

" 'Twasn't me, my lord. I came into the tent earlier and . . . and I greatly fear your friend Lord Erwin did something to the lemonade."

"Ridiculous," Kate said. "Nothing wrong with the lemonade." She clung to him, allowing her weight to sag against his frame, nearly tipping Harry off balance. Harry cursed Erwin under his breath, his mind filling with a vision of what

330

he would do with the bounder the next time he laid eyes upon him.

"To hell with lemonade," Julia called out. "We want champagne. Go fetch it." She gave Gravshaw a ringing smack on his rump.

The butler appeared about to have a fit of apoplexy at this affront to his dignity. As appalling as the situation was, Harry's chest rumbled with the desire to laugh. But it was nigh impossible to do so with Kate maintaining such a stranglehold on his neck. He managed to gasp, "Fetch water, Gravshaw, at once."

"Why?" The squire's wife trilled. "Is someone about to deliver a babe?"

Her comment provoked another gale of hysterical laughter.

"*Cold* water, Gravshaw," Harry shouted above the din. The butler looked only too relieved to scurry from the tent.

Harry tried to ease Kate away, but she hugged him tighter. "Schtop giving so many silly orders and kiss me, you foolish boy."

"Kate . . . Kate! Behave yourself and sit down."

"I am behaving very badly, aren't I?"

"Yes, you are," Harry said with all the gravity he could muster.

" 'Tis great fun." She chuckled, then stood on tiptoe until she brushed the tip of her small nose against his. She stared owlishly into his eyes. "Harry, I . . . I don't know how. But I think I may have shot the dog."

"I fear you have, love." Harry regarded her with tender amusement. She wriggled out of his arms. Although somewhat unsteady, she managed to keep her feet.

"Need some air. Need to find Mrs. Prangle."

"No!" Harry cut her off in alarm. "Believe me, Kate, this is not the time to go seeking out the archdeacon's wife."

To his relief, she nestled quite contentedly back into his embrace. Harry felt beads of perspiration gather on his brow. This was the most damnable coil he had ever found himself in. If he did not wish this day to end in complete disgrace and scandal, he had to keep all these women confined to the tent until they could be brought to some state of sobriety.

331

"Ladies, please. All of you sit down," he commanded. "We're going to have some tea."

"Tea be damned," the incorrigible Julia shrilled, shying her other sandal at him. "Bring us the bloody champagne."

While Harry wondered where Julia had ever acquired such language, Kate looked up at him, breathless with laughter. "You are so 'dorable, Harry, when you try to be stern. I do love you. I will never be vexed with you again."

"You will, my dear. Oh, yes, you will," he muttered. The next minutes that stretched out proved more nerve-wracking than those hours spent waiting the enemy's charge at Waterloo. Harry would have defied Wellington himself to keep order amid a parcel of very foxed ladies.

Mrs. Gresham nearly drew his cork, attempting to leave the tent, shrieking she was being held prisoner. Julia leaped upon the table, declaring that it was "Better to marry, than to burn," and launched into a sermon threatening him with fire and brimstone.

As for Kate, she began nuzzling kisses beneath his ear in a manner that was painfully distracting, while Mrs. Towers hummed quietly to herself. When Harry heard someone at the flap, he gasped, "Gravshaw, thank God."

But his prayer of gratitude was cut short. Instead of the butler, it was Reverend Thorpe that peeked into the tent.

If Harry could have done so, he would have thrust Adolphus right back out, but any such maneuver was impossible with Kate melting against him.

"My lord! Miss Towers!" The vicar's eyes popped with disapproval.

"Hell and damnation!" Julia cried with a sweeping flourish of her hand.

Adolphus's shocked gaze swiveled to his sister. "Julia!"

"We all know our names," Harry snapped. "Would you kindly do something useful like getting your sister down from there and, oh damn—"

While Harry's attention had been fixed on Adolphus, the squire's wife had managed to escape from the tent. As soon as Mrs. Gresham staggered out, Lady Dane stalked in.

332

"What is going on in here, Lytton?" she demanded.

Harry groaned, feeling the entire situation slipping beyond his control. As the vicar tugged Julia down from her perch, she burst into tears, wailing, "Oh, why wasn't I born a man?"

Even the gentle Mrs. Towers joined the fracas, tipsily shaking her finger at Lady Dane. "You're a mos' tiresome, meddlin' old woman. Hold your tongue and stop orderin' everyone about."

Harry was not privileged to hear Lady Dane's shocked response, for his attention was claimed by a bellow of outrage from outside the tent. Apparently, the squire had just encountered his wife. Harry rolled his eyes, not able to imagine how this horrific scene could possibly get any worse, when he felt a tug at his sleeve.

He glanced down to discover Kate's face gone alarmingly pale.

"Oh, Harry," she said. "I . . . I think I'm going to be sick."

Chapter 11

The day after the fête, morning dawned just as bright and clear, but Kate made no movement to bound out of bed. She lay flat on her back, the light striking against her eyelids only served to intensify the throbbing in her head.

Merciful heavens! If she had been a condemned prisoner, she would have begged the executioner to wield his ax. Amputation was surely the only cure for such agony.

By degrees, she came more fully awake and attempted to roll onto her side. A soft moan escaped her, her stomach muscles feeling bruised and sore. Her mind yet hazed with pain and sleep, Kate tried to recollect the reason for her wretched state.

What sort of mishap had befallen her? What dread manner of illness?

She forced her eyes open. The room pitched so precariously, she had to close them. Raising her lids just a fraction, she managed to focus, peering at her room through the thickness of her lashes.

The chamber appeared as ever a haven of serenity and order except for the frock crumpled upon the carpet, the same frock she had worn yesterday when she had—

Kate sucked in her breath as memory flooded back to her. Harry, the fête ... the lemonade! She groaned, flinging one arm across her eyes as though that gesture might serve to shut out the remembrance. But recollections, at first quite fuzzy, began to emerge with painful clarity.

She had been arguing with Miss Thorpe about the lemonade. Why had she not paid more heed to Julia's insistence that something was wrong? The vicar's sister had been odiously correct. Kate vaguely recalled Harry's conversation with his butler, something about Harry's horrid friend, Lord Erwin, tampering with the punch bowl. He had added ... what was it Harry had exclaimed?

Gin! That was it. Dear Lord! She had been gulping down gin. How oft she had heard Papa preach against that evil brew—the bane of the poorer classes, the bishop had called it. What would he have said if he had seen its effect upon his own daughter?

Kate could not say precisely all that she had done, but she knew, with dread certainty, she had been thoroughly intoxicated. Groaning, she massaged her throbbing temples, seeking to recall what was best forgotten.

The laughter ... everything had seemed so uproariously amusing. And Harry ... she had flirted with him. Flirted! Kate winced. Nay, she had pounced upon him in a manner that would have shamed a tavern wench. He had attempted to make her sit down, but she had kept right on kissing him before the entire assemblage of other ladies.

Kate's cheeks burned at the memory. And then ... oh, no. Had the vicar really come into the tent? And Grandmama?

She could not be sure for at that point Harry had helped her back to the house because suddenly all had no longer been so diverting.

Kate half pulled the counterpane over her head as she remembered the gleaming white chamber pot, Harry's strong arm supporting her while she had been hideously sick. After that, all was blank. She had no idea when she had been conveyed home or how she had come to be tucked up in her bed.

It scarce mattered, she thought, her face damp with humiliation. One fact emerged with painful clarity. She had made an utter fool of herself. She would never be able to face anyone in Lytton's Dene again—especially not Harry.

It afforded her no consolation that she had not been alone in her folly. Julia, the squire's wife, and . . . and Mama! Kate bolted to a sitting position, the sudden movement making her head feel as though an anvil had clanged down upon it. But the pain was as nothing placed beside the horrified remembrance. Mama, too, had drunk of that poisonous concoction. If Kate had been rendered so deathly ill, what had it done to one of Mrs. Towers's delicate constitution?

Thoroughly alarmed, Kate flung back the covers. Although her stomach did a series of flip-flops, she managed to stand. Never sure how she accomplished it, she crossed to the washstand and sloshed some water from the pitcher into the basin.

The chill liquid stung her flesh, but it revived her enough that she could struggle into her silk wrapper and mules. Padding down the hallway to her mother's room, Kate did not even pause to knock. She thrust the portal open, expecting to find Mrs. Towers at death's door.

But the rose-colored chamber was empty, the bed already made, the shawl Mrs. Towers habitually wore missing from its peg. Far from being reassured, Kate stumbled from the room toward the stairway. She started down, grimacing at every step. Why had she never noticed before how badly each riser creaked?

At the bottom, she nearly collided with Mollie, the plump maid bustling from the small dining room with empty plates. Kate took one look at the china, greasy with the remnants of egg and broiled kidney. She shuddered, clutching her hand to her stomach.

"Good morning, miss," Mollie said cheerfully, the scarlet ribbons on her mobcap fluttering in a perky fashion that seemed an affront to Kate's eyes.

Kate stared fixedly at a point past the offending crockery and the ribbons. "Where is my mother?" she rasped.

"Why, gone out, miss, with Lady Dane, to take a turn about the garden out back."

"Mama is . . . is out *walking*?"

"Yes, miss. She and her ladyship have already breakfasted and said as how you were not to be disturbed."

Kate scarce heard the girl, her mind reeling with relief and confusion. How was it possible? Mama had drunk at least as much of the lemonade as she, hadn't she? Obviously her memory was none too clear.

"Are you all right, miss?" Mollie asked, peering closely at Kate. "Will you be wanting your breakfast now? There is none of the kidney left, but I believe Cook has some kippers—"

Kate took a deep gulp. "Just a little weak tea, please."

Motioning Mollie to remove the congealing dishes from her sight, Kate leaned up against the oak banister. She could not quite face the prospect of mounting the stairs again, so she retired to the parlor. They would not be likely to have any callers at this hour and, in any event, Kate never intended to receive anyone for the rest of her life.

Within the parlor, she drew the drapes across the bow window, shutting out as much of the sun as she could. Not only was the funereal gloom more soothing to her eyes, but it cast Papa's portrait into shadows, preventing the bishop's stern gaze from glaring down upon her disgrace.

Mollie bustled in and settled a tray near where Kate collapsed onto the settee. After much ruthless rattling of the teaspoons and the cup and saucer, the girl finally left Kate to sip her tea in merciful silence. The brew fortified her somewhat, but she could do naught to dispel the overwhelming burden of shame weighing down upon her.

When Kate heard a muffled sound that told her of an arrival

in the hall beyond, she shrank down against the cushions. In her current state, she was uncertain she could even confront her own mama and grandmother.

But the rumble of voices that followed sent a shaft of uneasiness through her. That did not sound like Mama.

Mollie poked her head in the door and announced with a pert grin, "Beg pardon, miss. What should I do? Lord Lytton is here, and he threatens to cut off my cap ribbons if I don't—"

"No!" Kate bolted to her feet, her cup and saucer clattering to the carpet. "Send him away! Tell him I am sick, dead, gone on a long voyage."

"Perhaps you had best tell me yourself." Harry squeezed past Mollie, regarding Kate with a quizzical gleam in his eye. He had obviously taken great pains with his appearance, looking almost irritatingly handsome and full of vigor in his crisp, navy frock coat and whipcord breeches.

He thrust the highly interested Mollie out of the parlor and closed the door. Kate spun away from him, one hand fluttering with dismay to the disheveled curls tumbling about her shoulders, the other clutching at the neckline of her wrapper.

"My lord, you . . . you can see I am in no fit state to entertain visitors."

"You look as lovely as always, although more pale than I could wish." She heard the tread of his boots as he stepped beside her, stroking back her hair. Even that featherlight touch caused her to tremble.

"My poor darling." Harry's voice rumbled sympathy close to her ear. "You must have had a very devil of a night. You ought to be taking something more than tea. Believe me, I have had . . . er . . . a little experience in these matters."

"Oh, Harry, please! Please just go away." Her voice broke and she retreated toward the window, burying her face in her hands.

"Kate!" He followed her. Placing his hands upon her shoulders, he tried to bring her about. She twisted away from him, sinking down upon the window seat. But there was no escape. With tender persistence, he hunkered down before her, gently forcing down her hands, gathering them into the strength of his own.

Tears gathered in her eyes, one escaping to trickle past her nose. "Please," she whispered. "Don't look at me. I am so ashamed."

He caught the tear, one rough fingertip brushing it aside. "Kate, dearest, you've naught to be ashamed of."

"Indeed I have. My behavior yesterday—"

" 'Twas no fault of yours."

"M-my conduct was dreadful, and the fête was r-ruined."

"It was nothing of the kind. We still contrived to hold the supper after I had sent you home. I told everyone you had been taken ill, and, hang it all, Kate! Don't cry." He intercepted another tear. "You know I can endure anything but that."

But now that she had begun, Kate could not check the flow, though the release of the emotion brought no comfort, only increasing the pounding tempo in her head.

Harry squeezed her hands. "Devil take that villain Erwin," he muttered. "Damned if I don't call him out for this."

His words sparked a bitter anger in Kate, as unexpected as it was unreasoning. She wrenched her hands away. "Aye, isn't that just a man's solution to everything. Blow a hole in someone, and that will mend matters at once."

Harry frowned, straightened slowly to his feet. "What would you have me do, Kate?"

"There's nothing you can do." Leaping up, she brushed past him, swiping at her eyes. "The damage is quite done."

"You might be interested to know that I discovered who purloined that invitation and posted it. It was your good friend, Julia Thorpe."

Kate started only a little to hear her worst suspicions confirmed. "What odds does that make? It was *your* friends who put the gin in the lemonade and . . . and you promised you would not let them do anything to spoil the fête."

Her voice sounded childishly petulant and, deep in her heart, Kate knew she was being unfair. But her head ached so abominably, she wanted to scream.

338

"I did my best, Kate," Harry said. She heard him sigh as though regathering the ends of his patience.

He approached again, making one more effort to ease her into his embrace. She backed away, and his arms dropped to his sides, a hint of exasperation in his voice. "You are making far too great a piece of work over all this, Kate. No one else is taking it so seriously, I warrant you."

He could not have said anything less calculated to soothe her. She was miserable, about to perish from humiliation, and no one regarded it seriously?

Harry plunged on, making bad worse. "By the end of the day, the squire was laughing over the affair and even Adolphus was most understanding."

"That is all very well for them," Kate said. "But I assure you my father would not have been amused. It might be thought tolerable for a squire's wife to become drunk on gin, but . . . but—"

"But you are a bishop's daughter," Harry finished bitterly. "I fear I had allowed myself to forget that."

"So did I! Every time I am with you, I end up in the most improper—" She broke off, clutching her head, which felt nigh ready to burst. "Please . . . please, can you not just leave me alone?"

A heavy silence ensued, then Harry said softly, "Yes, I rather think that it would be better if I did."

There was no rancor in his tones. He sounded so subdued that, despite her own agony, Kate glanced up at him. He looked neither angry nor even irritated, those expressive green eyes frighteningly empty. The powerful set of his shoulders slumped as in defeat.

As he moved toward the door, Kate half whispered, "Harry." If he heard her, he pretended otherwise. He bade her farewell, his parting adieu brief, sad, and heartbreakingly final.

Then he was gone.

Kate kept to her room for the rest of the day. By the next afternoon, she continued to send down her excuses, declining to join Mrs. Towers and Lady Dane for luncheon.

339

The meal was a simple one, consisting mostly of cold meats and fruit. Mrs. Towers picked at a few grapes. Although she had not fared as badly as Kate from the lemonade episode, she bore little appetite, being consumed by worry about her daughter.

Yet she put on a placid front, unwilling to admit as much to Lady Dane. That formidable dame was far too quick to criticize her precious Kate. At the opposite end of the linen tablecloth, her ladyship tapped her fork irritably against the crystal.

"How long is this nonsense going to continue?" she said presently.

"What nonsense is that, Mother Towers?"

"You know full well what I mean—this sorry business of Kate hiding out in her room."

"The child has been ill."

"Humpfh! Just the same as that Thorpe chit has been ill?"

Mrs. Towers winced. Lady Dane's acid comment referred to the visit the vicar had paid earlier that morning. Reverend Thorpe had come by to convey Julia's farewell to Kate. It seemed Miss Thorpe was journeying up north to stay with an elderly aunt in Scotland, "for reasons of Julia's health."

"Running away—that is what Julia Thorpe is doing," Lady Dane continued, slamming her fork down. "I would have hoped that a granddaughter of mine would have more bottom than that."

"So Kate does. She will come out when she is ready," Mrs. Towers said, although she was not sure herself. What a cruel contrast it was. Kate had been so sunny and smiling the morning of the fête. It seemed Lady Dane's interference might have done some good after all. Mrs. Towers had been certain that her daughter's most unusual courtship with Lord Lytton was about to be brought to a happy conclusion. Then that disaster in the tent! Mrs. Towers had wracked her mind ever since, wondering if there was something she could have done to prevent it. If only she had not been so quick to agree with Kate about the lemonade.

These tormenting reflections were interrupted by Lady Dane. With a mighty scowl, she said, "I hope you have noticed that Lytton has not been back since we saw him ride off so hurriedly yesterday morn. I have had no chance to speak with him, but it is my belief that foolish child has sent him away again."

She flung her napkin down, scraping her chair back. Leaning on her cane, she rose, the familiar martial light coming to her eye. "I can see 'tis more than time I shook some sense into Kathryn."

Mrs. Towers believed that the last thing Kate needed was more of her grandmother's bullying. "I wish you would not."

As Lady Dane ignored her, stalking toward the door, Mrs. Towers hastened to intercept her. Although she trembled a little, she planted herself in front of her ladyship.

"I . . . I thought I had made my feelings clear to you before—"

"So you did, Maisie. You said a good many disagreeable things in your state of intoxication. However, I realize you were not yourself, so I am disposed to pardon you."

"I was not that drunk."

Mrs. Towers's admission seemed to crack through the room with all the force of a thunderclap. Lady Dane was stunned into a rare moment of silence. Mrs. Towers's courage nigh failed her, but she realized she had already passed the point of no return.

"I . . . I do not think your meddling has always done Kate good, my lady. And . . . and I forbid any more of it."

This last she said so quietly, Lady Dane had to bend slightly to catch it. As she drew herself up stiffly, Mrs. Towers half expected to be struck aside by her ladyship's cane.

"And what pray tell do you intend to do?" Lady Dane demanded. "Allow the girl to remain closeted abovestairs until the end of her days?"

"No. I intend to speak to Kate myself."

An amused expression crossed Lady Dane's features, like a mighty eagle hearing a sparrow offering to take over the task of seeking out prey.

"Then I suggest you get about it before Kate takes to wearing hair shirts as well." Her ladyship stalked to the door and opened it for Mrs. Towers. Lady Dane, of course, did not smirk, but the expression on her face was akin to it.

Mrs. Towers had little choice but to accept the challenge. Gathering up her dignity, she rustled past. With Lady Dane's fierce gaze upon her, she mounted the stairs to the second floor, her heart fluttering with trepidation. She had never borne any influence with Kate before. What on earth was she going to say to her daughter now?

At her timid knock upon the bedchamber door, Kate's lackluster voice bade her enter. She stepped inside the chamber to discover Kate seated upon a low stool by the fireside. She was bent industriously over a tambour frame, although Mrs. Towers had a strong suspicion the embroidery had only been snatched up with her entrance.

Kate glanced up, her appearance neat and trim, but her wan smile and the hollows beneath her eyes were enough to break Mrs. Towers's heart. "Mama! I thought you would be taking your nap."

"Not this afternoon, dear." Mrs. Towers closed the door behind her. "I came to see how you were feeling."

"A little better," Kate said with forced cheerfulness. She ducked her head, concentrating on her needle. Mrs. Towers noted that the delicate stitching had not progressed much from when she had last seen the work in Kate's hand. Gently, she removed the frame from her daughter's grasp.

"I think it is time you got out a little."

Kate flinched with dismay. "Oh, no, truly, Mama. You must not worry about me."

It was the old evasion, but this time Mrs. Towers knew she could not accept it. She caught Kate's face between her hands so that she could look into her troubled eyes.

"Worrying is a mother's prerogative, Kathryn. Now tell me what is wrong."

"N-nothing." Kate gave an overbright smile.

"I don't believe you," Mrs. Towers said. "The day of the fête I nigh expected Lord Harry to ask permission to pay his addresses."

"Harry would never have thought of anything like that and

c-certainly not now that I—" Her eyes filled with tears and suddenly she cupped Mrs. Towers's hand, holding it to her cheek. "Oh, Mama, I am s-so unhappy, I just want to die."

She broke down completely, weeping. Mrs. Towers plunked down upon the carpet, her skirts billowing about her, gathering Kate into her arms as though she had been all of six years old.

"N-no, Mama," Kate sobbed against her shoulder. "I—I shouldn't burden you."

"Of course, you should," Mrs. Towers said, her own throat constricting. "Please. Tell mama what is hurting you."

It was a most foolish thing to say, as though Kate were yet a babe with naught but a skinned elbow. But her daughter nestled closer, entwining her arms about Mrs. Towers's neck. Maisie Towers closed her eyes, briefly recalling all those times she had allowed Kate to be borne away by the nurse or the governess for "the sake of Mrs. Towers's delicate health."

To have Kate at last turning to her for comfort was most bittersweet.

Kate's words came haltingly, but gradually she poured out the entire story of her quarrel with Lord Lytton. "And. . . and I know I was being most unjust to b-blame him, but he should have seen how miserable I was. Th-then I just let him go. I suppose 'tis . . . 'tis just as well."

"Why, darling?" Mrs. Towers murmured against her daughter's silky curls. "If you love him—"

"But Papa always said we would never suit. You know he did."

Mrs. Towers sighed. "The bishop was full of wisdom, but sometimes even the most clever men are less than wise when dealing with their daughters. I always thought your Papa a shade overprotective. I oft wondered whom he would have considered good enough to wed you."

Kate drew away, regarding her with surprise. "But surely, Mama, Papa's fears were justified. Harry's reputation was so shocking. Marrying him would have been a great risk."

"Any marriage is a risk. Your Papa and I went through quite a period of adjustment in our early days."

343

Kate's tear-drenched eyes widened. "But Papa was never wild like Harry."

A gentle laugh escaped Mrs. Towers. "Well, I do recall him telling me about a time before he had taken holy orders, one Season when he went up to London. I fear he did some things that were quite scandalous for a future bishop."

"Papa?" Kate gasped.

Mrs. Towers nodded, although she could not quite meet her daughter's eyes.

"But he always seemed so perfect," Kate said.

"He tried to be, perhaps rather too hard." Mrs. Towers smoothed a stray curl from Kate's petal-soft cheek. " 'Tis a failing I fear you often share, my dearest Kate."

Kate's blush acknowledged the fact, her lips parting in a rueful smile.

"Now, if you love your Harry as much as I think you do, you had best be giving him another chance."

Kate's smile quickly faded. "I fear this time he has given up on me, Mama. He has asked me to marry him so many times. I . . . I do not think he will be asking again."

"Then you must ask him."

"Mama!"

"There are ways, Kathryn, that a lady may arrange her proposal without being unmaidenly."

They regarded each other for a moment, then Kate flung her arms about Mrs. Towers in a brisk hug, with a conspiratorial laugh that only two women could share.

Mrs. Towers got to her feet, wincing at the stiffness in her joints. She was getting a little old for sitting upon the carpet. Shuffling toward the door, she took affectionate leave of her daughter.

She had no notion if her words had had any lasting effect upon the child, but as she closed the door, Kate's eyes looked soft and luminous, the set of her brow extremely thoughtful.

Mrs. Towers sighed. She had come to this mothering business rather late in her life. It was not simple by any means. She could only hope she had made an adequate job of it.

* * *

344

As Kate fetched her cloak from the wardrobe, she felt suffused with a warm glow from the recent scene with her mother. It was most strange how one could live in the same house with one's parents for so many years and not truly know either of them.

It saddened her to think, having at last become better acquainted with Mama, she was now thinking of leaving her. Of course, that rather depended on Harry.

Kate stopped in the act of swirling her cloak about her shoulders, her courage nigh failing her. But she forced her fingers into brisk movement, fastening the braided frogs. Then she bolted from her chamber and down the steps lest she lose heart and change her mind.

For the bishop's daughter was planning to do a very shocking thing. She proposed to call upon a gentleman, completely unchaperoned, without even a maid in attendance. Stepping round to the small coach house behind the cottage, Kate had the Towers's groom hitch the pony to the cart.

In less than half an hour, she was tooling along the lane with all the expertise Harry had taught her. She cast an anxious glance skyward, the succession of bright days quite fled before the gray clouds gathering. She trusted she would manage to reach Mapleshade before the rain broke.

Passing through the village did not prove the ordeal Kate had once anticipated in the privacy of her room. No one regarded her as an anathema, Miss Lethbridge even cheerily waving her handkerchief from the door of her shop. It was a little difficult when she passed the squire on horseback and he shot her a knowing grin. Kate merely blushed and did not attempt to climb beneath the cart seat as she would like to have done.

As she clattered between the great iron gates and down the winding drive, Mapleshade's familiar red brick greeted her, rather solemn and subdued beneath the overcast sky. One of Harry's efficient grooms came promptly to take charge of the pony cart and Kate was left facing the tall pillars, the white-washed stairs leading to the imposing front door.

She moistened her lips nervously. Suppose ... suppose

Harry refused to see her. She had denied being at home to him often enough. Taking a deep breath to calm her wildly thudding heart, Kate marched forward and seized the huge brass knocker.

Her summons was so timid, she wondered if anyone could have heard it, but the door swung open promptly, not answered by one of the footmen, but by Gravshaw himself.

Remembering the last circumstances under which Harry's butler had seen her, Kate squirmed, unable to look past that redoubtable manservant's starched waistcoat.

"Miss Towers! Thank God you have come!"

The fervent greeting was so unlike the scornful disapproval Kate expected, she glanced up. The butler looked quite distraught.

As Kate stepped past him into the marble-tiled hall, apprehension clutched at her heart. "Is something wrong, Gravshaw?" she asked. "Pray, tell me. N-nothing has happened to Lord Lytton?"

"No, miss. That is, I trust not."

What did he mean he trusted not! Kate's fingers froze in the action of being about to remove her cloak. "What is it? What is amiss?"

"We are all at sixes and sevens here, Miss Towers, and that's the truth." His features contorted, and Kate could tell that he struggled with that natural reserve that prevented the elderly retainer from discussing the family with strangers. But it seemed a long time since Kate had been considered an outsider at Mapleshade.

" 'Tis Lady Lytton," he continued in a rush. "She . . . she . . . *She has eloped with that Crosbie fellow.*"

"Dear heavens! Are you certain?"

"Yes, miss. Yesterday afternoon her ladyship ordered up her coach to go into the village. I thought it a little odd, for as you know, she never does so. By supper she had not returned and Lord Lytton found a note in her sitting room."

The elderly butler shook his head. "There is no doubt, miss. The countess has most certainly run off."

Kate bit down upon her lip. "And Harry—I mean Lord Lyt-

346

ton. What was his response to all this?" she asked, nigh dreading Gravshaw's answer.

"He rode out looking for her ladyship at once. The master searched all night, but he could not overtake her."

Kate sighed with relief, at least rid of the apprehension of Harry being hung for the murder of poor Mr. Crosbie.

"Where is his lordship now?"

"He took his horse into the stables about an hour ago and then just walked off. No one quite knows where he went." Graveshaw's chin trembled. "The young master has taken all this very badly, Miss Towers. You see, he was her ladyship's trustee. According to his father's will—"

"I understand all that, Gravshaw, but you must not worry." She added softly, "I think I know exactly where his lordship has gone."

Kate had not been nigh Harry's Hill since the day of the memorial service. Hitching up her skirts, she labored up the slope, peering at the distant summit. The Hill was a bleak place on this chill autumn day, scatterings of dead leaves whisking by on the wind, Harry's memorial appearing abandoned and forgotten.

The site bore an aura of loneliness about it, a desolation that seemed centered in the man who hunched on the statue's base. Harry sat with his chin propped on his hand, staring vacantly across the sweep of his land, the woods with their half-bared branches stark against the leaden gray sky.

As she drew closer, Kate marked the unshaven line of his jaw, the shadows darkening eyes dulled from lack of sleep. He seemed so pulled down, Kate could scarce curb the impulse to fling her arms about him and cradle his weary head against her breast. But she hesitated, uncertain of her reception.

Harry did not notice her approach until she stood close enough that she could have stroked back the unruly dark strands the wind whipped across his brow. When he finally did glance up, his only reaction was one of mild surprise.

None of the joy that usually lit up his eyes at the sight of her, no uttering of her name with unbounded delight, not a hint of

347

that lightning smile. To Kate, it was as though the sun had indeed gone out of the world.

"H-hello, Harry," she said.

He bestirred himself, stretching his long limbs as he rose stiffly to his feet. "Miss Towers." He sketched a brief bow.

Kate's heart sank. This was going to be worse than she had thought. Giving him no chance to question her sudden appearance, she blurted out, "I ... I have been calling down at the house. I heard about Lady Lytton."

Harry grimaced. "I dare say everyone will have by the time the day is out. It should provide more entertainment than the most roaring farce." Kate thought she had never heard his voice laced with such bitterness.

He sneered. "Hellfire Harry for once tries to play propriety and keep his stepmother from making a fool of herself, but can't quite manage it." He expelled his breath in a deep sigh. "Damn! But that should come as no surprise to you. I never do seem to do anything right."

Kate wished she could caress him under the chin, saying as he had done so many times to her, "You are taking this all too seriously, Harry."

Instead she stood awkwardly, shuffling her feet. " 'Tis pity it had to come to this. But I fear the elopement was partly my fault."

"Yours?"

Although she shrank from his hard stare, she explained, "I promised Mr. Crosbie and Lady Lytton I would speak to you the day of the fête about their engagement. When I didn't quite get to it, I fear they became desperate."

"You were going to act as ... as emissary for that fortune hunter?" Harry did not appear angry so much as incredulous.

"I believe he truly loves her. Why, the elopement itself makes it obvious Mr. Crosbie cares not for your threat to cut off her ladyship's allowance."

"Even if that were true, 'tis a damned ridiculous match. He's a simpleton, and as for her! There has to be at least twenty years' difference in their ages."

Kate stared at the ground for a moment, then gathering her

courage, she said, "I have had much time to think these past few days. My belief is when two people are truly in love, all those differences in age, station, and family simply don't matter." She dared to look deep into Harry's eyes, hoping he would understand what she was trying to tell him, that she was speaking of far more than Lady Lytton and Mr. Crosbie.

But Harry looked away from her, the muscles along his jaw inflexible. "You don't understand at all, Kate. My father gave me the responsibility—"

"Of managing Lady Lytton's money. But do you truly think he expected you to act as her chaperon for the rest of her life?"

"No, but—"

"Of course, I know how dreadfully you are going to miss her ladyship."

An unwilling choked sound came from Harry. Kate felt hope stir. She had nearly broken through his grim barrier, made him laugh.

She continued gently, "You have done wonderfully well with the trust your father left you. I am sure he would have been very proud."

"You think so? I begin to harbor the fear the governor would think I have been making a great cake of myself, especially over this business with Sybil." A rueful smile touched Harry's lips. "Likely he would be right."

He turned to Kate suddenly, his voice gone low, earnest. "I know the old earl had a dreadful reputation. But he wasn't a bad man, Kate. I still miss him. Only there were occasions that I rather wished . . ." He hesitated. "I wished that he had been a little less my friend and a little more my father."

So rarely had Harry ever let his guard down, permitting her to see the pain, the more somber side of the handsome rakehell, that Kate heard herself agreeing softly. "I know. There were times when I wished mine had been more my father and a little less the bishop."

This admission astonished her as much as it did Harry. Their eyes met and in that instant Kate felt they had acquired a deeper understanding of each other than they had ever known before.

He unfolded his arms and Kate held her breath, half expecting to be drawn into his embrace. But he merely shrugged, returning back to the subject of Lady Lytton. "I suppose I will have to make the best of the situation and receive Crosbie at Mapleshade as Sybil's husband. Just as long as he doesn't inflict any more of his damned sculpture upon me."

Harry tipped back his head, peering upward at the naked warrior that towered above them. "But I do intend to have that cursed thing carted off my hill as soon as may be."

"No, don't." Kate said. "I have rather grown to like it." Boldly she forced her gaze up that disturbingly lifelike representation of male flesh. She faltered, "Of course, perhaps we should contrive to get some clothes upon him."

Harry's laugh did boom out then, hearty and deep. Kate thought she could feel it ring in her heart.

"What I had better contrive," he said with a chuckle, "is to get you home before the storm breaks. I thought I heard a rumble of thunder."

He tucked her arm within his, with a return of that familiar heart-stopping smile. As they hastened down the hill, Kate's pulses raced with anticipation. She was certain that at any moment he would ask her to marry him. Her answer, her lips, her heart were all eager and ready.

But to her confusion and dismay, Harry whisked her into his curricle and they were soon on the way back through the village. Thus far he had not said a word, at least none that she was longing to hear. He appeared to be taking great care to avoid any mention of their quarrel or the episode at the fête. With maddening cheerfulness, he chatted of the most insignificant matters.

Friends, Kate thought wretchedly. He now means for us to be no more than friends, just as she had always insisted. Would that someone had cut out her tongue.

By the time Harry deposited her at the cottage, Kate nigh trembled with her desperation. He did not even attempt to take her by the hand as he opened the gate for her.

"I am glad to see you are looking better than when we last met," he said.

350

"Yes," Kate agreed, regarding him hopefully. "Though I have decided I had better swear off the gin."

Her timid jest provoked a grin from him, but he made no movement to follow her inside the fence. To her acute dismay, he vaulted back into the seat of his curricle. Did he truly mean to leave without saying another word?

"Harry . . ." Kate began, then blushed. No, she could not do it. She could not be the one to ask him. Miserably, she stood, fidgeting with the latch on the gate.

"Good day to you, Miss Towers. My regards to your mother and Lady Dane." Harry gathered up the reins. He paused, adding somewhat wistfully, "I don't suppose you want to marry me, do you?"

"Oh, yes! Yes, I do." Kate cried out with joy and relief.

To her astonishment, he nodded glumly and set his horse into motion. Kate's jaw dropped for a moment, then she crowded close to the gate, watching in fascination, wondering how far he was going to get before her answer registered with him.

The curricle had not advanced as far as the turning in the lane, when Harry sawed back so ruthlessly on the reins, the horse reared in the traces. Kate realized that she must finally have been infected with his lordship's puckish sense of humor, for she took an unholy delight in observing how Hellfire Harry, that most notable of whips, became positively cowhanded in his frantic efforts to bring the curricle around.

As the vehicle thundered back to the gate, Harry almost leaped down before he brought the mare to a halt. He rushed panting to her side.

"Kate! What . . . what the devil did you just say?"

Laughter bubbled up inside her. "I said yes, you silly man. Yes, I want to marry you."

Harry let out a war whoop. Seizing her about the waist, he raised her up and spun her about until they were both light-headed and giddy with laughing.

Then slowly Harry lowered her to her feet, the laughter stilling, the expression in his eyes causing the breath to snag in her throat. He captured her lips with a hunger, a longing she felt

351

strike deep to the core of her own heart. Crushing her hard against him, he kissed her with a most tender ruthlessness, until even the gray day about her spun bright with promise and sunshine.

"Kate, Kate," he murmured, a shudder coursing through his powerful frame. "You must know how I love you. How much I . . . I— Damn it, I meant to make a much better job of it this time."

"If you think you can do any better than this, my lord," she said huskily, the heat rushing through her veins, "I am certainly willing to let you try."

Seizing him by the collar, she brought his lips crashing down on hers again.

At the cottage's bowfront window, the curtain stirred. Lady Dane peered out with a startled exclamation, then said tartly, "Maisie. Your daughter is making love to Lytton by the garden gate. I certainly hope this means they are betrothed."

Mrs. Towers joined her mother-in-law at the window. "I rather think it does," she said as she saw Kate locked in Harry's arms. The smile Mrs. Towers felt curve her lips was an odd mingling of joy, relief, and melancholy.

Her ladyship folded her arms in rigid silence. At last, as though the words were fairly wrung from her, she said, "All right, Maisie, how did you do it? Whatever did you say to that stubborn child?"

"Nothing, truly. I just talked to Kate a little about her papa, told her some of the wild things he had done in his youth."

"Wild? My Dylan?" Lady Dane stared at Mrs. Towers as though she had run mad.

Mrs. Towers squirmed. "Well, he did tell me he went to London once. He actually lost two shillings at whist and. . . and permitted a woman of most doubtful reputation to speak to him."

"Why, Maisie Towers, you lied to the girl!"

"No, I didn't. I only exaggerated," Mrs. Towers murmured a little sheepishly. "Being only a bishop's wife and not his daughter, I am not quite burdened with as many scruples."

A glint of amusement and newfound respect appeared in

Lady Dane's eyes. She gestured to where Kate and Harry lingered by the gate, yet lost to the world. "So what will you do now that you are about to part with your daughter?"

Mrs. Towers sighed. "I don't know. A small house in Yorkshire, perhaps with a hired companion. . . ."

Lady Dane cleared her throat. She said gruffly, "I don't suppose you would consider making your home with a most meddlesome and . . . and frequently lonely old woman?"

Despite her regal posture, there was a degree of humbleness in Lady Dane's request quite foreign to her nature.

After feigned consideration, Mrs. Towers replied, "I should be happy to come live with you."

Lady Dane seemed pleased, but so astonished by her response that Mrs. Towers hastened to explain. "You see, I know I would never have to have that dreadful Prangle woman in to tea again."

Lady Dane laughed so hard, the sound carried even beyond the cottage walls. Kate caught sight of the pair at the window, and wondered what Mama could have said to occasion her ladyship such mirth. But even the knowledge she was being observed could not curb Kate's desire to have Harry kiss her again.

It was left to his lordship to playfully wag an admonishing finger at her. Then with a tender smile, he linked his arm through Kate's and they marched up the cottage path together to solicit her mother's blessing.

Now on sale!

Torn apart by fate, two lovers struggle
to keep their love alive.

McKENNA'S BRIDE
by Judith E. French

Caitlin McKenna defied her family to marry her
sweetheart, Shane, on the eve of his departure for
America. While Shane promised to make his fortune and send for her, the summons never came.
Now, eight years later, Shane finally sends for
Caitlin to join him on his Missouri homestead, and
these two star-crossed lovers are in for a stormy
reunion. But can this fiercely proud man and
determined young woman learn to trust and to
love again?

Published by Ballantine Books.
Available wherever books are sold.

Now on sale!

A spellbinding new romance
from beloved and bestselling author
Jennifer Blake

*On a lush Caribbean island,
a hot, sultry passion is born. . . .*

PERFUME OF PARADISE

Beautiful Elene Larpent is terrified at the
prospect of her wedding to a wealthy Haitian
plantation owner and anoints herself with a perfume to bewitch her husband-to-be. Then her
wedding is interrupted by a slave uprising.
Captured by bandits, Elene is rescued by Ryan
Bayard, the handsome captain of a ship bound for
America. As their passion reaches a fever pitch,
Elene struggles to discover if Ryan has fallen victim to everlasting love—or to her love potion.

Published by Fawcett Books.
Available in your local bookstore.

Love Letters

Ballantine romances are on the Web!

Read about your favorite Ballantine authors and upcoming books on our Web site, LOVE LETTERS, at **www.randomhouse.com/BB/loveletters**, including:

♥What's new in the stores
♥Previews of upcoming books
♥In-depth interviews with romance authors and
  publishing insiders
♥Sample chapters from new romances
♥And more . . .

Want to keep in touch? To subscribe to Love Notes, the monthly what's-new update for the Love Letters Web site, send an e-mail message to
loveletters@cruises.randomhouse.com
with "subscribe" as the subject of the message. You will receive a monthly announcement of the latest news and features on our site.

So follow your heart and visit us at
www.randomhouse.com/BB/loveletters!

On sale now!

From *New York Times* bestselling author
Elaine Coffman
comes another tale of spellbinding romance
to enthrall you.

IF MY LOVE
COULD HOLD YOU

Charlotte Butterworth had sworn she'd never let a
man touch her. And she kept her word until the
day she interrupted a hanging party in her own
front yard. Suddenly a bold stranger was in her
custody, taking charge of her farm and challenging
her at every turn. Walter Reed intended to pay his
debt to the red-haired beauty of Two Trees, Texas,
and then disappear. But he did not count on the
passion that flared between them, a passion that
threatened to engulf them both in the flames of
everlasting love.

Published by Fawcett Books.
Available wherever books are sold.

On sale now!

The Berkeley Brigade is back
with a vengeance!

MURDER WHILE I SMILE
by Joan Smith

A beautiful comtesse of a certain age arrives to
unsettle the Berkeley Brigade. Prance is smitten,
Corinne is jealous, and Pattle is irritated. But
Luten suspects this mystery woman might be
embroiled in international intrigue and might
even be capable of murder!

**Published by Fawcett Books.
Available wherever books are sold.**

Coming in February 1998 to your local bookstore . . .

ON THE WAY
TO GRETNA GREEN
by Marian Devon

Prim Miss Claudia Wentworth and dashing Lord
Thornton are thrown together when her niece and
his younger brother disappear with plans to elope.
On a mad dash to Gretna Green to prevent a most
unsuitable marriage, Claudia and his lordship find
themselves waylaid by their own traitorous hearts
and a passion they cannot deny.

Published by Fawcett Books.

Coming in February 1998...

LADY MEG'S GAMBLE
by Martha Schroeder

Lady Margaret Enfield is determined to save her ancestral home, even if it means working in the fields herself. She has no time to play pretty with the imperious Captain James Sheridan, who is shocked and appalled by the eccentric Lady Meg. Sparks fly whenever these two meet, and threaten to ignite into a grand passion if this stubborn pair will take a gamble on the most wonderful game of all: love.

Published by Fawcett Books.